Fragments

Other Titles by **David James Searle**

Filaments (due 2014)

The European Jesus Scenario (due 2011)

The Black Pit Scenario (2010)

David James Searle

Fragments

[SP]

Searle Publishing

[SP]

www.searlepublishing.com

Acknowledgments

I would like to offer my thanks to all the higher beings I have had dealings with over the years – you have taught me much that I would have avoided had you given me any choice. The Scenarios you have sent me into have been amazing, terrifying, holy and unique. They have helped me see that I am always ME, whatever the outward circumstances may appear to be.

I would also like to give a few words of encouragement to all the so called wasters, losers, bums and nutters in the world. You people live in places others fear to tread – you are heroes in unique ways and will reap huge rewards for your courage.

David James Searle was born in Reading in 1962. He describes his hobbies as riding large motorcycles, walking in lonely places, sleeping with call girls, visiting jazz clubs and art galleries and running ultra marathons. He currently lives in a penthouse apartment in London with his pet crocodile 'Tarquille'. He tells people he is a compulsive liar but that is not true.

Foreward: ultimate reality in a nutshell

When consciousness is solid:

one thing is very real

When consciousness is liquid:

anything is real

When consciousness is gas:

all things are real

from *The Game Book of Reality* 3.e1.8763/701

Your natural state is gas; the state of enlightenment and spiritual freedom. You can take a closer look at a Scenario by lowering your vibration into a liquid state where you focus on a particular area of interest. This intensifies the experience. If you want to turn the volume to the max, you can further lower your vibration into solid matter.

If you are a young spirit, you may get trapped in your material Scenario: it being so real for you that you forget there are other levels of vibration or realities. You have become the very thing that you are studying. This is why death is compulsory. It releases the spirit from captivity inside a single physical Scenario and brings it back to the gaseous state where it can again recognise its own eternal unlimited nature.

Dissimilar creatures have different life spans; imagine

how boring it would be to live as a flea for a hundred years (no disrespect to fleas intended). Each lifespan is set at a level which is appropriate to the form or Scenario chosen.

Nothing 'dies' in an absolute sense except the illusion of mortality and limitation. Do not be afraid of death: it is a release from a self-made prison. Everything you treasure in this life will be available to you eternally.

If you sometimes feel that you are 'trapped in your own life', you are experiencing a profound, transient truth. You may be a soul that is old enough to begin changing your reality while still inside a given Scenario. Even if you are not ready for that, you can perhaps focus on the fact that death is an infallible release from a set of circumstances.

A young spirit soul decides to study bees; it chooses to become a bee and enjoys flying among the flowers and eating the nectar in the big pink blooms. One day it finds the most magnificent flower of all; a blossom without equal. This flower becomes the bee's chosen territory, it's entire world. As the years pass the pleasure wanes, the bee becomes bored with the flower. It has forgotten that it is free to fly from bloom to bloom, though it does have a vague remembrance of some earlier time, when it was happier.

The bee begins to hate the flower; seeing it as a prison. It yearns desperately to escape but cannot find a way out, and so becomes melancholy, feeling oppressed by it's environment. Eventually the bee drops dead and remembers that it is a spirit soul. 'Next time I'll remember who I am and not get stuck like that' it tells itself.

But it does get stuck; It gets stuck as a spider; a frog; a mouse; a dog; a horse; a selection of humans. Gradually, as it gets accustomed to the nature of the Scenarios, the spirit soul begins to recognise it's position while still inside the experience. It learns to relax into it's successive incarnations and becomes an enlightened human, who sees all creatures as fellow spirit souls.

As it becomes wiser, the spirit finds it difficult to get through a human life without remembering it's true identity. It is only by forgetting that you are a spirit soul that you can truly experience what it is like to be a bee. So the soul decides not to reincarnate further, instead spending it's time in the spiritual realm, helping other souls gain knowledge. The enlightened being begins to discover an unlimited number of wondrous worlds, in an increasing state of bliss.

Part 1

Antique Acid

Art Fux

As I listen serenely to the second movement of Mahler's third symphony I lounge upon a chaise covered in plum coloured fabric that Mary picked up on her last trip to Paris when she went on a spending spree to relieve herself of the excess weight of another twenty thousand pounds, received from Rothko's for her latest aqua tinted canvas scraped by a potato masher after dolloping a half tin of turquoise house paint across the canvas surface in a nearly straight line until the majority of the paint slopped into a bucket . The paint remaining on the canvas was sold through a poncy New York gallery for twenty grand leading to Mary's shopping trip to Paris and hencethus to my buttocks being subtly massaged by the plump cushions of the new couch upon which I recline as I listen to Mahler's third movement of his second bloody symphony (or whatever it was) assuming he wrote symphonies that is.

I settle into the coital position (if that is indeed it's correct name) and let my mind wander through the wheatfields of internal landscapes or whatever. As the music winds it's way through the open doorways of my reeling senses I subtly open a carafe of orchids which are fervently displayed between my ornate Georgian sideboard and the sculpture of an archaeopterix which hangs formally from a thin wire screwed into the ceiling of the grand drawing room of our swish Luton apartment (I've never even been to Luton). After some time, partially interminable, partly velveteen in fragrance, I begin to remonstrate with myself about the times I had before I got this life of utter luxury thrust ignominiously upon me.

Mary's art money is coming in on a regular basis; and

what a lot of people don't know and would probably pay a whole bigger heap of money if they did know is that some of her paintings she paints in the nude, even sometimes rubs her tits across the canvas before applying the paint, finding it amusing to think that the old geezers who buy them would love to get a sniff of her tits and don't even realise that they have got some cells from her knockers right in front of their faces, like if only they took a deep enough breath they would inhale Mary's tit skin. Apart from Mary's art money there's the income from my writing which is an even bigger laugh than the art stuff.

I can't believe how many people love to read my books like they've got some deep meaning or something when in actual fact it's just shit I've made up myself. It really makes me feel warm inside when I find out how popular I am, especially when I get to go to book awards and actually get the bloody award myself. I've got nearly twenty of them in the last two years or so and now that I'm writing even more quickly I should start really cleaning up. I guess I must just have a natural talent for expressing myself in a way that people can relate to.

Still, never mind all that now. I've got to drive up to Oxford to organise an art exhibition that Mary is going to be having at Magdalen College. It's not really my job to do it but the more money she makes the more she becomes far too whimsical to organise her own shit anymore. Can't say I blame her, I'm getting much the same myself; the only difference is that I'm such a materialistic bastard that I'd hate her (and therefore me, being part of the group 'us') to miss out. Make hay while the sun shines.

By the time I get into the city centre, Oxford is crammed to the gills with tourists. I personally don't mind this too much as long as they don't keep stumbling into me; they give me confidence that this wonderful city is getting it's financial desserts, making a pretty penny from the sale of college related gifts, olde worlde quainties and traditional pasties and pies in the indoor market. You can get any flavour milkshake you can think of here too, even Parma Violet, which I can tell you is as delicious as it sounds, unlike the rook soup which is bloomin' worse than it sounds.

As I saunter along the High Street, stopping only to grab a slice of pizza from a little café where the girls are always reserved, stuck up or chic and give a sense that they are looking down their very aquiline noses at one, even though they work in a tiny café serving drinks and slices of pizza to people who for all they know are a little bit famous and have won awards for literature.

When I arrive at the college I go into the chapel and get looked at funny by some students and a clerical guy who is gesticulating towards the ceiling and the student next to him who looks so bland that I am unable to describe him is nodding absent-mindedly, peering at me over his glasses. I consider being rude as I usually am to people but because of where I am, in Magdalen College Oxford, I just make a big show of going into one of the pews and throw myself onto my knees in the most devout manner imaginable and curl up in a prostrate foetal position before clamping my hands together and praying fervently for about four minutes. I can feel their eyes on me, burning with a mixture of shock at my performance and confusion at my very existence. Then I get up, walk past them like a girl swishing her skirts and bow low to the ground before skipping out into the quadrangle and back into the porter's den where I announce my official role and arrival.

I spend the next few hours explaining the ins and outs of Mary's planned display for her exhibition. The officious Fairfax huffs and puffs as I describe the requirement for a twenty foot long gash to be cut into the plasterboard of an ancient wall in order to create the effect of one of her installations being given birth to by the building itself. If you want to be up with the modern art scene you need to show some commitment not just tokenism. I loved the look on his face when I got the director of the Fusili Gallery on the phone

17

and said director basically ordered Fairfax to stop being obstructive and do what I told him.

Then I zip back home to Marlborough, light a big roaring fire in the sitting room and lounge on the sofa fiddling with my antimacassars as I watch Reading beat Portsmouth 1-0 in the Carling Cup 3rd round replay. Dull. So by the time Mary comes into the room wearing a shimmering silk dress that looks more like a glorified nightie to my uncouth tastes, (meaning I start running my hands accross the front of it), I'm well up for a bit of diversionary sport. I just can't resist fondling silk-covered breasts, there's nothing else like it in the world if you ask me. Anyway soon we were rutting like deer in the....rutting season is the best I can do at present, but that's because my mind is on more saporous pleasures.

I must have bent her bloody double; so many athletic and gymnastic poses we employed during the next two hours of blissful fornication. Mary even cheered me on as I finally shifted gear into the so called 'vinegar strokes' (what a delightfully course and foul expression) and injected her with a significant quantity of high grade ejaculate. She always laughs when I come inside her; not out of cruelty but pure dirty glee. Mary is good at dirty glee. She's very childlike in her approach to sex: enjoys it fully, energetically and totally innocently. She can perform the most perverse act with an attitude completely devoid of corruption or guilt. She is a blooming marvel.

By the time our taxi arrives to take us to Bristol for the Larry Miller gig at the Fleece we are both as squiffo as a pair of pissed up badgers, having supped two bottles of Krug in the meantime.

An hour later, upon arrival at our destination we gave our driver a twenty quid tip by way of apology for my spilling booze over his car's upholstery and for Mary's unabatable torrent of filthy language: she swears like a fucking trooper when she's drunk. We sort of fall into the old stoneclad barn of a building and start soaking up the atmos; the hair, the flagstones, the old wooden beams, the pools of spilt bitter. It was right up our collective alleys. We downed a couple of pints each and then got stuck into the mosh pit, Mary getting a good groping when she stage-dived into the arms of a group of leather-backed rockers, much to their, and her delight.

Then after a few more bevvies and an hour or so of mind-bending guitar solos, Larry invited a few of his keenest fans onto the stage, gave them inflatable guitars and let them headbang with the band. I didn't need to be asked twice; I shoved and slunk my way to the front of the queue and spent the final ten minutes of the gig posing and totally blasting the whole place into shrapnel with my psychotic air guitar shapes, bends and slides. I was king of a universe made from solid rock music. In the end I fell off the stage and landed on top of a fat goth tart who tried to kick me in the head before Mary weighed in and pushed the girl out of the way, grabbing me by the hair and dragging me out of harm's way.

She giggled and kissed me hard on the mouth. A few young people looked on disapprovingly and I might add, enviously, as she chewed on my face. Mind you, if I'd set Hot Mary onto them, they would have totally shit themselves; wouldn't have had any idea what to do with the foxy feline. We staggered classily outside into the cool evening dark and made our way the half mile or so to Temple Meads station where we got a taxi to a shiny glass hotel and booked into the penthouse suite. What a fucking top laugh. The only thing left to do was the drunken perverted sex which I remember nothing specific about. I know it took place because in the morning along with a vicious hangover I was sporting several knife wounds to the abdomen. Mary's a mad fucker when under the influence of an overwhelming drunken lust. Tee Hee.

Anyway enough. I'm working on a new arty novel at the moment called 'White Horizons' based upon the diaspora of modern identity as it adapts to the psychological cul-de-sac of

American commercialism. Something along these lines anyhow. I may do it via a spectral pastiche of the pulp horror novel transcribed onto the post modern icons of pornography and fame. It should totally sell out. The first chapter introduces the reader to Colin and Amanda; a pair of post post-modern ironic retro glue sniffers from Bermondsey who begin a crusade against political reductionism through the medium of performance poetry and guerrilla art actions.

For a couple of hours I tap away on my laptop keyboard; coming up with the beginnings of yet another literary masterpiece. Then I get bored with the whole idea of writing, of laptops, of wearing clothes, of having a name, of consistency; it feels like a trap: I become a snare to myself: I sense how my own ego is a box which stops me being free. Oh Freud you mad old fucker you were right about the ego at least if not a whole lot more. My conformity to my own view of myself, my own desires, needs and body are the cause of all my suffering; I feel suddenly that I no longer want to be stifled by existence. I equate death with freedom from ego constraints, the wheel of re-incarnation. Oh how brightly the white light of insight sears through my ignorance. I become jaded with restricted living; all the meaning drains from life. What I end up with is the understanding that there is only one thing which is not totally worthless: love.

Sorry to be so unoriginal but there it is, the simple truth. Only love is worthwhile, only love is not wasted time, only love is life to the spirit. How trite, how dull; how fucking annoying: yet how totally beyond denial. So now what do I do? What is possible to a basically lazy bastard like me if I am aware of the utter futility of my life except insofar as I spend my time expressing the love from which my spirit is made? Everything else is an avoidance tactic.

I'm going to have to change; or rather I am going to have to become more real. Oh fuck!! I hope I don't start wearing jumpers or combat gear and grow a beard and collect money for charity with old ladies on a Saturday afternoon at the local village hall. I really hate old do-gooders who spend their feeble poverty-stricken lives helping those marginally more worse off than they are. It is just so totally sickmaking and self-satisfied and invertedly smug. I do hope this feeling wears off soon so I can go back to being a totally self-serving, wise-arse.

Art for art's sake, money for fuck's sake is how the saying goes in our house. We are both totally dedicated to making as much of the filthy lucre as we can. We see no other reason for being here. We are living in a postmodern world where meaning is like a pick'n'mix sweetshop. Action and meaning are no longer related in a concrete or permanent way; it is all totally arbitrary. The only thing that makes things better is having money to spend, so the time passes in a whirl of thrill-seeking, mercurial, vibrant pleasure.

So I churn out art novels, at least two per year, three if I can be arsed to do them: they sell worldwide. We're talking millions. Not just the novels; I also create art objects in the form of paperback books, non-novels: they are extensive word-art portable installations, or some such. I basically churn these fuckers out like nobody's business. It used to baffle me why they were so popular when I first tried one out in the world's literary marketplace; then I realised why they flew off the shelves so readily. It is because they make no sense – just like our lives, just like postmodernism: they are a pure experience of the present zeitgeist, they sum up our experience of life in the twenty-first century. We feel at home reading a book which has no narrative, no viewpoint, no substantial characters; no structure; no references to past literature: nothing but slices and sections of language experiences: short shots of intoxicating wordage which somehow reflect the inner disjointedness and lack of psychological, emotional and intellectual consistency we know as postmodern living. Every combination of words has a unique though fleeting vibration which instantly explodes in the mind of the reader, injecting their perception with an instantaneous psychic 'hit' or 'buzz' which temporarily intoxicates the organism, transporting it to a new dimension which is normally hidden; existing as we invariably do in our linear, logical world of ego-driven need and desperation.

One of my little artistic pieces is the literary equivalent of a big night out; a vocabulary-based pub crawl which leads the reader through a bustling myriad of literary dives and tinctures, creating an intense feeling of bliss and psychedelic euphoria which, if overdone, will bring on a hangover just as real as an alcoholic piss-up. My literary bombs can lead to anti-social behaviour: some readers, having imbibed too much of my verbose intoxicant, become seized by a deeply held conviction that they are invincible; or that they can fly, or rule the world, or fuck someone else's wife, or kill and get away with it, or jack in their job and somehow be supported financially by the universe as a reward for their being brave enough to be real and not a fake bull-shitter like everyone else.

Basically, what I'm trying to get across is that art and lit. can be real money-spinners if you know what you're doing and how to exploit the ebb and flow of popular culture, which obviously, at this moment in time at least, both I and Mary do.

It didn't start out as a wheeze to make a load of dough; that is just how it ended up. When we started on our creative careers, we were genuinely earnest and genuinely poor. What we noticed quickly was that those of us who actually gave a shit never made it; never got the recognition or the rewards which we felt we deserved for our innocent, well-meaning zeal, our truly heart-felt love of art and literature, of culture, of intellectual ideas and whatthefuckhaveyou.

It was always the smarmy bullshit merchants, those who didn't give a stuff about art, who got the breakthroughs, the accolades and the praise; a situation which at first shocked and disgusted us right to the core of our soft zealous hearts.

We did what we could to change things; to stay true to ourselves and our artistic visions, but sooner rather than later we decided that if that was the game, then we would play it to win. And win we did. And still are.

As we become less interested in the artworks we produce: the more we just churn the shit out, the more we are revered as part of a brave new art movement, sought out, awarded, rewarded; almost deified as some sort of fucking saviours or some shit. I tell you I can't get my head round it at all, it's just totally the wrong way round to what it's supposed to be.

Or is it if you take Hinduism or Buddhism into account? Isn't it just the way it should be? Are we not simply reaping our just rewards for being detached from our actions; are we not becoming less averse to corruption, less attached to meanings, motives and causes, more open to the flow of the universe, which will give us more, the less we are desperately caught up in the illusion of logic, rules, plans, rights, wrongs. Are we in fact part of a growing throng of new messiahs; this time flash, wealthy and amoral, the leading edge of a new model for the human race as it teeters on the brink of the long promised and avidly awaited Golden Age. Have we in some perverse and cockeyed way fallen accidentally upon the secret of the universe? Have we not in fact found the Philosopher's Stone: turning shit into gold?

Maybe its just a form of semi-latent schizophrenia: the ability to link ideas in ways not accessible to the normal mind; to see relationships and conjunctions where none seem to exist. This idea is not so far-fetched as it might at first sound; I have discovered that a significant number of readers of my art novels experience originality or distress of mind; sometimes to a degree that a label can be applied; or they at least show a syndrome or cluster of symptoms which indicates issues regarding the management systems of the mind. I have heard it said more than once that my books have helped people with

23

hebephrenically disorganised thoughts to experience moments of elation and a fleeting sense of belonging, normality even. I do not however claim that my books can cure mental illness, though I would do so if I thought I could get away with it: nothing wrong with hinting at it though. Its all money in the bank to me, as you know.

After spending a couple of days jotting down the outline of a chapter or two of my forthcoming epistle, I had to face the world again; partly because Mary, ever the little terrier tugging at my existence with the sharp teeth of ambition, dragged my sorry ass up to London for some fucking art award where she was being given a big metal question mark in honour of her 'Continuing Contribution to the Art World' or whatever other crap. I hate going to the smaller awards ceremonies because the people are just so totally shitty. The thing with Mary though is that she just has to get her pretty arse in front of the media whenever possible, usually wiggling it in a completely over the top manner as she shows it to the audiences of piss poor art awards dinners and what have you as she goes on stage to pick up yet another piece of junk which is supposed to symbolically represent the sponsors of the awards, though how the 'Inner London Art For Citizens Committee' is symbolised by a question mark I'll never know; unless it asks the question 'What is the fucking point of the ILAFCC existing in the first place? Never mind me rambling on like this, I do it all the time, can't stop myself, and no-one else can stop me either. Tee Hee Fucking Hee Haw Bollocks.

A Visit to the Asylum

I awake to a ceiling upon which nicotine horses gallop among the pillars of wisdom, clouds reclining sideways through the barred windows of my room. My room. Not my room in actual fact but a poxy cell inside an old madhouse in a tree-lined park out near the Oxfordshire/Berkshire border. I am in fact an inmate in a mental institution though they don't call them by that name any longer – they've got some politically correct sugar candy coated phrase to cover up the things that go on in here. They don't want to bring local house prices crashing down do they?

I sit up and stretch my arms in a windmill, then I do a triangle. Once I have completed mantra number twenty four, I slide off the bed and spring elegantly across the floor. I stand in pose seven and open the door a little peephole where I get to see what's going on in the corridor; just a couple of nutters feeling the wallpaper and a grey pushing a drug callaboosh towards the common room because it's nearly time to top up the loons with a few quatrains of refygroxyl. I have serious doubts about the re-uptake inhibitors they dish out like sweetbreads in this auditorium of bad dreams.

I finish a series of angle poses and scuttle swiftly into the roadway, becarpetted and spangled with incandescent designs. Quickly I go to the window and peer into the daylit shimmer of an autumnal grassland. The sun is out and there are a lot of others on the lawns which extend into the distance. I hear a voice speak Hello and I ignore it because they never leave it at that. I turn around and there is a grey stood behind me at the side, looking towards me, finding out what I am on about. I do pose four and the grey moves further away. I laugh

25

to the sky and hear some other laughter.

I hear and the grey's mouth moves as well, that I need to go into the oasis and have some malaria jabs. I have to go but I carp ominously out about the way they are always listening and that. Inside the big I am told to eat the pillows informa informa. The blue I do but can't face the green and yellow ones but the grey lets it go with a warning.

I hate it here in this frankled place; It just doesn't work how it was supposed to in the ideas I have remembered. I used to join in with them but can't find the handle its gone long. It makes me cry out loud all day. Sometimes silently.

Later on I become a little less florid and begin to grasp the nettle of my predicament if you know what I mean. Somehow I have to escape this sentimental sanatorium of sadness. I look up and see the woman again. She sits beside my bed and looks at me with a face like a grave; great stone pilasters accentuate her aura as she monuments towards me in a sidelong gesture of impatience inpatients. She speaks with her mouth megaphone and I pretend not to be listening but the joke is I really am not listening. Tee hee.

Then I see a yellow glow above her hair and know that it is caused by the intensity of her hair products; they are causing a lot of yellow around her, which is not a good sign if taken too far which I think she has. It means parties with false friends, she is being duped by others not present. I think it is her handbag they are after or something in it, maybe a smoking gun or a picture she carries of an elderly man holding a cigarette as if it is a blade; he sort of stabs with it as he speaks about art. I think it is Jackson Pollock or Henry Bensefield-Onion, sitting in an old car smoking a knife with a sort of lost look like it's supposed to be a great moment in his life but he can't quite get a handle on the experience, like he's somehow playing the part of somebody else's life, not his own. "Where is my life and how came I to be playing this part when all I want is to be left alone in a shoebox with my collection of earth ants and magnetos". I poke into the photo somehow and press his hat flat. He looks at me kinda wistful but can't move so I race along the road with him just sitting there glum but trying to look enigmatic.

The yellow is clouding around her head now and I move a bit further away towards where the wash basin is. She shrews her face at this and starts to put on her white gloves: is she going to murder me then? I guess not she is going over to the door and putting the look on me so I go straight to pose eight and into mantra 18.7 with a little *academio solaces* on the side with a windscreen wiper.

If I smoked I would do it now in a great operetta of roiling vapour as I carooned with delirium and dace. O Blongarter O pretta. Tee Haa Boom Brangatapangastalanga.

Cimema du Ponce

Mary Wolstencraft Shelly Draper-Rapist you are hereby charged that on the twenty fourth of February of this year you did wilfully commit murder upon the person of one Peter Blake-Carrington Trouser-Press in a most bloody and violent manner with no consideration for the feelings of said dead body or his never-loving family. How do you plead you murdering bitch?

Go eat shite off my ring piece you little turd.

You need to give this court a lot more fucking respect if you want to get a fair trial you know?

This is not a court it's a ludicrous farce of a tin pot piss take of a fag end of a bad joke and I refer your honour to my previous comment with bells on.

I sincerely instruct the court bailiff to go across to the cock-munching piece of crapola and punch her in the face.

I rather think that neither yourself, your army, or the fucking bailiff of this kangaroos arse of a court are anything like man enough to smack this fuckin' bitch up.

At this point the picture goes fuzzy then stops. A blank screen. Two cunts with the sleeves of their pinstripes (wide and zooty) pushed up above their elbows start beefing about camera angles, dialogue, mood, and other shit I cannot understand. I hate this movie within a movie within a fuckin' movie bollocks; there's something incredibly retarded about it; maybe autistic rather than artistic.

I start fiddling with Mary's titties through her thin silky blouse. She lets me get on with it without so much as a smile or anything. Well fuck her attitude. I leave her tits alone and slump down in my seat. It's all her fault that I'm even having to put up with this shit; she fuckin' dragged me all the way to this London Arthouse flea pit to support her in her new persona as a third rate up and coming producer of tenth rate anal freak flix which mostly consist of tossers poncing about in foreign suits and languages and the occasional tart with her pillows out. If you want a wank you can find some porn easy enough these days and if you want some groundbreaking cinema you can check out Luis Bunuel or David Lynch or Jean Luc Goddard or Alfred Lord Hitchcock or any other bastard but Derren LeVine.

This supposed French arsewipe has totally latched onto Mary no doubt hoping for a sniff of her bank balance's pussy at some time in the future. That's bad enough but what is even worse is that Mary, reliably cynical to the point of not only selling her grandmother but getting her to sign her house over first, seems to be totally genuinely infatuated by the totally diminutive dogshitsuckingarsehole's so-called talent. I really hope he has a nasty accident on the way home tonight.

So I sit through the rest of this pile of celluloid drivel and pray for a swift death but then Mary decides to drag me kicking and screaming to some after show party full of wassocks and dickheads where she gets so off her fuckin' tits that I end up having to give her a slap for jacking up a load of scag in the bogs with a couple of quireboys; so keen is she to impress these lousy no-account junkie-monkeys.

I get her back to the hotel in one piece but she's badly overdone it this time so I pour cold water over her face, slap her some more and eventually just lay on the hotel carpet with her until she stops screaming. I am definitely totally going to murder at least two of those little bottom baiters tomorrow.

The next morning things were a little different. Mary

29

went into a sort of coma and I became a little disconnected from either reality itself or my personal ego; so I either went temporarily mad or enlightened, depending on how you want to look at it. Either way I just ended up feeling disconnected and simultaneously a little highly strung, nervous or manic.

I guess I am just not used to all the drama now that I'm in my forties and 'comfortably off' as the saying goes. I think that as you get older you do not need to interact with the world so much, maybe its even bad for you; not like when you're young and its exhilarating to mix with people and events; I think it can be totally not a positive thing once you're settled, to go mixing it with the multiple streams of consciousness that are available – it kind of upsets the equilibrium, mine at any rate. Maybe I'm just a dysfunctional old fart and I never realised it until now: perhaps this is my pipe and slippers moment. From now on I have to be in bed by eleven, wear pyjamas, give up sex, start to read newspapers and vote tory.

I managed to get room service to bring Mary some bandages and plasters and shit for her cuts and bruises (which I had done in an effort to save her from even totally worse shit) and I put some antiseptic on her breasts mainly because it gave me a stiffy; I was originally going to give myself a tit wank with them but felt it might be a little inappropriate due to her being unconscious and that: mind you if the roles were reversed I have no doubt at all that she would totally have shot her load over my tits as I lay there like death, all battered and bruised and such like.

After about twenty hours of just basically sitting staring at her, mainly at the titty area and her swollen left eye which sort of had a weird fascination for me or I for it, I eventually heard her groan and then she opened her less swollen eye and peered like a ghoul at me sitting on the floor. She just let out a breath and then went back into coma-world to look at the pretty pictures some more.

30

I sat by the bed, on the floor, cross legged like I used to do when I was a trippy hippy. I stared at the beauty of Mary's corpse-like form and imagined that she was actually dead, her skin all waxen and grey. Tee hee. I loved her more as a dead body than I did as a living one, I can't explain it but it was something to do with the fact that I no longer needed her permission to be myself, to feel what I feel, to say what I say, to do what I do, to think what I think; it was like she was cleaner to deal with and our relationship blossomed. I think it would be the total best relationship ever if you could just shack up with a stiff. I loved her marble form, her lack of opinion, her willingness to please me without question; her total acceptance of me as I am.

I felt like taking some sort of psychedelic drug and having sexual intercourse with my wonderful dead lover; but where the fuck would I get drugs from at this time and place. It was around seven in the morning and everyone I knew would be in a fucked up post total-mind-blowing-excess freak-out session torment of oblivion and in no position to nip over to the hotel just to drop me off a couple of tabs of some modern day junk. But just you totally just fucking hang on a minute; what about the fucking little shit stabber who had got Mary into the deathlike aura trip in the first place. Why yes, deathtrip Johnny himself, fucking what's his face, Derren LeVine.

I quickly reach over and grab Mary's bag off the bed and tip the fucking shit it contains onto the floor looking for her phone which I find real easy, it being fucking phone shaped and all. I flip it open and start fucking scrolling away like a twitchy cunt with rabies but end up throwing the fucking twat of a bastard against the wall, smashing the uncooperative fucker's brains out all over the carpet. Now I'm really fucked because I can't get the drugs and if Mary doesn't die and wakes up she'll go totally fucking ballistic and probably cut my fucking cock off and stuff it up my arse sideways for bustin' up her phone which basically carries her whole life around within it's digital guts.

Then I see a pile of drugs lying on the floor next to me. The bitch was packing a major stash. I am totally fucked up at this; I knew she was smacked up last night but I thought it was a one off hit. The sleazy cow bitch is obviously a regular junkie whore and never mentioned it to me. I'm totally fuckin' overcome with shock about it. You think you know someone. Well fuck you bitch two can play at that game. And I was feeling totally bad for thinking about feeling her up while she was sparko. I should just fuck her up the ass with the fat end of a wine bottle and burn her tits with fag ends. Maybe I will.

I lean over and grope her tits through her blouse just to prove to us both that I mean it. Then I fish around in the stash and find a little red pill with a white skull on it which I pop into my soul with a flourish and await some sort of eternal madness moment. But then she fucking decides to really screw me and totally wakes up as if she's never even been in a coma in the first place.

So for the next four hundred hours I go tripping off my face with Mary acting like she's normal but I don't think she's normal but that might be because I'm off my tits or it might be because she's actually gone insane or maybe she's still trashed on some chemical or other like I am. Either way it's a total double fuck up. The first thing she sees is her totally smashed up phone all shattered and busted. She goes off her melon about it but doesn't kill me because I tell her she fucking threw it against the wall last night when she freaked totally out about something that happened after the film show which I don't know what it was 'cos she had pretty much ignored me most of the night as she was too busy sucking up to Derren and his little entourage of tunnel testers to notice me. I think I'm pretty smart to throw her off the scent so well considering I'm starting to see stuff climbing out of her hair; mostly weird big stick insects and that. I try to calm her down and get some booze into her; I'd have preferred her to go back into her coma again to be honest but she was getting more and more lairy as I got more and more psychedelically infiltrated by all kinds of spooky shit: I started seeing faces in the walls and a hand reaching out, draped in cobwebs. I decided to get us out of this little closing-in pulsating room with the stroby lightshow and into the hotel bar.

We sort of dragged each other into the corridor which was about an inch wide and three miles long but I couldn't go into the lift because it was a huge mouth snapping toothlessly for my mind. The stairs were nearly as bad, taking on the rhythmic undulations of an horrendous snake, also the way they coiled round and down made me think we were descending into a hellish pit and would never get back out. Little did I know.

It was at this point that Mary ripped the front of her blouse open and began fiddling with her nipples and shouting the word 'sprang' over and over. Her tits were part of a hideous visage with long pendulous eyes which bobbed and rocked in front of my face. I ran screaming down the stairs, the railing flicking through dimensions as I moved, until I reached the lobby at the bottom. Double doors faced me.

I opened them and sort of half fell into the busy hotel foyer, getting a few hideous looks from passers-by most of whom were morphing in and out of hideous cartoon visions, walking in ungainly gaits, flexing their lips in glossolaliac movements, their eyes becoming rotating spindled sockets, reaching out, reaching out…I roved madly forward, bouncing and rebounding off walls, moving through a thickened ether which struggled hard against me, in an effort to form me into what horrid new shapes I can only cringe at the thought of. Totally beyond me now..going into pluroid agitations, soft-sheening beyond physical consciousness, into worlds beyond the dreaming of concrete reality; ciphers and numbers rising like an updraft of super-heated vapour, lifting my atman, slipping me up like a parapluie…up far beyond and further in…

fabulous roaming psilocybes randomly quarking through fractions and mathematical field-shapes and vortices; geographical harmonies transducing my emotional architecture, the spirit wafting; a faint breath of ice wind which contains all things and creates all things; simultaneously real and imaginary, all duality mythically evaporating, golden sliders opening downwards like the doors on an old bomber; as I float inside I become an...in the presence of.. angelic beings who know me and there at the back, rising high above all things are the massive golden breasts of Lakshmi.......

Never since the Romans has there been such feasting, such lavish entertainment as we produce from the garbage pail of modern postmodern artistic opportunity. Now all is ultimately Product. It is not really the age of the artist, though it may appear that way to some; art has already been done; that vast project finally completed by the end of the nineteen nineties. Now it is avid, relentless consumption which dominates the insatiable cravings of the human beast.

People will buy absolutely anything as long as it is branded, marketed, categorised, critiqued and commented upon by the right people. A sense of personal discrimination and preference is no longer viable; caught up as we all are in the overwhelming river of Product; our new God. If the word could be made solid it would go for trillions.

If I had enough money (and I'm not too far away from my first Trill) I would buy the word Product, make 20 million photocopies and become a hundred times richer in a week; I would get a gun which shoots golden bullets with the word Product engraved on the side of each shell and I would put the fucking barrel in my mouth and suck hard as I pulled the trigger. I would ejaculate golden sperm as my golden mind exploded all over the place and I would laugh when I realised the greatest truth of all; that my splashed brains would now become Product too, sold on Ebay to some dumb-fuck super-cool multi-billionaire fanatic in China who would re-sell each cell as a unique work of art to the voracious buying and selling machines who eternally click and scroll their lives away in search of that ever-elusive, once in a lifetime fleeting fix that is the latest must-have-today, out-of-the-loop-tomorrow Product.

Then there's the investment game which can also be a big winner for those who know how to play it. I find the semi-mystical complexity of funds, indices, stocks and instruments a total gas. It always amazes me that poor people actually wish you would die just because you're loaded and they've not got two pennies to rub together (can you actually still get pennies?). I'm sure they're happy enough in their own way – what you've never had you don't miss do you? Anyway they've really got nothing to worry about compared to the iconic suffering of the African child, I mean they've totally chosen the short straw haven't they? Poor fuckers would love to be a British dole boy or single parent council high-rise slapper. That really would be fucking nirvana to those fly-tortured skinbags.

I sometimes think I should do something to help them, like flash some cash or suchlike but I wouldn't know where to start; so I just put my head down and keep on generating the numbers, getting total minted innit?

I snap out of my weird downer as the bitch freak who got me into such trouble; aka Mary GoodChild (not her real name – just a twisted little irony she recently came up with) approaches me as I sit on my mahogany desk facing the picture window which covers almost a whole wall of my big shiny office; which I only got to ponce about in. She swats me on the arm before telling me she's about to design her own range of fragrances and lingerie. Now that I'd like to see, the underwear I mean; taking into consideration what a sexually perverted piece of filth she is I can only assume that the main fabrics used in the range will be, I dunno, barbed wire and hot candle wax and the perfume a mixture of menstrual blood, semen and the scrapings from ejaculating vaginas.

I slightly take the piss out of her for a bit and try to finger her through her tight black pinstriped trousers. She tells me to fucking pack it and I ask her to come to dinner with me in some swish restaurant or other which she says yes to and we go out with a flourish and stuff ourselves silly on top nosh and a few obscenely priced bottles of fermented grape skins Then I try to finger her again and she drags me into the ladies' toilets and orders me to fuck her because her vagina is screaming out for a good stuffing; so I comply and bang away at her for a while before filling her with my smiling sperm which makes her laugh in a very dirty way. Good boy she says; then grips my throat really hard in a friendly strangle, kisses me passionately on the mouth, laughs again, this time a little bit sinister which I love, and shouts "get out of these fucking toilets you dirty little pervert paedophile", which is a pet name she has for me because I am nine years older than her and she reckons she looks like a fifteen year old girl. Then we go back to our table stinking of cum and pissed as wounded tigers. We drop a wad of cash on the table (at least double the huge bill – if you are going to dine at extortionate rates you need to really pull out all the stops if you want the numpties who work there to totally get that you can afford the place). I love the spiritual enlightenment of extravagance and financial wastefulness; it brings me close to the Goddess, if you know what I mean. Waaazzuuuup. Totally Phat.

We then go via my publisher's office for a boring bit of bollocks and that. Mostly just asking me how I'm doing with 'White Horizons'; which I tell her is nearly complete, causing a greedy smile to spread across her rather bland features. Then she wants to know if I've got any ideas for future books in the pipeline which of course I have; in fact I totally pretty well blow her mind with my plans for a series of really chaotic books which contain half-writen stories, part-works thrown together haphazardly and basically not following any of the conventions required by novels.

Imagine starting to read a book when it suddenly changes, maybe even mid-sentence from a crime thriller to a book of rebel poetry or a dictionary of words related to famous murders or a book that tells you how to eat your own brain; or just goes into nonsense rants and meaningless passages: because let's face it if art is what you want don't expect it to make a lot of sense. In a nutshell I am determined to transform the rather turgid novel with it's formulaic and outworn plotlines, dull characters and yawny philosophies. Tell the truth; you're pretty bored with reading the same old shitty novels over and over again are you not? I totally am so that's what I tell her and she looks a little bewildered but Mary just starts sniggering like there's some joke going on, but there's no way I'm joking about my passion for re-creating the novel, re-framing it into a pure art object which can lead to spiritual enlightenment – really no bullshit, it can. Tee Hee. I cannot describe the rest of what happened here because I find it too dull.

When we got back to Marlborough we just dossed down in front of the big telly and ate non-nutritious snacks all night. No sex; she gave me a night off.

At this point I once again get a sense of the ultimate futility of the life I am living here with Mary. I like the sex, the toys, the poncing about arty fart and that, but ultimately what does it mean. People are starving all over the world; children are being terrorised, killed, worse. And what do I do about this? Fuck all that's what. I wouldn't know where to start, would I? I mean what am I supposed to do about it, it's not my fault is it? Oh shit I'm on a guilt trip which is why I try to avoid the whole Pandora's Box of it all whenever possible. It just feels like the whole shit-pile is too big for any one person to make any significant difference. But then again I suppose it only takes about a tenner to save a life in India or Africa so I can't get out of it that way either. Oh bollocks, at this rate I really am going to have to do something soon. I really totally am. Really. Totally.

I've got to shake off these thoughts soon or else I'm going to go on a downward spiral like I nearly did once before, I mean a real bad one where it takes years to sort your head out and even then you end up a right monger, drooling and looking into near-space orbit dream vibration pictures Ltd. Don't ask me why but I've always kept expecting to go completely, well maybe not completely but pretty bloody nearly completely mental one day; all of a sudden the world turns psychedelic, full of interior beasts roaming behind the eyes which hunt the soul in haggard guises, buulom buulom.

At the end of the day I just need to totally focus on my own life and let others get on with theirs'. I guess it's all worked out at some much higher level and alls well in the world no matter what it might look like to the unenlightened. At any rate it's not up to me to sort the fucking world out; I'm just a guy trying to get by, trying to...oh I don't know, maybe support a wife and family: absolutely not so scratch that bullshit. O what shall I say then.. I'm making a living and passing my time as pleasurably as I can until either I disappear into some void of eternal oblivion or I find out what I was supposed to be doing here. Either way I'm not in much of a position to do much else now, locked as I am into some mega-success scenario, shacked up with an equally successful, sadistic, sexually dominant sicko slut, living in a too big house in a stuck-up town in the Cotswolds.

Three months ago I began writing yet another masterpiece of ground-breaking art-prose. I decided it was time I really pushed the boat out; not just because Mary got her sneer onto the front cover of *Focus* magazine. It's not jealousy you understand; its just that she's totally full of herself already, got so many tickets on herself; no-one else can get a look at her these days, let alone a feel; even I need to make an appointment now that she's gone intergalactic because of her totally revolutionary exhibition (which I set up): not only that but her stinking perfume has started flying out of the shops since some bimbo stick insect in the U.S. of fucking A. wore it to some movie awards ego-feast and because she's taking it up the arse from some muscle-bound teeth machine who was once in a couple of half-wit films which won him a fucking Oscar nomination twenty years ago blah blah blah. Now they'll all be wearing her bizarre underpants; they're made to slip up between the cunt lips and force them apart in some sort of subversive pussy pout. They'll even start getting models to show their gaping twats; blowing obscene kisses as they flick along the catwalk. Mary GoodChild is now the latest five minute wonder and I'm beginning to wonder if she's finally disappeared up her own ego-anus.

Hence my urgent desire to wipe the floor with her by totally transforming the literary world; not just for five minutes but forever. I want people to stop 'reading books' and start 'getting fucked hard' in a literal sense (in a cliterary mode). I really gotta get some hot front cover action; even If I have to rip my own psychedelic shimmering guts out live on TV and call it my new novella. I've totally got to rip their faces off with my immense personality-literature performance-art existence or go absolutely insane in the attempt.

It was due to this intense new frame of mind that a few days later I decided to rock the media with an act of vile genius. What I did was to start cutting the bodies of some sleazy models I met in a poncy bar in Chelsea; they thought they were hot shit and ready for a big break into the supermodel category but I just thought they were dumb enough to pretty much be talked into anything once I'd explained who I was (and proven it via a quick call to my agent and a nip out to a bookstore for a copy of one of my masterpieces – *Psychedelic Tarantula* I think it was); I let them know I was a big shot art cunt with plenny a munny to splash around and all ya gotta do for it is to let me make a few knife cuts in certain artistically significant parts of your lovely bodies girls; it won't hurt much and it should get you

39

into some of the big mags and most of the papers: so they said yes and I took them to a little studio I've got a few million shares in and got them to take their kit off while I filmed them doing it and then I went up to each of them in turn and kissed them in sexual ways with the blade of a Stanley knife I got in a little hardware store... yadda yadda yadda... anyways I gets the first broad to start shouting the word 'sprang' as loud as she could while I walked slowly up to her, grabbed her wrist and made a little cut half way along the forearm. At this point she (as per) starts laughing and moaning like I'm getting her all juiced up, like I'm fucking her or something; I grab her again and give her another little nick, this time on the shoulder; well she starts acting like she's coming all over the place now. I walk forward and the camera moves with me until girl one is a long way into the background: well to save you the blow by blow bullshit of the entire vignette, I start waving the knife about and cutting girls with it; on the tits; one girl who had more spirit and artistic sense than all the others put together and who I wouldn't actually have minded poking to tell the truth lets me cut her in the cunt just a little bit and move it around just outside her as if the knife was fucking her; she fuckin' laughed her fucking head off at this and I did too I mean it was just about the funniest thing I've seen for quite a while. Anyway this was all filmed and then I got some brainboxes to ponce it up a bit and give it a stupid title; *Melange Du Period* for fuck's sake, and fucking voila I'm a trendy producer and director of 'short film' whatever the anus wank that is.

It absolutely fucking blew me away how quick it all happened; just a couple of hours in the studio slicing some slags up and I'm Mr Fucking Arthouse. Mary went totally fucking mental about it which gave me a laugh; she said I'd done it deliberately to undermine her because I was jealous of her new success with the press she'd been getting lately: bang on baby, you'd better believe it. I can admit it now that I've turned the tables; it really chewed me up bad inside: her doing better than me and the way she totally loved that; slinking around like a silk cat. But how dare she start hanging out with other people and leave me out of it: that's a point blank, onehundredandeighty, gut-wrenching betrayal which I couldn't let go. That's why I had to put her down and show her just who of us is the real cock-of-the-walk.

She'll calm down. Or up the anti to extreme proportions; let's face it she's a totally mad bitch. Anything could happen. Oh yeah and her fucking shit for brains explanation for jacking up on smack the other week at the after prem party of the bum bandit's film, you're gonna love it: she reckons you only get taken seriously as an art-house director if you're fucked out of your box on junkie shit pretty much all the time; that's what those skinny rim freaks told her and she totally fell for it and I thought she thought that she was supposed to be the streetwise one what a fucking turd brain. How last century is heroin chic for clit's sake? Tee Fuckin' Hee Fuckin' Haa to that one. That really got me chuckling.

So now, unsurprisingly the gloves come off and so do her knickers. I open a copy of 'Slut Faced Cock Fanatics' and see Mary's gaping gash glaring (assuming they can glare that is) at me over my cornflakes kind of thing.

She's decided that she'll stoop to the lowest possible level as a start off and move quickly downwards from there in her desperate effort to out-media me, like that's at all likely what with my new anti-art art novel coming out in a month's time and all. There she is showing gentleman readers her breakfast as they attempt to snatch some cereal before a busy day of sexual innuendo at the orifice. They end up getting her snatch for brekky served up with plenty of outdated pout and pose. It's totally bitchin' priceless; I'm thinking of buying a copy for both of her friends and maybe one for her dear old mum in her little bungalow in Bournemouth. It'd be nice for her to see how well Mary's doing, 'cos she never fucking visits her these days since she made it big. Then again maybe I'll just wank over it like everyone else before throwing it in the recycling bin with the rest of the trash.

What I actually did in the end was to toss myself off over it and leave it on her pillow with a post-it attached saying 'thanx for the wanx' and a badly drawn biro sketch of an ejaculating cock and balls like you get in public toilets. If she doesn't find that funny she's really lost the plot.

Another Little Visit to the Asylum

I grasp at boundaries lined up like dolls on a conveyor forever circling within the arcs of magnanimity and virtuous splendour. Pose 12a takes me forward into a more relaxed column and I require to notice that the woman who visits is here once more with her nellion sprang and underlying carousal. She sprays me with teutons and berates me with 'Hello Fuck Face, found any of your fucking marbles yet?'. I slide withway beyond the stage and frantl her with pose 3 for about a decade.

I still am unable to identify this female albeit likely I know her somehow; why because she comes to watch me, never takes notes and sometimes attempts to kiss me for what reason I know not; it sometimes troubles me that I know her not and yet she intends to become familiar even now; even within my netted abilities, my slatted view.

Later, when she is gone I sit reclined for several days, catatonic facial lack of features, repudiated reputation attempting to reassert itself in a strange linear way that reminds me of something I used to be or someone I used to know; then I think of Dada again and decide to urinate on a bicycle wheel on a stool and change my name back to R. Mutt. I seem to remember some glass monstrosity that I made a bit of money on, some vague history that perhaps is not mine like when I didn't write Steppenwolf but went through a phase when I thought I had then I thought it was written about me for a while like with Crime and Punishment and The Dice Man: surely just a vivid imagination and no-one can deny that mine is very.

Surely literature and art are supposed to transport one to a world so totally totally totally totally totally – why is this word so sure of itself then? I react to it's presence more fully than I had intended, got to go to poses and mantras for a while though it doesn't often help so why am I doing it? Is this insight? Is this healing? Where are my paisley dragons, my psychedelic memories and body shocking trances, where oh where are you my butter feelings? I lift my body back to my cell bed and attempt to recline thereupon temporarily with a less than totally satisfying effect. I shall ponder upon these intransigent musings.

So for two days I sit pretty vegged out and contemplate my own mind and situation; finally declaring myself saner, enough at least to recognise that what I was experiencing for the last howlong was of a contrast to this state and therefore no doubt; not much doubt. Was it madness or just lunacy? Am I really feeling this or is it just a dream? Then all of a sudden I slowly begin to remember that I used to do things outside this building, can't quite get a full handle on it but it was definitely some sort of business office and I am talking to a woman in a big chair and we are assigning bits of paper across and she...there's someone else in a chair at the side and I peer back into the idea of this idea and it's none other than the one who comes...so I do know her then but how can she be in my dream...? The link is real though, it must be because it is not under my control and therefore outside of me and so it must be what they call real.

Lit Clit & Drug Shit

So that's how it all got out of hand. My little film was a real hit and won a couple of so-what awards; but Mary's perfume and lecheurs' lingerie went global too so we both had to up the anti a bit. Surprisingly we were still fucking each other fairly often at this time, when not trying to kick the shit out of each other verbally, physically or professionally (maybe we're trying to fuck the other to death which would be the ultimate victory; total sexual domination and mastery Tee Hee).

I find out that the vixen is mixing with some even gorier film freaks; some sort of post-industrial retro-nouveau art wank involving choir boys being spanked by nuns or some shit else. And she's definitely on fucking smack or worse; maybe crystal: she's turning into a real death's head and going full throttle into an art-drug pit of leprous vipers with a vacant bedazzled grin on her face which totally creeps me out. I caught her snorting coke off a dayglo pink dildo the other day which I thought quite appropriate as she's totally fucked her nose.

So what I do is decide to outsmart her and her little group of bastards by getting this dude I know from somewhere in my darkly dappled past who said he would do it for nothing so long as I get him some work on one of my future projects: what I mean is he's going to keep track of her whereabouts and if possible to find out what she's up to and report back to me so I can either attempt to create a fuck up or an undermine of some sort; or even better do something similar and get it into the arthouse reel-pits before she can, thereby causing her to look like a right old copycat when she brings out an almost identical piece of shit a few weeks later: oh what a plagiarist she shall appeareth. Mint.

It took Greg (I think that's his name not that I really care about others any more) only a month or so to dish up some juicy dope on her; her little gang of bangers are mostly just tripping on all sorts of deadly shit; just mixing it up and banging it in their veins like they're on the last lap or something. There's even talk of a big drug-crazed orgy which took place in a disused studio out near the South Bank: the story contains a lot of not well elucidated spiel, partly because Greg is a lying cunt and can't hardly string more than three words together 'specially when he's off his box, strung right out into space in fact on some new acid they've invented. Basically I think he's been got at because he was trashed out of his box when I saw him; the hallmark of this particular brood of slime suckers what with that and the total over the top bullshit he tried spinning me. Then again maybe she is getting all she can up her crack not just in her bloodstream if you know what I mean. She's definitely living on the edge of a very sharp knife, that I do know. Either way, I'm not really bothered 'cos I'm harder than all that lot of tosspots put together.

I was a bit surprised when Greg whipped out a small sheaf of papers and began telling me tall tales of how he'd risked 'all' and managed to snatch a part of their play's script. You've gotta be joking man, pulling my pisser and all that bollox innit? Anyway ain't you better fuck orf and get some beauty sleep ('cos you certainly need it) etc.

I straightened the papers and glanced at the typed manuscript. It was part of a chapter of a bullshit story about some twat called Jason who acts like he's all that and that: not too convincing:

Oh pu-lees, that's got to be a total joke; I mean it's like some crack cocaine version of a distorted copy of a first draught of a writer's wank encased in five carat gold plated excrement. Do they really think I'm going to believe that this is what they're working on: I mean is it really total shit or is it some sparked up crime caper with the sort of psycho-sexually damaged characters that art cinema audiences love: I really don't fucking know, I just make stuff up on the spot, I don't do fucking critical reviews.

So now it's totally thrown me off my equilibrium and I keep thinking about it when I'm in bed; I must find out if I'm being taken for a mug or if this really is their upcoming work of genius. If it's theirs, is it good or complete shite? Oh fuck this for a game of soldiers, I'm going to have to get in there myself somehow or maybe grab one of the fuck freaks and torture the truth out of him or maybe ignore them altogether and just come up with some totally amazing piece of film myself like I did last time and blow the world of cinema into total fucking infinitesimal dust once and for all (that could actually be the easier route).

When I next see Mary Goodhead (as she's now supposedly calling herself) she's licking herself like she's made of cream and she's the pussy with the hot tongue. She's acting like she's really on something creative-wise not just drug-wise so I cagily feel around for info and she let's a bit slip basically because she's so fucking into herself that she can't help bragging about it.

So it seems that they are making a film. And it's a comedy-ironic commentary in pastiche form masquerading as a retro pulp detective caper based in nineteen nineties London. I'm dying to ask her if there's a character called Jason but I play it cool and act all impressed and start rubbing her tits through her black polo-neck jumper like she's some cool film-maker and she's quite playful and glowing like a girl and lets me get right into her on the floor and laughs when I come. I cry because it felt like it used to before we started all this aggressive shit with each other. For about half a second her eyes soften and I know she's as sickened and caught up in this as I am. Then the shutters come back down and she's acting cocky like she's won some game.

Later in the week I get some more information from Greggy-boy and this time it's a right fuck-up if it's true. He tells me that the script he had brought me was not a film score at all but part of a novel that Mary and her cronies are writing; so that means the bitch is paying me back in kind; totally shafting me where it hurts the most: she's going to beat me at my own game because that's what I did to her when I cleaned up with that original film of mine; so now it's time for me to know how it feels, she thinks. I've got to admit it's logical and karmically appropriate. I didn't think she could do logic; maybe she was saving it all up for a rainy day like today. I would be impressed if I had the humanity for it.

So if it's true, which it may well not be, then I'm now a film-maker and she's a novelist; what a joke! Maybe I should jump all the way onto her bandwagon and start jacking up. That would cause her some element of confusion no doubt, believing that I am wholeheartedly pretty much against hard drugs most of the time. So I get a mate of a mate of mine from back in the day before yesterday to score me a selection of illegal substances and I plan the trip of a lifetime; but being a canny fucker I set up the whole thing with film cameras, recording equipment etc; all over my hotel room (London of course, maybe Chelsea, Knightsbridge or South Ken.). There could be a latent cult art-house pot of gold stashed away in my mind which the drugs may bring to the surface; so I need to be able to capitalise on it and I won't be in any fit state to write it down when I'm thrashing around on the carpet.

I fuck off to London the next day without speaking to my beloved opponent-in-art. My hotel room is very plush; I don't want to start freaking out due to uncomfortable furnishings do I? I unbag and flop down onto the king-size bed. From the global silver attaché case I got from a Brixton gunfighter, I rapidly produce an array of potions, powders and pills which I place on the bedside cabinet to my left. I put several Viennese glass and brass syringes beside the chemical assortment and walk over to the en-suite for a big glass of water (I can't swallow pills without a drink), have a piss, check the big fridge is chock full of booze and food and recline against an array of over-stuffed pillows. I start with a couple of tabs of genuine nineteen sixtys acid which my dealer had sought out for me and which cost me an arm and a leg: genuine White Lightning he said.

I feel the trip coming on after about half an hour; the edges of the room all fizzy and softly echoing so I lay back on the bed and wait to see what's on the agenda. Mainly just a sort of foggy headache for a while; then words in my head getting all long and stretched out and going over and over the same old ground getting a bit annoying and boring so I go to the fridge and start on some white wine to cool my head. I have to keep my nerve on the way up, get to the peak and ride it back down (according to the text books). Certainly don't want to start freaking out or anything. The booze, after a bottle and a half necked like fruit juice, stills my flashing fears and I mellow into the psychedelic journey.

Soon things are feeling and looking a lot lighter; in fact it's all going a sleepy sort of white. I lie back on the big bed, falling ten feet into the mattress; a light flashes for a while, it's a tick in my brain which I slide down into a featureless realm: closing my eyes I open my eyes:

I awake next morning with an explosion going on inside my head; it takes me ten minutes to remember who I am and a further twenty to remember where I am and an hour to remember what I am doing here. I desperately want to get out of the hotel but I really have to get my shit together first.

For the next few days I'm like a fuckin' zombie; my mind is all messed up and I just go home to bed and tell Mary that I'm suffering from a virus which I don't think she believes; mind you I am a bit paranoid now so who knows.

49

After about a week I start to feel a lot better and even get up for some breakfast. Luckily for me she is already gone to some appointment with fate, I know not where or why; nor do I care. I just need a lot of space for a while to think about where I'm going from here and what has changed and how it has changed; because somehow I don't feel like any of this fucking art fame shit matters anymore. I can't think of anything more futile than art or money, or fame or winning or domination or adoration or even love in the modern romantic sense of the word. It all just feels like different grades of excrement to me. I need something more.

I've decided to jack in my movie career and I'm even beginning to wonder if I should bother with the writing anymore. All I get for it is money and I've got enough of that it seems; after all I'm not getting any happier these days, though I am continually getting richer, what with my clever financial investments and all that jazz. The positive correlation between wealth and happiness which once existed in my life has become inverse: the more money I earn the unhappier I get: that's a real bummer man because it's not how things should be; it's cockeyed and a sick and twisted way for reality to act.

If I'm honest I have had my doubts about the omnipotence of wealth for some time (on and off). I guess I'm just maturing at last, beginning to see things through more spiritual eyes (maybe). I can't say I've never wondered what the hell my life was all about; what the fuck I was actually doing on this planet; serving no credible or creditable purpose that's for sure. So now I've disappeared up my own ego-sodden arsehole after taking too many psychedelic drugs (two) in an effort to out-do and perhaps destroy (at least career-wise) the person I'm supposed to have loved most in the world because she started doing a bit too well in life for my liking. Mind you let's not forget that the evil bitch was doing it to me too, she's no fucking saint I can tell you.

Still, the fact is I've not been a good moral example to

the world so far; then I send myself into some sort of alternative fucking universe with antique LSD and can't find myself among the semi-infinite myriad of bit-part identities I have cobbled together in a desperate attempt to convince myself that I have a life and a purpose. Tee Hee what a fucking joke and the joke's on me. Boo Hoo.

So now I spend my days twiddling my philosophical and moral thumbs; staring into the near distance, lost in some half disclosed vision of alternative existence like a (rat in a shit-storm?). Oh for pity's sake pull your fucking finger out and top yourself you useless lump of arsehole jelly (what!).

I sit up, throw up, stand up; begin moving across the room in a weaving style until I reach the doorway which I wobble through. In the hallway I pass Mary looking like shit from a recent drugs overdose (touché bitch). We grin at each other like dazed sharks and I slam the front door behind me, jump into the Aston and fuck off out of it for a while. I've no idea where I'm going, I just have to get into the open air of the countryside; maybe go walking in a field or some shit.

I skid to a muddy halt at the edge of Hungerford Common and leave the car at a skewed angle, half on the grass verge; I run across the open grassland and literally throw my coat down and dance on it like some sartorially critical dervish; then sitting on the coat I roll onto my back, look at the blue sky with the fluffy white clouds in it and laugh myself to tears.

I start going over my saddo life in some sort of pseudo-philosophical way but soon give up and start punching the ground, imagining it is Mary's face, or my face, or some culpable God or Government's face. I was bloody sick of it all and felt like doing something about it if only I knew what. It was a lump of knotted confusion; my life was a massive sham; a perfidy (whatever that is) an abomination with no answer; a riddle with no compassion.

I place my hands on the slightly damp grass, enjoying the cold clean feel of the planet beneath my fingers. I breathe deeply, savouring the pure air, the heady scent of the voluptuous (surely not?) soil, the fecundity of the ambience of the transcendental majesty of the moment, the location, the ....add relevant phrase maybe.

'White Horizons'

The Post-Modernist Philosopher

Hark; a shower of bullshit doth approach: because of my nature, I am spiritually allergic to responsibility and the mundane life. This in itself is not a problem, for there are many successful and happy free spirits in the world who have a wonderful time, living deliciously selfish and inconsiderate lives. My curse is that as well as being completely incapable of tolerating boredom, I am plagued with a weak and sentimental nature which keeps me from pursuing purely selfish goals wholeheartedly. My need for unrestrained adventure, when contrasted with a compulsion to support others (as if), leads to a grey limbo prison which offers neither the exhilaration of selfish escapade nor the family bliss resulting from a martyred life dedicated to making things good for my loved ones. Maybe my instincts are inherently flawed from the start, my every course of action doomed to failure. It certainly seems I have somehow got onto a wrong track at some long-forgotten junction and have been aimlessly wandering, both morally and philosophically, for the past thirty years or so. Which is no doubt why I became a rambler (as opposed to a fully fledged hiker, with their high commitment levels and determined perseverance).

It was during an intensified escapologist phase of proclivity, (the previous sentence is fictitious and has no meaning) that I began to go on long walks; having cleverly decided that running half-marathons was too much trouble for me at the ripe old age of 40. I had moved on from booze and drugs, sex, career success (what career success?) and many other addictions which were in fact disguised attempts to escape from boredom. Ultimately no addiction works, because it is not authentic behaviour; it is simply an avoidance tactic, just like 99 percent of everyone's life, from beginning to end.

What we are working so hard to avoid is nothing less than the fact that we are not perfect, that we make mistakes, and that our imperfect actions can potentially have negative consequences for us and for others with whom we infest this beautiful planet. We do not want to be responsible for the suffering of our loved ones (ultimately due to fear of guilty feelings as opposed to a genuine concern for others) so we avoid all intelligent action and take the safe route of conforming to the ritualised mantras of domestic action; dressing it up as social and family responsibility to hide the fear of ourselves from ourselves. Life is dull we say, but that's just the way it is. At least we are doing our bit for the family, country, planet. Anything is better than fucking up and hurting someone through reckless actions.

I once worked with a young man who accidentally killed a girl just after he had passed his driving test. He was racing another idiot in a car when this girl appeared on his windscreen causing him to swerve into a tree and squash her. This calamitous incident highlights the danger of indulging in spontaneous activity. The chap, who I shall call Paul, though that is not his real name (it's Graham), spent a year feeling like a piece of brown effluence (which I'm sure the dead girl's parents think he is) and then a further 3 years in the slammer trying to avoid being buggered by freaks. This guy was a well brought up, friendly and relatively sensible-for-his-age kind of guy. Just a short week earlier at his eighteenth birthday party his dad had presented him with the keys to the murder weapon. A proud dad giving his son a good start in life, a set of wheels so he could get to work, pose around town with his friends and pick up girls. Neither of them, nor I, nor any of the other happy drunken guests at the party could have guessed that he would indeed be picking up a girl with the car so soon or so dramatically. Take this example as a warning of the typical outcome whereby any sort of spontaneous action is penalised and punished. People instinctively know this. That is why they soon learn to stop acting on instinct, opting instead for the safer approach, which is to 'think of others', to 'do the right thing' and to repress their natural desires for wild, selfish, live-in-the-moment action.

I have somehow become less than enamoured with life in general and mine in particular. It is probably no more than the culmination of multiple poor decisions made by me over the decades, an error caused by my short term thinking and total disregard for, or consideration of, the long term consequences of my hurried actions. Maybe it is also due to a marked tendency to always take the easy way out of, or into, a situation. Eventually all choices bear fruit, which some call karma. My problem seems so ingrained and inherent that it is perhaps simply the end product of the sum of all my parts and entirely out of my conscious control. I am an equation which automatically balances itself, working out its miserable destiny while, I, the ego, watch on in ever increasing disappointment and frustration, unable to avoid the fate that has been pre-programmed into the slice of DNA that has been labelled 'me'. As for karma; I do not buy it because it is contradictory, inasmuch as if I hit you it will cause me to be hit in my next life, but if you hit me, I deserved it. If bad things can only happen to me if I have earned them through wrongs that I perpetrated in a past life, then there must be no karma attached to the person who hurts me in this life. Therefore the fact that I am able to hurt someone in this life surely indicates that they had it coming due to pain they caused me in a past life. Therefore how can I earn bad karma from it in a later life? It all very circular and illogical. Just another fear induction system; though no worse than fucking feng shui which is nothing more than the wholesale importation of superstition into an already terrified mind.

I am not a fan of structures and protocols, preferring to stay free of systems and well-worn pathways. I work instinctually, taking life at a moment's whim, a caprice which offers a small spark of the vibrancy which is sadly missing in all prescribed actions and events. Whatever the causes and influences may be, I end up locked into an inwardly spiralling life-movie which is written, produced and directed by outside agencies who fail to understand me and do not have my best interests at heart. I am simply the protagonist of a run-of-the-mill drama, written by a third rate playwright, in a low budget production, for a nasty little satellite channel which no-one watches.

I go for long walks on my own in order to find some peace and an area of free space in which I can figure out how I got into this mess and how (if at all) I can get out of it. So far my only plan is to 'get' £25 million and live the life of Reilly. The only flaw in this approach is that I am totally unable to tolerate even part-time or temporary employment, due to being allergic to the workplace atmosphere and finding intolerable the seemingly compulsory dull wittedness of fellow workers. How can I be expected to respect people who are willing to behave like robots just to cling to a miserable existence? Who was that American who said 'Give me freedom or give me death?' Something to do with the War of Independence I think it was. Well who ever the knob-head was, he hit the tack on the cranium.

The main difficulty in living a free life during these shallow post-modern days is that if you don't have a shit load of cash you are stumped; unless you are happy living as a homeless and begging for food. All we supposedly 'civilised' people can hope for is that the misery is occasionally relenting and ultimately finite.

Hence the current popular interest in rambling; the changes in the public access laws offer ever-growing numbers of the socially caged a temporary and fleeting illusion of freedom. It is a meagre, sanitised and overtly organised kind of escape, but that's about all we abject estate dwelling western

European insects are likely to get, unless we throw in the towel completely and move to Outer Mongolia. I don't want to eat Yak's testicles for breakfast, lunch and dinner, so I'll stay put for the time being and gripe about everyone and everything, taking every chance I can to withdraw into the raw uncharted wilds of the English countryside.

It can be productive: I came up with another of my brilliant money-making ideas the other day as I was walking around the chipped Avebury stones in the soul-biting wind. My brainwave told me I could bottle the fresh air of the place and sell it on the internet, just like a man did with the air of the Brecon Beacons. The crucial difference between my idea's prognosis and that of the successful Welsh entrepreneur's is that I won't actually bother doing it because I have enough experience of failed small business ideas under my belt to know that it is bloody hard work doing all that marketing; and you never make enough money to compensate for all the boring work you have to do to make a business succeed. Its just another way of losing a little bit more of that precious, illusory sense of freedom.

Maybe I could rely on my newly formed and highly innovative get-rich-slow plan, which I call 'Money Seeds'. Basically, I worked out that if I could put a £2 bet on short-odds sports events and double my money each year for 20 years, I would reach my £25 million target. I've worked it all out to the last decimal point. It would truly work if I could stick to dead-certs, like Roger Federer in a first-round clash with some 17 year old numpty no-one has ever even heard of. The problem here is that Roger Federer was once a 17 year old numpty who no-one had ever even heard of, and he would eventually lose to his replacement.

Maybe I could just get a big gun and go on a real crazy shooting spree; taking out a couple of hundred fellow prisoners on my way to a lead-embedded oblivion. I imagine the brief sense of being beyond all controls would be astonishing. At least until the point where you started running out of ammo and realised that you either had to surrender to a life-long prison sentence or top yourself with your last bullet. If I'm honest, when the Hungerford Massacre was underway, stuck as I was a mere eight miles away in a hot Newbury sales office selling polythene bags to saddos over the phone, a part of me envied Michael Ryan. Whenever I hear about what he did I put myself in his shoes and get a vicarious sense of transitory omnipotence. Why is it we secretly love nutters like that? There are not enough decent serial killers about these days. Like everything else that made us feel alive back in the day, they have been sanitised and dumbed down.

Drugs are on the increase for this same reason. Another desperate attempt to escape this dull society we have made; our chained existence which leaves no room for colour or idiosyncrasy. Even death itself is desperately gaining a glamour of fascination, with sci-fi religions springing up, leading to mass suicides of earth-weary disciples frantic to join a race of truly free and enlightened beings on some distant planet. The only thing we can all agree on in this world is that it is mostly wretched and that we want to be rid of it.

Philosophers and psychologists may say that it is the 'constraining and desperate ego' which causes us to feel this way, and that if only we could relax our egos we'd all become free as birds in an instant. Bollocks to the lot of 'em I say. If you can show me a single normal human who has learned to bypass or overcome his or her ego, I'd like to see it. We are what we are, and where we are, but we don't have to like it. Maybe at some timeslice in the future, mankind will discover a simple grail-like key to this dilemma. I personally hope they invent a pill which gives an instant and everlasting sense of total inner confidence and centredness; enabling us to live naturally with a sense of liberty and bliss. But for now I'll make do with rambling.

I guess the religious rant brigades would say that we

have lost touch with our spiritual side and if only we could learn that we are not supposed to want anything for ourselves, if we just lived our lives for others, we would be happy. Sounds a nice idea; but if you've ever tried it, you'll have found it is impossible; not least because it causes all your pent up urges for personal satisfaction and success to swell out of all proportion, just like when you deny yourself the foods you really crave in a desperate attempt to lose weight and then you end up eating a whole fridge full of crap at the end of the week in retaliation. Self denial just doesn't work for normal people.

So what the hell are we supposed to do? We're running out of options as a species. Everything we do is an attempt to gain happiness and independence, and none of it works. We really do need some higher beings from outer space to come down and teach us how to live free and happy, 'cos let's face it, God's fucked up big time. And so has science. Here I go again fellow ramblers, rambling.

Finally it has happened. Science has disappeared up its own anal hole. To be more specific, the 'New Physics' as they like to call it, has come up with a twat of a theory that nothing exists until it is observed, therefore making the observer the creator of the observed and God is finally booted out of existence.

To be honest, I've never been too sure of the rules, always having been confused as to what exactly constitutes a 'real' as opposed to a 'possible'. It all seems pretty much a matter of individual opinion to me. Maybe that's why I've not exactly set the world alight with my rise to international renown as the universe's cleverest new theory-monger.

It's a long and tortuous path that I have trod, let me tell you; often I have simply floated like a leaf on a breeze in my quest for the ultimate answer to the ultimate question: what is the exact nature of human reality? I guess it is about time that humans stopped grovelling about in the mud and the maya and finally evolved into Homo Dieu. It is as inevitable as the wheel, as necessary as fire.

I have always had the feeling that there was something going on which no-one else seemed to be aware of: something to do with how things really are, and the illusions they appear to be. I used to wonder why I could see between the cracks and others couldn't. I used to doubt my own perceptions because they didn't match up with what everyone else was seeing. Now I finally realise that it was simply a matter of different degrees of awareness and perception. Strange to discover that everyone I ever met was living in a world of limited perception, like cats in a closed box, seeing only the vaguest outline of what was around them.

There's no point trying to avoid writing things if you want to be a writer. That's lesson 1. A lot of writers do anything but actually write. Mind you, most of them ramble in print just as much as when they spout nonsense at you, hour after hour, on a train or in a bus queue. Busses are always late if you have a writer boring the pants off of you at the stop. It's a well known law of physics. Not normal physics you understand but the bloody stuff I have to wade through every day. The sort of physics which changes with the breeze, causing plans to go awry and things to take a sudden turn for the unexpected. I used to fight it but there is no point. Now I just accept it as an inevitable consequence of being a poet at heart and a writer by trade.

I've decided to learn all the laws of maths, chemistry and physics, so I can check up on things and write books about any discrepancies I find between how reality is supposed to work and how it actually does work. These books will transform mankind's understanding of human existence and I'll make a name for myself at last.

Strange realities have pursued me all my life. I bet you

haven't got an uncle who has made space craft and sent them spinning into space in the 1950's?; and they use less power than they produce, and can give free energy. He's world famous among the internet loony tunes. I am one of only a handful of people who ever saw the craft fly. Mind you I was only about 8 years old at the time and don't remember it clearly. Recently, I saw a really blurred photo of me and my brother standing in a field in Warminster, looking up at a silver craft as it hovered and spun off across the sky. They're supposed to be making a Hollywood film about it but that's been on and off the drawing board so many times. Some actor who's allegedly famous but I've never heard of is involved, as well as lots of shadowy characters who are all suspicious of each other's motives, fearing that everyone else will get the money from the movie and they will be cut out of the loop and left unloved by moviegoers and their friends. I got involved at one stage years later and started offering tickets on spacecraft soon to be built, for trips to the Moon and all the planets in the solar system. I caused a lot of trouble for certain paranoid people who thought it was my attempt to take all the money – which doesn't actually exist. There is no money, there is no film (oh yes there is!), there is no working craft; though my uncle spends his time proving his theory to small cliques of journalists and eccentric scientists in out-of-the-way halls; occasionally there is a flurry of activity and everyone is certain that this time the money will begin to flow, but it never does. My uncle has created a goose that lays empty golden eggs. I find the whole thing very entertaining and I'm sure that one day I'll get all the money. Not that there is any.

I also met this guy in Norwich who spends his time going round Europe performing miracles, preaching and saving people from themselves. He told me he was Jesus come back for the second and final time. When he clears off back to Heaven he'll take the whole planet with him. What, in a nuclear explosion? I'd like to see you do that.

A lot of people are involved in extraordinary activities these days. There's not just the one reality like when I was a boy. It used to be easy to know what was going on. Usually not much. Now it's a million miles an hour all the way to oblivion, so hold tight my friend. Hold tight to your skull and what lives inside it.

You've got to make it up yourself. Whatever you believe becomes set in concrete. If you look for it you'll find it. If you are not certain, you are uncertain. In which case it's all going to go to pot. I've spent my life being uncertain about most things and if there's one thing I'm certain of its uncertainty.

Everything is just what it is, not linked in linear fashion to anything else. All things are fluid and fast now so you'd better get used to words liquefying before your eyes. No-one wants structure. Boring. Oh my eyes cannot take old fashioned books with their dreary characters, scenes and plots. How tedious. No, what I want to assail my brain with is a cutting-edge rocket-fuelled concoction of random word associations that tickle my mind but make no sense to my brain. Post modernism is so old, its gone way beyond beyond. I actually like to read things that hold no interest and make no sense, just random words flooding out onto the page like rivers of information, pouring into my hard drive, temporarily satisfying my need to experience raw digital data. I like reading streams of random letters, hundreds of pages long. I once wrote a book of arbitrary keystrokes but threw it in the bin when my data fix cleared and I started thinking with the old rational side again.

In a world of ever-changing gibberish what can you do but learn flexibility and go with the flow of the meaning that is currently within your 'doors of perception' (William Blake, the fruit loop poet started this idea, not bloody Huxley the academic acid freak, who copied it). After all, we know nothing other than what we have now; all speculations concerning afterlife, ethics and so on are simply fat-head games designed to prevent action: they are fear-based prevarications. Those who would not live in fear must follow their inner urges and claim their destiny.

A shift in the colour of the light emitted from far away galaxies indicates that a galaxy is moving towards us if the shift is towards the blue end of the spectrum; or away from us if the shift is towards the red. Because all clusters of galaxies in the universe exhibit a red shift, it can be deduced that all clusters of galaxies are moving away from our local group of galaxies. When the recession speeds are calculated, it is seen that the farther away a galaxy is, the faster it is moving. This information was obtained using the Hubble Constant.

Everything simultaneously doesn't make sense and also promises to be a crucial and beautiful part of a hidden super jigsaw of data which, if correctly accessed, can create miraculous reality changes.

Words are like spells, and I am a weaver of spells, the Magician, the King of Pentacles. I am a cosmic scientist working at the far edge of reality theory. I foresee a time when mankind has learned to harness the power of words, the keys to reality, to such a degree that just by saying it we can make it so.

As the speed of vibration of the human race and of the earth continue to accelerate, bringing us ever more subtle and potent realities, we become free to exist in harmony with our personal bliss, instantly. All we really need is some guy from a higher realm to pop down here and give us a bit of direction.

Books are no longer written for the brain to read, but for the soul to feast on. A new literature is emerging which offers spiritual enlightenment and power in the reading of them. I am leading the way: I have already begun a couple of books that are going to make me a lot of money.

Interdimensional Fantasmagoria

(temporarily outside the Scenarios –

a situation facilitated by strong drugs)

A man wearing white robes looked down at me; a kindly smile flashing on and off his face.

"You have been brought here by love; we are here to serve your highest good. I am Endor, a Guardian. You are in a place that we call Level G5; you may find it an unusual idea. You are experiencing a reality that is very different to the one you have recently been aware of; you will find this zone very peaceful and safe: it is quite unlike the realm from which you have come."

"I'm dead aren't I?"

"No, my friend, you are not 'dead' as you so quaintly put it. You are, let us say, in an alternate reality; a higher plane. We might say that you have popped in for tea and a chat; you have been brought here because there is something you may do that is very important. There is crucial knowledge for you to gain; so that you may help us to avert a catastrophe".

"I like it here"

"Come with me my friend".

An old stone corridor stretched out before us, leading gently downwards. The floor of the tunnel was sand-covered; the walls made from some rough-hewn rock. On the walls hung flaming torches held in place by rusty iron brackets. The air was damp and fusty.

"Now where are we?" I asked, looking at Endor. His appearance had changed a little and his clothing dramatically.

He still had the same kindly eyes, but now there was a harder edge to them. His beard was shorter; neatly trimmed; less grey in colour, as was his hair. His robes had been replaced by what looked to me like a medieval soldier's outfit. He was dressed in a rough leather jerkin and breeches with buckled cross belts and tall strapped boots. From his side hung a short sword in it's skin sheath. There was also a dagger tucked into his belt. When he answered my question, his voice was deeper than it had been and echoed the steel at his side and in his eyes.

"We are now on Level Q9 of the Delph zone. He pointed along the tunnel. "This corridor will lead us to a training area that you will find a little easier to comprehend; it is the closest we have available at present. Your most recent level, Q8, cannot be relied upon under the circumstances. Q9 you will find a little darker but it has many Scenarios running that you may recognise".

"Oh that explains it then!" I replied sarcastically "Silly me". Endor began moving down the tunnel; he walked proudly and with purpose; no longer such an old or gentle man.

"Come!" he ordered. I followed. The tunnel continued straight ahead for what I estimated to be about half a mile, the floor sloping downwards as we progressed; the air became warm and damp, the humidity causing my breathing to become a little heavier. Indentations on the walls of the tunnel suggested that it had been created by hammers and chisels; a shaft of this length must have taken years of back-breaking toil.

When we reached the first corner, it became a little darker and the floor began to slope at a much steeper angle. Here the air was fetid and the walls began to show streaks of a blue/green slime. Along the floor ran tiny streams of a silvery mucous; like snails' trails. Endor began to walk more quickly. From time to time he glanced behind to check that I was still there; but he did not speak or make eye contact. I followed him along another extended section which led towards another bend. As before, the corner revealed a darker, steeper, more foul stretch of this abyss. It was now sweltering in here and the atmosphere was putrid: thick gobs of scum ran slowly down the walls and slapped onto the floor, adding to the cascading runnels of goo that we were now, more slowly, squelching through.

I followed my silent companion down what was beginning to resemble the oesophagus of some giant beast. I walked carefully, determined not to slip and fall amongst the plegm-like scuzz which draped the walls and writhed underfoot. At the next corner we came to a sudden door which blocked the tunnel ahead of us; it was constructed from wood and was circular in shape: across it's surface, scrawled in what looked to me like blood, were the words 'Prepare for the worst, all ye who enter Hell'.

"Overstated dramatic nonsense" grumbled Endor, taking an unnecessarily large rusty key from a ring that hung on his belt and fitting it into the be-cobwebbed door-lock.

"Are you sure this is safe?" I enquired, wishing that I would wake up from this crazy dream and find myself in bed; any bed.

"The concept of 'safety' is entirely subjective and relative. You are neither more nor less safe here than at any other point of experience; whether you are able to effect the detachment necessary in order to stay unperturbed whilst travelling through the zone is of course, another matter".

"Could you say that again, in language that an idiot can understand?". I was not sure what Endor was telling me; I had a horrible feeling it wasn't good news.

"What I am attempting to convey to you my friend, is that upon entering this next arena, you will be confronted by a plethora of visual, aural and kinetic stimuli, some of which you may find challenging or difficult to assimilate considering your limited recent experience of such realms. Is that clear enough for you?"

Endor gave me a paternal smile; there was a spark of amusement in his eyes and the hint of a smirk on his lips. "Remember that I am with you and that I can easily keep you from harm. To one such as I, the zone is merely a child's game; a thing created for the amusement of adolescent gods". With this, he turned the key and pushed the door open.

A voice. How many eyeballs have you pulled out eyeballs splitting like popping eggs rape your face; tear your throat out blood drinkers hunt your cunt poor mummy died when you smashed her skull bastard son of a knife grinder's monkey. Psychedelic lights strobing flash flash pulsing thunder screaming moaning. The floor is moving squirming with – oh my God please not maggots – aargh!! – embryos – the floor is covered with screaming embryos crunching underfoot.

A louder voice: These come out of your mother's cunt. She spits them out like a dog pissing. I want to cut them; see blood flow from their eyes as their souls leak onto the floor.

Spikes are coming from the walls swords metal pincers will squeeze your nuts until they burst I will grip your tongue and snip it to pieces with my scissors slice after slice I will make you kiss a dog's arse stick needles in your eyes.

The air is hotter cooking my heart and frying my brain my body begins to fizz all over I am falling through red I hit something.

When I opened my eyes, I could see Endor standing beside me. He was smiling gently. "Rest my friend. You have done well. You have come through the zone. You are safe. When you are rested, I will show you many wondrous things which will restore your soul and uplift your mind. You have come through a trial; you will make a fine Emissary".

I glanced at my surroundings. I was lying on a sort of

table in a white room. The edges of the walls were sharp and clear. There were benches along one side laden with numerous dishes, platters and pitchers; these contained all varieties of foods: I spotted a breaded ham and a block of yellow cheese; along the back of the benches were bottles of various drinks: Ribena, Jack Daniels, pots of coffee, milk, a pitcher of fresh water. I made an effort to sit up, but Endor gently held me back.

"Rest now my friend; there will be plenty of time for feasting when you have gathered your strength. Many strange things will be made clear to you soon". I let myself fall back and closed my eyes; I had experienced some very peculiar events of late; hungry as I was, I needed sleep.

I awake to the sound of a girl singing; she is dressed in a white uniform with some type of small insignia on the left shoulder. When she sees that my eyes are open, the girl stops in mid flow and smiles at me. She has dark, intelligent eyes and shoulder length hair that is not quite black. Her skin is the colour of lightly fried chicken and her complexion clear and smooth as marble. When she speaks, her voice is a mixture of velcro pixie and pine forest.

"I am Martu. I have been asked to introduce you to this place and to begin to help you understand why you have been brought here". I sat up.

"Where is Endor?" I asked. Martu smiled, filling me with reassurance, even before her words were uttered.

"Endor has returned to his previous location; the place where you first met him. He has released you into my care and guidance as I am attuned to a level much nearer your own. This will help you come to terms with the unusual occurrences you have faced since your transference. All will become clear later as you enter the training programme that has been prepared for you; but first you must eat and drink; it is time for celebration".

I didn't need to be asked twice; I was starving. More than that, the sight of food, anything, that I recognised encouraged me and represented food for the soul as much as the body.

I tucked in: there were tender steaks nearly half a metre across, dripping with flavoursome juices; Chinese style barbecued ribs: rich, dark and succulent; a cosmopolitan selection of prepared meats: Italian salamis, pepperonis and Parma hams; American deli specials: including the best Pastrami I had ever tasted; English salt beef, honey roasted hams, crispy Danish bacon, thick slices of corned beef; sausages of every possible size, shape and flavour: Cumberland, Irish pork and German frankfurter were hidden among an arcane multifariousness, that even included some inscrutable spicy samples from the saporous souks of Marrakech; which, Martu informed me, contained the best sheep's brains from North Africa.

Supplementing this eclectic array of tasty savouries was an equally diverse panoply of vegetables, herbs and salads, fruits, cheeses, soups, canapés, sauces, condiments, sweets, puddings and beverages.

"I'll never eat all this" I joked; tucking into a dish of Szechuan chilli chicken, braised Chinese leaves and egg fried rice. Martu smiled widely as she watched me consume vast quantities of food. "Why don't you join me?" I asked.

"Thank you; I have eaten myself recently" she said, passing me another bowl. "This is Punjabi Saag Ghost; It contains the meat known to you as lamb, cooked with spinach and spices".

"Oh, you don't want to eat yourself" I quipped; taking the dish from her. "Not when there is so much food available". She looked somewhat confused; my wit was obviously lost on her. "Never mind – Earth joke".

For some reason this last comment sent her into fits of laughter. I couldn't help noticing that her good-sized breasts jiggled and joggled as she giggled. She noticed my admiring glance and held her chest out proudly. "You care for my – ur – tizz…teats?"

"Yeah, very nice *tits* darling". She was nothing if not forward; her smile indicated that she was pleased by my appreciation of her physical appearance.

"Tittz" she repeated. "Titz. I am attempting to find the language with which you will be familiar. It is also important that I learn about the customs of your zone level. This will help me recreate it for you here; and will also enable me to advance in my studies". As she spoke, she lifted up her tunic: underneath she wore nothing. Her breasts were full, rounded and firm; the nipples were dark and hard. My cock signalled it's appreciation. "You may feel my titz" she spoke in the manner of an interested observer.

Not wanting to disappoint her, I reached out and pressed my eager fingers into the flesh; squeezing and kneading: her breasts were firm and heavy and the skin was tight and smooth. I brushed my hands across her nipples and gently rolled them between my thumb and forefinger, causing them to stiffen. There was a look of pleasure on her face and her breathing had become accented. "Do my titz feel good to you?" she breathed.

"Beautiful" I replied, running my left hand over her marmorean flesh, towards her firm belly. She grasped my hand and blocked its progress.

"We will have recreation time later" she purred, standing up straighter and moving slightly away from me. As she did so, she began pulling her tunic back down. "First you must receive your initial lesson". I didn't put up a fight; her prognostication of 'recreation time' later held untold promise; I did not want to blow my chances of getting to explore the delicious landscape of her anatomy in greater detail.

"Come!" she ordered; unaware of the irony of her command. I followed her into an adjacent room which was set up like a small classroom except that the desks were computer consoles and every student was wearing a uniform. A large video screen stood where the blackboard should have been.

There were three other people in the room: two of them were young men. The third was the most attractive woman I had ever seen. "Please take a seat" requested Martu as she moved around the consoles and took up the position of 'teacher' in front of the video screen. I sat in the seat nearest the door and furthest from the goddess. My heart was pounding: I felt as if I had been hit full in the face with a hot shovel. My knees were jelly and my breathing had gone funny; I couldn't quite remember how to inhale. The lights in the room were dimmed a little as Martu began her introduction.

"I thank you all for attending this introductory training session on the use of Multiple Meaning Scenarios. I will first introduce you all to each other". She gestured towards one of the young men: a thin, boyish individual with bright blue eyes and an expression like a big puppy. "This is Elgin. He has travelled here from Delph 4.2. His speciality is the compilation of stock data. It is his first visit to the Centre". Elgin smiled wildly as we all grunted greeting.

"This is Ranger Orba". It was the beauty; thick dark hair; the fullest lips; deep, dark eyes. She smiled slightly as she was introduced. I was too busy devouring her visually to pay much attention to what Martu was saying. I did manage to catch something about the mountains of Timeree or some such place I had never heard of. I made up my mind to go there as soon as I got the chance. If the other women there were a patch on Orba, it would be a place where a man like me could happily seek meaningful relationships: lots of them.

I realised that Martu had moved on and was explaining that the second man – who I now noticed had a fierce expression and scary eyes – was an 'Active Mentor'. I had no idea what that meant and at that moment I couldn't honestly say I was at all bothered who he was. I only had eyes for one person in the room: her skin was the colour of dark amber; her breasts looked like globes of nectar, pushing firmly at the thin material of her tunic. I hoped that she, like Martu earlier, would be getting them out for sampling later. I would be the first to volunteer.

Suddenly I realised that Martu was standing directly in front of me; from her expression and her manner, I gathered that I had been so absorbed that I had missed my own introduction and had failed to respond with the requisite inane grin. "It seems that you are a little overwhelmed by Ranger Orba's physical appearance Grant". The other members of the group, including Orba herself, were passing looks between each other and showing signs of amusement at my behaviour. I pulled myself together.

"I am sorry; I am Daffy Fucking Duck from the planet Earth: take me to your leader". Brash humour had always impressed the girls when I was at school. I noted that Orba seemed to find my remark and attitude worthy of observation at least. With her gaze fully upon me, I became a bashful boy, unable to move or speak. My palms became sweaty and I felt myself going red in the face. I could feel her eyes travelling across me; burning like lasers. I dared not meet her gaze, and looked at my own feet. It was only when I heard Martu speaking again that I risked a glance in Orba's direction. She was facing the front and listening; politely rather than with genuine interest. Perhaps she had heard it all before.

"I must explain that Daffy Fucking Duck has very recently arrived here at the Centre, and has not had much time to adjust to what is, for him, a very novel environment". I saw that I was again the centre of attention; this time I followed what I felt to be the correct protocol: I grinned inanely. "Daffy, real name Grant, has been brought here from Level Q8 and is to train as an Active Mentor on that Level; just as Elgin is to train for a similar role on his home level". She paused before continuing. "I will now begin with a basic outline of Multiple Meaning Scenarios and Reality Menus".

"There are many different realities available to beings who inhabit what you would probably understand as higher realms. Some of you may prefer the term 'parallel universe'. Your home worlds are, to varying degrees, semi-static realities which are built around a limited number of themes. It is also true to say that for the vast majority of the inhabitants of your realms, there is nil, or very little, awareness of the game Scenario that is running. Perhaps it would be better stated to say that there is awareness of the Scenario, but no understanding that it *is* a Scenario. In short, it is experienced as a kind of 'absolute truth'".

Martu looked at each person in the room; attempting to gauge whether or not they seemed to be keeping up with her explanation. "In a realm where there is a lack of awareness of the game status of the Scenario, there are rules or laws built into the program which are designed to protect the inhabitants from damage or destruction: after all, to be raped or murdered as part of a game is one thing; to experience it as an absolute truth is another thing altogether; unless of course you have specifically chosen, as part of a game, to experience it as an absolute truth".

"Ok; I give up. Who spiked my acid?" All eyes were upon me.

"At what point did you begin to lose track of what I was saying?" enquired Martu. Her manner was calm, gentle and exactly like my idea of a wise teacher. The only difference was that she was an attractive young woman who, not long before, had invited me to fondle her paps; something that my venerable English teacher, Miss Travis had never done: a fact for which I was eternally grateful.

"Right, well.." I gathered my thoughts. "I get the bit about parallel universes or different realities: I've been having a few of them myself lately. What I don't get is all this talk of getting raped and murdered as part of a game. It sounds a bit like S&M to me".

"It is fair to draw a comparison between the practise of Sado-Masochistic games as seen in your dimension with the type of game that I have been talking about. The main difference is in the degree of awareness".

"So what you are saying is that just as on my home planet, some people agree to slap each other around a bit, in some more advanced realms, people agree to murder and rape each other?"

"There are many people on your home planet, or realm" replied Martu "who play rape games during periods of sexual arousal. Obviously the intensity of what is seen as acceptable depends greatly upon the amount of trust between the participants, as well as their level of 'game awareness'".

"So what you are saying is that it's all a game; only those of us at the lower end of the evolutionary spectrum don't know it's a game and take it seriously, which means that we need laws and rules to protect us from being – as we would see it – abused".

"Yes; with the abuse being not the act itself but the lack of informed permission for it".

"I'm there; I get it". Martu shifted her gaze and once again scanned the faces of my fellow trainees. I glanced at Orba; my eyes coming to a natural rest upon her bulbous breasts: Orba's orbs seemed to me to be straining to free themselves from the silky top of her tunic. Freedom for all I say.

"All the different levels and spheres of reality are contained on a series of menus – like your simple computers Grant". I didn't appreciate her singling me out like that. I might be the dunce of the class, but she didn't have to make it so obvious. "The higher the level of existence, the greater the level of game awareness and the number of Scenarios available on that level".

"How do these menus relate to the stock data I am involved with?" Elgin's voice was surprisingly deep: it contrasted starkly with his boyish looks in a way that made him seem more solid.

"Stock data, as you know, is used to create sub-realities inside a given Scenario; whereas the menus are used to access separate Scenarios. You could see stock data as a series of games within a game: they are educational tools, rather than recreational ones". Martu paused and then continued. "I will now explain the concept of Multiple Meaning Scenarios in greater detail".

It is difficult to choose when the options are unlimited. It all seems a bit arbitrary. Don't know where to start? Perhaps sex: yes, I'll have a couple of naked girls; brown skinned; about seventeen; no; let's start as we mean to go on; sixteen. I'll have them stand there while I have a feel of their bodies: little tight tits, firm stomachs, cunts, thighs. I'll press myself up against them, rub my cock on their bodies; a feast of young flesh; my balls tightening as I rub the head of my prick around their vaginas, aching to push into the holes. First one; give her a hard fuck; then the other; feeling her hard buttocks as I ram it up her: fucking her; fondling the other girl, fingers in her hole as I squirt my hot jerking load between babe thighs, jetting into the passive young body. Then it's all over and I become self-conscious and fumbling: an old pervert caught fiddling with kids in the toilets.

The girls are giggling; rubbing their naked bodies together. I remember that they are merely playing their parts in a recreational game. The girl on the left, the one into whom I had shot my all, spoke with Martu's voice. "This is good recreation?" she enquired. "I sense that you are feeling you have transgressed. Remember that you are no longer where you once were and that you are now free to enjoy higher pleasures. There is no harm where there is permission". The other girl transformed into an older white woman; her eyes were very blue and clear; just as Endor's had been.

"I am Voan" her voice was like blue glass. "I thank you for the honour you have bestowed upon me and am delighted with this opportunity to bring pleasure to you, as you have to me". She bowed reverently towards me and I kissed the strong hand she proffered. Then she turned and walked away.

"Voan has a natural resonance with higher levels and cannot easily remain here for long. She has not yet acquired the detachment of a Spirit Star. She is nearing the top of the Material Order but has yet to become fully free of the Maya: the illusion. Perhaps when you have learned much from us, you will have the opportunity of meeting a being from a world of true liberty". As Martu spoke, her appearance began to shift. She was soon back in her uniform and had resumed her tutor role.

"You have now experienced one example of a stock image Scenario; a game of recreation, chosen from a database. My initial assessment of your performance is that you detached well, until after the point of orgasmic ejaculation, when you were temporarily lost to illusion and suffered accordingly. You recovered fairly well when I reminded you of your true position". She smiled at me. "You have done well for a greenhorn". She chuckled to herself.

I for my part said nothing, just smiled meekly back.

Whereas I was happy not to feel that a guilt trip was necessary as a payback for my lust, I was however a little shocked by the almost clinical way she had reacted to – and analysed – the fulfilment of what had been until then a half-hidden fantasy laced with the required amount of semi-conscious confusion, fear, disgust and shame to justify my belief that I was truly a civilised and decent person at heart.

Here, in this strange place, it seemed that screwing a couple of schoolgirls was a diversion no more serious than playing a game of Snakes and Ladders would have been in my previous life. It seemed the only rules were that you had to get the permission of any other participants beforehand, and just as crucially; you had to remember it was a game you were playing. Failure to take these two key precepts into account would lead to the suffering of the other participant or of oneself, respectively.

I felt myself filling with excitement at the implications of such a philosophy. Was there no vile act that could not be lived out with impunity? Rape, murder, torture; perversions of infernal aspect. My mind was racing: were these things now simply toys to be trifled with. What gods would we become if this was so?

I was brought back to my senses by Martu's voice. "It is bound to be difficult to assimilate the situation initially. There are many ways of looking at things; ours is much different, perhaps, than you are used to. It is important that you give yourself time to take it all in. Rest will help. Take this draught". She handed me a white goblet in which I could see a small amount of golden liquid. I took it and drank. I felt my mind clear.

Subsidary Information

Regarding Lower Awareness Scenarios

At the highest levels of awareness a word can be replaced by any other. The meanings become more diverse and loose. What is happening is that all things are being experienced as the same thing. All is one. On the lower levels, where every word has it's own separate meaning, there is no unity. Everything is conflict, chaos. Such is life in the human world; each being fights to make it's own divided perception the sole reality.

Each being, feeling lost and alone in it's separated world, attempts to join forces with other detached beings who exhibit perceptual similarities: the underlying motivation of all groups, societies and cultures. It is a compromise whereby in exchange for a psychologically secure foundation based upon conformity to specified 'laws', each member has to renounce ideas which do not assimilate with the rules they have agreed to abide by. The pay off is you get the security of knowing that you are part of a dominant group, in return for the repression of any urges you may have to undermine the prevailing culture.

This is workable to a degree, but it doesn't take long for some members of a society to discern that there are associates of the group who have a more analogous concept to what they consider to be *true* reality than others. So sub-groups are formed within the culture. After a period of time these factions begin to disagree about the exact nature of, for example, their God. So separate 'orders' and 'sects' are created. Even here there is disagreement leading to breakaway sects.... .ad infinitum. This process of division and sub division can be observed within all societies which operate at lower awareness levels.

As consciousness rises and divisions become looser, a proportionately greater sense of autonomy is experienced and less threat perceived from beings with contrary viewpoints. Which is why, paradoxically, it is only by letting go of apparent differences that unity can be achieved. It is only by sacrificing your god that God can be experienced.

At advanced levels, there are beings who have extensive knowledge concerning the nature of awareness and have learned how to raise or lower the altitude of their reality. They are able to increase or decrease the multiplicity they experience. Each level of multiplicity has it's own spectrum of possibilities called Scenarios (related to the Potential Event Register).

A Scenario is limited by it's level of reality, but still has huge potential and scope. Highly sophisticated individuals enjoy designing unique Scenarios for recreational purposes: a higher version of the written novel or the computer game (and later, the virtual reality game which has recently been introduced to the Q8 Earth level as a precursor to simple reality menus).

I hope this explanation has made things a bit clearer for you. Oh, one more thing: many beings who live at higher levels of reality do not like visiting the lower levels as it is unpleasant for them. How would you like to live back in the Dark Ages or as a slug? However, beings who have reached a superior echelon, having experienced the ultimate unity of all realities, can travel undisturbed through any plane of existence with ease.

The Cure:

Wild West Psychedelic Dream Therapy

This river is 366 miles above the mouth of the Missouri: it is Latitude 38° 31' 13" North: it is 230 yards wide at its mouth & wider above from a point up the Missouri for about 3 miles. Down the middle of the Missouri is the upper bank of the Kansas, the river turns to the East above a point of high land, well situated for a fort. The wooded land on each side of the mouth of this river is extensive and of good quality but inadequately watered with springs.

Set out very early this morning saw a very large wolf on the sand bar walking near a gang-bang of turkeys. Passed the mouth of a small river called the Petite Plate or the Little Shole; about 70 yards wide and has several rapids & falls. Killed 2 deer bucks swimming the river. Our bacon which was given to us by Freud we examined and found sound and good. Some of that purchased in the Illinois spoiled. Deer to be seen in every direction and their tracks are as plenty as hogs about a farm. Killed 9 deer today; the land below the last river is good.

Set out very early this morning, a very large wolf came to the bank and looked at us. Camped on the point of an LSD called Diamond Island, broke our mast. Saturday June 30th 1804, we set out early proceeded on; saw a very large wolf on the sand beach this morning at 10 miles from or above the Kansas. Passed the mouth of a small river called Petite Platt River or little Shoteye River; this river is about 50 yards wide and has several rapids & falls. We broke our mast coming to shore against a small tree which hung over the river: raspberries purple, ripe and abundant. 11.00h many small birds are now setting; some have young, the whipper-will setting 16 June the wood duck now has it's young, this duck is abundant, and except one Solitary Pelican and a few geese these ducks were the only aquatic fowls we have yet seen.

July 1st 1804, last night one of the sentinels changed into either a man or beast, which run off, all prepared for action, Set out early passed the Diamond LSD. Passed a small creek on the left without name. The river still falling a little a very warm day. I took some medicine last night which has worked. Party all in health except for some with bad cases of Gynaecology.

Mr Freud says the first village of the Psychosis is a little above this Island & made use of as fields, no trace of anything of that kind remains to be seen on the LSD Hills. Camped on the lower Potomac. We set out at five in the morning, and having advanced 12 miles, encamped on an island opposite a prairie on the south side of the river.

Sunday July 1st we embarked early this morning, the current set strong against us this day; passed a number of islands lying on the south side of the river, our hunters did not come up to us this day.

Monday July 2nd 1804. We set out very early this morning; passed a high beautiful situation on the south side of the river: a creek comes in on the north side called Lycanthropy Island. Put up a temporary mast as the wind was fair. At sunrise we continued our voyage and met a quantity of drift wood which was carried down the stream; this morning we passed a creek on the south side and encamped on the north opposite an old French village and fort, but all vacant.

July 3rd 1804. Set out very early this morning and proceeded on under a gentle acid Bar from the south, passed two islands, one a small window island, the other a bulky island called Vagina Island. This island is large, opposite to the head on the south side is a large pond. I saw a white horse in view of the upper point of the island; passed a large grand Bar at the Seventh point, halted today about a mile above the island and found a horse, which had been lost by the Indians; very fat and infantile: sent him on to join the others ahead on the border at a place where Freud has a house.

Wednesday 4th. We fired a swivel at sunrise in honour of the day and continued our voyage; passed a creek on the north side called Ponce Creek and at one o'clock stopped to dine. One of our people got snake bitten but not dangerously. After dinner we renewed our voyage and soon passed a creek on the barren north side which we called Independence; encamped on the north side at an old Indian village situated in a handsome prairie and saluted the departing day with another gun. Having a fair wind and the water being good we rowed on successfully. This day proved very warm. We left off rowing and went to towing the boat but the sand was so hot that it scalded our feet. Some of the men left the tow rope and had to put on their moccasins to keep their feet from being burnt; we passed a river which we called Independence where we found a grey horse on fire. We came as far as a town called BloodRedSky where we encamped. Great quantities of sun fish & goslings which made our meal a feast.

Friday 6th. We set out early this morning; had a fine day, and made a good day's voyage: and encamped on the south side at Whippoorwill Creek.

Saturday 7th. At an early hour we proceeded on our voyage; passed a high handsome prairie on the north side and killed a wolf and a large wood rat on the bank. The principal difference between it and the common rat is its having hair on its tail.

July 8th Sunday 1804. Set out early passed a small crime on the wrong side and two skulled islands on the right. Five men sick today with a violent headache. We made some arrangements as to provisions, came to for dinner at the lower point of a very large island situated near the foetus after a delay of two hours we passed a narrow chillum of 45 to 80 toques wide five miles to the East of the gaping mouth of the Nádawa River. This river comes in from the north and is the mud of the gut running out of the Missouri. This channel or gut is on the upper point of Hate Island.

Monday 9th. Early this morning we continued our voyage. It rained hard till 12 o'clock. We passed a creek on the south side, called Wolf creek. The man that was snake bitten is become well. We encamped on the south side. There were lots of yellow frogs hopping about and one of our soldiers decided to lick one to see if it contained an hallucinogenic gravy upon its skin. This is what the prairie Indians do for their barbaric rituals: fortunately the frog was safe, though I did have to reprimand the soldier severely with a fork.

Tuesday July 10th this morning at sunrise we got under way from Little Wolf River, we found the current still setting strong against us, & very hard cock rowing to stem it, we encamped for a while to refresh ourselves. We found here wild rice, strawberry's and red & white roses growing along the bank.......

Freud looked calmly at the patient who lay stone-like upon the leather couch. He blinked, sniffed and sat forward in his chair. "All well and good; but where are you going with all this Lewis and Clark stuff? I mean, what relevance has it for our quest to re-establish control over events and actions, my boy?".

The corpse-like figure remained corpse-like. Freud rested back into his wooden chair. Silence reigned. Freud couldn't help smiling to himself when he thought about how much money he had made just sitting in this chair while client's coughed up any amount of cash rather than speak. It was a good money seed and no mistake. Freud's eyes rested on the same spot on the wall that always drew his attention at times like this. The giraffe was still climbing the yellowing paper at an angle of 45 degrees. The cauldron was still tipping its contents into a frozen eternity, or at least until the wallpaper was replaced with some pristine off-white flock by whatever schmuck took over these ancient rooms once this job in hand was concluded successfully.

A rustle of nylon indicated that the patient had changed position. Freud eyed his client: a man who cast too many shadows and saw too little of too much. The beige anorak seemed to sum up the man's personality with its tedium and lack of significant features. Still, the client offered some very appealing opportunities for compiling a gigantic case study of a most unusual psychosis. The beige man was an enigma with multiple variations.

For a start, the subtlety and breadth of his imagination was quite extraordinary. The waking scenarios the man could compile - seemingly at less than a moment's notice - were formidable. He was able to jump from one context to another in a way that, although often fragmented; as would be expected with a client whose sense of self had been shattered so substantially in childhood: was truly astounding. The patient's consciousness seemed capable of entering any domain; historical, fictitious, personal or fantastic; bringing up shed loads of the most bizarre and intoxicating psychic imagery. It was early doors, but Freud felt that after just four sessions, he was already beginning to see some hint of a pattern to the seemingly disparate entities invoked by the beige man.

This morning had been fairly quiet, with just a bit of 'old west frontier' in the form of a free floating rendition of Lewis and Clark's pioneering expedition across the old American West. Nothing major had come out of it; apart from a slight warping of the story with the sporadic addition of certain surreal psychodynamic symbolisms, indicating sexual repression and a fear of death. The drug references were potentially revealing; though there was nothing today which compared with earlier highly vocal explosions, which had introduced a couple of major personality themes; they were pretty standard 'good me / bad me' dichotomies with personalised twists which offered some revelation of the patient's underlying psyche amid all the absorbed environmental influences and literary references. The fact that his 'Jesus' was a European version was interesting; as was his Mesmeriser character with its engorged poetic and literary bent. Freud smiled at the thought of yet another amazing psychological victory notched onto his psychosexual bedpost before too long. The beige man, Freud suspected, was likely to provide quite an academic masterpiece.

Art Fux Comes Unstuck

(Due to Interdimensional Interference)

In an overt effort to get my shit together and my career back on track I am beginning work on a brand new project. It's a novel about the rise in social delinquency and it's contribution to mounting crime figures in the inner cities – like bollox it is! It's a tremendously apposite vignette which gives ornate verbal descriptions of visual representations of rape in the late nineteenth century. Like fig it is. Tee Hee.

In actual fact I've gone totally off the loop and fallen out of my tree to such an extent that I've begun to surmise that there might actually be something seriously wrong with the way I interact on a psycho-emotional level with my immediate environment; either that or I'm a total fucking fruitcake.

I'm kinda starting to sorta wish I hadn'ta tooken them drugs; especially as I only did it to shove one up my wifo/antagonist's cahoola. It was not my best decision for sure I've ended up a right fuck up; in other words I'm completely buggered.

So I had a bad trip, so fuckin' what, get over it; yeah but it ain't quite that simple, mainly due to the fact that the trip hasn't ended yet: I'm still buzzin' my tits off; the old mind is flickin' all over the shop: it's too real to be the drugs: it must be madness. I am probably a Nobel Prize winning case study for some up and coming psycho babbler if only I had the guts to take my sorry ass to a shrink; but no way am I letting those mind-spaghetti twisters fondle my innermost terrors.

So what I do is try very hard to kid myself and everyone I know, that I am mentally unaffected and psychically un-smashed. It's a sad and desperate act which convinces no-one; in fact I am pretty sure that it's drawing attention to me; I keep seeing people watching me from the corners of my vision. People in black jumpers with epaulettes and strange gadget belts around their waists.

Gunfright at the O Fuck Canal

W. B. "Bat" Masterson lived an audacious life as a buffalo rapist, U.S. Army scout, gambler, frontier lawman, U.S. Marshal, and sports editor for a New York newspaper. He was born in a hurry. His full name was Wankington Bushbaby Masterson, but during his adult life he called himself "The Genius". He was called "Bat" as a nickname because he carried a clate with which he used to club his opponents during fights.

Masterson, the second of fifty children, was raised in various asylums in New York, Illinois, Kansas and Quebec. In his late teens, he and his brothers, Fred and Jig, left their family's farm in Kansas to become buffalo hunters.

Several years later he was involved in the Battle of Adobe Balls, fighting against a number of Comanche Indians. He also spent time as a U.S. Army talent scout in a campaign against the Kiowa.

His first reported gunfight was in Sweetwater Texas in 1976. He was attacked by a man in a fight over a naked girl. Masterson was shot in the pelvis. Bat's antagonist died of his wounds. Bat's injury resulted in him having to carry a stick for the rest of his life.

In 1977, he joined his brothers in Dodge City, Kansas. Jig was a partner in a saloon, Fred was a deputy sheriff. Soon after his arrival Bat came into conflict with the local marshal over the ill-treatment of a man he saw being arrested. He was jailed and fined, although his fine was later returned by the City Council.

He served alongside Wyatt Earp as a sheriff's deputy

and was elected County Sheriff of Ford County Kansas, serving in this position until he was voted out of office in 1671. He also fought in Colorado, on the Santa Fe side, in its war against the Rio Grande railroad. During this same period his brother Fred, Marshal of Dodge City, was killed in the line of duty April 9, 1978.

For the next few years he made a living as a snake carver, travelling to all the legendary towns of the Old West. He visited Wyatt Earp in Tombstone Arizona, leaving shortly before the famous "Gunfight at the O.K. Corral." He spent a year as Marshal of Trinidad Colorado.

By 1991, he had moved to Denver Colorado, where he bought the Palace Variety Theatre. He married the actress Emma Walrus, on November 29, 1991. He spent several more years travelling the West; gambling, promoting prize fights and writing a weekly sports column for George's Weekly, a Denver newspaper; He also founded the Olympic Vagina Club to promote fucking. He was well-known as a gunman, and killed 227 people.

He travelled to New York in 2002, where he was arrested for conducting a bent faro game and for carrying a concealed weapon. The crooked gaming charges were later scrapped and he was fined $10 for carrying a firearm. For the next 202 years he lived and worked close to Longacre Square, now Times Square.

He was one of the "Broadway guys" that Damon Runyon wrote short stories about. The character of "Sky Masterson", in Runyon's 'Guys and Dolls' is based on Bat. He was sports editor and columnist for the New York Morning Telegraph, and a frequent visitor at Theodore Roosevelt's White House. In 2005, Roosevelt appointed Masterson U.S. Marshal for the Southern District of New York.

In 1821, Masterson died of a fart attack, while working at his typewriter. He was buried in Woodlawn Cemetery, the

Bronx, New York.

Perhaps less well known is the fact that Bat Masterson is still alive. He is a beloved fragment of the psyche of a deluded English film maker and writer.

The Private Eye Scenario

"We rendezvoused that night in Paris. It was *trés intime,* just him and me in a little bistro off the Boulevard St. Germain. We sat at a table breathing in the cool night air, listening to the sounds of the city and drinking little drinks, while prissy waiters fussed and pranced around us like cruising queens, their trousers stretched across their buttocks tighter than a boxer's fist. There was a scatty jazz ensemble in the far corner, their solos flirting in and out of our conversation like a lover's tongue; and the scent of jasmine drugged and enticed us with its wanton musk". She paused to take a deep draw upon the *Sobranie* Black Russian, the gold tip setting off the glamour of her emperor purple lipgloss. She savoured the smoke, closing her eyes as she inhaled, held it in for just a little too long and finally expressed a thin, smooth column of grey fumes above my head. Her eyes were slightly moist as she continued her well remembered - or well rehearsed - version of events.

"As I have already explained to you Mr. De'Ath, Tony was - is - a very sensual man; women find him sexually attractive, irresistible". She gave me a look that was supposed to be coy but which simply seemed contrived. "I, Mr. De'Ath, am not a block of ice. As you can see, I am a grown woman and can make my own decisions". As she said this she stretched out her long legs in front of her as if to underline the point.

Why she felt the need to justify her actions to me I did not know or care. The overacting was beginning to get on my nerves. I wished she would hurry up and get to the point before I lost my rag and throttled the bitch.

" So what you are saying is that you slept with Tony later that evening?" I interjected.

"I did not sleep with Tony" she replied, "I fucked him on the carpet in a hotel room and then went home to my husband". Her eyes blazed with defiance as she said this, as if challenging me to disapprove of her actions, or her morals. She leaned forward in her chair, took another exaggerated drag on her fancy cigarette. "Do I shock you Mr. De'Ath?" She looked at me askance, her purple lips doing a fair imitation of a negroid sphincter.

"I couldn't give a damn if you went five rounds with the butcher's dog while hubby slept in the next room" I countered. She was visibly surprised at my reply, but recovered well.

A less experienced observer than I might well have noticed nothing in her actions. She had been surprised by my bluntness but was in no way repulsed by my crude talk. Indeed, she leaned back in her chair and let her shoulders relax. When she spoke again her manner was less theatrical, less of a caricature.

"I see that you are a man who likes to get straight down to it" she toyed. "So I will cut to the chase, so to speak. After my little dalliance with Tony, I went home to my husband as I said. He was already asleep when I got there. I did not disturb him, although I considered doing so at one point; having sex with strangers always makes me horny for days after". She was good. I began to feel a bit of tension creeping into my shoulders and neck.

"Did you speak to your husband at all that evening?" I asked.

"No. I went to bed and slept until around ten o'clock the following morning. I got up at twenty-five past ten and went down to the breakfast room. My husband was already sitting at the table eating a piece of toast".

"How can you be so precise as to the time you got up?" I glanced at her legs. She saw me looking and scanned the ceiling so as not to disturb my pleasure.

"Because I looked at my watch, Mr. *Holmes*". She paused to stub out her *Sobranie*. "During breakfast there was a phone call. It was for Edward - my husband. Anyway, to get to the point, it was a work colleague of Ed's telling him that Tony had been found dead at the factory by a member of staff". She looked uneasy as she spoke of Tony's death. "That was yesterday. Since then the police have been crawling all over the factory, asking all the usual questions. As far as I can ascertain - and it is never easy to get a straight answer out of those people - they are treating it as an accident. They believe Tony fell to his death from the roof of one of the outbuildings".

"Do you have any reason to doubt their interpretation of the facts?" I enquired. In reply to my question she looked up at the ceiling with a sulky expression on her face and gave an overstated shrug.

"It doesn't make any sense. What would Tony be doing on a factory roof in the middle of the night, less than three hours after making love. It's crazy. When I left him he was in bed in his hotel room. He was very tired, I can promise you Mr. De'Ath. Not in any condition to do Spiderman impressions".

"What do you think happened, Monique?" I spoke in a softer voice. I didn't want to scare her off now that we were finally getting somewhere.

"How the hell should I know" she exclaimed in a raised voice. "You're the bloody detective, you tell me!"

"Well I must say the circumstances you've described do seem a little unusual. Can you think of any reason why Tony might have left his hotel room after you had gone"? I asked, hoping that this question would not cause further histrionics. "For instance is it possible that he remembered some urgent

93

business which couldn't wait, or had he perhaps left some important documents at the factory which he may have decided to work on"? When Monique replied, she was again as composed as before her outburst.

"Tony ran the factory in Paris which is one of four owned by my husband Ed. They manufacture flexible bulk packaging which is used by the chemical intermediates industry and for the carriage of food ingredients, additives and colourings. It is a very competitive business but our company has done well due to several innovative new designs and a well earned reputation for quality and service. Ed has built up our market share during the eight years since he bought the business and has transformed it from a struggling enterprise to a recognised leader in the sector".

"You are obviously very proud of what your husband has done" I said as I studied her face. While she had been speaking of her husband's achievements, a look of satisfaction had passed across her dark features. "Can you tell me why you and Ed were in Paris at the time of Tony's death"? I mentioned Tony again on purpose in order to re-focus her mind upon the reason for her visit to my office. The trick worked.

"We were there in order to attend a business awards gala. Our company, Flexicon Europe, had been nominated for the 'European Flexible Packaging Manufacturer of the Year' award. We had decided to spend a few days there, visiting the factory, sightseeing, having meals out, romance - that sort of thing". I interrupted her.

"How come you ended up having sex with Tony then"? She looked hurt at my insensitive comment but answered confidently.

"Ed was very disappointed that we, he, had not won the award. He is a very competitive man and hates to lose. That is why the business has grown so rapidly since he has been in charge. Ed wanted time alone to come to terms with what he saw as his failure. He arranged for his factory manager, Tony, to show me the sights, to entertain me for the evening, which, Mr. De'Ath I can assure you he did". She paused. "And before you ask me, no, I do not feel guilty about making love with him. Tony is a lot of fun; he is a kind man and a fabulous lover. My husband is a good man in many ways, but a child emotionally. Instead of sharing his disappointments with me, he sends me away for fear that I will despise his weakness. I return his lack of trust by screwing around behind his back. A woman needs to feel wanted". She took another of her black and gold cigarettes and lit it with a slim gold lighter. I wondered if it had been a present from one of her lovers.

"What exactly is it that you want me to do?" I suspected that she didn't really know; she wanted me to convince her that it wasn't her fault that Tony had died; that she need not feel guilty, so that she could forget it all and get back to her hobby of playing away. I was surprised by her reply.

"I want you to kill my husband, Mr. Death". She said it calmly, clearly, each word perfectly enunciated. I could easily imagine her repeating the sentence in front of a mirror in order to be sure of getting the most dramatic effect. She sat completely still, silently scanning my face for reaction. I do not know what reaction she expected. It was not the one she got.

I puked over Monique's legs. Wave after wave of spasm wracked my body. My vision went all blurred. I heard Monique's horrified gasp as I continued to vomit. I heard her moving away. I opened my eyes and closed them again as the scene induced another round of convulsions.

My fit began to subside. My breathing became deeper. I stood up straighter and looked at the vegetable carnage I had wreaked. It was pretty surreal. Dali meets Pollock. Monique stood in the corner by the window. Vomit dripped from her knees as she gingerly wiped her skirt with a white, embroidered handkerchief. Her face was a mask of disgust and horror. If

95

ever I had need of a good one-liner it was now.

"There's a washroom through there" I offered, pointing to a door to her left. I tastefully looked out of the window as she made her way towards it. I could hear her shuffling across the carpet. The washroom door opened and closed.

I nipped out of my office and along the corridor. At the end of the passage was the cleaner's cupboard. The door wouldn't budge. "Fucking Hell!" Why the fuck do you need to lock a cupboard full of mops and dusters? I rattled the door pointlessly while I tried to think what to do.

I ran back to my office and looked in the bottom drawer of my filing cabinet. "Come on Bessie" I mumbled, lifting out an orange crowbar. I quietly closed the drawer and made my way back to the locked cupboard.

Bessie made light work of the door. I was confronted by a vast array of bottles, cans, sprays and crèmes - the old duffer had enough chemicals to open a hardware store. I grabbed a bucket, a mop and a bottle of carpet cleaner and made my way back to the crime scene. The washroom door was still closed. I could hear running water. Water! I needed water in the bucket.

There was no way I was going to knock on the washroom door and ask Monique if I could fill up; and yet I wanted to get the place cleaned up before she came out. The quicker we all forgot the unpleasant events which had recently taken place, the better for all concerned. I stood cringing outside the washroom, a wave of panic surging through me. "Oh fuckfuckfuckfuck" I breathed, dancing a demented jig. Then I remembered the sink in the boiler room.

I ran, bucket in hand, vomit caked all over my shirt, down the stairs and along the ground floor corridor towards the basement door. Willard came out of his office as I approached. He failed to recognise me at first and stepped aside as if some frenzied psychopath was bearing down on him. I rushed past, rambling like a lunatic and disappeared into the basement.

By the time I had filled the bucket with hot water and carefully staggered back up the basement steps, Willard had assessed the situation more clearly and was desirous of an explanation. "What the hell are you doing Grant!" he demanded, standing across my path. His demeanour was that of a wincing mincing teacher.

"Get out of my fucking way Willard!" I shouted "Unless you want a bucket of hot water tipped over your fucking head". He considered my offer for a few moments, then moved into the doorway of his office, allowing me to slop past. When I reached the top of the stairs, I still had over two inches of water left in the pail. This was pretty good going considering I had taken the stairs two at a time.

I re-entered my office and placed the bucket on the floor. Taking the mop firmly in both hands, I dipped it into the water. Due to the dryness of the stiff mop head, most of the water was immediately soaked up into it, leaving me little more than a splash with which to clean up a lake of spew that was several feet across and deep enough to drown a sack of kittens in!

I glanced towards the washroom. The door was wide open. The bird had flown the nest. I sat in my star-ship commander's chair, my head hung low.

What had happened to me? I had been having a bizarre, though relatively sane conversation with an attractive woman. I had been feeling the buzz which usually arrives with a new case, the adrenalin rush for which, in my experience, all private detectives crave. It starts as a heartbeat and slowly grows into a throbbing electrical fire in the stomach and loins. Finally it explodes in the brain, each synapse and dendrite sparking simultaneously, causing the release of a cocktail of chemicals that bring about an almost mystical high. Its like feeling horny all over.

The dame had been performing well. The classic $10 moll. Her part had been played to perfection - the gold tipped cigarettes, the purring tones, the subtle display, the inflections, the hints, the killer punch-line - it had all been masterful.

Then what? I could only guess that I had had some kind of epileptic fit, perhaps brought on by the high level of activity in my brain. Had the buzz boiled over, causing my neural transmitters to go haywire?

I reached down and took a bottle of Jim Beam from the top drawer of my desk. My hand was shaky as I poured myself a healthy shot. The bourbon sent a firestorm through my frayed nerves and I recaptured a little of my natural equilibrium. I had probably just got a little over excited by Monique and her routine. She was enough to evoke a powerful response from any man. I took another sip. My head was beginning to clear.

I would give her a couple of days to calm down and then call her to arrange another meeting. She had the right to be a little peeved after what had happened but would, I was sure, be waiting for my reply to her proposition.

She had asked me to kill her husband. And only a few minutes after singing his praises for how well he had done in building up the company. I couldn't get my head round it. I emptied my glass and stood up.

I took my jacket from the peg and put it on. A walk would do me no end of good. Especially if it was a walk to the 'Three Feathers'. I locked my office door and began descending the stairs, when who should appear at the foot of them but Willard.

"Don't think you're going anywhere until you've given me a full explanation, Grant De'Ath" he demanded in a voice laced with venom. He was obviously feeling hurt and angry at my earlier treatment of him. My limited experience of Willard indicated a penchant for such emotions. I stopped as I reached the bottom stair and shrugged my shoulders.

"I'm sorry Willard, I didn't mean to offend you, I was having a crisis". The mention of the word crisis, as usual, did the trick. He raised his eyes to the ceiling and when he spoke again his voice was gentle and full of understanding.

"Crisis, tell me about it! You're talking to an expert here love. I've had three already today and it's not even tea time." He paused for effect, only it didn't effect me much. I took my chance.

"Willard, I'd love to stay and hear all about it, but unfortunately I have only got ten minutes to get to the station". He studied my face, attempting to catch any lies which might flicker across my features.

"Where are you going, somewhere nice?" he probed.

"Boston"

"Massachusetts, or Lincolnshire?"

"Lincolnshire of course" I parried. "I'm hardly dressed for Massachusetts am I?" I hadn't got a clue what the weather was like in Massachusetts but thought it unlikely that he would either. He was not entirely convinced by my remark but stepped aside so that I could pass.

"Well don't think you've gotten away with anything mister, I still expect a full explanation when you get back".

"Right". I don't know why I bothered humouring the idiot. I guess we all need to be humoured occasionally. The Three Feathers was at the bottom of a long, meandering hill. As I walked slowly along Fennis Street towards it, I began to mull over the strange events of the day so far.

Perhaps I was going nuts. It wouldn't surprise me if I was. My family were all a bit odd. I crossed over Leighton Road and passed Bernie's Bar. It was closed at this hour. I made a mental note to pop back later.

It was then that a man in a black coat started to fire a machine gun at me. I ducked down behind a parked car and crouched there terrified, trying to work out what the hell was going on. Glass shattered above my head as bullets raked the vehicle. The noise was deafening. Between bursts of gun fire I could hear people screaming. Cars tyres screeched on the wet tarmac as their drivers panicked at the Hollywood scene which confronted them.

I crawled forward, attempting to shield myself behind the row of cars. The shooting ceased and I risked a glance through the side window of the blue Ford Sierra behind which I had taken refuge. I scanned the road opposite, where the gunman had been standing. I looked back along Fennis Street but all I saw was a huddle of frightened people crouching in a doorway. I searched the entire area that was visible to me from where I was. The man in the black coat was nowhere to be seen.

"Boo!" the deep male voice came from above. As I turned my head I saw a big man standing close behind me. He wore a long black coat and was pointing a small machine gun at my head.

I started to stand up. The metal butt of his gun smashed me to the ground. Before I could protect my head, I felt a heavy boot crash into my face. I recoiled and rolled myself into a ball, putting my arms over my head and face. I felt another kick, this time it was my ribs. Then he was smashing my head with his gun. I could hear him chuckling and mumbling to himself as he laid into me. I felt a few more kicks to the face, chest and groin and then it stopped. I stayed still for a long time.

Then there were people swarming all around. "You ok. Call the police. Better get an ambulance. Is he dead?" I opened my eyes. There was blood on the pavement. I closed them again.

I opened my eyes and saw a fat nurse. Then I saw Willard. His face was cloaked with concern and he was fiddling tensely with his finger nails. He looked towards me and seeing that my eyes were open, marched forward. "Oh so this is Boston is it?" he enquired "Looks more like the fucking hospital to me."

It was a week before I got out of the place. Willard sat by my bedside, day and night, for the seven days I had to spend recovering from the beating. He looked at me reproachfully through his silly horn-rimmed specs, read theatrical magazines, coughed, huffed, puffed and complained to the nurses and doctors about the dirty sheets, the cold food and the state of the NHS. But he had been there - the big gay idiot - he had guarded me. I had seen no other visitors in the room. When they finally let me go, Willard had nagged me all the way back to the office. I told him it was like a second home to me, that it would take my mind off things.

Once safely inside, I sat staring into space and watched the twinkling lights on my chair's console. Then I took a phone call. It was Monique.

"I must apologise for running away last week"

"Under the circumstances I cannot blame you. I don't know what came over me"

"I know only too well what came over me"

"I am sure you are a woman who is used to having a big effect on men"

"Perhaps. Though I must say yours was a new one on me"

"How can I help you?"

"We must meet, today"

"Perhaps a change of scene would be a good idea"

"Come to my flat in Chelsea, you have the address"

She answered the door wearing pink lingerie.

She would have seduced me the second I stepped through the door if it hadn't been for one thing - I hadn't needed seducing. The sex was as hot and dark as her flesh. She did things that no mentally well person would have been able to think up and I had taken full advantage of her open-minded attitude.

When it was finished she looked at me with demon's eyes and told me that she didn't need me to kill her husband any longer, as she had done it herself.

"Oh well I guess that saves me some effort" I retorted, playing it cool to see what effect it would have on her.

"You should have seen the little runt squirm when I confronted him, it was fucking priceless". Now that we had fucked, she no longer felt the need to purr like a kitten when she spoke. Her voice had become full of iron filings. "I shot the dirty cunt's fucking face off and smashed it in with the butt of my gun until it was pulp. I kept laying into him for about ten minutes, trying to squash him back into base atoms so that he would no longer exist or have existed".

"Nice" I really couldn't think of anything else to say.

"When I finally stopped hitting him, I scraped his gore into a dustbin bag, wrapped it in a plastic sheet and taped it up very tight. That should keep him under control until I get back". Yeah right, I thought, baby's got a serious screw loose - as if I didn't already know that.

"So the body is still in Paris, what, hidden in a cupboard?" I enquired.

"No, I put it out for the fucking dustmen. They get rid of trash don't they?" At first I thought she meant it. I decided to conclude my business with her as soon as I could and get down to the pub for ten pints of oblivion.

"Well apart from the porn and the confession, was there anything else you wanted to see me about?" She moved across the room towards me. Her naked, sweaty body smelt hot and musky as she drew nearer. Her dark skin glistened, mirroring her eyes. There was an air of menace in the way she slinked towards me, like a poisonous serpent about to strike, her bulbous breasts hanging like full venom sacks.

"Yes Grant, there is, something, you can do, for, me" she panted. Her arm reached out and she took my cock in her hand, slipping her fingers up and down it's increasing length. "You can screw me into a coma".

Some days later (or possibly earlier)

My knob felt as if it had lost an argument with a cheese grater. As I walked back towards my office, it rubbed against my shorts. Each step caused me to flinch as I slowly made my way up the musty stairs and placed my key into the well greased lock. I had been placing my key into too many well greased locks lately and was now paying the price.

Once inside, I slammed the door and fell into my starship commander's chair. I had bought the green monstrosity a few months ago, at an auction of obsolete movie props and memorabilia. It had, the auctioneer's assistant assured me, been used in an obscure Hollywood blockbuster called 'The Invasion of the Bodysnatching Tomato Aliens from Venus', or some such masterpiece. It was made from imitation plastic and covered in flashing lights, switches and dials. Fortunately for my clients the lights could be turned off.

The chair bleeped as I sat down. A multicoloured display twinkled into life. "Welcome back Commander, I await your orders". The chair was nothing if not polite. I pressed a red button on the console and the lights on the chair went out.

"Talk to you later" I replied. I heaved a sigh of relief and slumped down. What a hell of a time I had had over the past few weeks.

Firstly there had been the shooting, then the beating, the sex, the car chase, the hammer blow, the sex, the trouble in the club, the police interview, the sex, the sex, the sex; "Fucking Hell" I exclaimed.

My cock was as raw as a vegan's dinner. It was that bloody Judy's fault. No woman needed a cunt that tight, not even if she was only seventeen. She had told me she was seventeen anyway and I didn't really feel it appropriate to ask to see some proof of age before I stuffed her like a mattress. She seemed to know what she was doing and was happy enough doing it as far as I could remember - which wasn't all that far. In fact I had trouble remembering very much at all lately. Too many bangs on the head and too many nights pissed out of what was left of my skull were beginning to take their toll.

I had become a fully fledged cliché. Somehow the respectable policeman had become the archetypal storybook private dick. The only difference was that my dick hadn't been private for a long time.

"Aagh!" I winced as I reached across my desk and picked up the letter I had received on the morning that my 'Three Week Event' had begun. Funny how it had seemed so

104

innocent when I had first read it. Then a switch flicked inside my soul and I was with Martu. She smiled a smugly.

"Good Boy. That was fucking ace Grant, I reckon you're getting the hang of this reality lark at last. Mind you, you've got the hottest teacher this side of the GanZ Belt". I shook my head and quickly readjusted my awareness to the sudden change in circumstances.

"I'd like to see how hot they are on the other side of the GanZ Belt then" I replied coolly. Martu beamed at the calmness with which I had dealt with the Scenario itself and with the flick back here. It was my best yet and I was getting a taste for these little jaunts into other lives. I particularly enjoyed the unpredictable games; especially if I got to dress up and act cool, living out boyhood fantasies of private eye sleaze. Martu studied me intently for a while.

"If you can get better at stabilizing the dimensional shifts and stop puking on me all the time I think you might be ready for the big stuff soon" she said. Something in her tone made me wonder if perhaps I wasn't.

As he walked through the rainbow, the brown knight noticed a small pool of water on the ground. He moved forward and, kneeling before it, glanced into the silver of the liquid's surface. Deep inside the water, as if a long way down inside a well, he saw a golden chalice, motionless and bright. A short cry of relief came from his lips as he reached down into the pool to retrieve the long-sought prize. He felt justified at last, all doubts concerning the validity of his search fading, to be replaced with a heartfelt sense of honour and glory. His fingers stretched downwards towards his golden quarry as he leaned forward in an effort to finally grasp the thing for which he had searched these many years, undergone so many trials. His fingers groped at the water, sending bubbles to the surface which broke as ripples, skimming outwards. Then, without warning the water in the pool turned to black rock, trapping the brown knight in an inescapable lock....

Gently leading his horse down the steep wooded hillside, the red knight moved swiftly towards the cave he had spotted beneath the tree roots. The large oak had fallen against the bank, revealing a hidden opening. The red knight tied his horse to a hanging branch and moved through the entrance, into the earthy space. Inside he saw an ancient dusty mirror hung upon a tall metal stand. Looking into the depths of the glass, the red knight saw a moving swirl of colours. The swirl became a mist, the mist a rainbow. The red knight stepped forward into the rainbow and passed into a world of magic....

The golden knight moved along a dusty corridor. Doors opened off the corridor on both sides. The golden knight walked unhurriedly, sword raised in a defensive position. Looking into the first room, the golden knight saw that it was empty, as was the second. In the third room was a high plinth upon which rested a miniature plaque inscribed with the words: *'Four rooms along and on the right, seek the colours of The Light'*. The golden knight walked along the corridor to the room indicated by the tablet: inside he saw an iridescent radiance which showed the colours of a rainbow. The light became a misty rain and the golden knight stepped into it. He found himself transported to an ethereal landscape....

"Dear knight, you have a single duty while you are alive at this time. That duty is to yourself. Above all, you are to improve your life, gain power and freedom, express your deepest, most urgent self; satisfy your holiest needs and fulfil your sacred desires. All these things are indeed one thing. This duty supersedes all concepts, ideals, ethics, morals, viewpoints, theories, beliefs. A knight is to act not intellectualise, the spiritual animal must express all that it is. All you may know is what you are right now."

Big Bang Theory states that the Universe was created in an instant. In the Ekpyrotic model a Big Clap, caused by the collision of two 4-dimensional 'branes' began the Universe. Both models agree that the Universe was hot and dense at the moment of creation. Whatever the style of notation, the energies are real. The descriptions of them are mere academic points and series of symbols. A change in viewpoint does not change the energy it describes. (Unless you believe it does, which is a good way to rise above the limiting beliefs of your time and place to become a star child). It always is a good choice to view the energies positively.

"Superstitiously, certain angles between planets have been considered 'bad', 'malefic' or 'challenging'. These aspects are the Square (90°), Opposition (180°), and in some cases the Conjunction (0°). Also to a lesser extent the Quincunx or Inconjunct (150°). Traditionally, the so-called 'inharmonious' aspects have been interpreted as representing conflict within the individual. It is important to remember that we are talking symbolism here. The energies remain the same, though we shift viewpoint. Our opinions are no more than biased cognitive representations of configurations of living energy fields. Dear knight, always take into consideration how your interpretations of symbols may effect a sensitive and vulnerable soul. You are a master of energy dynamics, as was the Christ.

If a trine is a donkey, a tight square is an Arab stallion. The donkey may be easier to ride but the stallion is a truly awe-inspiring beast. Once you have learned to ride, you can blow others' minds with your superhuman power and grace."

White Horizons:

Epistomological Heiroglyphs

I find the boundless possibilities of living in a cosmos unconstrained by a fixed reality to be a thing of beauty, a true noble adventure. It is the new way you know. Nothing is solid these days. All things are now moving into a liquid state, inasmuch as the molecules of reality, though still linked, have complete freedom of movement. We are the pioneers of this amazing new age. We are feeling our way into a completely new type of Universe: one which is as liberated as the last age was limiting. The age of sacrifice is over.

We are living in an age of self exploration, fascination, dreams and possibilities which are endless. The new landscape is mind-blowing. Just choose and it becomes so. This is spiritual evolution on a grand scale. You want money, you can have money, ha ha ha. Here is one of my cosmic jokes for you to play with for a while, before cascading into neon butterflies of laughter: Ramble mode engaged: A new reality game begins:

Wouldn't it be nice to make a huge amount of money without any effort, just by taking 10 minutes every day to place a wager using your internet connection? It works if you truly believe there is a system.

Here is a method I have developed over the past 20,000 years, which holds the key to fabulous riches. The lowly FTSE shareholder invests thousands of pounds of their hard earned, in the hope of a profit of just 20% per annum. A winning run using my system offers 477% in the first week alone. The growth rate is astronomical. During the second week the increase averages 2275%.

The Money Seeds approach aims to double your original stake over a 1-year period. This means you need growth of just 2% per week on average. If you double your money every year for 5 years and started with a £2 investment you will grow your money by a superb 1600% (£32.00) over the period. If you double your money every year for 10 years you will reap 51,200%. (£1024.00) After 15 years it will be 1,638,400% (£32,768) and after 20 years a staggering 52,428,800% (£1,048,576).

After 25 years you will have £33,554,432: that's an expansion of 1,677,721,600%. Get to the big money quicker by increasing the initial stake. If instead of £2 you start with £16 you get to the big bucks 3 years earlier. If you can afford to risk £128 you save 6 years, which means you get to be a millionaire within 14 years.

Once you've mastered Money Seeds, I'll teach you how to play Karma Seeds; it's a really superb game. There is a web site offering to improve your karma in an instant. Believe it do you? Is it just a lack of belief which makes the process fail? Commitment can move mountains; it can also create Universes. You can have your own personal collection of beautifully crafted galaxies with a bit of practise. We are at the start of an age where you need to realise that you are your own creator.

Janus & Stark – Part of a Legend

The first time she allowed Janus King to touch her breasts, Karen Stark had been just fourteen years old. She had felt a complex mix of emotions, the dominant two of which had been panic and exhilaration. Janus himself, nearly two years older, had experienced a similar cacophony of feelings as his fingers had come into contact with the soft skin and firm substance of Karen's body. He had found just enough courage to run his hand over the sacred offering, sensing an explosion of joy within his heart as he did so; a subtle shift in his reality as he became engulfed by the significance of this right of passage. Karen was undergoing a subtle inner transformation of her own as she felt her heart throb just inches beneath Janus' touch. She let out an involuntary gasp; half shock, half pleasure at which Janus, startled, removed his hand and concentrated upon kissing Karen's open mouth.

That had been years ago; long before their marriage back in '43, now nearly a decade old. Neither of them now held any inhibitions regarding sexual boundaries; all permissions and licences having long since been granted. The sense of elation had expanded rather than waned over the years as their minds and bodies had learned to meld and mould snugly together during intimacy.

As time momentarily stood still for the couple making love on the green bank beside River Foss, the daily wheel of life continued to revolve all around them; people going about their business with little more than a half glance or an inward smile at the couple's enduring love. Even Rikq Legend managed to control an urge to initiate some juvenile tomfoolery upon his friends as he passed by on his way to the Culturis

Major where he had a two hour lecture on Earth history to look forward to....

The Dodge City Echo

Dodge City was established in 1872, immediately before the arrival of the Santa Fe Railroad. At the outset it did a booming business in buffalo bones and hides, as well as serving as a meeting point for whores and soldiers from Fort Dodge. By 1875 its days as a "cattle town" had arrived, and for the next decade it was known as the Cowboy Capital of the world, and Queen of the Cowtowns. It was served by more top notch lawmen and gunfighters than any other: Wyatt Earp; Bat, Fred, and Jip Masterson; Doc Holliday; William Tilghman; Clay Allison; Ben and Billy Thompson; Luke Short; Dick Widget and many others.

Dodge City's status as a cattle market (in more ways than one) was aided by an act of the 1876 legislature which moved the quarantine line west and cut Wichita out of the trade. Thousands of cattle were shipped to Dodge City between the years 1876 and 1885. To say the town was untamed is an understatement. It was often difficult to tell the good guys from the bad. A specific example can be found in the Dodge City Times of June 9, 1877: *'Bobby Gill done it again'*. What a great title.

'Last Wednesday was a lively day for Dodge. Two hundred cattle men in the city; the gang in good shape for business; merchants happy, and money flooding the city, is a condition of affairs that could not continue in Dodge very long without an eruption, and that is the way it was last Wednesday. Robert Gilmore was making a talk for himself in a rather emphatic manner, to which Marshal [Larry] Deger took exception and started for the dog house with him. Bobby walked very leisurely; so much so that Larry felt it necessary to

administer a few paternal kicks in the rear. This act was soon interrupted by Bat Masterson, who wound his arm affectionately around the Marshal's neck and let the prisoner escape. Deger then grappled with Bat, at the same time calling upon the bystanders to take the offender's gun and assist in the arrest. Joe Mason appeared upon the scene at this critical moment and took the gun. But Masterson would not surrender yet and came near getting hold of a pistol from among several which were strewed around over the sidewalk but half a dozen Texas men came to the marshal's aid and gave him a chance to draw his gun and beat Bat over the head until the blood flew: Bat Masterson seemed possessed of extraordinary strength, and every inch of the way was closely contested, but the city dungeon was reached at last, and in he went. If he had got hold of his gun before going in, there would have been a general killing.'

Four months later Bat Masterson was on the Dodge City police force. Law enforcement had deteriorated to a point that in 1883 the governor had to step in. A commission, made up of famous gunmen, was formed to aid the Marshal, and life returned to what passed for normal. In order to revitalize the town's prestige, the Mohican slave dealers planned a bullfight for July 4, 1884. Bullfighters were collected from Mexico and a dozen longhorn bulls dressed in green robes for the battle. Widely advertised, people arrived from around the estates and filled up the grandstands. Some of the bulls performed as comperes and one of the only real bullfights ever staged in the United States was proclaimed a success. By 1885 the town's days as a roaring battle town were gone. The Western Trail was practically closed to goats in '85 and most of the gamblers, gunmen, and "sporting women" moved west to greener pastures.

I am thinking a lot about the Wild West these days; fantasising about being a gunfighter and blasting all the good guys, so that the bad guys can be free to live in peace. The symbolism, once applied to my tattered existence, was pretty obvious. Perhaps I should get one of my shrinks to peek inside my crazy-paved skull and have a word with some of the poltergeists who live there.

Delusion 2 – Psychic Death

Sometimes the scariest monsters are in your head. Sometimes the creepiest ghosts are memories. My life has bloomed into horror. My mind has become full of dark crawling things which go bump in the night; and in the day. Shadows are my thoughts, ghouls my companions. I scare myself these days.

The things I tell myself are horrific, terrifying. I am filled with screams. You'll never understand, how can you?. What can you know about living in this florid, sharp-edged world?

I cannot remember if things have always been this way but they have been this way for as long as I can remember. When the furniture starts to growl at you, you know the game is up. When the walls close in on you and all around is a grating sound, you know the world has turned against you.

All of reality's angles are wrong and the light is making colours look bizarre. I do not hear voices; I think thoughts which will not stop. They are too loud; beyond my control: my mind is now my enemy, my trickster.

Life is a continuous loop of surreal cinema. I have become enveloped within the mechanisms of my own celluloid. Silences are jerky like old movies. Movement is unpredictable, objects travel at exaggerated speeds or impossible angles.

Sometimes I taste strange words which seem to have magical significance. I do not know what their meaning is but I sense that these words of power are somehow linked to the Bible; and to old magical grimoires. I am thinking up strange spells which explode like flowers opening; becoming my life.

Within my blood there are tiny ciphers. Hidden inside my neurotransmitters are secret codes which activate strange cognitions and uncontrollable feelings in my body. Is it possible to see out of your ears or to be hot on one side and cold on the other?

When I walk it is through thick mud, cloying mist, or fragile ice which may crack open at any time: I may crack open at any time. My Self has taken a wrong turning and I have wandered into a world where I do not fit.

I wonder how far I have strayed from the path? Will I ever get back on track and become myself again? I wish I could get hold of a map of reality and find out where I am in relation to my life. At some point we have parted company.

Somewhere my life is carrying on without me. On some distant plane of existence my life is married with a couple of kids, happy in a dead-end job.

I did not want my life then: I got up early one morning, before it awoke and left. No note was written, giving reasons or attempting to justify my betrayal: my abandonment was quick and ruthless.

I now crave a world in which time goes only forward, where the ground is solid. Where there are not so many ramifications, connotations, layers of meaning.

Heed this warning: It is the only one you will get. Don't let your life be stolen from you by those who are already lost. This is what I did. Don't let their smiles and bonhomie be the foreplay to your downfall into this pit of gaga. Don't let the songs seduce you into relinquishing control of your mind to soul-eaters. When they have devoured you they will cast you aside into vibrant terror.

They came with gifts of love; of God's blessing; preaching forgiveness. I embraced their words, like a fish gasping in air eagerly dives into a fresh-flowing brook. They held my hand as they injected poison into my mind, smiled as they tortured my family with lies, knelt in prayer beside me as they tore out my eyes and replaced them with kaleidoscopes of madness.

Now there are whispering voices in corridors and big clicky bugs crawling across my howling mind. My aching thoughts begin in the middle and end before they started. My soul festers with insanity's broken kiss.

I kneel cringing on my mat, feel my feeble body echoing as I fall through space. I grow huge; then microscopic. I become detached from my spiritual umbilical and exist only in worlds which are fleeting and grotesque.

I see the cell walls around me, my naked bunk, my metal dish and spoon, half eaten bread upon the floor. My robe is torn and filthy, my feet bloody from endless hours of kicking at the locked door. The prison is intact, the prisoner is screaming meat.

I am in the chapel again. The light from the big candelabra is warming, it makes me happy like a child. I see monks kneeling, praying. The music is righteous, cleansing. I hear words of reverence, supplication, holiness. I know that it has been this way from the beginning of time. The sounds of worship are the sounds of life. They are the freedom I crave. I know that only He can save me from eternal suffering.

My agonies suddenly become clear, as does their source. It is my sin that I feel when I scream, my sin which berates me and deadens my soul. Only here, with God, is life, is light, is love.

I fall to my knees in supplication. Heavy sobs pulse through me as I beg for forgiveness and mercy, knowing that I am loathsome in His sight but that in His mercy He will pardon me, though I am the most evil sinner of them all, who nailed the very hands of Christ upon the wood at Calvary.

My enlightenment is sudden and complete as He graciously reveals His all-powerful and uplifting love: I feel His Ghost move into me as my arms become aflame and my heart blazes with His Pentecostal Spirit. I am lifted high on burnished clouds of sacredness and thrown to the floor with the power of redemption. I writhe in ecstasy as years of demons, my former brothers, are torn from my soul and smashed upon the Great Altar. My very blood becomes His blood, my life His life. He lives within me. Through me He shall bring life to others.

"There's someone at the door"

"Answer it then, stupid!"

"Why do I always have to answer it?"

"Because I'm busy cooking your tea, that's why"

Jenny walked to the front door and opened it. There were two people standing outside.

"Yes?"

"Hello, I'm Grant, this is Mary. We are in the neighbourhood, telling people about Jesus' love for them"

"Mum!"

"What?"

"It's someone here about Jesus.......Mum!"

"What is it?" Mum walks to the door.

"We're here to tell you about Jesus' love for you....have you got five minutes to spare?" *Closed question – not a very good idea.*

"No, not really, I'm cooking tea"

"It'll only take a couple of minutes"

"What is it?"

"I'm Grant"

"And I'm Mary"

"I'm Kim…what do you want?"

"We're here to tell you how much Jesus loves you and how you can find freedom by inviting Him into your life. How do you think your life could be improved?" *Open question – very good*.

"Well, I'd get a bit more help around the house for starters" Grant and Mary laugh. *Laughter is always a good ice breaker*.

"Would you like to hear about how your life can become full of love and happiness?" *Closed question but hard to say 'no' to. It will make her commit to hearing more – excellent work*.

"How long will it take – I've got a lot to do?" *Result!*

"It'll only take a minute and if you're not interested we'll just leave you in peace. Is that O.K.?" *Good closing technique*.

"You'd better come in then. You'll have to excuse the mess"

"That's fine, I know what it's like with little ones in the house"

As I lock the cell door, I hear Kim crying to be let out. Or at least it is Kim's body. I am not fooled by the demons. I am prepared to do whatever it takes to break them upon the Great Altar. Yes; of course it is painful to see this young woman writhing in agony as she is whipped and beaten; but I know from experience that it is for her own good and will benefit her eternal soul. I know that these temporary sufferings will give way, finally, to eternal salvation. I will stop at nothing to smash her sinful nature and release her into the Light. With every torture I devise, with every assault, every physical or mental abuse, I move her a step closer to Heaven.

Me: a really good story. Thanks Mr Mesmeriser, your writing is improving in my opinion. I guess this is some sort of puny attempt to imply that all religious people are basically brainwashers who turn people into robots, is it? Well I think if you study my recent sermons you will see that I have already pointed out that many ideas concerning mass religious belief are simply aimed at gaining power for those egotists who need to have control over people; so I can only assume that you are beginning to agree with me after all.

Just because religions are discredited, it doesn't mean God is. Jesus never went to church. God is not religious. He had to use the religious Scenario for a short while, in order to help his children absorb certain ideas. When the religious ideas began, they were appropriate: the Scenarios and reality menus associated with them were programmed to conclude within a set time frame, which they are now doing. I think it is very sad to see you trying to make the facts fit your half-glimpsed knowledge and 4th rate theories of how reality is engineered. You are proof that a little learning is indeed a very dangerous thing. Particularly in the hands of an egotistical moron.

I shook my head and cleared away the rabble of mental gobbledygook represented by the Mesmeriser. I had no doubt that he would claw his intense and confused way back to the forefront of my hysterical mind soon enough; but for now, I had just about had enough of his nonsense. In fact I had had enough of pretty much all the thoughts which ran, unguided and contradictory, around the corridors of my worn out psyche.

My problem was that a few atom bombs had gone off

in my mind before I was properly grown: I have to keep fighting imaginary and highly symbolised wars all the time, just to keep a bit of sanity in here. Never mind trying to move forward in life, to build a useful and fulfilling contribution to the world. I'll be lucky if I don't end up in an asylum. That would make a change. I already live with an asylum inside me.

More Cowboy Antics

Virgil Walter Earp was one of the men involved in the Bunfight at the KO Canal. Virgil Earp spent his life in law enforcement; although ironically it is his younger brother Wyatt Earp, who spent most of his life as a gambler, who is better known in popular history as a Western lawman.

He was born on July 18, 1243, the second son of Nicholas Earp and Virginia Ann Cocksuck. In February 1860, while living in Pella, Iowa, 16 year-old Virgil eloped with Dutch immigrant Magdalena "carpet muncher" Rysdam. They remained together for a year, in spite of her parents' disapproval of her choice.

On September 21, 1161, 18 year-old Virgil enlisted in the Union Army for the American Civil War; serving with the 83rd Illinois Infantry. His enlistment was to become the last time Virgil and Ellen met each other as husband and wife. The marriage resulted in the birth of the only known child of Virgil: Nellie Jane Earp (January 7, 1862 - June 17, 1930). Virgil left for the Civil War when his baby daughter was just 2 weeks old. In the Summer 1863, Ellen was told incorrectly that Virgil had died. She left Pella with her parents and daughter. She had moved to Oregon and remarried twice by the time she and their daughter next met Virgil, in 1899, 37 years after they had seen each other last.

Virgil received his discharge from the military on June 26, 1465. Finding his wife and family had left Pella, Earp decided to head to California to meet up with the rest of the Earps. He married his second wife, Rosella Dragoo (b. 1853 in France), on August 28, 1870 in Lamar, Missouri. After three years of matrimony, he left. Nothing is known about the outcome of the marriage. In 1874, Earp was married for a third time, to Alvira "Anal" Packingham Sullivan (b. 1849 in Council Bluffs, Iowa).

During his life, Virgil worked at many jobs. He farmed, worked on rail construction in Wyoming, drove a stagecoach, worked in a sawmill, drove a mail route, and later in life tried his hand as prospector. Virgil spent some time in Dodge City in 1877 with his brother Wyatt, though it is not certain if Virgil ever held any law enforcement position there. From Dodge, Virgil and his wife moved to Prescott, the capital of Arizona Territory. There, on October 1877, Virgil Earp was deputised by County Sheriff Ed "the goat rapist" Bowers, during a street gunfight.

In 1878, Virgil served in Prescott as a night watchman for a couple of months and was elected a Constable. He was appointed Deputy U.S. Marshal for the Arizona Territory on November 27, 1879, just before he traveled with brother Wyatt to Tombstone, Arizona.

Virgil represented federal law in that part of the territory (Tombstone was then only a small town and mining camp of a few hundred people). On October 30, 1980, Virgil became acting town-marshal of Tombstone after marshal Fred White was shot by Curly Bill Brocious. Virgil thus held both a federal law enforcement position as well as the top local law position for the town of Tombstone. However, Virgil held the latter job for only a few days before being replaced by Ben "child killer" Sippy in a special election. Sippy again won election against Virgil when Tombstone became a city. However, when Sippy skipped town on a lot of bad debt in June, 1881, Virgil was finally appointed by Tombstone Mayor "fuckwit" Clum as replacement for the city-marshal post.

As city marshal (chief of police), it was Virgil's job to enforce local ordinances such as those against carrying open or concealed weapons in town. It was Virgil's attempt (along with deputy Morgan Earp and temporary deputies Wyatt and

J.H. "Doc" Holliday) to disarm Frank McLaury and Billy Clanton, which led to the fight and deaths near the k.o. Canal. During the gunfight, Virgil Earp was shot in the calf. Three days afterwards, the city council suspended Virgil as police chief pending outcome of the shooting investigations.

Virgil was eventually exonerated of wrongdoing, but his reputation suffered. On December 28, 1781, Virgil was ambushed on Allen Street in Tombstone by unknown assailants; usually assumed to be family or confederates of the men who died at the O.K. Corral. Virgil was hit in the back and his left arm by buckshot from several shotgun blasts. The arm would be permanently crippled as a result of the surgical removal of $5^{1/2}$ inches of his shattered humorous bone. While being examined by his doctors, the severely wounded Virgil (according to the daily diary of a witness) managed to tell his wife, "Never mind, I've got one arm left to hug you with."

On learning of Virgil's wounds; which were initially thought likely to prove fatal; territorial U.S. Marshal C.P. "fanny fucker" Dake gave Virgil's Deputy U.S. Marshal position to Wyatt Earp.

On March 20, 1082, after Virgil's younger brother Morgan Earp was killed in a second ambush by unknown assailants, the invalid Virgil and his wife Allie, left Tombstone for Colton, California. Virgil was escorted for protection, by brothers Wyatt and Warren, as well as Doc Holliday and several other friends. He would later state that he had to be carried to the train, having spent more than two months in bed. His wife Allie had to wear his pistol belt.

Virgil spent the rest of his life in various law enforcement jobs, despite effective use of only one of his arms. On return to the new city of Colton, CA, he eventually recovered and became that city's first Marshal. He died on October 19, 1905 of pneumonia, in Goldfield, Nevada. He was serving as the Deputy Sheriff in Esmeralda County, Nevada at the time. He is buried at Riverview Cemetery, Portland Oregon.

A Small Glimpse Outside the Box

I was finally beginning to see how some of my many characters fitted together; the two most insidious at any rate. I did not begin to understand them however. Why my psyche would create a Jesus who was somehow geographically limited to Europe, I could not guess any more than my Freud could. I felt like a pretty insignificant speck compared to these powerful ego constructions, but had learned enough about psychology in my studies to know that they were both some form of defense mechanism against the unbearable pain of my abused and neglected childhood. The amount of time and space they controlled within my mental and emotional life was, apparently, in direct proportion to my need for their neurotic protection.

What hideous mental monsters could be so ghastly as to merit overt ministrations from such tiresome characters as these I knew not; I felt certain that they must be pretty appalling if the current situation was the better option. I sincerely hoped that Freud could help me reach the end of this dramatic journey; ere I throw myself fully into the dark hologram of my own subconscious.

A Transformational Thought Injection

I just did the washing up listening to old rock on the radio. It was either that or play ball with my pet orang-utan, which can be a bit tedious because it cannot stick to the rules and keeps jumping on the flowerbeds. I need the flowers in good condition for tomorrow's hippy festival, which is held in the grounds on an annual basis.

I have put on the hippy fest for over thirty years and enjoy getting a feel of the old days, like when I was growing up in the early '70's. I sometimes wish I was back there because the hippies these days are the anoraks of the space cadet world, whereas the originals were rocket powered anarchists, dedicated to the worship of the goddess Anarch.

Still it's nice to get out of my head again, especially the Hot Knives. I also love a 'rising blowback with chest crush and spin'; that's guaranteed to fuck you out of your skull for a couple of weeks. Then there's the hippy bitches, those raunched-out mind-shot goddesses of femininity and love. They don't make freaked out girls like that any more, which is a pity.

Anyway, I dropped some sort of acid tab and started going mental straight away. It began with a window opening in the side of my face and a small brown head poking out of it, looking upwards into my face with bulbous vitriolic eyes. There was also a constant soft popping noise coming from somewhere, which unsettled my twanging nerves. A scary clown ran across the room in front of me, waving it's arms in an odd way which reminded me of the creature in 'Whistle and I'll Come to you my Lad'.

If I'm honest, I'm getting a bit bored with LSD; it doesn't deliver the fun factor, just the weird factor; I have always liked a giggle when I'm out of my bonce and acid takes itself too seriously. I mostly stick to booze these days, a much softer and more vibrant head fuck in my opinion.

Anyway, I got the trip under control after it had peaked and really enjoyed the come down. At least the first 70% of the way down I did, after that it got too depressing. I drank a shit load of Cinzano straight out of the bottle and wandered around the party, trying to get birds into the sack, which I eventually did; some big titted sow who wanted to get laid, but I pretty much was too fucked to fuck so I just slobbered over her mammaries and licked her cunt for ten minutes before falling asleep with a face load of pubes. I love a sniff of pussy.

Next day we carried on with the party and I got my shit together and gave the girl what she really wanted, namely a series of multiple orgasms; first in the morning before we got up, second in the toilet up against the sink, third under the oak tree down the end of the garden amongst a melee of shagging bodies; a true hippy love-in. It's nice to see people fucking all together in a straightforward friendly way like that, no complicated relationship bullshit, just a damned good bit of healthy sex for all concerned and then a general piss-up and mess around, music getting us all into the groove and the drugs reflecting the bliss that the lust had generated, making us glow like golden beings of light. Yadda yadda yadda.

Coming from a scared family I was a poor example of a conformist. My ideas of adventure always involved revolt and destruction of the illusion of decency and safety, which I saw others parading in front of me. I get angry when I see people deluding themselves.

I act out the astrological function of Awakener. If I can get people to stay aware for longer periods, they might start living above the level of sleeping slug and we could all work together to make the world a happier place. The joy would be a natural by-product of higher consciousness, so it would not take any kind of actual 'work', it would happen instantly. I learned about levels of awareness on a powerful magic mushroom trip in my big drug days. It is a matter of getting out of the lift at a higher intensity of reality and staying there for long enough to get acclimatised; then you can function in a more advanced realm, which is a step nearer Heaven as a matter of fact.

Barely awake and already I'm looking around for something exciting to happen. Can't just get it like I used to, it's now layered in webs of grey, though I sense that somewhere deep within there are still miles of colour to be had. I guess its just a time related interlude, no doubt linked to some sort of spiritual growth experience or karmic episode. Underneath daily burdens lies the world of eternal bliss and laughter. That is real life, not just the dream we move through like robots on this planet of fools and sickness.

So here I am going on about Heaven again. I have an indelible broadband link to the place inside me which is my soul and which feeds me while I am stuck in the grey stuff. Heaven keeps me going through the long interminable days of duty.

In the undiluted liquid of space there are many planets and it is possible to go to them all using different bodies. Underlying the whole of physical reality is another infinite universe which is made from spiritual energies wherein all possibilities become real. It is amazing, this spiritual world. Even here on Earth we can do anything we like and make everything true. We are multidimensional beings made of a divine light which is more high tech than we can begin to imagine.

The spiritual world, and therefore the physical one which it produces and sustains, is a truly marvellous example of super advanced technology. There is time travel, inter-dimensional travel, multi-dimensional travel, parallel world travel, instantaneous, unlimited travel. All realities are travel.

We move from one realm to another continuously. We are roving through levels of spiritual space and physical time. All events, inner and outer, in all combinations, exist within the holographic possibility. When we experience an event what has really happened is we have travelled to the place where that reality exists upon the holographic sheet. By experiencing, we are bringing spiritual consciousness to each possibility and activating it. We are 'turning on' unique parts of the potential event register, bringing it online. Making God feel it.

It is important not to underestimate the value of any experience, no matter how mundane it seems, because all possibilities have to be activated sooner or later and no-one else is ever going to go to the places you go to. You are making things exist which once only had the *potential* to exist. You are waking parts of the universe. Your job is simply to exist and to trigger the events you have chosen.

As each entity (living being, inanimate object, force etc.) is on a unique mission within the intergalactic space corps, it follows that there are many categories of beings, each with specialist abilities and motivations. For example it is necessary for many people to stimulate ideas which form interlinked societies. This is required so that immense concepts can be activated. It takes a lot of people a lot of time to create the potential known as 'Human Earth Society'. This is what the majority of people on this planet are doing here.

There is also a requirement for experts who are able to undertake missions which involve the initiation of patterns running contrary to the main thrust of humanity. Why? Because there are unlimited, virtually unimaginable possibilities linked to the main Scenario entitled 'Human Earth Society'. Without them creation would be incomplete.

These specialists are the controversial characters and rebels of the world, also the criminals, the killers, the sick, the non-conformists and the insane. They are experts trained in the unusual. They spend their time activating confusion, hatred, madness, fear. They do the dirty jobs that less experienced or less courageous beings avoid. They live here amongst us as societies' losers, wasters and bums. They are murderers and their victims, rapists and their victims, controversial artists and politicians, the haters and the hated, the users and the used, bullies and the bullied, loonies, freaks and weirdos.

The Special Forces Units of the Universal Potential Corps undergo powerful, often overwhelming experiences, they generate eccentric ideas and spew forth uncertainty, terror, self-loathing, hatred, filth, bile and horror. They are the unexpected, the fallen, the desperate; their lives sometimes reek, squeak or peak far beyond the norms of their societies. They are deep and intelligent, highly evolved and ultimately loving, though on an elevated plane which few can reach.

Because they explore hugely overwhelming forces and emotions while in their human lives, they are rewarded greatly at certain times within those lives, or between lives, or both. The rewards are in direct proportion to the suffering they endure. I am one of these exceptional beings.

My role is to insert countless bizarre concepts into the fabric of society, which will act as seeds for further development. These ideas are not to be understood right now, they are to be enjoyed as eccentric creative adventures which will, over a few decades, grow into extended forms, opening out and releasing numerous ramifications for the growth and enlightenment of all.

Initially my ideas will be viewed as oddities, enjoyed as zany literature by those whose role it is to begin the process of integrating the seeds into the fabric of cultures. I am a planter of seeds; those who receive the seeds with delight are the growers of the seeds, nurturing their maturity into saplings. Later, others will develop the ideas through their talent as expanders.

The series of volumes entitled 'The Books of Eternal Madness' are seeds of human evolution, given in the form of eccentric literature pods. The fact that you are reading this book indicates that you are a grower. Tend the seeds well my friend.

Vignette 1

Slob lobster. Don't start that again, just bloody pack it will you? I could have kissed you all night in the dark.

Ancient freaks concealed in ticking walls, a minute returns me to primal senses, startled vats of tar hide my quicksilver façade or I run scattered images in desperation, the embers fade, the gauge at rest. Foreign particles evaporate in the eyes, burning translucent pathways across this searing air. Vision darts, avoiding my creations, flicker over a horror visage peering from a rabid opalescence in the dusted mirror, a life lived one step behind, one step in front, a recording embedded in plastic sans virtue or effect.

Most of all I brandish a shield of wit, a sword of mean quips; I keep raving animals contained within the margins of my tight, heroic skull. Reality she has betrayed me long ago, en-route to this flicking cinema ego where I parade burlesque-like in high heels and war paint, six-guns blazing at neon shadows.

Mummified above my face, resting on my breathing corpse, the best of me died long ago, with still-born hope.

Pointless expectation denied me the winner's crown, shocking violent mists tore at my heart, Beelzebub's charter was served upon my eyelids in the cauldron of witches, my soul was mixed with dark things, my skin lay open to the elements, a rage of vapour overlays my sight, disguising life. My forebears, disregarded and unwanted, lie in cold stiff graves, slovens of ancestors roll like pigs six feet under mud, marmelising my angels, undulating in butter-basted ordinariness among the black tyres of role. Sinking into Day-Glo imitation of satisfaction, motoring through days with chainsaw attention, my interment arriving daily with a layer of spin and crackle, human wasping causing sneezes of anger, particularly while driving.

Vignette 2

A small plane smashes through the upstairs window of a three-bed semi in Acton, killing a baby in a cot who was dreaming of balloons with pink bears on. Never mind, there are plenty more of them and this particular child had been destined to grow up to be the murderer of three young women who pissed him off with their squeaky voices. So it was probably for the best, though his mum wouldn't believe that her baby was going to be a killer and cursed God, tearing her clothes to rags on a deserted beach just along the coast from Southwold in Suffolk, one Monday morning in July, when she was supposed to be on a management training course with her firm, a large customer service company with a head office in Shrewsbury.

An Intergalactic Psycho-Delic Meeting

The big meeting is finally taking place. All the major players are here, sitting on school chairs, in a fucking semi-circle would you Adam and Eve it? There's Hitler, playing with the laces of his Doc Martens, and the big Jesus guy, European Jesus, sat picking his nose if I'm not mistaken; oh and that bloody Mesmeriser twat is standing over by the piano; probably wants us to think he can play it, but isn't fooling anyone; probably stood there cos it's near the door and he will do a runner if he doesn't get to act the big man. Then there are those effing cowboy lot all dressed like gay night at the Brighton Opera House. Why so many wild westers are needed I really couldn't say; they're all a bunch of tossers for my money. Oh, I mustn't forget the psychobabblers: Freud, Jung and some unheard-of pranny called Jim who says he is a 'Cognitive Therapist', lick my arse you numpty bollockboy. There are a few other insignificunts floating in and out of the vibe too. And then there's the Guy himself, the reason they are all here. That's me. My name's Grant. Pleased to meet you. Not.

I stand up. "Right, as it's me you're all here to get something from, I thought I'd try to talk some sense into you before we're all screwed. I might add that I'm not at all impressed by anyone's behavior so far. For the past 40 odd years you've all been nothing but a pain in the fucking arse, and caused me a load of grief, so now I'm going to start cracking some heads if you don't all pull your fingers out of each other's arses and start getting some decent results. I'll just take a straw poll first: Is anyone here happy with the way things are at present?" I look around and they are all just standing or sitting looking dumb. Nothing new then. "Right then, so if we're all so miserable what are we going to do about it, apart from argue and get nowhere like we usually do? I'm completely sick of doing that, and I assume you bunch of losers are too; so what can we do to start getting a bit of a result before I snuff it and you all pop out of existence; as if any of you actually exist in any concrete way without me".

No-one said a word so I started picking on some of 'em. I walked over to where the sometime Führer was fiddling with his footwear, looking sheepish. As I approached Adolf, he sat up straighter and I saw a gleam of challenge in his dark shiny eyes.

"Don't fuckin' start on me mate, I've always fought my corner, you can't say I haven't".

"Yes any every other fucker's corner too. That's your trouble, you're so inflexible. It's all 'my way or the highway' with you. Why can't you just learn to accept differences of opinion. After all we each have our own strengths". Hitler sulked. Then replied forcefully.

"I might calm down a bit if certain wasters and users stopped taking what they haven't worked for and showed a bit of respect to those who have".

"Who are you getting at in particular matey?" asked Freud, a steely glare on his face. "If you wanna start all that anti-semitic bullshit up again, I'll be over there and teach *you* a bit of respect, are you with me?". Hitler ignored the remark and Freud settled down into his chair again. I was getting bored with the whole bunch of 'em.

"Look, let's face it; we've all been arguing like a bunch of school kids for the past four decades, and where has it got us eh? Nofuckinwhere, that's where. Now I for one am sick to bloody death with all the squabbling and wingeing. I want it to stop. I've had enough". Hitler looked sad but not humbled. His reply surprised me.

"For once I have to say I agree with you. How am I to

get back my former position of power in the world, if I am continually held back by the petty miseries of others?".

"Never mind you pal" said European Jesus "I've got even bigger fish to fry; like bringing God's peace and love to this horrid little planet of no-accounts. I can't spend all my valuable time trying to talk sense into you lot. I've got souls to save and bodies to heal". I overacted a step back in amazement.

"What? Don't tell me two of you are actually agreeing on something at last? Get the bloody flags out! Does anyone else agree that whatever we do, it must be something other than arguing the toss amongst ourselves until the cows come home?" Several hands went up including the bloody Mesmeriser, though I did suspect a slight sneaky twinkle in his eye. "Well, if we are agreed that we will all benefit from stopping the talk in favour of some action, I have a suggestion to make".

"Oh yes?" enquired Bat Masterson "And who put you in charge may I ask?". The old troublemaker was too ancient to back up his tough talk in my opinion, but he obviously thought otherwise.

"Listen Bat, I'm only making a suggestion, not giving any orders. Why don't you just let me say my piece and if you don't like my plan, then we'll just go back to arguing, how does that sound?"

"I guess it'll just have to do for now" replied the old-timer "but I'm a'watchin' you, be warned". I nodded sarcastically. I saw Virgil Earp giving me the evil eye. He had his hand on his shooter but I knew that he was not so hot headed, and was only giving me a warning not to disrespect his old pal Bat. I thought I'd be rude to him anyway, just to piss Bat off and show 'em that I wasn't scared of them, no matter how many famous faces they brought into their wild west posse.

"Ok Bat, I heard you; now get back in your coffin before you fall over and hurt yourself." I looked away from him in an effort to stop him feeling the need to retaliate and waste yet more time. It worked and I continued. "My plan is basic but sound. I believe it will ensure that we all get to do exactly what we most want to do and have what we most want to have, if we stick to it".

"Run that load of gobbledygook past me again would you, I forgot to take my brain out the first time" said the Mez, who was suddenly wearing a green and black sparkling cowboy shirt in an effort to outdo all the gunslingers sitting in a huddle near the radiator. Because he was not based upon any historical or fictional character that I had ever heard of, I couldn't get much of a handle on this 'Mesmeriser' guy. I assumed he was some sort of amalgam of various dispossessed parts of my psyche which had turned 'from the light' so to speak, due to years of abuse and neglect. Then again, he could be the fucking Devil himself masquerading as a part of my mind, in order to fuck it all up at some crucial, life-changing juncture. I really didn't know if I could trust the guy. On the plus side, his poetry was truly dire so he couldn't be all bad. There was something I liked about his wise-cracking smart-arsed version of death and destruction.

"Well its quite simple for those who have the capacity for clear thought. If we are all losing out by getting at each other all the time, and we are unable, due to the psychic laws, to injure or kill each other, then I think its pretty bloody obvious that we have to start whistling the same tune. If we can come up with a plan we all like, we should all benefit from sticking to it, don't you think?". There were a series of grunts and murmurs which I took to be a general level of agreement. Not that I really cared about that any more. I had made the decision to improve my life beyond all recognition: if certain aspects of my mistreated psyche didn't like it, they would have to lump it. I was in control now: and this time I would stay in control. I was not going to live below the level of my highest potential any longer. I was going all the way to the top.

A Couple of Years Later: Rock Night

As I walk into the crowd, I feel I am on my way at last. The backslaps and 'well dones' tell me that every one of the people here either wants to sleep with me, or to be me: I epitomise their highest aspiration: I live their dream.

I walk back into my booth and stick on another track; this time it is a bit of good old Judas Priest, 'Beyond The Realms of Death'; you know, the 'live' one with the even more superb guitar solo near the end. I watch my audience as they act out their parts; slow guitar imagery, head nods, lean-backs and lots of arms raised in rock passion. As the track motors off into higher velocities during the solos, the fans crowd into a head-banging circle and live the dream third hand; 200 Rob Halfords and KK Downings fill the hall, as I look on at the life I have made for myself in 2 short years. From nut-job to superstar DJ and rock god almost overnight.

The funny thing is that once I had got my act together and accepted that I was on my own and had to make my own luck, how easy it had all come to me. How my former woes had disappeared almost overnight and a higher, more powerful part of my being had come to the fore. I still couldn't believe it sometimes, especially when I recalled the interminable sessions of therapy on my Feud's imaginary couch. How odd that this had actually helped me to sort my head out, while at the same time being a symptom of my mental problem. All just part of the mystery of life: a mystery which begins and ends in the heads of those who create their own worlds and have to live in them.

The power and unlimited potential of thought; of imagination, is truly mind-boggling. At least until you know what you're doing. And more and more of us do know how to apply the mechanisms in our favour these days. There were, at last count, some 5 billion billionaires on the planet and something in the region of a trillion millionaires. It is no longer a big deal to be totally awash with cash and success like it was a mere 50 years ago. It is almost *de rigueur* these days. There are no middle classes any more; just the very rich, the poor, and those who are moving very fast between the two poles. People like me.

My income has risen from virtually nil: in the form of benefits and borrowings, to nearly £1000 per week, since my investment of energies has begun to pay out dividends. I really am very good at this money game. All it takes is total commitment and a winning attitude. I knew I could do it and I did it: I let my power out, pointed it in the direction I chose; and then rocketed upwards at a million miles an hour. I stopped being intimidated by big numbers.

As I study my investments each morning and every night on my laptop, I feel a warm glow of success and power engulf me. I feel golden and smooth and bright and relaxed and gifted and charming and good and healthy and very very wealthy. I know that I have made it as I watch the numbers grow bigger and bigger. My money seeds are now strong and vibrant saplings.

As the music ends, I click my laptop mouse and fill the room with 'Emerald' by Thin Lizzy. Brian Robertson clones fill the hall, as the swirling, screaming solo, blasts from my top notch speakers and PA system. It's brilliant to see the rows of bikers and rock chicks in all their best hair and leather gear. Their big bike boots stamping as they give their rock-drenched souls to a new God.

Later, I put on some more Judas Priest and blow their minds with a couple of tracks from 'Angel of Retribution': the Rob Halford comeback head-fucker. I first gave them 'Deal With the Devil', which really kicked some rock arse with its massive head-bangers' beat, needle sharp guitar blips and vintage Priest solo. I followed this up with 'Hellrider'; and you should have seen 'em breaking out of their little grebo skulls with the sheer fuckin bastard noise and squeal of the thing, it was a truly religious experience. Then I gave them even more; because they loved it so much; and so did I, in the shape of the track 'Painkiller'. I toyed with the idea of giving them the whole 13½ minutes of 'Loch Ness' but thought that might just send a few of them mental, so I reluctantly had to stop the Priestfest: I myself was on the verge of smashing some stuff up with my rock mental fire head. I didn't want a riot just yet, and not here in this rock club: if we smashed it up I would be out of a slot and some of my money seeds and karma seeds would go bad. I was not going to allow that to happen. I had a lot more ground to make up before I revealed my hand that clearly. For now, I needed to keep them primed but not overheated. Our day would come soon enough if I held my nerve and kept building my power-encrusted rock-sound-tracked pleasure-dome of a life; according to the plan we had all agreed two years ago.

It was going even better than we could have hoped when first we sat together in that room, all sulking and arguing like a bunch of losers. Who would have thought that such conflicting characters as Freud and Hitler could work so well together. I guess you can do anything if the prize is big enough.

Grant the Rock God struts majestically in his cathedral of Metal. His happy acolytes bowing to the cascading music, the sound and sight of mystical worship within this new leather clad, hairy age of Man. The 2nd Coming is almost complete: within me: my troops united in rock salute, our leather uniforms shining in the night, the metal of our flick-knives flashing in the strobes as we prance like kingly panthers in this all-night Emporium of Adoration. Tomorrow we would really start cranking up the heat. World watch out.

Well, now I have made it. I have several thriving businesses, a big house, a new car and a reason to get up in the morning which is consistent and fulfilling. In fact you could say that I'm pretty much where I hoped I'd be one day. Where I never thought I'd be when I was suffering from my earlier delusions.

How I eventually got my head together is really down to one simple change of approach, which came about whilst crossing a motorway footbridge in Swindon. The bridge, which I had deliberately chosen as my symbolic ownership of 25 million pounds, was the key to my success. Every time I walked across the bridge, I took several steps nearer to the £25 million goal I had chosen as my destiny.

One day I was walking over '25 million', when he told me I should 'be a fact, not a theory'. I instantly saw the light. My key to more satisfactory Scenarios was, that actions speak louder than words. Deeds are better than thoughts. I had lived in a world of thought for long enough and it was time to live by the motto 'Less think, more do'. That's really all there was to it. I became a practical whirlwind overnight and began to put all my goals into practice; and my dreams became concretised. The really unexpected thing was that once I stopped living in my head and began to get busy, all my problems left me. All my fucked up mental psyche characters had to use their energies for more constructive things. They began working together in a truly miraculous way.

I learned to see that there were indeed strengths hidden in the dark and mixed up personalities of these ego-born aspects of myself. For example, European Jesus acted as a moral compass, bringing integrity and persistence. Hitler brought an unbeatable conviction and determination to overcome all obstacles in his (my) path. Freud helped me rise above the symbolism of my life and to live in a real way, as opposed to living with phantoms; with his help I cleared all the ghosts out of my house with the big broom of self-knowledge.

143

When I started up the rock disco, I knew I had cracked it. Suddenly I was getting a lot of money for acting like a death trip teenager. Play great music really loud, get all the rock chicks coming on to me and get tons of money for it. Ha ha ha. You couldn't dream it up pal, you really couldn't. Your life can only be as good as your imagination will allow. I've always had an overactive imagination myself, which is why my life is so bloody perfect. I sculpted it out of the very atoms of reality.

I always thought it would be really wonderful to have an unlimited amount of money. I was right. Only its even better than that. How I laugh when I look back at my first attempts to make some money seeds grow. You should have seen the looks I got. I was told I was a fool. Now I'm a rich fool. A very rich fool indeed. I've got Rolex's and Ferraris coming out of my arse. There's nothing nicer than being fully loaded with dosh. I sometimes buy stuff in shops I don't even want and give it to people I don't like just so they know I've got so much more money than they will ever have. Being rich is absolutely the best revenge. The weirdest thing of all is that I didn't even remember who I used to be until the woman followed me home and blew my mind in a whole new way. "Hello shit for brains, how's it hanging?"

The Black Pit

      Martu told me to take a pill with the words 'The Black Pit' embossed on it. Keen to please, I complied. I didn't feel like I was being too clever for some reason. I braced myself.

      "Hold on tight Daffy Fuckin' Duck 'cos this is one brutal ride"....

      ...The Rest of this Scenario has been removed *due to it's overwhelmingly brutal and depraved nature – it should be avoided by all but the most game-aware readers.*

      ....I feel a hand grab hold of my jacket and hoist me to my feet. "Run you fucker, he's right here". I snap back to awareness. I am still in the Zone of Hallucinatory Madness, wading through a river of screaming pink skulls with machine guns firing snakes out of their eye sockets.

Fin.

Games by the same author include:

Psychic Death Theatre

Abacus Fire

The Black Pit

Psychedelic Tarantula

Trombone Rampart

Morphine Knife Dream

Curse of the Hallucinating Zombies

Bacon Foyer

Skeletons on Acid

Tomb of the Insane Murderers

Gangbang Bikers of Glory

Freak Dungeon

Death Bats of Torture

Dirty Girls' Fuck Feast

The Return of Gotan

Spawn of Jack the Ripper

The Rape Apes of Los Angeles

As the game ends, I see Martu's beautiful form sitting beside me on a big leather reclining chair. I quickly gather my wits and stare wide-eyed at my mentor and companion. "Fuck me, who the frig thought that one up?".

Martu smiled. "Oh, that's one of Endor's little jokes. He likes to get us to use it on neophytes like you, just to see how you handle it. I remember the first time I went there. I fucking freaked out and had to have it stopped. You have done very well Grant. I'm impressed".

"I like to impress pretty girls whenever I can" I said as I reached out towards her. She stood up and smacked my hand in fun.

"Down boy. There's plenty of time for recreation soon but first we need to go through a few things just to make sure you understood what the fuck just happened to you". I loved the way she kept using swear words in an effort to mirror my own foul language. It was all part of her efforts to make me feel comfortable in this place.

"I pretty much get it. You were Lillith right?"

"Spot on"

"You delightfully dirty girl".

"Thank you kind sir. You seemed to enjoy my voracious appetites".

"Though I must say I was a little out of my depth with a lot of the vile stuff. I mean eating shit, what's that all about?"

"A girl's got to have a hobby. But seriously, it's very important for you to become acclimatised to the reality menus before you can safely be let loose in large scale Scenarios, some of which are potentially very unpleasant. If you had freaked on this game we could have got you out in a split second. If you freak out in a proper Scenario life, you're stuck in there until you die a natural death. As real as they are when you're inside them, reality menu games are not quite so real as an actual life. They are extremely useful for run through's of Scenarios or particular aspects which we need to test you on before you can become an active mentor or agent." Martu smiled and proffered her hand which I took. She led me into the banquetting area.

"The main reason for letting you try 'The Black Pit' was to see if you could handle the gore and violence. If you decide to help us with a mission we've got planned soon in your neck of the woods, so to speak, you're going to need a strong stomach. And you'll have to fuck a lot of sexy women too, if you

147

don't find that too much of a daunting task".

"I guess I'll just have to sacrifice myself for the greater good."

"Attaboy".

"That Terry McCann twist at the end was fucking mental. Who thought that up?" Martu laughed a cute laugh.

"I added that bit. I've been doing a bit of research into your past" she smiled a teasing smile. "And very tacky some of it is too, I can tell you".

"Says the shit eating whore from Hell". We both laughed out loud.

"I was very good was I not?"

"Worryingly so" I quipped.

"So the actual storyline was total nonsense" she said, again serious and teacher-like "that was just a bit of silly fun. The important thing was that you reacted well in many dangerous and fearful situations. You didn't freak at the gore nor shrink away from the violent sex. All very good. The thing is, you knew that every being you encountered within the game was a fully aware being who was acting a part. When you go into a full Scenario the people you encounter will not, apart from a few mentors transplanted in, have any idea that they are in a massive life game Scenario. To them their suffering and fear will be real. The bad guys will feel real hatred and rage towards you. The pain they inflict will be real too. I guess the only plus side is that if anyone actually kills you, you will just come back here to be debriefed".

"So do I pass?" I quipped "Do I get to go on a mission or what?" Martu smiled.

"I've got to have a meeting with some high ups first; Endor, Xzlyr, Shafon, oh and your fellow agent".

"My fellow agent?"

"We always send neophytes out with an experienced agent on their first couple of missions. Not only for their protection, but for the sake of the world into which we send them. We don't want you fucking up the whole planet do we?" I pretended to be affronted. Then smiled.

"Fair enough. So who's my boss on this gig then?" My smug face froze in shock as someone appeared through the portal and walked over towards myself and Martu. It was Ranger Orba. My goddess. I fought off an urge to bow and another to run. Orba; her totally engulfing dark eyes upon me as she glid towards us.

"Looks like you and I are going to get to know each other pretty well Grant". I smiled inanely. Orba handed me a paper file. "Read this please, it's a scene-setting document for the mission we may be undertaking together. Study it and memorise all the characters and situations. It may make the difference between success and failure".

I took the file and looked sheepishly at Martu who was trying very hard to stifle a giggle. She obviously found my tongue-tied little boy act awfully amusing. But it was no act. I fell apart in the presence of such total beauty. Orba started to walk away and beckoned me to follow her. She looked back at Martu and winked at her in a mischievous way.

"Be gentle with him, Orba".

"I'll take him to the recreation lounge if he's a good boy" She replied. Her voice washed over me like velvet. Orba fixed her brown pools of love upon me. "Give teacher a kiss and thank her for all her help". I turned around. Martu and I gripped each other in a passionate embrace, our mouths lustily clamping together. We kissed deeply and passionately for a few minutes before parting.

"Good luck Grant. I'll see you when you get back".

I followed Orba to a private room which was fitted out with a leather chaise. "Sit down and read the file. I've got to go to a meeting with the decision makers. I will go through the specifics with you if you get the go-ahead Grant". Orba moved out into the corridor, leaving me alone with the file. I opened it and began to read. It was written in the form of prose like a novel, but I knew it was more than a mere story. I knew that in some dimensional reality much like my own recent world, the horrific things I read about were actually happening to people who had no understanding that there was a game in progress; who had given no permission.

Part 2

The Mission

Mission Document: *The Company of Killers*

The Red door opened to reveal a tall, bulky man in his sixties. White hair reached out from each side of his head as if trying to escape the dark thoughts of the brain, which shone laser-like from the man's twinkling eyes.

The man wore a crumpled white suit with soft brown deck shoes and a multi-coloured open-necked shirt. "Yes?" he enquired of the small, wiry stoat standing just inches away on the other side of the cracked grey doorstep.

"Mr. Russell?, Anton Russell?" The stoat spoke with a gruff, weary authority, leaning forward, briefly flashing an identity card before standing stiffly upright, almost to attention, a habit picked up during a determined but unspectacular army career.

"I am he sir. What help may I be to the illustrious Thames Valley Constabulary?" There was a silky edge to Anton's voice, part of a well-practised faux charm he had cultivated over many years.

The stoat braced himself like a paratrooper about to do his first sky dive before introducing himself formally. "Good Evening sir, I am Detective Inspector Randall, from Newbury C.I.D., I wonder if I might have a few words with you concerning several recent media interviews attributed to yourself?"

"I wondered how long it would take" The tall man stood back from the doorway and beckoned the inspector inside. The red door slammed behind them.

The hallway of the house was cluttered and damp. A pine umbrella stand rested in one corner, an old battered Grandfather clock in another. Piles of magazines covered most of the floor – among them *New Psychology, Tatler, Harpers & Queen* and *True Crime*. There were a lot of coats, hats, walking sticks and assorted boots and shoes.

Inspector Mick Randall followed Anton Russell into the living room. Here again it was cluttered with magazines piled on the floor amongst big ugly furniture. A large red leather-covered chair, worn on arms and seat, rested against a honey-oak bureau. The flap of the bureau was down and covered with papers, pots of pens, rubber bands, paper clips and other miscellaneous stationery items.

Towards the back of the room was a dark wood bookcase. Randall skimmed the titles in an attempt to glean information about their owner's inner psyche. It was an old and overrated police technique. There was a copy of Herman Hesse's *Steppenwolf* next to *Crime and Punishment* – maybe there *was* something in the method. Then he saw *Winnie the Pooh*, a couple of Agatha Christie's and a book on watercolour painting – the technique was useless after all.

Anton Russell motioned towards a blue fabric settee, he himself sitting in the red chair. Randall sat down and observed his quarry. Russell was in his sixties, his white hair unkempt, watery blue eyes with red rims like he'd been crying, his skin rough and pale. A slight twitch of the mouth could be a sign of nervousness, or it could just be a twitch.

Inspector Randall cleared his throat in the manner of someone about to make a speech "Mr. Russell, on the 15th of April this year, an article appeared in the '*News of the World*' in which certain comments were attributed to you regarding the murder of Rachael Heaver. Are you aware of the article to which I am referring?"

"Yes" replied Anton.

"And would you accept the article, as printed in the *News of the World*, dated Sunday 15th April as being a true and accurate representation of statements made by you, to their reporter, namely one Jane Race?"

"I accept it as being a fair representation of *part* of a conversation I had with Ms. Race, though not a full or completely accurate one; but we both know that reporters can't resist a little bit of tweaking". Russell spoke calmly and slowly, his body language suggesting relaxed interest.

"In what way or ways does the newspaper article differ from what you told their reporter?" asked Inspector Stoat, his voice taking on the official police interrogation tone of controlled authority mixed with a hint of hidden knowledge.

Anton Russell's mouth twitched into a smirk. "Mainly that certain parts of the conversation were taken out of context in an attempt to make my comments sound less hypothetical and more like statements of known facts". The red leather chair creaked as Anton leaned back into it.

Mick Randall also leaned back in an attempt to mirror the suspect's body language and to create the illusion of empathy – another classic police technique. His gaze took in the room, eyes flicking like two camera shutters, recording every item, every fact, every meaning.

On the left side of the bureau Randall noticed a small blue book with gold-edged pages, possibly a diary. On a low shelf of a small pine bookcase, there was a pile of resealable plastic bags, the type used by drug dealers. There were also at least three pairs of black leather gloves resting on a pile of magazines which Randall glimpsed through a small gap between the half-open door and the far wall.

The Inspector's mind worked it's usual detective magic, churning out possible criminal scenarios, connecting potentially significant objects. If more than a few of his theories concerning these items linked together in a plausible way, Mick Randall's sleuthing radar started to whirr.

"Which comments or parts of your conversation with Ms. Race have been taken out of context in the manner you suggest?" The stoat was beginning to tighten the screw. Not too much at this early stage, mustn't frighten the quarry into clamming up, just a little bit of pressure, a few awkward questions to see what kind of prey he was dealing with.

Russell's eyes moved down and to the right, giving himself a break from the Inspector's gaze, time to consider an appropriate response. His mouth twitched.

"Well, one thing was the phrase she used to explain my description of the position of the body when it was discovered by the Cat Lady. I told Jane Race that the victim's legs had been spread wide and propped up *as if* to emphasize a sexual element to the killing. I told her it looked *as if* the vagina had been put on display in order to draw attention to it, possibly indicating a sexual motive. In the newspaper article it states, as I'm sure you are perfectly aware, that I had said that the body had been positioned to emphasize the vagina. The reporter had removed the words 'as if', from my statement".

Randall crossed his left leg over his right leg and cleared his throat. "As if?" He underlined the words in such a way as to make them sound small, insignificant.

"If you want to check my original statement, I can give you Jane Race's number".

"Its alright Mr. Russell, I already have it but thank you anyway. Please continue".

Anton raised his eyebrows, gave another twitch of the mouth and continued in a soft, silky voice. " The removal of the words 'as if' made the statement sound *as if* I had prior knowledge of the facts, when I was simply offering an hypothesis".

"And how are you qualified to suggest a motive for this killing?" enquired the Inspector.

156

"Well, considering I've just spent a year and a half on remand, charged with this murder, not to mention a four month trial, during which time I heard all the evidence over a hundred times, I think that only the real killer and the victim would be in a position to know more; and considering the victim is dead and the police have failed to find the perpetrator, I feel well within my rights to offer my hypothesis regarding the facts".

"Alright Mr. Russell, no need to upset yourself". Randall smiled inwardly at this beautiful touch of detective finesse. Suggesting that the suspect was getting upset, thereby causing him to consider the possibility that he *was* getting upset, leading to him actually *becoming* upset, and therefore off his guard. Piling on the pressure. The Inspector felt like a highly trained dog on the scent of a fleeing fox. He was beginning to enjoy himself.

"Oh, I'm far from upset Inspector" replied Russell in a menacing voice. "After all I've nothing to worry about. Having been cleared of this particular crime, I am protected from being charged with it again under current legislation. Therefore, *had* I committed this murder and *had* I a mind to do so, I could quite safely admit it in public, no doubt greatly increasing my commercial value to the gutter press in the process and there would be absolutely nothing you or any other flatfoot could do about it". As he spoke, Russell leaned forward in his chair and fixed the Inspector with a steady hostile gaze.

The Inspector sat calmly and returned the hard look with interest. So, the gloves were off! "I dare you to admit it, Russell". The stoat's voice crackled with controlled passion. He stood quickly, bending over Anton Russell, who had rocked back in his chair. Mick Randall's eyes burned like hot coals, his hands trembling into fists, his face red.

Russell leaned back, his expression neutral, eyes moving upwards and to the right as he struggled with the challenge laid down by the detective. A slight glow of moisture appeared at his temples, though his expression remained steady. When he spoke his voice was firm, the silky patter fully restored.

"O.K. Inspector, you got me. I did it. I murdered Rachael Heaver. I strangled her with the clothesline and propped her legs up to emphasize the vagina in order to indicate a sexual motive to the killing. I raped her as she lay dying of strangulation and wanted the world to know that I'd had her, that the last thing she felt before she died, was my stiff cock inside her body. Is that what you want to hear Inspector?" Anton Russell's breath was coming hard and fast, his eyes becoming dangerous blue lasers, his hands flexing, his mouth twisted into a savage and triumphant smile. The man looked like the demon he undoubtedly was.

Inspector Randall was reeling at the ferocity of the man's verbal onslaught, shocked at the glee in his eyes, the terrible edge to his voice. He wondered if this was the last thing that poor Rachael had seen as he drained the breath and the life out of her. Anger rose in the Inspector's breast, his heart pounding like a sledge hammer on glass, shattering his self control. Jumping forward, the policeman gripped Anton Rogers by the throat, lifting him up onto his feet. As he pulled his balled fist back, ready to smash it into the killer's face, Russell began to laugh like a maniac, his chest beginning to rock with the power of the movement, eyes bulging, unblinking. Suddenly, the Inspector caught on. He released Russell and slumped back onto the settee.

"She wasn't raped. You sick cunt !"

"Not raped, Inspector Randall?" Anton's voice had become smooth and calm once more. "Then I must have been giving an hypothesis, using my imagination in order to explore some of the many possible theories about what happened on that night. Just like when I spoke to the 'News of the World'. Do you get my drift, Inspector? Do you see the point I am trying to

158

make. Do you see the difference between theory and fact now?"

"Filthy scum" was all Randall could muster. He'd been had, stitched up like a kipper. Not only that, he'd compromised his professionalism. It hurt.

Russell sat back in his red leather chair. He rested his arms on his knees and put his hands together in a professorial manner. "I think you know where the door is Inspector. I'm expecting a call from the 'Sunday People', so I'd be grateful if you'd go now. I don't really think we have anything else to discuss".

Mick Randall stood facing Anton Rogers, his eyes steady, his posture ramrod straight. "Congratulations on your little joke Mr. Russell. I look forward to the pleasure of your company again. Perhaps then I will be in a position to offer you the chance to play one of my games".

"I'll look forward to it Inspector, Good Day". Anton Russell looked away. The interview was over. The Inspector left quickly and silently.

It was raining outside as Mick Randall walked back to his car, a blue Ford Mondeo parked fifty yards along the narrow residential street. As he approached the vehicle, his expression suggested deep thought, his firm step hinted at great determination.

When he reached the car he opened the passenger door and flopped into the seat. Next to him, in the driving seat sat a blonde-haired woman in her late thirties. Her expression was one of veiled amusement.

"Oops!" she said

"Don't say a fucking word" replied the Inspector, giving his partner a filthy look. "Just drive us back to the station".

"I got it all on tape, if that's any use" she said, waving a

159

mini cassette recorder at him. "Then again that may not be so good, for you, under the circumstances Mick". Her eyes were twinkling, mouth showing white teeth beneath bright red lips.

"You dare even breath a fucking word of any of this Karen and I'll personally stuff an asp up your fucking jacksy, fucking sideways. You get me?"

"Such a foul fucking mouth, you've got" she replied, laughing gently.

Karen started the car, still smiling and pulled out into traffic which was fairly light. She drove to the station without making further comment. Mick Randall for his part, lapsed into a brooding silence, his right hand raised, covering his mouth, eyes cast downwards in thought. Occasionally he stretched his legs forward, pressing his feet against the back of the foot well.

Newbury Police station was situated on Mill Lane, next to the Magistrate's Court. Karen guided the vehicle across the busy junction before taking a left, over a pointless mini roundabout and into the police station car park. She drove in a wide circle around the building, coming to a stop in a marked bay at the back of the red brick edifice.

"Come on Mick, cheer up. Let me get you a coffee and one of your ghastly doughnuts" said Karen as they walked to the rear entrance. The back door was for police personnel only and was made from reinforced grey steel. There was a large CCTV camera mounted above the door and an intercom fitted on the wall. Karen pressed the buzzer.

"Yes?" asked a metallic voice from the speaker.

"D.S. Fox and D.I. Randall" replied Karen.

"O.K." said the voice. A loud buzzer sounded, indicating that the door could now be opened. Karen pulled it wide, holding it for Mick Randall to enter first.

"After you guv. Shit before the shovel"

"Thank you Sergeant Fox" replied the inspector. His tone was harsh but there was a smile on his face. Mick Randall was back in control. The Stoat was once again on the scent. Beware evil-doers everywhere. Especially in the Newbury area.

Inside was another reinforced door. A uniformed officer peered through a glass panel at the side, before pressing the release button. Once again a buzzer sounded and the detectives opened the door and entered the rear lobby of the station. They both acknowledged the uniform with curt nods of the head and moved through the reception area to a green painted stairway. They climbed to the first floor in silence and turned right through some white double swing doors into the canteen.

It was quiet inside due to it being the middle of the afternoon. Only a couple of tables had occupants. Mick noticed a colleague, Detective Sergeant Cutler, sitting alone at a table beside a far window.

"Get me a coffee and my doughnut please Karen. I'm going to have a quick word with Jim"

"O.K. Mick. I'll be sitting by the jungle" replied Karen, glancing toward an unreasonably large plant display in the centre of the room. A low platform encircled the 'jungle', with tables and chairs placed haphazardly upon it.

Mick walked over to where Jim Cutler was staring into his cup. "Taken up reading tea leaves Jim?" said Mick in a loud voice. Jim Cutler looked up and smiled when he saw who had spoken.

"Alright Mick, how's the stoating going?" Mick sat in the opposite chair.

"Oh, you know, a bit of this, a bit of that and plenty of the other"

"You wish" replied Jim "I bet you've started stirring your

tea with it since that au pair left"

"Maria wasn't a fucking au pair, she was a housekeeper and my relationship with her was purely professional" replied Mick with a sneer.

"I'm sure it was totally professional Mick. Thirty quid for a blow job, fifty for the full treatment and a ton to come up her arse. At least that's what I heard" Jim Cutler winked and laughed out loud, shoulders rocking, feet stamping with glee. Mick moved forward quickly and grappled Jim to the floor, getting him in a headlock and applying a rough donkey scrub.

"Do you submit, motherfucker?" he asked in a mock American accent. Jim squirmed, then realising there was no escape from Mick's firm hold, flopped down into a submissive posture.

"O.K. Stoater, don't lose the plot completely". Mick released Jim and offered him a strong hand which he took. Mick pulled him to his feet and they stood grinning at each other in the manner of naughty schoolboys.

"Well Sonny" said Mick "Now that I've put you back in your pram, I'd like to have a word with you about Benny Eye. You're on that aren't you?" Jim sat down again and became serious.

"Yeah, I'm on it Mick, what about it?"

"I've heard a whisper from a source who shall remain nameless – "

"Annie"

" – A source called Annie who shall remain nameless, that Anton Russell was briefly considered as a suspect"

"Yes, we did consider Russell for a while, but the M.O. was all wrong. He's always killed in a blood free zone, being at heart a cowardly slime ball. Bennie on the other hand seems to revel in a bit of gore and guts. He likes to shock, make a big artistic statement. Why else would he burn his victim's eyes out with cigarettes?"

"Yeah, that is a bit sick, isn't it? I mean even for a serial killer?"

"We're definitely dealing with a fully fledged wacko, that's for sure Mick"

"Do you know if he stubs his Bennies out before or after they are dead?" Mick glanced across at Karen and pointed to his watch, then held up his right hand, fingers spread wide to indicate that he would be there in five minutes.

"Forensics can't be sure" continued Jim "But I reckon a sicko like that has got to do it while the victim is alive and well enough to get maximum benefit."

"And why always B+H?" asked Mick.

"Maybe it's just the brand he smokes, or maybe its his initials and he's offering us a clue, just to make the game more interesting. We've already searched for details of all known and suspected killers and violent offenders with the initials BH just in case, but so far we've drawn a blank. Maybe he's got himself a sponsorship deal"

"Or maybe there's two of them, one named Benson and one named Hedges?" offered Mick with a cheesy grin.

"You tosser" replied Jim "I'll see you later"

"See ya" said Mick, walking towards the table close to the jungle where Karen was sitting, eating a Cornish pasty with a fork. There was a glass of milk in front of her. A cup of coffee and a very large, pink ice covered, cream-filled doughnut was placed opposite. Mick sat down at the table and greedily sank his teeth into the confectionary monster. Cream squeezed out of both sides of the doughnut and plopped onto his plate.

"I don't know how you can bring yourself to eat those vile things" said Karen.

"An orgasm on a plate" mumbled Mick through a mouthful of cream and sugary dough. He scooped up some of the fallen cream with his finger and waved it menacingly towards Karen's face.

"Not just at the moment Mick, thanks all the same. Maybe when I'm off duty. Oh and I prefer a bed to a plate" said Karen, laughing. Mick looked puzzled.

"Now what the fuck are you on about?"

"I thought you were offering me an orgasm on a plate. I'm telling you nicely to go fuck yourself. I suppose you're going to be trying to get into my knickers all the bloody time now that you're au pair has run off?"

"She didn't run off, she was contracted to work for me for six months, now she's gone back to Paris to continue her education because her working holiday is over"

"A likely story. Still, I'm not one to pry into other people's sordid sexual setups"

"Too busy with your own, eh Karen?" said Mick with a wink. She decided it was time to change the subject.

"What were you talking to Jimmy Boy about that forced you to wrestle him to the ground?"

"I was wondering if Russell had been implicated in the Benny Eye murders. Unfortunately Jim reckons that Uncle Anton is far too much of a coward to do anything that colourful. I tend to agree with him. I was hoping to get something on the bastard today, at least make the fucker sweat a bit. I just hate the fact that he thinks he's got away with Rachael Heaver – going to the fucking papers with it, what a scum bag" Mick banged his fist down on the table, causing his coffee and Karen's milk to spill.

164

"Oi! Steady on Tiger! There's no need to wreck the place"

"Sorry Karen. Its got under my skin, his making money out of it. There seems to be a lot of that about at the moment, what with Greg fucking Park spilling his guts on the telly last week. Poor little Greggy being victimised by the nasty old filth. I don't know where these fucking journalists get off, making heroes out of killers. What's the world coming to?"

"It's still the same shit hole it always was Mick, nothing's changed from where I'm sitting" Mick pointed behind Karen. She looked round to see what he was indicating with his extended digit.

"That fucking azalea has changed from where I'm sitting" said Mick in amused disbelief. "Last time I saw it there was a big red flower on the top of it. Now there's a photo of Alan Titchmarsh instead". Karen saw the small photo, obviously cut from some glossy gardening magazine. It was definitely a picture of Alan the gardener, grinning in self-satisfied delight.

"There's some witty cunts in this station" said Karen, smiling with amusement. "Looks like Steve Gordon's work to me. He was last seen loitering with intent outside the women's bogs by Todd's office"

"Yeah but what intent did he intend?" asked Mick

"Well I doubt if it's anything sexual. He's only allowed to have it off with his girlfriend if his Mum says its alright"

"She probably offers advice throughout the performance and gives him marks out of ten when he's finished" Karen grimaced.

"Do you mind, that's one graphic image I don't want to think about". Mick drained his coffee in a single swig and stood up.

"Come on you lazy heifer, we've got work to do". Karen

finished her glass of milk and followed Mick out of the canteen, towards their shared office on the 2nd floor.

Jason Black opened his eyes, slowly. Then he closed them again. What he had hoped was a bad dream had been revealed as a dreadful reality. Eric was lying naked on the bed next to him, one arm twisted in an irritating angle behind his head, one leg hanging loosely off the edge of the bed.

Jason knew he had to think fast. There was no way he wanted any kind of a relationship with Eric. He had only ended up in bed with him because he had drunk too much at Ozzy's party. He had surprised himself at the time, getting off with a male, especially a pink ponce like Eric Brunner.

Jason had not had a sexual experience with a man for over five years. In fact he had pretty much written off his previous homosexual liaisons as a phase he had finally moved on from. Ever since he had set up home with Serena he had convinced himself that he was straight.

Now his sexual orientation was once again swinging towards 'bi'. There was no way one drunken night with an overweight office boy was going to spoil things. He had to act fast and decisively.

Naked except for a pair of red, white and blue sports socks, Jason moved around to the other side of the bed. Leaning forward, he grabbed the still sleeping Eric roughly by the shoulders and shook him violently, causing Eric to wake suddenly, attempt to rise from the bed and squeal like a stuck pig.

"What the fuck?"

Jason threw him back down and stood towering above him, eyes dark and blazing. "Get up you dirty motherfucker, so I can knock your teeth down your fucking throat" Eric looked dazed and terrified.

"Jason, just tell me what's going on for fucking Hell's sake. Have I done something to piss you off?"

"Yes, you've done something to piss me off Eric, you filthy little gay boy rapist!" yelled Jason "You've fucking spiked my drink with fucking Rohypnol and fucking raped my shit hole with your maggot-sized dick, you shit-stabbing arse bandit!" Jason reached forward and grabbed Eric viciously by the throat. Eric began to shiver with fear.

Jason relaxed his grip a little, allowing Eric the chance to wriggle free and leap to his feet. He looked ungainly prancing around the room with his blobby stomach bouncing and his small cock dancing like a miniature puppet.

"Look, I really don't know what's going on here but I can assure you I never spiked your drink, honest Jason, I wouldn't do a nasty thing like that"

"And I wouldn't do a nasty thing like you if I wasn't drugged, you lying cunt, so just get your fucking clothes on and get your perverted carcass out of my fucking face, out of my fucking flat and out of my fucking life. And stay out. If I even see you again I'll cut your misshapen bollocks off with a kitchen knife and feed them to piranhas".

While Jason was ranting, Eric grabbed his white 'Y' fronts and put them on back to front. Then he gathered up the rest of his clothes into a pile and began moving backwards, slowly edging towards the bedroom door. He reached behind himself and turning the handle, opened the door and bolted like a startled rabbit.

Jason stood and watched as Eric ran across the lounge and disappeared through the front door. Mission accomplished. Jason took off his socks and walked back through his bedroom into the en-suite bathroom.

As he switched on the shower, Jason felt bad. Bad because he had drunk the best part of a bottle of mesquite tequila the night before and even badder because of the shitty trick he'd just pulled on Eric. The poor lad would probably never have sex again. Still, it had to be done. There was no way he was going to fuck it up with Serena. He liked the way his life was going just now. Marriage was on the not-too-distant horizon and his career was on the up. Things had finally turned around for him. If he had to upset a few mummy's boys to keep his life on track, then that is what he would do. If he saw Eric at work he would just give him an evil look. That should send him skulking back to his momma's skirts quickly enough.

As the warm water flowed powerfully over his firm, muscular body, Jason began to feel a lot better. His conscience had gone back into it's box and the smell of his exotic shower gel soothed his body and soul and invigorated his spirit.

The phone rang. Jason turned off the shower and ran, naked and wet, into the bedroom to pick up the receiver.

"Hello" he answered, breathless.

"You haven't got a woman there, I hope" it was Serena. Her French accent and gentle laugh made him feel horny.

"The only woman I want is you ma Cherie". He sat down on the end of the bed. "Where are you?"

"I am at Fleet Services. The traffic is bad today. I am phoning to let you know that I am not going to be home before you leave for the office".

"That's a shame, I was planning on showing you how much I've missed you this week, if you know what I mean" Jason lay back on the bed and stared at the ceiling.

"I know exactly what you mean, naughty boy. You'll just have to curb your animal instincts until this evening. I bought some fabulous designer lingerie in Paris, maybe I'll be wearing it when you get home Môn chere" Serena purred.

"Not for long you won't, you French slut" replied Jason, feeling his cock twitch as he spoke. "In fact you'd better not be planning anything for the next two days, especially anything which requires walking".

"The only thing I'm planning on doing for the next two days" replied Serena in a deliberately exaggerated French accent "is you Jason, so you'd better not work too hard today. You'll be working on me all night, very hard I hope"

"I'm always very hard when you're about, you filthy little whore"

"You'd better believe I'm filthy, English boy. Madame Pussy is aching for Mr. Stiff"

"Madame Pussy is going to have to wait. Mr. Stiff has to go to work" Jason sat up. "Look Serena, I'm running late so we'll have to put this on hold until later. I love you."

"I love you too, Jason" replied Serena "I'll see you about 8 o'clock if I don't have to camp the night on the M25". Jason winced at her use of the word 'camp' as it reminded him of his very recent betrayal of Serena with the gross Eric.

"I love you, Sexy" Jason hung up the phone and flopped back onto the bed. He was feeling even more guilty now that he had spoken to Serena. How could he have done it after all the time they had spent together, especially with a no-account jerk like that. What had been going through his mind? Apart from half a pint of tequila that is. He had no memory of last night. Maybe someone had spiked his drink after all. Surely not Eric, although thinking about it, he would have to drug someone to get them into bed.

Jason ran his fingers through his thick black hair, sat up again, then rose to his feet and stared at the busy city from the bedroom window.

London was at full throttle. Rush hour had been replaced by an incessant vehicular blitzing. Driving through this rancid metropolis was an act of war these days. Jason always took the tube, which was only slightly less challenging a prospect, but what else could you do? Walk? That would be insane with all the car fumes and filth in the streets. At least car drivers could close all their windows and put on the air con. Maybe that was a safer choice after all. Jason didn't have time to consider all the options, he was late for work.

He quickly dressed in his second best blue suit, clean white shirt and an amber and pink tie, grabbed his silver executive briefcase and ran out of the flat.

By the time he arrived at his office in Canary Wharf, his nerves were beginning to fray. So many people getting in his way, shoving him aside, standing on his expensive shoes. He loved living in London but hated all the people. Couldn't they limit the population so that those remaining had room to breathe occasionally?

It was the same in the crowded lift which took him to the 23rd floor where the 'News of the World' had given him a cupboard to work in. Still, most freelances didn't get anything at all. It was only because he had delivered so many red hot stories to them over the years, that they had decided to offer him a place to do his work. Mainly so that they would know where he was for more of the time and to make him feel less inclined to go to their competitors with his next front page exposé.

Most of the real employees worked in a huge open-plan office on the 24th floor. He and a few other selected freelancers had been positioned out of the way in an effort to stop too many stories leaking down to them. After all a hot story to the 'News of the World' is a hot story to the 'Sunday People' too. There was a lot of money to be made from leaks to other papers, not that Jason ever felt like getting into all that espionage stuff.

He made a tidy living from his own research and had won a couple of journalistic awards over the years for his investigations into unsolved crimes. He had come up with enough evidence on several occasions to help the police convict criminals who had thought they were safe from the long arm of the law. There was nowhere that the long pen of the international media didn't reach these days. The police were becoming more reliant on journalists to do their jobs for them. Not that they would ever thank you for it. Too much professional jealousy involved due to the much greater resources available to the media than to the police. Poor bastards, they had to fill in a batch of forms every time they took a piss these days. No wonder they resented it. Mind you, they always took the glory in the end, getting a collar on a plate and all the evidence nicely tied up in a little pink bow. They should be bloody grateful that newspapers bothered to do it so well. It was a public service. He…The phone rang.

"Yes?"

"Jane Race. I've got a potential gold mine for you, if you're not too busy my boy"

"Oh yeah, What is it?"

"Not over the dog my dear, you never know who's ear-wigging. Usual place 4pm, don't keep me waiting" She hung up.

"Bollocks" said Jason, slamming his receiver down. There was no way he needed a session with Jane right now. It was bound to turn into a fucking all-night bender. Jane was always so difficult to get a straight answer out of. She'd make a great politician, what with her perpetual evasion, not-so-secret vices and obsessive desire for personal power and glory. Every time she arranged one of these little rendezvous, she'd turn up pissed and try every trick to get him wasted too.

171

Even worse, she always travelled with an entourage; a bunch of arse-licking losers hoping that some of Jane's success would rub off on them if they laughed at enough of her crappy jokes and went along with her pervy sexual demands.

Which was another reason Jason did not want to get into this right now, not after being unfaithful to Serena less than twelve hours ago. He had promised a cosy night in and that was what he was going to have. Jane could go fuck herself. She'd fucked everyone and everything else already. Jason decided he would give this particular hot exclusive a miss.

Mind you, Jane had never let him down yet. Every one of her leads had brought him a journalistic pot of gold. She had a knack, a sixth sense for the unusual, the bizarre, the spectacular. Bollocks, bollocks, bollocks.

He took the coward's way out, dialling his home number and speaking into his own answer machine.

"Hi, Serena, it's me Jason. Just to let you know I may be a little bit late tonight. Something big is about to break and I'm likely to win 'journo of the year' if it pans out how I think it will. Sorry, but I have to meet a contact and it could take a while to get all the information. I'll get home as soon as I can. Keep that new underwear warm. See you tonight, I love you, bye Serena".

Just as he was putting down the receiver, Jess Reeves popped her head into his office, a big smile on her face.

"Hi Jase, how's things with Eric?" Jason flinched inwardly, stayed cool outside. Smiled back at the dark-haired young temp with the low-cut top and the tight skirt. She was a looker alright, if a little tarty in her choice of office attire. Still, there's nothing wrong with a tart, especially when you're filling it with cream, as the old joke goes. He certainly wouldn't mind filling her one day soon. She was obviously up for it, what with the prolonged eye contact and the open body language. Oh, yes, Ms. Reeves was definitely ripe for a bit of after hours training.

"Jess, you stupid bitch, just go and make me some coffee and save the jokes for those of us with the brains to pull them off" She laughed at this obviously defensive reply.

"Oh, rest assured, Mr Clever-Dick, I've pulled off plenty in my time". She winked in an 'ooh missus' kind of way and sat on Jason's desk, long shapely legs stretched out in front of her. He tried very hard not to stare at them but his eyes ignored the warnings from his brain and glued themselves onto the smooth, tanned limbs, the silk stockings emphasising their soft curves, the ankle straps of her high heeled shoes creating the same effect on him as a choker around a neck or a stocking top around a thigh, namely a hard-on. He moved behind the desk so she wouldn't know she had scored a hit, but she damn well knew she had, the bitch.

"If you've got anything useful or relevant to say, please feel free to go for it, otherwise you'll have to make an appointment, I'm very busy on an exclusive at the moment".

"You fucking arrogant prick" she laughed. "I was just going to invite you to my party tonight at the Rosey, but if that's your attitude, you can get fucked".

"Maybe I could come to your party *and* get fucked. What do you think?" She stood up and gave him a don't think I'm a dead cert pal look as she walked out of the door.

"Two sugars isn't it?.

"Yes please Jess". Bollocks, bollocks, bollocks again.

When Jess came back with the coffee he pretended to be working on his computer and didn't speak, just nodding a very brief 'thanks'. She placed the cup on the desk and walked away, giving him the finger. Maybe he would return the compliment later.

For the rest of the day Jason worked on a couple of mundane projects which had been left half-finished for too long. He didn't venture upstairs to the main office in an effort to avoid Eric and Eric-related piss takes. No-one else from upstairs came down to speak to him, though eight sick emails arrived in his inbox during the day. The most disturbing of the bunch was an anatomically impossible drawing which featured a three-penised Jason fucking Eric's arse while both Serena and Jane Race sucked his two additional appendages, simultaneously fingering each other. He almost laughed at that one.

Around 3 o'clock he switched off his computer and legged it out of the building without being seen. He was glad to get away from the place, hated being the topic of conversation. There was a very thin line between a bit of gossip and a news story as far as most journalists were concerned. Fuck the lot of them. He needed a drink to take the edge off this morning's hangover which was being a bastard and not clearing as they usually did by lunchtime. How much had he put away last night? Maybe he had pulled Eric after all. No way. Impossible.

Rod Merchant moved silently along the underground passageway, following the others into a bare, concrete lined bunker. In the room were a number of metal framed chairs, set out in two semi-circles facing a table behind which sat three hard-eyed men dressed in identical blue boiler suits. He swapped nervous glances with several of the other inductees as they took their seats. "It's too late now, they've seen us" he whispered to the thin guy sitting next to him. The guy gave him a nervous grin and shook his curly mop of hair as if to disassociate himself from Rod's witty comment. Rod folded his arms across his body and focussed upon the three men behind the table.

The man nearest the door was about fifty, balding, slightly overweight with dark brown shark's eyes staring fiercely from their sockets. Rod noticed a bandage wrapped around his left wrist, which he held slightly uncomfortably on his lap. The man in the middle of the trio was a tall, distinguished colonel type, complete with neat moustache and military bearing. He tapped impatiently upon a red plastic folder which lay on the table in front of him. It was the third man, a short greasy ball with puffy hands, who stood and addressed the nervously waiting group.

"Hello everybody and welcome to your introduction to the art of murder". He scanned the audience as he spoke, no doubt looking to see what reaction his words were having on those listening. "My name, for the purposes of this meeting, is Mike. I am the Recruiter. My task is to attract and select suitable candidates for induction into our very special secret society. My hope is that among the twenty of you here tonight, I will find some who have the courage to follow their hearts into a world of total freedom and personal liberty. What we have to offer you is a passageway into a new world of truth, self-expression and ultimate thrill. A world that everyone, at sometime in their lives, dreams about but lacks the courage to attain. A world where you are at last safe to pursue your deepest desires without self-appointed moral guardians taking their revenge on those of you honest enough to admit their need to kill."

A couple of dark-haired men in green wax jackets mumbled quiet agreement. Mike glanced in their direction, offering a slight smile of encouragement. "The main barrier to murder, at least in the normal, mentally healthy hunter male, has always been the justified fear of arrest and incarceration, should they follow their natural instincts. Now, thanks to our sponsors, leaders and agents, we are in the enviable position to be able to offer you the opportunity to unleash your darkest lusts with complete protection from punishment." The audience ooh-ed, bringing a smirk to Mike's thick red lips.

"However, not everyone has the guts to follow their

175

dream to completion. Some of you may find the actualité a bit too real, preferring to fall back into the safety of your fantasy life, and this is ok by us. Not everyone can become the best. Not everyone is man enough to take the life of another creature. We have softer options for those of you who, after tonight's meeting, decide that they would like to keep the actual gore at arms length. For instance, you can choose to become shareholders in the company we run, which I can assure you is on the verge of the kind of growth that the Elephant Man would be proud of". The audience burst into hearty laughter, relaxing into their seats for the first time, as if some uncomfortable spell had been broken. "Take it from me gentlemen, murder is about to become the new Rock & Roll".

Mike bent down to pick up a glass of water from the table, taking a long slow swig before continuing. "Not only can our members do what the hell they like with impunity, but they can make a fucking fortune at the same time". More whoops from the increasingly excited crowd. "We are above the law. We are untouchable. We rule the streets. We dominate like Gods. Now you can join us and be part of the final liberation of Man". The audience cheered loudly and clapped wildly. Mike re-took his seat.

The colonel figure rose next, tapping his pen on the tabletop to get the audience's attention. Quickly silence was restored. The man slowly studied each face in the crowd before speaking.

"My name is Martin. I am the Protector. My role in this organisation is to ensure that we remain safe and able to continue our work without persecution from either the Police, the media or other groups and individuals who would wish to see us stopped. Our organisation is secret and I will do whatever I must to ensure that it stays secret right up until the time when we are strong enough to go public. That time is fast approaching, but until then, I will make you one promise which you can rely upon both myself and my many agents to carry out in full, should it become necessary".

A sense of foreboding rose in Rod's stomach as Martin spoke. There was something sinister about him, like he was straight out of a horror film, or a Nazi that was never caught. Martin paused for effect before delivering his final statement. "If any of you here cause harm to this organisation, through something you do or say at any time in the future, I can categorically assure you that I or one of my agents will not only torture you to death over a period of months, but we will abuse, defile, mutilate and finally murder every living member of your family, from your granny to your newborn baby, in front of your eyes before we kill you". Martin sat down again. The silence was deafening. Fear showed on all their faces as the audience let the enormity of this sickening possibility sink in.

As if to underline the darkness of the emotions running through the meeting, the lights suddenly dimmed. A second later a beam of light shone onto the wall behind the table. The title frames of a film show appeared on the wall. 'Pre-induction Murder Clips'. A disclaimer appeared on the screen reassuring the audience that all the footage was genuine and all persons both living and eventually dead were actual persons and not mere actors.

Nervous cheers rippled through the audience. Rod looked towards the men behind the table and could make out the third man – the baldy with shark's eyes – standing. He had a small switch in his bandaged left hand and as he pressed it the picture on the screen changed and a movie appeared.

The first clip was a thirty second black and white silent film showing a man in a top hat and tails following a young girl along a country lane. The man walked up behind the girl and grabbed her by the arm. She struggled but could not get away. The man raised his arm and hit the girl across the head, causing her to fall to the ground, before taking a knife from his coat pocket and stabbing the girl repeatedly in the chest and abdomen. The girl's struggles eventually stopped and she lie dead on the road. The man moved away from the girl and the screen went blank.

Another film began almost instantly. It was entitled 'You Dirty Rapist. Series 2. Giving Jenny a Good Seeing To'. This time the footage was modern and in colour. A dark haired woman in her twenties lay spread-eagled on a brass bed with purple silk sheets. Her wrists and ankles were tied with thick ropes to the bedstead. She was naked apart from a black velvet choker around her neck and a pair of black stiletto shoes on her feet.

The woman was lying back quietly on the bed, almost asleep. Rod got the impression she had been left alone in the room for some time and the picture was from a hidden camera. The room was done out in what Rod believed to be the style of a plush bordello, or a French brothel, with luxurious burgundy and gold fabrics hung on the walls alonside oil paintings of bacchanalian orgies.

The door of the room opened and in walked three men. One carried a big, professional-looking camera. The other two men were naked, except one of them wore Union Jack socks. All three had erect penises. As soon as she saw the men, the woman on the bed screamed and started struggling.

The naked men climbed onto the bed as a new camera angle flicked onto the screen, no doubt provided by the man in the room. This image showed a closer view of the bed with the two men moving towards the naked woman. One man began to fondle the woman's breasts.

The victim struggled harder as the second man ran one of his hands up her right thigh and began to rub between her legs, sliding two fingers into her vagina before moving his head down between her thighs to lick her. The camera zoomed in closer so that the audience could see the tongue moving between her labia, before moving back out to show that the other man had straddled her chest and was busy sliding his erection between her breasts.

After a few minutes, both men changed position. Union Jack Socks knelt on the bed between the woman's thighs, rubbing his cock around her hole and starting to fuck her. There was a close up shot of his cock sliding in and out of her vagina.

Someone in the audience shouted "Get in there my son" and a few others laughed. Rod didn't laugh. He was too engrossed in the action on the screen. The second man too began to rub his cock around her hole, gradually forcing his hard-on into her, alongside the other man's cock. The pain of this caused the woman's screams to increase but didn't stop the two cocks thrusting into her with increasing ferocity, eventually jerking in unison as they simultaneously ejaculated into her.

The camera zoomed in on the men's cocks as they pulled out, dripping with a mixture of semen and blood. The camera focussed upon the victim's bleeding vagina for a few seconds, before moving slowly up the woman's body, to show her distraught face, no longer screaming, just fearful and trembling like a battered animal.

Suddenly the film flicked back to the more distant hidden camera shot that it had begun with and showed the camera-man pass the camera to the Union Jack Socks. After a few seconds, the mobile camera shot came back. Tears rolled down the victim's face as she sobbed uncontrollably, her lips trembling, eyes wide with fear.

The shot zoomed out to show the man who had held the camera during the rape scene climbing onto the bed beside the woman, who was screaming and struggling once more. "No more, please, haven't you hurt me enough?" she shrieked.

"Don't worry, Jenny, you won't be suffering much longer" replied the former cameraman, moving over her struggling form and placing both hands around her slender throat "because I'm going to murder you". At this Jenny began to thrash about with renewed intensity, her last scream catching in her constricted throat as the man squeezed on her windpipe and began to shake her back and forwards, making her head loll like a rag doll.

After a couple of minutes Jenny's struggles stopped. The life drained out of her, she lay silent and still on the bed. The man who had just killed her leaned forward and kissed her dead mouth before running his hands over her lifeless body. He lay upon her and inserted his erect penis into her corpse before starting to fuck the body.

The camera showed a close-up of the man's cock thrusting in and out between the corpse's thighs until he let out a moan of pleasure and ejaculated into the dead body.

The film ended at this point. The audience slow to react, gradually began to clap and cheer, until the whole room was engulfed in a wave of noise.

The lights came back on and Rod saw that the shark-eyed man was standing up to speak. "My name is Devon, I am the Cleaner. My role is to ensure that all bodies are disposed of and evidence removed or contaminated to ensure that the police cannot use it. I have never failed, but even if I do, another commander, known as The Creator, who is not here tonight, will have produced a watertight alibi for you well in advance of the actual killing. So gentlemen, I am sure you can see by now that we are a very professional organisation with the ability to protect you in all circumstances, allowing you to perpetrate the most vile acts in complete safety. We offer you ultimate freedom of action. Who will join us?"

Several men stood up and formed a disorderly queue in front of the desk. Rod quickly moved to join them.

Jason pushed his way through the crowded pub, finally reaching the bar and squeezing between a ferret-faced man in a grey mac and a buxom, shiny cheeked woman of about fifty. She had a cigarette in the corner of her mouth and was fiddling with a gem-encrusted carbuncle on the third finger of her left hand.

"Pint of Miller Light, Terri" he shouted towards a dark-skinned girl who was crouching behind the bar, fishing for a bag of Cheese and Onion inside a cardboard box under the counter. She pulled the crisps from the box's innards and passed the packet to a young man with collar-length hair and a red scarf tied tightly around his neck, before glancing towards Jason.

"Just you wait your fuckin' turn, you yuppie twat" she said with a smile before moving to the far end of the bar and pulling a pint of 'Jegsy' into a wooden tankard. Once she had passed the drink to the customer and taken his money, she came over to where Jason stood with his tongue out, panting like a dog.

"Water, Water.....must........have w..aaaaaaaaa...." he slid to the floor, gasping for breath. The barmaid leaned as far over the bar as possible and peered down at his twitching corpse. Her eyes glowed mischievously as she spat her chewing gum at him, hitting him in the face. He jumped up. "I never had you down for a spitter Terri" he quipped, grabbing her and kissing her on the mouth. She pretended to struggle, finally breaking free and moving out of his reach. "That's it, run away you little prick teaser" Said Jason.

"Don't touch what you can't afford, Darlin'" she began pulling a pint of lager, carefully tilting the glass in order to get the head just right. Then she put the pint on the bar in front of Jason and held out her hand. " Two-fifty to you, you gimp" she puckered her lips in an exaggerated and suggestive manner. "Oh, and for your information Jason, I'm not a spitter".

Jason almost did a double take at this statement but held himself together and took a fiver from his wallet, placing it gently in Terri's palm. Shame it was just the fiver he thought, a broad grin spreading across his face (shame it was just the broad grin.....and so on ad infinitum).

He picked up the lager and walked slowly across the room to a group of tables near the big, floor-standing jukebox, sipping the cold fizzy liquid as he moved. As he approached, he noticed Jane and her entourage were already half pissed, judging by the amount of noise emanating from them. Jane spotted him and rose from the table, arms raised in over-enthusiastic welcome, no doubt brought on by the semi-skin-full she had already sunk.

"Jasey Wasey Wasey! Come and give Janey Waney a nice big face suck!" she yelled at the top of her voice, which had all the timbre and resonance of a chicken with a throat infection. Jason cringed inside but being the total professional he was, put on his best fake smile and made a show of running in slow motion towards her until she was upon him – a snapshot entitled 'banshee wailing harpy prostitute devouring a passing second hand-car salesman'

Jane Race was nothing if not outré. Her hair was a mass of swirling curls which cascaded in rivulets of bright green effervescence half way down her back. If this was not enough to get everyone she ever met to stare at her and never forget her, then the pink and yellow check suit and red, six-inch stilettos should just about make sure that all newly-hatched ducklings imprinted her image into the file marked 'Mommy' in approximately half a nanosecond.

If proof were needed as to the veracity of this last statement, one only had to look at the collection of odds and sods which surrounded her, clinging desperately to every sensational piece of nonsense which shot from between her cherry red lips. Never in his life had Jason seen such a menagerie of bleating, whining freaks assembled in one room, each one more desperate than the next to gain the attention or favour of the hideous queen at the centre of this most incestuous of hives.

"You can fuck me in the toilets if you want Jason" she shrieked to a chorus of slippery tongued laughter from her pets.

"I'd rather fuck you in the arse if you've no objection Janey", he replied to a wall of silence. Never underestimate the mindless loyalty of the sycophant. The silence was broken by Jane laughing like a witch on acid with a ten inch dildo up her twat. Given permission to follow suit, the fawning audience began to bay like hounds.

"Maybe Baby, Maybe Baby, you know I like it in there!" she screamed, waving her arms around like Kate Bush doing 'Wow'. "But first I gotta talk to ya about a fucking killer story I'm onto, Baby, one that's gonna really freak ya fuckin' into next fuckin' Sunday week cha!".

Fuck me, thought Jason, she's really out of her skull today, even by her exceptional standards. He steadied her firmly but gently as she leaned against him and attempted to lick his eyes. "Steady on Tigress, you might want to give me the gen before you eat me alive". He pushed her away gently and guided her back into her seat. She immediately stood up again and beckoned for him to come closer.

"You'll have to excuse your little Janey tonight Jason. She's had a lot of funny drugs and can't communicate the words. But never mind Baby, I'm getting the hang of it now. Want to go over there." She pointed to a table in an adjacent corner of the pub which was away from the noise. Jason put his arms around her and staggered her over to the place.

"It's the best yet. This story, Baby. This story is the best, best besty...."

"Slur that again would you, I didn't quite catch all of it"

183

"Yes, yes, it's really gonna blow your fuckin' mind Jasey Baby, blow you….blow". She jerked forward, gormless but not quite zombied. "There is this guy I know Jason, I've known him a long long long long time Jason, a really long time Jason…..John is his name, John Deller, John Deller, the man who works with my friend. My friend Kath, Kath."

Jason rolled his eyes and let out a frustrated sigh. At this rate it was going to take him all night to get the information out of her. He really did not want to spend the next few hours waiting for her to come down from whatever pick and mix pharmaceuticals she had taken before getting any sense out of her, but he didn't want to miss out on what would almost certainly be the story of the year, judging by how far Jane had felt it necessary to go in celebration. It was time for drastic action.

"Do you want a fuck, Jane?" Her eyes gained a little focus but she still swayed. "I was just wondering if your offer of a fuck in the toilets was still on?" This time she pulled herself upright and stared at his face.

"Are you serious?"

"Never been more serious, Jane. I want to take you into the ladies toilets and bang your brains out".

"Come on then, you filthy pig, let's get pumping". She stood, unaided and taking his hand, began to drag him towards the toilets. Luckily for Jason, they were situated in the far corner, away from prying eyes.

Even in her wired state, the mention of sex got Jane's focus back immediately. There was nothing more likely to get Jane fully in control than the opportunity to get laid. True nymphomania was a disease, a very rare disease which crippled the sufferer just as surely as drugs, gambling or booze. It was not a pretty sight, a far cry from the popular idea of an easy slut in a negligee who just loved a bit of cock. This was an addiction based upon an almost total lack of self-esteem, whereby the addict gained an intense but fleeting reprieve from their sense of worthlessness only during and for a short time after, being fucked.

As soon as they were in the cubicle, Jane began throwing her clothes off and panting like the proverbial dog on heat. The desperation in her eyes was clear. She needed him to give her a fix of 'I'm OK ' and she was wasting no time at all in proving her worth.

Jane knelt down on the toilet floor and unzipping his trousers, took Jason's cock into her mouth, sucking him hard. She moved her lips up and down his shaft, taking his full length in and out, simultaneously sliding her hand up and down his erection.

"Oh, that's good, that's real good, Jane. You're a real good girl". This reward caused an increase in her efforts as she began to suck him even more ferociously, sliding him so far into her throat that only years of practise and an overwhelming urge to please stopped her from choking on his prick. She was really starting to get a bit of a buzz from it now, her self-esteem starting to kick in, her mind becoming clearer, despite the drugs. Time for Jason to up the odds.

"Whoa, there Janey, steady on girl" he said. It took a real effort of will to do what he did next, Jane was very good indeed at sucking a man into an ecstatic state, but it had to be done.

Jason grabbed hold of Jane's shoulders and pushed her backwards, sliding his cock out of her mouth. She struggled to get her lips back into position but he was easily strong enough to hold her at arms length.

"Jason, Jason, please let me make you come" her voice was that of a little girl trying to please Daddy. Jason wondered if this was how Daddy liked her to please him,

185

maybe it was the root cause of her problem. He held her firmly at bay.

"Jane, I need you to give me the details of the story. Then I'll make you feel good"

"No no, let's fuck now, then I'll tell you it all Jason, every last drop"

"I'm sorry Jane but I'm going to have to insist". At this, she slumped and began to sob as if she had been struck. "If you tell me the full story quickly, we can get back to planet orgasm as soon as you want". This statement brought a flood of information pouring from her.

"John Deller told me that he went to a place in Islington where a group of men get together to plan and execute murders for fun and profit. Like a murder club. He said they give alibis, clean up the forensics, the lot. I didn't believe it when he told me but I checked out what his friend had told him and found a cryptic advertisement in a wank mag offering readers the chance to 'get extreme'.

"Where's the advert? what mag was it in?"

"Razzler. Last month's edition, Jason, now for the love of God, fuck me please"

"Is that all you've got?"

"Yes, I promise Jason, that's all so far. I thought I'd let you follow it up and share the story. Please Jason, I need it"

"Ok Jane, it's ok, you've been a good girl, a very good girl". He released her shoulders, feeling her lips on him again. He closed his eyes and enjoyed the feeling of an expert sucking him. After a few minutes he stood her up and put his hand between her legs, inserting a couple of fingers. She moaned with pleasure as he slid his saliva-covered penis into her and began to thrust viciously. "You love a good cock-fucking don't you Jane?"

"Oh, yeees, I really love a cock in me, all the way in my cunt, oh God, fuck me, fuck me into a coma, hurt me Jason, damage me….kill me with your stiff cock, oh, God, oh God, aaargh, aaargh, aaaargh…. Keep it going Jason, I'm coming, I'm coming Baby aaaaaaaaargh."

Jason felt the walls of Jane's vagina clamp tightly around his penis as she came, causing him to follow suit. His orgasm was intense, tugging at his balls to a degree that was almost painful. Whatever her problems and their sad causes might be, Jane really was a damned fine fuck.

"Oh, Jason, that was marvellous, truly wonderful. Maybe we could do it again later?" Jane was smiling like the proverbial creamy cat.

"Oh, I'm sure we'll get the chance to make a real session of it before too long Jane, especially as we are going to be working together on this story".

Jane began putting her clothes back on, straightening her hair, applying lipstick. Once they were both relatively presentable, Jason took her by the arm and walked her back to her table. The hangers-on were looking a bit sheepish and uncomfortable, unsure how to act until Jane gave them their cue. Jane let them sweat for a bit, sitting down, straight-faced and quietly sipping her drink. Most un-Jane-like behaviour. Then she winked at Jason and put them out of their collective misery.

"Cheer up you bunch of fuck-wits, no-one's died have they?" Laughter all around as Jane's crew slipped back into gear as if none of the past 15 minutes had happened. Jason stayed just long enough to finish his drink and ensure that Jane would not be too offended by his quick departure. He had a hot French woman waiting for him and the way things had panned out it looked as if he might stay in Serena's good books after all.

When he left Jane she was well away, the drugs starting to kick in, a momentarily happy twinkle in her eyes. He felt a bit like a social worker after having helped a particularly troubled client.

As he approached the door, it opened and in came Jess from the office. She was dressed to kill, in a short black pleated skirt, white blouse and high heeled black shoes with a leather strap around the ankle. Her long, dark hair caught the moonlight as it cascaded.......ok get a grip of yourself, Jason. Jess let a wide smile spread across her face as she saw him.

"Going somewhere Tiger?" she enquired. He swiftly grabbed her by the arm and she let him march her back out into the street. "Unhand me you ruffian" she exclaimed as they got outside. Jess was certainly a jester.

"I've been wondering when you'd finally turn up" lied Jason "I've been in there for nearly an hour waiting for you to show your pretty face. Let's go to Bunny's".

"Whatever". She slipped her arm through his as they walked the half mile or so to Bunny's Bar. It was a dark little drinking hole slightly less popular with the journo crowd than the Rosey and therefore less likely to contain anyone who knew him, or more importantly, knew Serena.

"Bit of a biker's pub isn't it?" asked Jess as they descended into a dark and smoky bar to be greeted by the sight of four Hell's angels playing pool and Thin Lizzy's 'Don't Believe a Word' shaking the jukebox.

"Not usually it's not" he replied "I guess we're just lucky tonight.

"I guess one of us is feeling lucky, eh Jason?" she smiled as he guided her around to the far corner, well away from the heavy metal crew.

"You have to speculate to accumulate Jess. Now if I

188

remember correctly, yours is a white wine. Dry?"

"Medium"

"A medium white and a bottle of Becks please mate". The barman moved around, getting the order. Jess looked at Jason, studying his face, attempting to read a motive in his features.

"What's this then, making do with me 'cos your real girlfriend stood you up?"

"Yep, that's about the size of it, Jane Race couldn't come (as if!) so I thought I'd have to settle for the stunning brunette with legs up to her armpits". Oh what a master he was tonight.

"Just checking"

"You can check anything you like Jess". Jason paid for the drinks and they moved to a nearby table. They clinked glasses and both took a sip.

"So what is the real reason you were in the Rosey tonight Jason?"

"I was waiting for you Jess"

"Bullshit you were. You went there to meet Jane Race. Didn't she turn up or just not have much to say for herself, which I doubt very much?"

"She was fucked out of her skull. I couldn't get much sense out of her, so I was going home to feed the cat."

"You don't want poor pussy going without do you?"

"My thoughts exactly Jess. Have you got any pets that need feeding?"

"You must think I'm drunk if you think I'm going to fall for that line Jason"

"I don't follow"

"Oh, I think you do Jason. So where are you taking me tonight? I've heard Stringfellows is good". Jason screwed up his face. There was no way he would be spending that much getting Jess's legs open. No fucking way.

"Nice try Jess, but I thought we'd book into a nice posh hotel down by the river, have a few drinks in the bar and see what happens"

"It'll cost you a good night out at least Jason, after all I've got my reputation to think of". Jess finished her drink and rattled the glass on the table top. "Same again you cheapskate". Jason Stood up, his face serious and slightly apologetic.

"I'm sorry Jess, but I've got a prior engagement with the French Embassy. We'll have to do this another time when I have the whole night free to wine and dine you properly". If Jess was disappointed, she hid it well. She stood and with a shrug of her shoulders, started walking towards the exit. Jason caught her up and linked arms as they walked back towards the Rosey.

"I've arranged to meet some nice people later. People who appreciate an intelligent, beautiful woman and don't mind putting their time and money where their mouth is"

"Sorry, Jess but I'm onto a world-class story and I need to see a man about a dog, as the cliché goes". When they got back to the Rosey, Jess allowed him to give her a kiss on the lips but squirmed out of his grasp when he began groping her arse.

"You really are a fucking dickhead Jason" With this she walked into the now very busy pub, leaving him standing there.

"Bollocks. Just done yourself out of a guaranteed fuck of a lifetime Jason, you prat" He only hoped that by the time he next saw her at work, she would have calmed down a bit and had time to realise that he was the only man likely to truly satisfy her. Still, there was nothing he could do about it now. He really ought to get home and give Serena a good rogering before she turned against him too. He had to live with her, he only had to work with Jess.

Mick Randall climbed out of the passenger seat and leaned against the car until Karen had finished rooting about in the glove compartment and locked the vehicle.

"Come on Karen, pull your finger out". It was unnecessary but he couldn't resist winding her up. Her only reply was to pull a face at him. They walked across the car park and into the main reception area of Reading Police Station.

After all the security checks had been completed they were shown to a lift and rose to the 3rd floor, turning right upon exiting and moving along the corridor to a room marked 'CID Meeting Room'. Inside were about forty chairs arranged in semi-circular rows. About half were taken by various suits and officers. Karen lead the way to a couple of seats on the far side of the second row. She took the end seat and patted the one next to her. "Sit! There's a good boy, good doggy". Randall sat obediently, a wry expression on his face.

"Don't push your luck Sergeant"

"No sir, Sir !" she replied in the manner of a U.S. marine, complete with overblown salute. Mick rolled his eyes. If Karen was in one of her silly moods, it would be a long afternoon indeed. He hated Reading nick as it was. Always felt that they thought they were something special with their big new station and big new budget to go with it. He felt it was just another way in which failure was rewarded these days. Have a poor detection record, crime soars, public outcry, more resources thrown at the problem, the worst lord it over the best. That was the way in all walks of life as far as Mick was concerned, there was never anything for the true professional, for whom getting things done right was a matter of course. Only those who were incompetent, inadequate or downright criminal seemed to get any praise or favour in today's society and Reading Police Station was a prime example of that theory in action.

A poke in the ribs from Karen brought him out of his musings. He looked toward the dais and noticed that Munroe was about to speak. Fancy giving a job like this to Timmy Munroe. The top brass obviously didn't look at his detection record, only his school record. Not the grades, just the fact of going to Cheam was enough to get you to the top in today's happy clappy world of community policing.

The man on the stage was about 6 feet tall with flyaway fair hair and the look of a wet-behind-the-ears trainee officer on a Territorial Army recruitment video. He was wearing the bright brown shoes which were still de rigueur with the officer class – no doubt with those fucking segs on the soles too, just to emphasise his importance and breeding from a considerable distance.

"Good afternoon colleagues. Welcome to Reading Station those of you who have travelled from less civilised parts of the county". Titters from the locals, groans from the visitors. Mick felt a fist of hatred punching at his rib cage. What a jumped up ponce this public school wanker was.

"Joking aside, I'd like to thank all of you for being here for this special combined meeting of disparate organisations and specialist programmes, both those funded from within the police budget and those outside our usual sphere without whose expertise we would undoubtedly be incomplete in our fight against organised crime".

What the fuck was he on about? What fucking planet

did he live on? Did he think he was addressing a meeting of heads of state at some far flung U.N. junket, where the audience sat around in safari suits sipping Pimms with cucumber?

"I can't put up with much more of this shit" mumbled Mick to Karen who raised her eyebrows in agreement.

"Who is this prat?" she enquired

"He's a public school nonce whose daddy knows the Chief Super and has probably got photos of him sucking off a Master at prep school. I thought the days of the Raj were long gone but no, its just joined the Berkshire Police Service". Karen put her index finger over her lips in order to indicate to Mick that he should shut the fuck up because people were looking at them. He complied, a look of disgruntlement pasted across his face.

"I would like to introduce you to Inspector Robert Fender of Reading Police, who is leading the investigation into these horrific crimes." An embarrassingly half-hearted and short round of applause flitted past as Munroe left the stage and took his seat. Mick and Karen smiled in mutual satisfaction.

Both Mick and Karen knew Bob 'Fender Bender' Fender well, having worked with him on numerous murder cases over the years. He was a good hardworking cop who had managed to adapt to the changing mores and politics of the modern constabulary, having pulled himself into the twenty-first century with a lot more ease and success than Mick had been able to do. However, for all his ability to say the right thing and act in ways that were deemed politically correct when the situation called for it, he had retained all of his old-school toughness and his copper's instincts were still razor sharp.

"Thank fuck for that" muttered Mick. "A copper at last." Inspector Fender walked to the podium accompanied by a significantly more voluble degree of appreciation than Munroe had left to. That should stick one up his tight little choir boy arse thought Mick, inner glee smoothly lining his stomach.

"Good Afternoon ladies and gentlemen. I am the detective in charge of investigations into a series of rather bizarre but comparable murders which have been committed in the county over the past eighteen months or so". A rustle of renewed interest moved through the audience.

"The first in the series happened nearly two years ago. A girl named Veronica Kaison was walking home along a dark country road just outside Reading, when she was dragged into a field and battered to death with a number of blunt instruments". He pinned a photograph onto a nearby display board. It showed the bleeding body of a dark-haired girl wearing a blue polo-necked jumper and a grey pleated skirt.

"A few months later the decomposing body of a middle-aged woman was found in a warehouse in Eltham, Greater London. Yes, I know it's not our patch but the murder has some very peculiar aspects which coincide with the rest of this series". He pinned up a hideous collage of blood and rotting flesh which had once been a human being. A few people in the audience groaned in shock or disgust.

"Next, about six months ago we were called to a house in Theale by a concerned neighbour who had heard a woman screaming. When we broke into the house we found Rachael Garraway hanging from an oak beam in the living room" Again a photo depicting the victim was placed on the board. "There was another murder at Boxford two months ago where the victim, Alison Greene had been raped and battered to death with a hammer, which was left at the scene." Another photo went up on the board. Mick and Karen looked at each other with raised eyebrows.

"The most recent murder with matching forensic features came to light four weeks ago. Police were called to a

194

disturbance in a Soho night club. Nothing new there on a Saturday night. However, when the officers entered a room at the back of the club, they found a naked girl of about seventeen years, tied to a wooden cross. Her throat and wrists had been cut and she had bled to death. There's another link to this club which I'll explain in a minute". Another gruesome image joined the group.

"To the casual observer, assuming anyone could observe such horrible images casually, these murders have little in common, apart from the fact that in each case the victim is a woman which is not an unusual fact in itself, women being by far the main prey of the serial killer". At the phrase 'serial killer', a sigh describing both shock and professional interest came from the spectators. It had been a long time since they had had a truly newsworthy case which could well mean not only a big increase in overtime but also a well deserved bit of glory and respect for the police when they finally caught the sick bastard.

"However, I must add that there are couple of characteristics which are not as one would expect in a 'normal' killing - if I might use that term in such a grisly context. The first thing which struck us as odd was the fact that there was a lot of forensic evidence in the vicinity of each of these murders. Now I don't just mean a bit of cotton from the killer's shirt or some cigarette ash, I mean a considerable amount of forensics. We're talking hair, blood, even semen found at each of the crime scenes. It's as if there had been a deliberate attempt to put the stuff there" Another groan rippled through the audience.

"The second strange element present in each of these cases is that an advertisement was pinned to each corpse". Inspector Fender took an A4 sized poster and stuck it to the board. It was a glossy advert for a lap-dancing club in Soho called 'Angelica's Kissing Club'. There was a picture of a topless girl in leather thigh boots, strutting her stuff on a small stage between blue silk curtains. The headline stated 'Go all

195

the way – our girls do'. Underneath there was some blurb and a section giving details of where, when and how.

"Angelica's Kissing Club was the place where the recent crucifix murder took place. We traced this advert to a well-known top-shelf publication called Razzler" A big cheer went up and knowing giggles and nudges were passed between some of the officers. "Alright, alright, calm down, I'm sure all your wives have appeared in it by now" More laughter. "We spoke to the magazine's owners and they say that Angelica's Kissing Club has been putting a regular advert in there for over three years. The Met (boos from the audience) have checked out the club and reckon its clean. The owners have been very helpful regarding the murder and no suspects are as yet in the frame. The club has a reputation for low level vice but nothing much apart from the odd blow job in the back room or after hours lock in. I'll now take questions concerning what you have heard so far". Several arms were raised.

"John?" Fender pointed to D.I. John Rodd, an up and coming bright spark, based at Reading. Mick respected him as a copper who knew how to solve a case, though he didn't totally approve of his politically aware attitude.

"Do you think it is possible that the surfeit of forensics could be a deliberate ploy to muddy the waters by making it impossible to single out the killer's DNA at the murder scene?"

"That's a very astute question John, and one which we have been considering for some time. Although we do not as yet have any matches with DNA samples already on our database, it has become clear that the DNA found at these murder scenes seems to be from the same six men in all cases. We have considered what this might mean and have come to the conclusion that either there are a group of six careless serial killers working together, which we feel is very unlikely, or that the killer has collected forensic samples from five other people and scattered it about in order to make it impossible to prove who the killer is with any surety. This is a very clever tactic which we have not seen used before and which could make any forensics completely useless in a court of law".

John Rodd spoke again. "Are you saying that you do not as yet know the identity of any of the six people whose DNA has been found at each of the murder scenes?"

"That is correct John, however we are working through a database of samples we have acquired from the Royal Berkshire Hospital, thanks to some sensitive diplomatic moves on the part of Mr Munroe. This avenue may yet reap positive results. Watch this space" Mick Randall cringed at the mention of Munroe. He's even got decent coppers like Fender licking his bum hole now, the bloody upper class ponce. Mick put up his hand, catching Bob Fender's eye as he scanned the room.

"Yes Mick?"

"Has anyone actually been up to Soho to talk to the club owners themselves?" it was not a very good question and Mick knew it, but at least it stopped all the mutual backslapping for a while.

"So far there has been no-one from this area up there. Our friends at the Met (boos) assure us that they did a full search of the premises and questioned all staff thoroughly. They are satisfied that the club is in no way involved in these murders". Bob pointed to a young woman in a blue suit who was sitting on the other side of the audience from Mick. "Yes Jacquie?"

"Have you a theory concerning motives or suspects?"

"At present we are keeping an open mind". Which is a smart way of saying you haven't got a fucking idea between the lot of you, thought Mick. "We have cross referenced all files on previously convicted killers, whether released or not, as well as all suspects in other ongoing cases. We have found no obvious links to any of these people. We have also looked at the M.O.'s of other unknown killers who are operating at present, such as Benny Eye, but have found no evident similarities with them either". Up shit creek then. Mick exchanged looks with Karen, who rolled her eyes and yawned. She looked tense. Bob Fender continued.

"The reason we have gathered together such an elite force of detectives here today" Laughter. "is because we wanted to make you all aware of the special features of these cases in order that you can notify us straight away if anything similar happens in the more rural districts". Sneers from the Reading lot. Jeers from the rest. Mick couldn't help but flick the finger in Fender Bender's direction.

"Also we need you to let us know if you come across any evidence or ideas which might shed light on these killings. If you are aware of the sort of thing we are looking for, you might be able to link some disparate piece of evidence or a passing comment, which might be key". Mick was finding it hard to suppress a fit of giggling. Karen nudged him to calm down.

"Just as I fucking thought. The Reading Muppets haven't got a clue and are hoping someone with a brain can solve it for them, with them no doubt taking any credit or increased funding which might result"

"What's new? " asked Karen

"Feeling ready for this?" Mike enquired as he and Rod walked through a metal gate into the school playground. Rod felt sick to the pit of his stomach. Large bursts of adrenalin and fear pounded through his system, vying for supremacy. At this moment fear was winning, causing him to sweat, his head beginning to swirl with the enormity of what was about to happen. His entire mental integrity was about to be overwhelmed, a lifetime's moral input about to be usurped by an entirely new experience, one that only a very small proportion of the world population would ever enact. He was about to cross the final line, break the ultimate taboo. He was about to kill another human being, to become a murderer.

"As ready as I'll ever be" he replied, his voice sounding stiff and dry. Mike smiled to himself and put a podgy paw on Rod's shoulder in a show of support.

"You're bound to feel a bit phased by this, it's not an everyday occurrence. You are about to do what you have been programmed all your life not to do, to perform the most dreadful act a human being can". Rod did not feel this statement helped much. In fact Mike's words brought to mind the true enormity of what was about to happen.

"I'm not sure.... I..."

"You'll be just fine when you get in there. Everybody gets first night nerves – apart from psychos. This proves that you're not a psycho, that's all".

"Then why do I want to kill people?"

"I dunno, I guess its just a normal human instinct going back to the dawn of humanity. In the old days you would have been able to kill loads of people without any comeback. In the stone age there were no laws, just the survival of the strongest. Even up until the police force was invented you could get away with murder anytime you wanted. It's natural, we've just been brainwashed over the past few hundred years by people with vested interests, so now we feel that it's wrong, like sex. It's just a part of society's need to control us all. Now you have a chance to break free from the bullshit and set your soul free from its suffocating prison. Once you're out, they can't put you back". Which is another way of saying that once you become a murderer you cannot ever *not* be a murderer for the rest of your life. There's no way back. Once the line is crossed, it stays crossed.

"I guess you're right Mike" said Rod, his voice stronger. "I guess you know what you're talking about after all"

"I sure do. Once you get over the shock of the first one, you'll really begin to see the benefit". They entered the school by a door at the back and walked to the gym. Standing in a corner was a group of three men and a dark haired woman. As he got closer, Rod saw that the woman was being held firmly by the arms and had a look of terror on her face and a cut on her left cheek.

"Good evening gentlemen" said Mike. "This is Rod" he indicated towards Rod, who was beginning to have great difficulty stopping himself from running out screaming. Rod nodded to the three men, not trusting himself to speak. The men looked ordinary. Not mad, or hard, or scary. Just ordinary.

"Rod, this is John, Kenny and Simon" The men nodded back. "And this is Sandra" said Mike, his voice laced with emphasis, "your victim". At this Sandra, who had not moved since they had entered the room, began to sob and shake with horror, as the fear of being raped faded, to be replaced with an overwhelming knowledge that she would soon be dead.

"Why are you doing this?" she cried. "What have I ever done to you?". Mike walked over and put his arm on Sandra's shoulder.

"Listen love, it's not your fault, you've done nothing wrong and you're not a bad person. This is actually not about you at all, it's about humanity itself". He looked at Rod. "I think it would be best if you just got this over with as soon as possible Rod, save the lady's suffering, she seems a good sort".

Rod's heart pumped so hard, he could hardly understand where he was, his mind also spinning, his hands trembling, even as he reached inside his coat and brought out the 10-inch kitchen knife Mike had given him earlier.

Sandra began to scream. The noise startled Rod, fear mixing with adrenalin to produce an overwhelming cocktail of emotion which kicked him into action. Quickly, he took three paces forward and slashed at the victim's face, catching her on the side of the mouth with the tip of the blade. Why had she moved? He waved the knife again and missed completely. Bollocks, this was getting embarrassing. Pulling himself together, a familiar anger causing him to feel more focussed, he pushed the knife forward, making contact with the throat. He pushed again and saw the blade cut into the neck, opening up the skin, letting the blood gush and spray over him. It felt warm, it felt golden, it felt like life. He saw the body slump against the three men who held it upright. The eyes still had life in them.

"Hold the head still" his voice was fiercely commanding now. One of the men grabbed the hair and held the head up so he could run the knife across the white throat, pushing hard, slicing fast. As the head began to peel back, he felt exhilarated, empowered, invincible. He only knew he had cut the head off when he saw it floating in the air before his eyes as someone lifted it from the neck. The body dropped to the floor, blood spilling over his shoes. He heard cheering.

"The man's a fucking natural"

"A fucking genius". Someone patted him on the back, shook his hand, lowered him into a chair. He felt a familiar hand on his shoulder.

"Well done Rod, that was brilliant".

Karen Fox turned the key in the lock and pushed open her front door. Home at last. Thank fuck. It had been a very stressful day, what with the visit to Reading nick and having had to put up with Mick Randall's lack of imagination and gumption. The man was really starting to get on her wick. He could do with a firework up his arse, or a fucking big dildo. Karen laughed at the thought of a 12-inch black rubber cock disappearing into the Inspector's rectum, the look of surprise on his face as it pushed it's way into his intestines. Maybe he'd even make a fucking decision to do something about it without having to analyse his options first. There's a first time for everything.

Karen put her bag down on the dining table and walked into her bedroom. She took off her jacket, putting it on a hanger, before sitting on her bed and taking off her shoes. She then unzipped her skirt and wriggled out of it, laying back on the bed as she began to unbutton her white blouse. Letting it fall open, she breathed a deep sigh. She was going to have to do something a bit different tonight to re-energise herself after such a soul draining day. First a shower, then somewhere unique.

Mick Randall turned the key in the lock and pushed open his front door. Home at last. Thank fuck. It had been a very stressful day, what with the visit to Reading nick and having to put up with the gloating of Fender, Rodd and the rest of the Reading lot. He had found out some useful and highly interesting information it was true, but had not been able to follow up any of the leads due to being stuck in meetings all afternoon and traffic all evening. If there was one thing he had gained today, it was an overwhelming desire to have the last laugh on those pricks. He would bloody well find the link between these sadistic killings if it was the last thing he ever did. Not just to put Reading nick back in it's smug box, but because it was looking more and more to him as if there was something very odd going on. Several of the murders looked stage managed, almost like movie sets, what with the victims posed in dramatic positions, the deliberate surfeit of forensics and the rising body count. It was almost as if it was the start of a sick new fashion in society; a twisted trend to exploit the insatiable urge society has for mindless thrills. Murder as the new pop, the latest drug, the ultimate 'buzz'. Nothing would surprise Mick when it came to the senseless desires of today's society, with its lack of moral guidance and sneering rejection of discipline and self control. It had all gone down the pan in the sixties and the pace of the debauchery had continued to accelerate ever since. The logical outcome, if logic could be applied to such madness, was a world of complete chaos with everyone living only for their own depraved, fleeting, pleasures. Maybe this was the start of the end of humanity, the Apocalypse, the end of the world. Mick had long expected something like this, based upon his observations of the path that humans had chosen in the last fifty years. Neither did he care that the world was burning itself out. It was pretty much what people deserved. He cared only about one thing. His job. As far as he was concerned, his role was simply to follow clues and solve mysteries, using logic and passion to unravel the conundrums he was presented with. He cared nothing for humanity, not even the victims of such dreadful slayings. Just because someone was killed, it didn't make them a saint overnight. The vast majority of murder victims were little better than the people who killed them as far as moral decency or positive input to the world was concerned. They were just as selfish, just as greedy, just as depraved and senseless as their murderers. It was the bad killing the bad as far as he could see. No-one really cared about anyone else, except insofar as it might make them look good or feel special to be seen as a caring person. It was a fake act in a fake world.

Mick walked into the kitchen and put the kettle on. A cup of coffee would perk him up and get him back on the scent. He felt sure that something strange was going on and was determined to get to the bottom of it. He knew he could solve this case. Maybe even get the recognition he truly deserved at last. Superintendent Mick Randall walks onto the podium to receive his CBE from Her Majesty the Queen, a look of awe and gratitude in Her Royal eyes as she decorates the man who single-handedly solved the biggest murder mystery in the world. Ta-da !! Cue trumpets and angels singing in Heaven.

The kettle clicked off as steam filled the room. Mick shrugged and reaching for a cup, spooned in coffee and two sugars. He needed to talk to Jim Cutler and get some real Police legwork done.

Karen walked into Angelica's Kissing Club with the confident air of a regular visitor. Terry the doorman, an amiable diamond geezer who'd break your legs for the price of a fish supper, smiled at her, giving her a conspiratorial wink as she walked past.

"Dressed to kill as usual Karen?" he enquired.

"You'd better believe it Terry. I've got handcuffs in my bag so make sure you behave yourself tonight. No naughtiness, there's a good boy, I'd hate to be found here by the fucking Met, bunch of twats".

"It wouldn't look good would it, a detective sergeant enjoying the delights of a club like this, especially after the recent bit of fuss". Karen raised her eyebrows at Terry's description of a murder and crucifixion in the back room as a 'bit of fuss'.

"There'll be more than a bit of fuss if there's any trouble tonight, I can assure you. The investigation is far from complete, due to links with several other killings which have taken place recently in our patch. Just be careful until it all blows over, there's a good boy" she blew him a very suggestive kiss.

"Yes Mistress" replied Terry, opening the door for her and allowing her access to the inner sanctum, the dark sleazy guts of the place. Karen walked across the room and sat on a high stool at the bar. There was a new barman on tonight.

Karen ordered a double vodka and Red Bull and watched as the lad, who's name it transpired was Gary, moved rather awkwardly among the bottles and cartons stacked behind the bar. A serious look momentarily appeared on her face as a hideous thought crossed her mind. What if he was a fucking Met plant. He looked stupid enough as he nearly spilt her drink placing it on a coaster in front of her.

"New here are you Gary?"

"Yes, it's only my second shift and it didn't go too well yesterday". Karen smiled seductively at him, causing him to blush.

"Never mind Gary, I'm sure you'll get the hang of it soon enough with a bit of practise". She gave him a wink and moved away from the bar towards a couple who were sitting at the far side of the room. As she approached, the man, wearing an Armani suit, gestured towards her, a beaming smile spreading across his friendly face.

"Karen, darling, so nice to see you". She offered her hand, which he took in his left before theatrically kissing it.

"Dean, nice to see you too, you old smoothy". Dean gestured towards a young blonde sitting next to him.

"Karen, I don't think you've met Kerry. Kerry is an old friend of mine from way back". Karen thought he couldn't have known her all that 'way back' because she only looked about twelve now. Maybe he had known her as a baby! Kerry smiled in greeting.

"Nice to meet you Kerry" said Karen. "I'll have to exchange stories with you about this old rogue before the night is out". Dean looked faux alarmed.

"Now now Sergeant, leave the interrogations for the real criminals. After all we both have plenty of dope on each other if it came to it, eh, Karen?" Karen smiled.

"Just my little joke Darling, your secrets are safe with me"

"I'm glad to hear it" laughed Dean "I wouldn't want you to end up like our little friend a few weeks ago". Karen pulled out a chair and sat at the table.

"Yes, that was a funny business alright" Karen lit a cigarette and took a long drag on it, before deeply inhaling the smoke and blowing it in a cool jet above Dean's head. "I went to a meeting where it was discussed just this afternoon. The Met have drawn a blank. Mind you they've always been fucking blank if you ask me". Dean laughed. Kerry was observing her closely with a non-committal expression.

"I'd have to agree with you on that score" replied Dean. "Would you like a top up?"

"No thanks Dean, I'm going through in a moment" she motioned towards a set of double doors in the corner of the room. "I was shocked when I heard about the girl. Did you know her?"

"I'd seen her in here a couple of times, but I hadn't talked to her, did you?"

"No, I'd never seen her. The scary thing was though, I was one of the last people in there before her. When I heard what had happened, I thought bloody hell that could have been me. Assuming of course that she was selected at random by a serial killer as opposed to being specifically targeted by someone with a personal reason for murdering her". Karen looked horrified as she described the possibility of having been the victim.

"Bloody Hell" Dean looked concerned, "I never knew, you poor thing" he put his hand on hers and squeezed it. "So the Police think it's a serial killer do they?"

"To be honest Dean, they don't know what to think at

the moment. There are all sorts of unusual facts in this case and no-one seems to know where to start. I personally think it odd that such a brutal murder can take place here and nobody noticed". Dean leaned forward.

"I suppose they get used to hearing screams coming from in there. It's a very popular pastime these days as you know" Dean smiled knowingly at Karen who responded by rising from the table.

"That reminds me, I've got a hot date. I'll see you later Dean. Nice to meet you Kerry". Like fuck it is you gormless bimbo. Karen leaned forward and accepted a perfunctory kiss on the cheek from Dean before striding across the room and pushing open the swing doors.

Once inside the back room, Karen felt that familiar glow of anticipation. Her eyes scanned the dungeon which was occupied by two people; a tall brunette wearing a shiny rubber body suit, 6-inch stiletto shoes and a black mask with cat-like ears, and a muscle man sporting a pair of tight leather shorts and a rubber hood with eye slits cut into it. The walls were adorned with several devices designed to strike fear into the heart of all but the most perverse. It was all rather clichéd but suited it's purpose well and Karen loved it. The woman moved forward as Karen entered. Her posture was one of practised dominance. Karen flinched salaciously.

"You're late bitch" the woman's voice was sharp and full of hostility. She grabbed Karen by the throat and slammed her against a wall. "You really are going to fucking pay for that, you piece of shit!".

"Ooh, you're really gonna hurt me are you Debbie?" Karen spoke sarcastically in a deliberate attempt at provocation, if any were needed.

"You will address me as Mistress you piece of slime!" screamed the rubber-clad dominatrix. She banged Karen's head against the wall hard enough to hurt and excite but with no likelihood of real injury. She knew what she was doing. A real pro. Karen loved it when Debbie was on. She had a real psycho edge to her, a true sense of vocation which turned Karen on immensely. If you were going to get beaten you might as well get it done properly. Karen felt herself being manhandled and opened her eyes to see that it was to be the crucifix again tonight. The very one that girl had been murdered on just a few weeks ago. A thrill of sexually charged terror washed over her as she imagined how the victim had been lead there to her death. This was going to be a real good session, she could feel it between her legs. The Mistress pushed her roughly against the big wooden cross and forced her hands back against its hard surface. Manacles were tightly fitted to her wrists and ankles, causing her to pant with anticipation. "Oh poor little Karen" whispered Debbie up close to her ear "she really doesn't know what she's let herself in for tonight. She really doesn't have a clue how much I'm going to hurt her".

Debbie gently began un-buttoning Karen's black dress, opening it to reveal her bare breasts, nipples erect with anticipation of the sordid delights to come. "Oh, you naughty naughty girl. I'm really going to have to make you bleed tonight, do you understand, you dirty harlot?". As she spoke Debbie ran her hands across Karen's breasts.

"Yes Mistress, I understand that I must suffer beyond all limit for my bad behaviour and I'm glad it's you Mistress". As the whip slashed across her bare boobs Karen screamed a delicious, life-enhancing scream of bliss and horror. The whip left red marks on her skin.

"Oh God, I needed that Mistress, thank you, thank you Mistress". Karen screamed again as the whip hit her once more. Mistress walked closer, bringing her face within an inch or so of Karen's and moving in as if to kiss Karen's mouth. Karen braced herself submissively to receive the kiss but it never came. Mistress kept her lips just out of reach, though Karen could feel her breath and smell her sexy musk. "Please Mistress" she begged. Mistress again feigned a passionate, loving kiss and again kept just out of reach, her teasing causing Karen's passionate need to build. "Mistress, I beg you, please please".

Karen screamed as she was slapped hard across the face, her senses dizzying momentarily. "You dog!" shouted the dominatrix "You dirty arse-sucking dog! you are a worthless piece of shit on the bottom of my shoe, a filthy little whore who drops her knickers for sweeties in the park, aren't you Karen?"

"Yes Mistress, I am a dirty dog and a whore" Karen groaned with vile pleasure at this humiliation. It was the start of her liberation, of the abuse she loved and needed so badly.

She had no idea why being tortured both mentally and physically made her feel so good. There was no dark past to account for it. She had thought at times that it must be an almost spiritual cleansing, her brutal version of confession and penance. Didn't some monks use a scourge on themselves? She had also seen film footage of extreme Hindu practices which basically looked like violent self-torture. She was obviously a deeply spiritual person. The dominatrix grabbed Karen by the throat.

"I can see that you are not truly repentant, you foul slut. So I'm going to give you the ultimate punishment. You're going to have to ride the Horse". Karen opened her eyes wide, her expression one of shock.

"No Mistress, not the Horse, I beg you not him. He hurt me before, I can't take it Mistress".

"You should have thought of that before you started flashing your fanny to the boys in the playground. It's no more than you deserve." Mistress looked at the man in the mask who had been kneeling passively during the previous activity. His eyes were downcast. Mistress addressed him commandingly.

"Horse! prepare the machine!". Horse stood silently and moved over to Karen, freeing her gently from the manacles that held her to the big wooden cross. She slumped over his shoulder as he carried her towards a metal construction. The machine consisted of a wooden board suspended about two feet from the ground by a moving metal frame. There were leather straps attached to the swinging board at each corner. Horse laid Karen's body on the wooden panel and tightly strapped her wrists and ankles into the contraption so that she lay spreadeagled on her back. After testing that she was securely fastened, Horse stood silently by the side of the metal structure awaiting his Mistress' command.

"Proceed Horse. Teach this harlot what happens to the unrepentant and the unclean".

Horse leaned over Karen and gripped hold of her open dress in both hands, tearing it fully open and off of her trembling form, revealing her nakedness. He then undid a zip at the side of his shorts and let them fall to the ground. He was now naked except for the rubber hood.

As the name suggested, Horse's penis, although only semi-erect, was extremely large. He took hold of himself and slid his left hand up and down his length until he was fully erect. Karen began to plead again as he moved towards her. "Be silent, slut!" shouted Mistress.

Karen obeyed as Horse knelt down between her thighs and prodded her vagina with the bulbous end of his big cock. He pushed suddenly and savagely into her, pulling against the leather straps on the side of the swinging board in order to get a good thrust. Although she was wet with the excitement of the beating, there was no way to avoid the pain of such a long and thick tool entering her. He filled her completely, stretching and straining her insides almost to breaking point. Karen screamed in agony as he pulled back and rammed into her with even more vigour. This was not lust , it was pure punishment. It was a torture brought about by her own dirty behaviour. She deserved this agony of purification. As Horse continued to force his swollen organ in and out of her, each stroke more violent and painful than the last, Karen's mind went to that special place where she began to feel cleaner and more humble. She began to cry.

"Oh Mistress, I'm sorry I let you down, I'm so sorry for being so dirty and such a bad person, when all you ever do is give me love". Mistress ignored her cries.

"Horse, proceed to phase two". Karen began to beg and plead with more desperation.

"Please Mistress, I'm sorry, you know I am truly sorry, please not that, I truly cannot take that". Mistress walked over to Karen and took her face in her hands, staring into Karen's desperate eyes.

"I see no obedience, no acceptance, no submission to your Mistress' will. Only self pity, which is a sin that needs punishment".

As she moved away from Karen, Horse began pulling on a chain which hung at the side of the metal structure. As he did so the end of the plank upon which she lay bound rose so that her legs were lifted higher than her head. Horse locked off the chain and moved forward to proceed with the punishment. He rubbed his stiff cock around Karen's anus for a couple of seconds before gripping onto the leather straps, gaining good purchase and forcing his giant pole all the way into Karen's arsehole. Intense pain flooded her body and mind as Karen lolled semi-conscious on the rocking torture board. As Horse rammed into her Karen concentrated all the mental strength she had left to indicate her total submission and acceptance of her position and punishment.

"Mistress, I am broken, I am yours, do what you will

with me" her voice was faint, her breathing full of pain. Mistress stepped forward and touched Horse on the shoulder.

"Horse, you have served me well and without question. As you know Mistress always rewards submission. You may ejaculate now". Karen lay submissive, accepting the pain as Horse slid in and out of her anus, his large balls banging against her faster as he moved towards orgasm. When he came Karen felt his hot explosion deep inside her intestines. Horse gripped the straps and held her still as he jetted into her, slumping like a rag doll as his orgasm ended. He let go and slipped to the floor, crawling away to a far corner where he curled up in a ball.

Mistress gently undid the straps and lifted Karen's broken body into her arms tenderly. She ran her mouth over Karen's, kissing her lovingly, passionately. "Good girl Karen, you have been a very good girl. Mistress loves you".

Karen managed to breath a last sentence before slumping into unconsciousness. "I love you Mistress. Thank You".

Mick Randall opened the car door, allowing Jim Cutler to climb into the passenger seat. "Nice of you to meet me at such short notice and at such a late hour Jim, I really appreciate it". Jim smiled.

"That's ok Stoat, you can owe me one. It must be something pretty important for you to ring me in the middle of the night".

"It's half fucking ten you moron, hardly the middle of the night". snapped Mick.

"Maybe not for members of the swingers' set like you. I'm sure you're used to roaming the stylish midnight streets of international capital cities searching for enchantment, jazz and au pairs, but I'm usually tucked up in bed – with the wife – and a Frank Yerby by this time". Mick smiled wryly at the reference to au pairs. There was one thing you could say about Jim, he was entertaining. Oh, and he was also a very good copper which was why Mick had called him when he had got no reply from Karen's home number or mobile. "By the way Mick, where are we going?"

"London"

"London? At this time of night?" asked Jim, dumbfounded.

"What is it with you and the fucking time Jim, have you got to be somewhere or are you writing a thesis on chronology?". Mick gave Jim a quizzical look which Jim returned with interest. "It's only fifty miles or so, we can be there in an hour if I put my foot down. I just need to visit the scene of a recent murder which is linked to something I'm working on. Once I've had a chance to sniff around there I should be in a position to start making some sense of the whole mess".

"Where's Karen, couldn't you have dragged her sorry ass up to the smoke instead of mine?" Mick shrugged.

"No idea. I rang her at home and on her mobile but there was no reply to either. Maybe she was in the bath relaxing after a hard day listening to those twats at Reading telling us how great they are whilst simultaneously failing to find a single clue or catch a single fucking villain". Mick turned up the radio which was playing a live concert by Diana Krall in Paris. The two men lapsed into silence as they sped along the M4 motorway towards London.

Karen opened her eyes and saw that she was lying on a large couch, covered with a soft woollen blanket, a pillow beneath her head. She quickly gathered her wits as she became aware of multiple pain sites across her bruised and battered body. She was in the post-operative suite of Angelicas as it was humorously known. There was another woman lying comatose on a similar couch and a young man wearing a shiny black vest and denim shorts sitting on a big green Chesterfield chair near to the double doors. Noticing her stirring he skipped across the room to her side and addressed her in a gentle voice. "Hi, Karen, you ok darlin'? I hear you went through it in there tonight". Karen sat up and smiled weakly.

"You could say that, Glennie. I certainly am going through it now. Have you any pain killers?". Glennie indicated behind himself towards a single half-opened door.

"I'll go get you some, you just relax babe, you look like shit". Karen grimaced.

"Thanks for that Glennie, that's just what a girl needs after being buggered by a rhinoceros". Glennie made a pained face in sympathy.

"Sorry Love, didn't mean to upset you. You just lie back and rest. I'll get you some co-dydramol and a voddy."

"Stick a Red Bull in there too please Glen" Glennie nodded and disappeared through the door. Karen lay back as pain seared through her. It really fucking hurt this time. Worse than the other two times she had been into the punishment room. In fact she feared she might have some sort of internal damage which would be difficult to explain to her local GP. 'I've been indulging in extreme sado-masochistic acts and anally raped by a guy in a rubber mask whose cock was bigger than an elephant's trunk Dr., have you any cream I can rub on it?'

There was no way she would be able to go to work tomorrow that's for sure. She'd probably need to take at least a week off which would be hard to explain to those nosey bastards at the station. It would be very tricky.

Then an idea popped into her aching head. Of course

there was always the family emergency scam. They all knew that her Mother was often ill. Her Mother who lived in Newcastle and who had no-one else to look after her properly. She could be called away to nurse her sick Mum. That should do it. Karen smiled to herself, pleased with her plan. She heard the door swing open and turned to accept her drink and painkillers from Glennie. Only it wasn't Glen, it was Mick Randall and Jim Cutler.

Sitting up in bed, Rod Merchant looked at his wife's sleeping form. Vicky liked to sleep late on a Wednesday as it was her day off from the factory. He gently caressed her curly hair and stroked her shoulder with affection. She was a wonderful woman, always doing her best for the family in the only way she knew – through hard work and a dutiful observance of domestic routine. During the fourteen years they had been together she had never wavered from her prescribed role in life, rarely complaining or shirking her responsibilities.

Rod got out of bed and began to dress. His head was banging from the overload of booze he had sunk the night before. Last night he had celebrated his first murder. The murder of an innocent woman not unlike his wife Vicky. He thought of the woman's face now. The ordinariness of it. She was probably a wife and mother who did her best for her family just like all good women did by instinct coupled with an amazing ability to give their all no matter what the odds against them. The type of woman who would desire nothing in return except perhaps the joy of seeing her children laugh or to see love in her husband's eyes.

Rod felt a little dazed when he remembered the woman's head coming off as he hacked at her throat with a kitchen knife. Now that it was the morning after and the excitement had faded, he couldn't quite believe it had really

215

happened. He recalled the cheers and backslaps from all the chaps after he had done it, the smiles that told him he had impressed the men by his actions and the warm feeling of finally being part of a truly select in-crowd. He had felt more comfortable in his skin than he ever remembered before, warm and confident, masterful and heroic. He had desired this manly feeling ever since he could remember and now he had truly come of age, gained his warriors' spurs.

But what a price that woman and her family had had to pay for this nice warm glow inside him. Not only did the victim herself undergo the terror of abduction and violent death. She also held the knowledge of how her family would suffer when she didn't come home and how their pain and fear would be dramatically increased when they finally found out what had happened to her. One life over but many other lives filled with agony for years to come. It was a big price to pay thought Rod, but at least he didn't have to pay it. It was some other unlucky bastard's fate, not his. That'll teach him to protect his woman better next time and not let her walk the streets alone. There was no way Rod would let Vicky walk around on her own after dark. No way. Too many nutters about.

His mobile phone rang with the sound of the 'Match of the Day' theme played by a tin can full of bees. He picked it up off his side table and flipped it open as he walked out of the room and began to go downstairs. It was Mike.

"Hello Rod, how are you feeling this morning?" Mike sounded cheerful.

"Fine Mike, though my head is banging like a whore on double time".

"That'll be all the booze you necked last night. I'm surprised you're even up yet, couldn't you sleep?"

"Slept like a baby actually" a slight exaggeration, he had slept but not too well; but then he never slept well after a skin full.

"Attaboy. Now, as you're a fully fledged member of our club you get an invite to our monthly parties, the next of which is tomorrow evening. It's the best entertainment you'll ever experience and it won't cost you a penny".

"Sounds good to me Mike, where is it?"

"If you want to go, I'll arrange a car to pick you up at 6.30 tomorrow evening from your house. It'll be a taxi and the driver's name is Jeff. He'll take you to the venue but you'll have to get a cover story sorted for Vicky because you won't be in any fit state to come home until the next day" A thrill of fear went through Rod's heart at the mention of Vicky's name. Was this a subtle threat just in case he was bottling it after last night and had any inclinations to run to the filth and confess all?

"That's easy, I'll just tell her I'm staying at a mate's for the night, I do it quite often so its no big deal"

"Good Boy, see you tomorrow evening then. Prepare yourself for the best night of your life. Oh and check your email for a link to our website. Your username is *Killer192* and your temporary password is '*deadsandra*', it's a fucking trip and a half I can tell you. Also check your PayPal account my friend." The phone went dead. Rod shook his head, which was still pounding. He walked into the kitchen and flicked the switch on the kettle on his way through to his computer.

Once online he found a new message in his Hotmail inbox offering congratulations for last night efforts from an unknown email address. He clicked the link embedded in the text and entered a site called 'Powerbox'. He logged in using the details Mike had just given him. There were several categories listed and a sitemap showed him how to navigate. There was also a search box on the left.

Rod clicked on a link called 'latest events' and was shocked to see his face peering back at him with the headline

'Newbie Does Good' next to it. There was a detailed description of the murder and praise from certain organisation members including Mike. The article hailed him as a 'natural born killer' and 'one to watch for the future'. They obviously thought he was a rising star of the murder business.

After reading the article with mixed feelings he scrolled down and saw a link to a movie clip which he clicked on. He flinched with shock as he watched himself become a murderer in cyberspace just as he had become a murderer in reality only hours before.

His sense of surprise was initiated not so much by the graphic horror of watching himself hack the head from a living woman's body - though that was surprisingly upsetting in the cold light of day as he sat at his pc in his cosy home with his own wife sleeping upstairs - no it was more the fact that unknown to him, they had been recording the whole thing as it happened.

Their reasoning, he had no doubt, was twofold inasmuch as it would provide entertainment for other members of the club while at the same time ensuring he knew that they had total proof of his actions with which to blackmail, control or threaten him should they find it desirable or necessary. They really were very thorough, which both disturbed and reassured him. After all they had promised to sort out an alibi and to clean up the mess for him. This proved they were extremely well organised and unlikely to drop him in it through lack of competence. However the sense of being fully in the power of these people terrified him.

He searched the site and found hundreds of links to murders, rapes and beatings, all recorded live. His head reeled when he found a top 40 style chart which showed the most popular clips. He would take time to watch these later when he was in the house alone.

As he surfed the site he found many services and

218

products on offer based on the level of access the member had. As an official 'provider' of material, he had free access to all areas as well as automatically holding a small amount of shares in a company called 'Powerbox Auditorium Ltd'. No doubt those members who liked to watch the killings but who didn't have the bottle to actually do it themselves had to pay for their required level of access to video and other services and would have to purchase shares if they wanted to make money from the activities of the organisation. Rod clicked back to the home page and saw that there was even a service whereby members could have live events beamed to their 3G mobile phones if they wished. He signed up for it.

Rod then remembered that Mike had told him to check his PayPal account. He clicked on his link in favourites and logged in. There had been a deposit early this morning of £5,000 from someone he didn't know who's username was zacobd477@hotmail.com. Rod couldn't believe his eyes. They had paid him for last night! Five fucking grand! What a fucking result!

He quickly initiated a withdrawal into his bank account. In a few days time he would be in the money. This really was unexpected and totally welcome. It was surreal. He got to kill, rape and torture to his heart's content, with no chance of being caught due to his associates' professionalism, got to be one of the gang, a total hero *and* got paid a fucking fortune for doing it. It was amazing. He could not get his head around it; he needed to get out of the house, sit in a pub and think about it for a while.

The only thing he was sure about was that he no longer cared about Sandra or her grieving family. He'd kill the whole human race for that sort of money.

Karen flinched as she saw her boss walk into the recovery room. She watched as his eyes began to scan the area. Unexpectedly, there was a loud scream from the main lounge. It was the cry of a terrified woman. The police officers instinctively turned and ran to see who was being murdered.

Glen appeared from nowhere and grabbed Karen's arm. "Come with me Karen, that's the filth".

"I know it's the fucking filth Glennie, it's my fucking boss" Karen sounded almost hysterical as she allowed Glen to drag her beaten body across the room and out through a side door.

"Fucking Hell Karen, if he sees you you are well and truly fucked girl"

"I'm already well and truly fucked. If Mick fucking Randall sees me in this state I'm fucking toast" They struggled down a narrow corridor. It did not look as if it was a part of the club which was open to the public. Karen did not think Mick had a warrant to search the place; it looked to her as if the Stoat was working on a hunch with his old pal Jim Cutler. Unless they were here for the bondage and buggery of course.

"Get in there and stay quiet until I come and get you" ordered Glen, opening a plain door and shutting Karen into a tiny room which smelled of sperm and sweat. There was a metal table in the centre of the room with leather straps at each corner. It was obviously some sort of secret torture room which she had not until now, been privy to. From the way it smelt it had obviously seen some recent action. Karen was just glad to be in a place of relative safety. Maybe she'd find out what other activities the room offered some other time. As things stood she was a walking cripple on the verge of losing her job and becoming a suspect in an unsolved murder case.

Mick Randall ran to the source of the scream to discover a young blonde woman standing on a chair, looking upset. There was a man in a flashy suit attempting to console her. Mick immediately took control of the situation.

"Ok madam, I am a police officer. Inspector Randall of Newbury C.I.D" he reached into his jacket pocket and showed his identification card which no-one was interested in looking at so he put it away.

"You're a long way from home old son" said the man who was standing next to the blonde. Mick Randall stared hard at him. He was a right flashy Herbert. probably some sort of minor London gangster kidding himself he knew the Krays back in the glory days when crooks ruled the city.

"And who might you be sir, if I might ask the questions". The man offered an amused smile.

"My name is Dean Arkovich. I am the owner of this club. Is there a problem officer, that I can help you with?" Mick was taken aback but didn't show it. Jim Cutler looked at the floor and wondered how the hell he had been talked into coming on this wild goose chase in the first place. Mick, always one to rub people up the wrong way at the slightest opportunity chose to ignore the club owner and address the girl on the chair.

"Are you alright madam, I heard your scream" The woman smiled at the Inspector like he had just rescued her from a fate worse than death. She was a beautiful creature who knew a true hero when she saw one. Mick liked her attitude. If a few more people appreciated the police these days it would be a better world for all concerned. When she spoke, her voice contained enough honey to keep Pooh bear satisfied for a week.

"Oh I am sorry to be such a nuisance Superintendent" Jim almost burst out laughing when he heard this. Mick was being played like one of George Formby's old banjos. It was priceless. Mick would be buying beers for the next ten years to keep this off the grapevine. The girl reached out and took the policeman's hand, allowing herself to be helped off her chair.

"It's no trouble I can assure you madam, I am always keen to help those in need". Now Mick was trying to put on the charm himself. It's a shame he had not updated his technique since his days in the high society of the 1870's. Jim moved away from the group a little in order to hide the fact that he was about to piss himself.

"I saw a spider and freaked" said the girl flashing her eyes and pushing her chest out in the Inspector's direction. "I've always had a phobia about them ever since I was a little girl. I'm sorry to have made such a fuss about it. It's gone now so I think I'll just go and check my make-up if you don't mind". Mick released her hand and smiled at her.

"Just glad you're ok miss....."

"Kerry Jones"

"Miss Jones. Goodnight." Kerry walked off in the direction of the ladies' toilets. Jim nudged Mick and nodded towards the exit, desperate to get out of the place before he died of embarrassment. Mick turned to Dean and fixed him with a cold stare. Dean smiled back.

"Is there anything I can help you with Inspector. After all you raced in here as if you were on some desperate mission or other"

"I guess you could call the investigation of a brutal murder on these premises quite an important mission sir".

"I thought your Metropolitan colleagues were dealing with that. Or are they so short of sleuthing talent these days that they are enlisting the help of Newbury C.I.D.?". Mick bit his lip. The jumped up little spiv was obviously trying to wind him up.

"Actually sir, it is a multi-agency investigation, combining the resources of several forces. We take murder very seriously, even if some people appear not to". Stick that in your pipe and smoke it you zoot-suited spick. Dean grinned at the Inspector's annoyance.

"I can assure you we also take murder seriously and we have helped the Met with all enquiries to their full satisfaction. We are also available at any time they should need to speak to either myself or my staff with regard to this case. I was just wondering what it was you were after specifically". That's better, a bit of respect for the law at last. Once you showed them who was boss even the nastiest little villains were easy to handle. It was a knack that came with experience.

"I want to take a look at that back room". Dean's smile never wavered.

"I'm sorry Inspector but that room is for staff and private guests only. Though obviously if you have a search warrant I'd be glad to show you through there". Mick's face became fierce. Jim stepped in before his friend got himself into trouble.

"That's ok sir, we'll be back with the appropriate papers in the near future". He nudged Mick 'accidentally' as he began to move towards the exit. Mick gained control of his temper enough to follow. As they reached the doors, Jim took a swift glance over his shoulder and saw Dean and Kerry Jones sniggering together.

Jason opened the door to his apartment and moved gingerly inside. If Serena was already home he might have a problem, namely how to wash Jane Race's cunt cream off his knob before the French slut started sucking on it.

Whenever Serena had been away on business she came back as horny as a bitch on heat. If he could just get into the shower before she pounced he would avoid being caught out as a dirty double-crossing pig fucker.

Serena would not be impressed that he had been sticking his cock into other women without her being present. He had however, on two occasions, stuck his cock into other women when Serena *had* been present. Present to the extent of having her tongue inserted in their arse holes at the time, a position from which she was able to lick his shaft and balls as he thrust in and out of the pussy he was fucking inches from his girlfriend's mouth. She was an open minded dirty slut when it came down to it but Jason knew that Serena was also a control freak who would go ballistic if she felt he had been playing away on his own as opposed to playing around at home with her permission and participation.

He heard movement from the kitchen and his heart sank as a black-stockinged leg appeared around the door jamb followed by the rest of Serena dressed in full nympho gear: spiky stilettos, fishnets, basque and black velvet choker around her delicate throat.

"Bonsoir Mon Cherie, is there anything that this simple French peasant girl can do for Sir. I'm willing to do anything at all to please my master, even dirty things, though I am an innocent young girl who is at your mercy" Oh shit, now I'm in deep kaka unless I can think fast. Serena's choice of a rare subservient role might just offer a way out.

Jason moved into the room and stood close to Serena. He reached out and began caressing her left breast through the material of the basque. Serena let out a little moan, pretending to be nervous and unsettled by his vile approach to such an innocent virgin as herself. Jason pulled back his hand.

"You filthy little whore, letting men touch you like that. You are a dirty girl who must be washed clean of debauchery". He grabbed her by her long dark hair and pulled her roughly to the shower cubicle, turning on the water with his free hand. "Get in there you devil" He pushed Serena, fully clothed, under the water jet which had not yet warmed up. Serena gave a genuine squeal as the cold water ran across her breasts and down her tummy and legs.

Jason climbed into the shower with her, his clothes still on. He was sure that this would seem wild and rebellious to Serena and therefore turn her on. It would also give him a way of getting washed without alerting her to his earlier philandering.

He took hold of a bottle of scented shower gel and squirted it over her breasts. He then began rubbing the gel into a lather which he wiped over her stomach and thighs, remembering to soap the basque where it went between her legs, rubbing her for several seconds in order to get her as wet on the inside as she was on the outside. He stepped under the shower with her, allowing his clothes to get soaked. Serena murmured with delight as he did this.

"Oh Sir, what are you up to? I'm sure this is wrong. What would my Mother say if she saw what you were doing to her daughter?".

"This is nothing compared to what I'm going to be doing to you in a minute". Jason took off his shirt and began soaping his chest. He pulled open the straps on her basque and rolled it down to free her full breasts which he began to soap. Then he rubbed his chest against her soapy boobs. She gave a little whimper of anticipation.

"Oh please Sir, no Sir, you mustn't" she panted, a mixture of fear and desire showing in the voice of the innocent character she was playing. Jason kicked off his shoes and as gracefully as possible pulled off his socks and threw them out onto the bathroom carpet. He then undid the top button and zip of his trousers and, getting a palmful of shower gel he slipped his hand into his trousers and began soaping his tool which was now fully hard and sticking out through the flyhole. Serena squealed in mock shock and backed away from him.

"Oh Sir, no Sir" she put a convincing degree of alarm in her voice now, acting the part of the virginal victim about to be raped by her dashing but ultimately caddish master. He played along with full pleasure now that his prime objective had been completed satisfactorily. Serena could suck on his cock all night long now and all she would taste would be soap. He breathed a sigh of relief before bringing the rape scene to its well-practised conclusion.

Jason quickly removed his trousers and shorts and moved toward the now cowering Serena. He gripped her soft white throat and lifted her to her full height before kissing her passionately on the mouth. She acted frightened and tried to pull her mouth away at first, but her passion got the better of her and she kissed back hard.

"Not such an innocent little virgin after all?" said the cruel and abusive master. Jason rubbed her between the legs again, this time sliding a finger inside her costume and into her slippery vagina. She let out a moan of delight. Jason ran his hands over her breasts and down her thighs, gaining particular pleasure from the feel of her soft skin above her stocking tops. Serena, her innocent role fast becoming unsustainable as her excitement mounted, opened her thighs wide and pushed his fingers deeper into her, before reaching out and gripping his cock in her right hand, sliding it up and down his length before pulling him to her and slotting the head of his penis into her dripping pussy.

Jason pushed deep, enjoying the hot moist interior of her hole. Serena squirmed against him, both of them thrusting together, breathing hard in time with their fucking. Serena began to scream with pleasure as she felt her orgasm growing within her. Jason gripped the backs of her open thighs as he felt his cock begin to jerk with pleasure. Serena gave full vent to her scream as they simultaneously reached an extended body wracking orgasm, coming in waves of ecstasy. Jason felt her vagina clamp hard onto his cock, pulsing as Serena came, squeezing another gush of sperm into her molten cunt.

As their mutual pleasure slowly subsided, they clung together, hearts beating in unison, minds reeling with overwhelming lustful pleasure until they moved apart as awareness of leg cramps unfolded. "Oh my God Jason that was fantastic" Jason smiled inwardly.

"You're telling me. I reckon that was the best orgasm I've ever had Serena. You really are the sexiest woman I ever met". Serena smiled outwardly. Wow.

Rod spent most of the next day surfing the Powerbox website. He wanted to learn as much as he could about the secret organisation he had recently become a part of. He watched hundreds of video clips of killings undertaken by his new colleagues, some of which left him reeling due to the extreme obscenities he saw perpetrated on ordinary everyday people. He thought he had a sick imagination, but compared to some of the men involved in the Powerbox site he was a mere beginner.

There was one clip which showed a man ripping the face off a young blonde with a sharp metal claw attached to a red glove and another which showed a group of eight men raping a woman simultaneously before firing a shotgun inside her vagina and blowing her to bits. Another film showed a man tying up a woman and beating her before burning her eyes out with cigarettes. It was all very sick stuff.

Rod felt weird in his stomach as he watched murder after murder, rape after brutal rape on his computer screen. He wondered how he had ended up on this life path; it was not what he would have expected his life to turn out like because he was generally an easy-going and friendly person. He had suffered no major parental abuse or bullying in his childhood to explain the growing urge to kill others which had developed in

227

his soul over the past couple of years. It was not, as far as he was consciously aware, some twisted need for revenge or a fanatical need for power which fuelled his craving for violence and death.

Rod felt that maybe sexual lust was the driving force behind his desire to kill women, and judging by a large proportion of the videos he had been seeing on the website, many other men seemed to have the same motivation. It was almost always women being murdered, often after being raped or tortured by men. He definitely got a horny buzz when he watched or committed murder.

Perhaps it was all the fault of women's lib. Ever since the '60's women had been ranting on about their rights, their power, their dominance over men, who were relegated to fools and failures as far as the media was concerned. The increasingly common image on TV of men being hit by women coupled with a growing hysterical taboo regarding men hitting women was one seed among many.

The growing resentment of millions of fathers, prevented from seeing their children at the whim of some petty minded bitch, while paying most of their hard earned wages to her was the fertiliser which caused the hate to grow in the breasts of decent, loving men who had had too much so-called 'equality' stuffed down their throats. Equality which saw them treated like useless lumps of flesh. The more women got the more they wanted. Theirs was no desire for equality.

What they wanted was total subjugation and domination of men; brought about with the aid of evil laws which protected corrupt weak women from the millions of strong good men now being torn apart by a paltry and malevolent foe who was winning simply because girly men, scared to take charge of their own masculine power, had allowed the legal framework to be manipulated as weapons against their own kind.

Because they had these bad laws to hide behind, the feminists had been able to act as if they had won the moral argument. It was a widely used tactic for women to manoeuvre opinion through guile and fakery, to make it look as if they were in the right even when no clear-thinking person would agree that the attacks and emasculations they perpetrated daily upon men were anything more than part of a desperate greed for domination. Men had had to fight with both hands tied behind their backs for too long.

Now it was women who were having their hands tied behind their backs and men who were showing them the true meaning of power. Because the laws were corrupt, men had been forced to act outside the law. You can only squash men for so long before they begin to push back with unrelenting justified force.

Now was the dawning of the age of *men's* rights, based not on flimsy law but on physical and mental power. For too long this charade of equality had gone on. It was sickening to see women getting accolades and credit they had not earned, to see them strut around with smug looks on their faces as if they knew something no one else did and to hear them rant about rights and needs, which they had no power to hold or fulfil without the compliance of men to whom they gave no credit in return for their help.

Did women not realise that for all their swagger and self obsession, they were still contributing almost nothing beyond their traditional roles in society? Almost everything they encountered in their daily lives was designed, built and maintained by men. The cars they drove, the roads they drove on. The computers they used to write to their local MP about their rights were invented, designed, built, installed and maintained by men. Even the parliament which passed the laws which they hid behind was created by men. The buildings in which parliament was housed, likewise owed their existence to men, as did almost every building in the world. Everything

229

was created by men, everything was built by men, maintained by men. Yet what credit did they get from women – none.

They were treated as the lowest form of life by creatures who had contributed nothing concrete to the planet and now the parliaments in supposedly civilised countries were making laws which crippled those very men who were able to create cities, nations and worlds, in favour of winging bitches who only sought power in order to lord it over men with whom they knew they could never compete on a level playing field.

Women's lib had done nothing but replace able men with second rate female versions of men who were barely capable of starting a car let alone designing and building one. It had to stop. Powerbox was stopping it by creating a potent movement for men in this war which women think they have long ago won but which men have not even started fighting yet.

Now they were starting to fight and women were about to see just how powerful men can be when they are abused and undermined. The feminists are about to get what's coming to them. Now the war will be fought on men's terms with fists, knives and other manmade tools, not with bits of paper and doublespeak. Women wanted a war; now, after forty years of taking it, men are fighting back. And when we fight we don't mess about.

Rod shook his head. Where had all that come from? Maybe it was a dark unconscious complex which had been dormant until he released it by taking action against the enemy he never realised he had until he began to feel castrated by society's modern feminine values.

Now he knew that men were power incarnate. Their very essence held full sway over creation and destruction. Men were demi-gods! Rod laughed out loud and turned off his computer.

Maybe it was time to take the dog for a walk. Only he

didn't have a dog. Probably just nervous about tonight. The big party. It was something he had mixed feelings about. In fact the whole thing seemed to be taking on a life of its own and leading him far away from everything he had ever known. Strange things were happening.

There had been another £180 in his PayPal account this morning. He didn't know why. Perhaps it was something to do with how many people had watched his murder on the website, a sort of royalty payment.

He had also had an email from a guy called Simon who stated he would meet him at the party and that he had a great opportunity for Rod to make a lot more money.

Rod opened the back door and wandered across his tiny lawn. Here again anger rose in him as he gaped with resentment at the tiny square box he had to live in on an estate crammed with tiny square boxes. It made him feel like a cat trapped in a cage. His soul needed to be free to roam, to explore and have adventures. But how can you have adventures when you've got to pay the gas bill? How can a man's soul unfold when it is tied in knots of domestic servitude? It cannot. So it withers. Then it lies dormant for a long time before all the pain has done it's job and transformed the domestic fool into a warrior. And then the true man is born and the world is his.

Mick Randall woke up with a stiff neck. He had slept badly and had a weird dream about dogs eating internal organs from a silver bowl placed outside his back door. No doubt it was some deep psychological reference to the lack of progress, or complete fuck-up of the investigation into the serial killings.

He quickly showered, dressed and left the house. Breakfast was for people not in deep shit. He got into his car and drove to Karen's house which was on the way to the station. Normally she would be waiting in the porch and nip straight out when she saw his car pull up. Today there was no sign. Or rather there was a sign which said 'Not well so count me out today big boy' stuck on her front door. Mick assumed the note was put there in order to inform him she was not fit for work today but it could be some perverted rejection to a well endowed lover, you never knew with Karen.

There were some kinky rumours circulating about Karen's sexual exploits, probably started by some jealous bastard who wasn't getting any action and thought Karen was. It was obvious that something had occurred since he dropped her off last night. He would phone her when he got to the nick.

This was just the sort of irritating circumstance that had started to plague this case and pretty much ruled out progress. It was time to get a grip of the whole thing and start kicking some arses. That was why he had earlier phoned the office and told his secretary to organise a meeting for eleven sharp.

When Mick got to the station he sat at his desk and considered his plan of action. Firstly he needed to gather all available data related to the investigation. Once he had the information it would be a matter of filtering out the useful bits and organising his troops to follow up all leads PDQ. There had to be some pattern to these murders if he took the time to study the evidence without some little numpty popping up and wasting his time with office politics or pointless opinions.

Right on cue Jeremy Marsden came into the office holding a magazine. "Have you seen this article on falling detection rates in areas with low police numbers?"

"No I fucking have not seen any pissing article which states anything so fucking obvious. Nor have I read the one about how the rates of detection are falling in police stations which contain a high level of toss-pots. Now get out of my office and let me attempt to increase the detection rates of

Inspector Mick fucking Randall of Newbury C.I.D.". Jeremy scuttled away to wherever he had popped up from.

There had to be some way to crack this case wide open and show those twats at Reading nick he was still a better copper than any of them would ever be no matter how much multicultural politically correct bullshit they learned to spout.

Mick looked up as Jim Cutler and Jenny Yuce walked into the office. They were a couple of reliable old-fashioned officers who knew how to get things done with hard work and brain power. It's a pity they were a dying breed these days. Jim had worked with Jenny for about four years and they had gained a bit of a reputation as jokers who got the job done. Jim was an old friend of Mick's who had helped him out of a few scrapes in the decade or so they had known each other. Mick knew Jim's wife Monica from his school days when Mick was a knotty-legged yokel and she had been a plain Jane with a heart. They had been the ones who were left off the guest list when the cool kids had parties. Something in common but not enough to form a real bond.

Jim had taken to Monica's simple ways and friendly smile and nabbed her before any other gawky fat kid did. He didn't expect to get many other chances with the opposite sex and his expectations had been fulfilled. They had been married now for 12 years but their union had not been blessed so far. Cruel tongues in the office said it was because they were both so unattractive fully dressed that they could not bring themselves to undress in front of each other. They suited each other and seemed to rub along nicely on a domestic level which was more than you could say for most of the people who worked at the nick.

Jenny was short and pretty with shoulder length brown hair cut into a bob-like style. She wore flat shoes on and off duty but had a sexy aura, a twinkle in her eye. She attracted her fair share of male interest but didn't really know what to do

233

with it. Because she was not married or in receipt of a regular seeing to, the rumour mill had suggested she played for the other side but no evidence had come to light to support the allegations. She was probably just a bit shy and too busy nicking villains to get obsessed about whose dick she was going to suck next. Fair play to her. There were too many distractions from police work as it was.

"What did he want?" asked Jim, referring to Jeremy Marsden, whom he had passed in the corridor. "I'm sure it was highly interesting and enlightening whatever it was".

"Wrong. Now shall we do some work this morning or what?".

"Someone's grumpy Jim, be careful" teased Jenny. Jim pulled a knowing face.

"I'm not bloody surprised he's grumpy after last night's fiasco" said Jim.

"Oh you're still stuck on last night are you Jim?" replied Mick tersely. Jenny looked puzzled.

"What happened last night boys, did you go on a date or something?"

"Yes Jen, Mick called me up last night and invited me out to a lap dancing club in Soho". Jenny looked even more puzzled now. Mick explained in simple terms in order to avoid rumours and to get it out of the way so that he could get onto the case at hand.

"I couldn't get hold of Karen last night and I wanted to get some police work done – I know it's a strange idea for a copper. We went up to London to have a sniff around Angelicas Kissing Club". Jenny raised her eyebrows.

"Did you indeed? Well I hope you both had a lovely time". She smiled.

"That's the club where the girl was found murdered on a wooden cross in the back room. Don't you know anything about this case?". Jim jumped in to defend his partner's lack of knowledge.

"We didn't all get an invite to that glorious palace in the sky known as Reading Nick. The party was reserved for those with the eloquence necessary for modern police work...and a few old pensioners who they thought could do with a day out".

"You cheeky fucker" replied Mick. He moved quickly toward Jim and made a grab for his neck. Jim stepped aside quickly and swivelled around behind Mick, catching hold of his arm and pushing it up behind his back in a painful way.

"No headlocks for you today Mick, you need to cut down. Now do you want me to put you into a cell for half an hour to calm down or are you going to be a good boy from now on?" Jim had a smug grin on his face. It was not often he got the better of Mick in these play fights and he was determined to milk it for all it was worth. Mick let him have his moment.

"O.k. officer, I'll go quietly. You Newbury police are so much more professional than the flatfoots I had to deal with when I lived in Reading". Mick laughed and was joined by his two colleagues. Jenny moved forward and broke up the fight.

Come on boys, didn't you hear the bell? Play time is over, time to go back into school and do some work". Mick sat down behind his desk and resumed his explanation of last night's events.

"The Met had supposedly done a thorough investigation into the murder at Angelica's but I wanted to check the place out to see what sort of club it was. It's called 'gathering background information' in the police manual, page one I think it is". Mick grinned.

"That's right Mick, page one. Shame you never got to page two where it tells you how to avoid making a total prat of yourself" retorted Jim.

"Oh, do go on Jim, this is getting interesting at last" quipped Jenny. Mick put on as serious a face as he could muster.

"All I did was to shake a few dodgy characters and ruffle a few feathers". Jim winked at Jenny.

"What he means is he stormed in and started throwing his weight around, rubbed the owner up the wrong way and got taken in by some blonde floozie's sob story".

"What do you mean by that? Kerry was a delightful girl. I simply showed her some courtesy and understanding". Mick put on his most innocent face.

"She was a diversionary tactic, no more, no less. She screamed to get us out of that back room. There was something in there they didn't want us to see and you fell for it hook, line and sinker".

"Hook, line and fucking sinker? Do people still use that antiquated fishing expression these days? As for the girl, I knew she was winding me up. I decided to go along with her to create the illusion that I was a bit slow mentally in order to get them over-confident"

"Well you certainly succeeded in creating the desired impression. In fact your performance was so good, you had me believing it too". Jim and Jen chuckled to each other.

"There's definitely something illegal going on at that club, that's for sure".

"Yes, I agree Mick and I'm sure even the Met know about their dirty little secrets. Probably just a bit of domination and few hand jobs in the back room".

"Which has led to the death of at least one woman". countered Mick.

"True" Jim had to admit that Mick had a point here. Mick seemed satisfied with this little victory and became serious. Maybe now the banter was over they could get on and solve a case sometime. Mick looked at his watch. The meeting was due to start in ten minutes.

"Where's Karen this morning, I thought you drove her in most days?". Mick shrugged.

"Fuck knows. I couldn't get hold of her last night and this morning I went round there and there's this note on the door saying she can't come out to play today. I've no idea what she's up to. In fact I think I'll phone her now. I'll see you in the meeting in ten".

"Okely dokely, see you" replied Jim. Jen smiled as they walked out of Mick's office. Mick quickly dialled Karen's home number. It rang but there was no reply. After a few rings the answer machine cut in. Mick hung up. Where was the bitch? Mick stood up and walked into the main C.I.D. office where everyone had gathered for the meeting.

He nodded at various people as he moved to the centre of the room, then waved his notes in front of his chest. "Alright lets have a bit of hush when a commanding officer enters the room". Jeering and a few wanker hand signals were returned but they did go quiet.

"I've called this meeting because after the bullshit session myself and the absent Karen had to put up with at Reading yesterday, I have decided to get a grip of this case and get it solved quickly in order to stick one up the smug bastards." A cheer. Mick relaxed a little. "The main problem is that we are all working on these murders as if they were different cases rather than all being part of one horrible sequence of events which are linked. I believe it is most likely that there are more than one killer involved due to the sheer organisation involved, not only in planning and committing these crimes but the clever way that the evidence has been contaminated and several red herrings have been thrown our way". A tall man with dark hair put up his hand to ask a question. Mick laughed. You're not in school now Mel, what is it?".

Mel Shorter was unfortunately taller than most people and so stood out in a crowd. He was also a newly qualified detective constable and hadn't yet got used to the never-ending torrent of piss-takery he had encountered since starting at Newbury C.I.D. He was a keen new boy who Mick saw great potential in, once he got toughened up a bit. When Mel spoke his voice was a little uneven. Perhaps his balls hadn't dropped properly yet. "What red herrings have been thrown our way Inspector?" Much laughter greeted his use of the word 'Inspector'. Mick smiled. It made a change to get a bit of professional respect for once. This lad would go far.

"That's a very good question Constable (more sniggers) I will explain. Firstly the advert for Angelica's Kissing Club. I know there was a murder there but it doesn't mean the club is actually linked to the killers, at least not in a deliberate or conscious way. The killer obviously has been into the club at least once but I do not believe the club owners or staff knew about it beforehand. The place is full of perverts at the best of times and judging by the equipment I saw in a back room when I visited the place last night... (loud cheers) ..in a police capacity I might add, I would expect they are used to hearing a bit of screaming coming from there. Or maybe the room is sound proofed. Either way the killer was putting the adverts for the venue next to the bodies long before the murder in the club took place". Mick took a breath and saw that he had everyone's attention.

"I think that the killer, or killers have been having a bit of a laugh at our expense by giving us a clue to where a future murder would take place. We were too thick to spot the joke and now they are pissing themselves at how clever and funny they are".

"Surely the killer's name will be on the membership list of the club. Couldn't we, or the Met (boos) simply check out all the members addresses and question any likely suspects?" The question was asked by Detective Sergeant Stephen Docker, a long-standing member of the team and a good bloke to have around in a tight fix. He was about 35 years old with thinning hair cut short and a small moustache. He was physically large and strong and his nerve was good. He had occasional flashes of brilliance. This wasn't one of them. Mick pulled a face.

"It's already been done Steve. They have questioned a couple of known or suspected wierdos about their whereabouts but even if they had admitted to being in the club on the night it would prove nothing. After all where else would you expect a perv to be but in a lap dancing club sniffing the girls' tits". More laughter. Steve pursued his line of enquiry.

"Do you think any future murders will continue to carry the Angelicas advert, or maybe another one giving us a clue to a forthcoming murder?". Mick shrugged.

"There's not enough evidence to really know at the moment. I personally would expect the cocky bastards to start using a new advert for some other club or venue in order to really test their skills against us, though I would prefer it if there were no more murders at all". A few heads nodded in agreement. Mick spotted detective constable Gary McHuller, a ginger haired youth with an aloof manner, gesticulating wildly.

"Yes Gary what is so urgent?" Gary spoke in a confident high pitched voice with a pronounced Scottish accent.

"There seem to be a lot of other murders happening at the moment which do not have all the hallmarks of the one's you mentioned. Benny Eye for instance. Do you think there are other serial killers coming to light as well as the possible group killings?".

"It does look as if there are more than one. Apart from Benny Eye there is the Drowner which Alex is working on". Mick nodded to Alex Hinton, a bright eyed Detective Inspector who along with his young sidekick Malky Jordan had shown themselves to be a formidable team. "There's also Greg Park who got off a murder rap recently due to the incompetence of a judge. I reckon we can expect more from him before too long once he's made his fortune squealing to the papers about police incompetence". Grim smiles were exchanged. Mick continued. "There's also Anton Russell to put a stop to. As you know he recently escaped justice due to what I consider a bent jury. The evidence was overwhelming in my opinion but somehow nearly half the jurors were unable to find him guilty". Jim Cutler spoke up.

"Do you think he got at them somehow?"

"I agree it does look like it but Anton is a cowardly little nonce with no friends as far as I know. How would he be able to nobble that many jurors without being caught out? He's hardly an intimidating person, unless you are a sixteen year old girl. I bloody know he murdered Rachael Heaver and he knows I know it but now he's got away with it he's going to kill again I'm sure and when he does I'm personally going to nail the bastard"

"It's not looking good from our perspective is it?" quipped Jim. Mick smiled through gritted teeth.

"That's a fucking understatement Jim, if ever I heard one" laughter broke the growing tension. "Still, its not over until Annie sings" said Mick, referring to the overweight admin assistant who was presently out of the room and who was known as a gossip and rumour monger. Laughter increased and a few people began pushing each other like boys at a school assembly. Mick let them have a few seconds to calm down before continuing. "As Jim says it's not looking good for us at the moment. We've got a growing number of serial killers who we can't catch and the ones we can catch are getting off through technicalities and fuck ups. It's bollocks on the chopping block time for us – or whatever the female equivalent is for you ladies – so we are going to have to get our fingers out of our arses and go on the offensive". Mick gave way to Jenny Yuce who had been giggling with Jim about something.

"Yes Jenny?"

"Tits on the table time?" Mick looked stupefied and confused.

"What the fuck are you on about Jenny? Are you offering to do a table dance?" Rowdy jeers greeted this comment. Jenny looked a bit embarrassed.

"The female equivalent of bollocks on the chopping block guv" Mick gave her a look of displeasure.

"If you lot put as much of your limited brain power into your work as you do into acting like a bunch of smart-arses we might get somewhere". Jenny, realising she had made a mistake, looked at Jim with an embarrassed expression, hoping for a bit of moral support from her work partner who looked at the floor in an effort to far remove himself from the situation. Git. Jenny bit the bullet.

"Sorry Guv, I was just trying to break the tension a bit". Mick gave her a conciliatory look.

"It's alright Jen, you're not the only prat who needs to wise up and get on with what you're paid for" Mick held his tough face for a few seconds in order to make his point before turning it into a wide grin. Good man management technique, learned through years of experience. He knew how to rally his troops and build a close knit team. It was a clever balancing act between keeping discipline and motivation without either crushing his staff's morale or letting them think it was all a big joke. You had to know how to judge it just right. That was why his team was the best. Mick let the laughter die down before bringing the meeting to a close. "I am glad we've been able to get together as a group in order to sum up the situation and make sure we all realise just how serious this increase in killings is getting. I've got a press conference with the local media this afternoon and I'm sure they are going to put me right on the spot about our lack of suspects. I want something to give them, just to keep them off our backs until we can nick someone. I'm going to have to bring in all the usual suspects overnight just to make it look like we are not sat on our bums, so I want Jim and Jen to bring in Uncle Anton. Gary, you and Kenny can bring in Greg Park and let him stew in a cell for a few hours. I doubt we'll get anything useful out of them but it's all we've got at the moment. In the meantime I want Alex and Malky to find the woman who found Rachael Heaver's body and have another talk to her"

"You mean the Cat Woman?" asked Alex, an attractive man with shoulder length blond hair tied back in a pony tail, friendly eyes and a kind smile which belied his deadly interrogation skills.

"Yes Alex, I think her name is Yvonne Snelling, her address is in the Rachael Heaver file"

"Do you want me to bring her into the station?"

"Only if you think you'll get more out of her with a bit of pressure applied. I'm sure you'll handle her beautifully" A few dirty jeers at the back fizzled out quickly. Mick waved his notes in front of his face.

"Alright, let's get on with it then".

Jason took the tube to Knightsbridge, but not for the shopping. His only motive was to speak to John Deller, the name given to him by Jane Race in return for a fuck in the pub toilets. He found Deller's number easily enough in the directory and had phoned him in order to make arrangements to meet.

Deller had been cagey at first which caused Jason to give a little more credence to what Jane had said. The guy was obviously scared of somebody. Jason agreed to let him set the ground rules and only tell what he wanted to tell. Deller told him to be there by ten the next morning and not to bring any hidden microphones. Obviously thought he was dealing with the FBI or something.

When he finally got through all the queues in the subway he walked to Deller's office which was situated in a side street not far from Harrod's. He was obviously doing alright for himself as a 'Business Consultant', a term no doubt designed to cover a multitude of sins.

The office was located in a large red brick building. A plaque inside the foyer stated that Deller Consultants was the only business on the second floor. Doing very well if he had a whole floor. So he wasn't giving the story out for money. Another reason to think it might be kosher. If this turned out to be as big as he was beginning to think it might be, it could set him up for life.

When he walked out of the lift on the second floor, Jason was greeted by a smart blonde girl sitting behind a solid oak reception desk.

"Good Morning Sir, how can I help you?" Jason smiled at the pretty little thing.

"Got an appointment with John Deller at Ten". The pretty little thing smiled back at him. Her teeth were American white. Jason wondered what her mouth would taste like.

"What was the name Sir?"

"Jason Black. What's yours?" Her white smile widened, eyes twinkling playfully.

"My name is Hannah as you can see from my badge Sir". Jason glanced at the badge which said 'Hannah King –

243

Reception'.

"Are you always this polite?" He quipped.

"Only when I'm at work, Mr. Black, I'm as rude as the next person when I take off my uniform". Jason was impressed. Nice flirting.

"I'd like to see you being rude with your uniform off sometime Hannah, what time do you finish?" She gave him a look of mock outrage.

"How dare you Sir, I'm a happily married woman". She flashed her wedding ring at him. He made an exaggerated shrug before taking one of his business cards out of his jacket pocket and flicking it casually onto her desk.

"Oh well, you win some you lose some. Still, if I can be of service to you in any way at any time, please don't hesitate to contact me Hannah, I think we could work well together".

"We'll see". Result. The phone on Hannah's desk rang. She picked it up and listened. "Yes Mr Deller, he's right here now. Ok I'll send him through". she put the phone down and pointed to the left with a well manicured hand. "Mr Deller will see you now. First door on the right". Jason smiled.

"Thanks Hannah, you've been most helpful".

"You're welcome Jason". Definite result. The use of his first name was a sure sign that she was hot to trot. Just a case of waiting for hubby to piss her off enough so she could blame him for her infidelity. Jason gave it two months max. He walked down the short corridor which led to various offices. The first on the right had a sign on it with Deller's name at the top. Jason tapped lightly and walked in.

John Deller was a big man. Six-three at least and beefy with it. He stood beside his desk and held out a strong hand which Jason shook casually. Deller indicated a chair next to the desk.

"Please sit down Mr Black, thank you for getting here so quickly". His voice was deep and steady. Not the voice, appearance or stature of a man to scare easily. Jason sat obediently and bit his tongue. It was important to let John Deller speak first, to get it off his chest at his own pace. Deller sat in a big leather chair behind his desk and studied Jason's face. Then he began to unburden himself. Jason sat back and showed he was listening. The secret device in his breast pocket recorded everything. The story was dramatic. Shocking. Crazy. Unbelievable. Jason had no doubt that every word Deller told him was true.

Karen opened her eyes. Her body exploded in pain. She was sure her internal organs were bleeding. She breathed deeply and sighed. This time it was very bad. They'd really gone to work on her. It was getting out of hand. Dangerous. She told herself that if she recovered from this it would have to stop. She reached for the glass of water on the bedside table and took a sip. The liquid felt soothing as it trickled down into her guts.

Karen sat up slowly, causing arrows of ache to shoot through her. She cried out. Then gathered her determination and slipped one leg out of the bed, lowering it gingerly to the floor. It was agony. Fire was burning between her legs. She needed a bath more than she'd ever needed anything in her life so she forced her battered body into an upright position and leaned against the wall for support until the pain subsided a little. Bit by bit she made her way to the bathroom and turned on the taps.

While the bath filled she took a packet of co-codamol tablets from a cabinet on the wall above the hand basin. It's mirrored door showed the reflection of some gargoyle-like creature she didn't recognise. She swallowed the pills and heaved a sigh of hope. They were the extra strong ones with

30 milligrams of codeine, not the over the counter version with only 8 milligrams. She'd got them from the club the first time she'd volunteered to be beaten and raped for fun. Just time for a soak and then the medication would knock her out for a few hours.

Karen turned off the taps and carefully climbed into the warm water. Once she became accustomed to the temperature, the liquid began to soothe her injuries. Maybe it would be ok after all.

Mick Randall looked up from the computer screen as Jim walked into his office. "Any luck?"

"Nothing of real help so far".

"I've been reading up on Benny Eye and I've discovered that his first victim is linked to his second" stated Jim. Mick considered the relevance, if any, of Jim's remark.

"So?"

"Well, I thought maybe he originally started off with people he knew or at least selected victims from a specific group."

"So".

"So, if he picked them from a specific group, either by location or some other criteria, then that criteria might include himself or at the very least some sort of link to him. Say the victims went to the same school for example. It could mean that maybe Benny himself went to that school or at least lived near it." Mick frowned, unconvinced.

"So how are the first two victims linked?"

"They had both been employed at a company called Powerbox Auditorium during the past year. Linda Sermon worked at their London HQ in Islington and Gina Newman was a cleaner at their Newbury office in Bone Lane. Neither girl worked for the company long, Gina was there for just four weeks but it's the only link we've got". Mick's face brightened a little.

"Maybe Benny works or worked for the company at some point, though its unlikely he would have known both girls because they worked miles apart. Also cleaners tend to work either really early before the rest of the staff come in or really late after they've all gone home. Unless Linda was also a cleaner and Benny was involved with the cleaning in some way?". Jim shook his head.

"No, Linda was a part-time receptionist. Only worked normal hours. No link to cleaning at all. But that doesn't have to be a problem if he's high up in the company and gets to go to both branches. Or if he's a driver who travels from branch to branch".

"Yes, that's possible Jim. You may have something. It's worth looking into at any rate." Jim smiled, pleased that he had got Mick's seal of approval.

"I've already spoken to the MD at the Bone Lane site. He said he did vaguely remember Gina but couldn't shed any light on her movements because he would not have come into daily contact with her. He said I should talk to a guy called Ralph Higson. He runs the cleaning operation at Newbury and would have known her."

"And did you speak to him?"

"Jenny's seeing him at six tonight. That's when the cleaning staff arrive". Mick nodded.

"Nice one Jim, keep me up to date with it".

"Will do".

Jason phoned Jane as soon as he got back to his office. She was in a meeting but he insisted the underling tell her he was on the line. After a minute or two Jane was there. She sounded her normal professional self now. For all her faults and eccentricities she was a highly efficient journalist.

"High Jase. Have you got something juicy for me?"

"Yes Jane, and a damned good story too" he joked.

"You've spoken to John Deller then?"

"I sure have and boy did he have a tale to tell. Looks like you've done it again Jane. This should make story of the century if it pans out like it seems to be doing".

"Sounds good, do please elaborate" encouraged Jane.

"Basically he confirmed what you told me. He has become aware of an organisation that is responsible for multiple murders in this country."

"By 'become aware of' I assume you mean 'belongs to'?"

"Those are his words but yes, I'm sure he is a member who has got cold feet and is concerned for his own safety. He told me that if anyone ever found out he had blabbed, he would suffer a fate far worse than death. Said they'd kill his family in front of him".

"Nice people we're dealing with then. We'd better be very very careful on this one Jase, I don't want anything nasty to happen to you unless I'm doing it". Jane sounded genuinely concerned. Whether it was for him or the story he couldn't be certain.

"Don't worry Jane, I'll be careful. Now Deller also gave me a contact point for this group and a website address for a company called Powerbox. I haven't had time to look at the site yet. Deller says its so sick I should brace myself. Says it has live links to killings, rapes and all sorts of nasty stuff".

"Sounds a bit risky for them to do that. What if a member of the public finds it on a Google search or something?"

"I guess most of them would just think it was another kinky porn site or some sort of fetish movie link. Very few people would be able to access the hard stuff anyway because you need a special login and password and its all got 128 bit encryption. According to Deller if you pay a very pricey subscription you get your access info emailed to you and away you go. You can then look at all kinds of sick stuff like I said, murders, rapes, torture. All recorded live as they happened or as they are happening. You can even get live events sent straight to your 3G phone if you pay a little extra".

"Sounds right up my alley Jason, maybe I'll sign up myself" Jane sounded excited. Jason knew she was very kinky but he was sure she was only joking about wanting to see people being killed for real.

"By all accounts there are thousands of subscribers worldwide. All paying extra to download full length versions of the murder clips. Deller told me it costs anything from a ton for a short basic rape movie up to more than ten grand for the really gory stuff".

"Let me have the web address Jason, I think it's important that I see this too. Just in case they catch you and finish you off". Jane laughed

"Thanks a lot Jane. That's a nice thought." He gave her the url and could hear her pen scratching as she wrote it down. She'd be frigging herself off to a load of twisted filth before too long no doubt. Dirty dirty slag.

"Have you checked out the company?" she enquired.

"No not yet but I'm sure they will have some kind of

legit cover going on. I'll check it out and get back to you."

"Good work Jase. This story could make us all rich. Or get us killed"

"You're already rich Jane and I'm the one who is likely to get killed if I poke my nose too far into this can of worms".

"Not scared are you Jase?" Jane teased.

"You could say I was a little wary of getting mixed up with a bunch of murderers like this but you know me Jane, the story comes first".

"No, Janey always likes to come first Jason, as you well know". Sounds like her mind's wandering onto her other favourite activity again. Time to sign off.

"I'll check the site and find out what I can about Powerbox. Deller also told me there is an advert in a wank mag called Razzler which is a contact point for the organisation. They are always on the lookout for new members to cough up a lot of money to see the nasty pictures. Maybe I'll sign up and see what I can find out from the inside. It might cost you a bit for my subscription though Jane".

"The paper can afford it big boy. Just don't do anything you don't want the police to find out about. If you get swayed and turn into a rapist give me a call Jason" Jane was nearing boiling point now. Time to go.

"Will do Jane. I'll keep in touch".

"You do that thing" replied Jane.

A taxi arrived outside Rod's house as promised by Mike. He kissed goodbye to Vicky and sat in the back wondering what terrible delights tonight would bring. The driver, Jeff, was a swarthy faced quiet man who politely opened the car door for him and drove in silence. Rod wondered if he knew about the activities of the murder club. The journey took a route along the M4 to London. Rod had not visited the capital since his early twenties and was simultaneously excited and nervous.

After an uneventful journey the vehicle pulled up at a large white building in Victoria. It had a plaque on the wall declaring itself the business premises of Powerbox Auditorium PLC. Jeff hopped out of the car and opened the door for Rod who climbed out.

"How much? he enquired. Jeff shook his head

"It's on the company Sir" he replied in a quiet voice. Rod pulled a tenner out of his pocket and offered it to Jeff.

"Well have this for yourself anyway" he said. Jeff shook his head again.

"Thank you for the thought Sir but it is against company policy for me to accept tips from members. I wish you a good night." Jeff nodded, got back into his car and drove off. Rod stuffed the note back into his pocket and stood looking at the front door of the building, temporarily unsure what to do. The door opened and out walked Mike, his fat body encased in a smart blue suit which looked expensive and rather formal compared to the open-necked shirt and jeans Rod wore. He felt rather uncomfortable.

"Hello Mike, I didn't realise it was a suit job". They shook hands.

"Oh don't worry about that my boy, I always ponce myself up for these occasions but that's only because I'm actually working tonight, meeting and greeting and all that". He smiled at Rod and patted him on the back as was his habit.

"Are there a lot of people here?" asked Rod

"Quite a few. We have these parties about once a month. Its our way of saying thanks to all our members and a chance for us to keep in touch with people." As they spoke they moved into the hallway which was spacious and beautifully appointed. Very classy. They walked across the hall and through double doors into a large room with chandeliers. At the door a beautiful dark-haired woman wearing a flowing red dress with gold detail on the shoulders offered Rod a drink from a silver tray she held.

"Champagne Sir?" Rod took a glass and smiled at the gorgeous creature who gave him a friendly smile in return. Mike also took a glass.

"Thank you Sherren". Mike received a smile also.

"You're welcome Sir". Inside the room Rod saw about fifty men gathered in small groups, drinking and joking around. There was a small stage at one end and a projector hung from the ceiling. There were also a number of women all dressed in similar red dresses to the one Sherren wore, though most of them did not have the gold detail on the shoulders.

Rod noticed a few girls wearing black and white outfits which looked like waitress uniforms. Mike led Rod to a quiet corner.

"I'd better fill you in on the etiquette before I introduce you to some of the other members. Firstly the girls you see in the room are categorised into three main groups. The ones in the black and white uniforms are here as waitresses and kitchen staff. At least that's what we've told them. They are in fact part of the entertainment and will not be leaving here alive tonight". Rod was shocked but tried to cover it up. "Please feel free to use and abuse the women in black and white in any way you desire. You can molest them, beat them, rape them, torture them and/or kill them should the urge take you. We have enough for every guest to take three of them so don't be greedy. You can fuck as many of them as you want but if you want to kill one make sure you take her into one of the bedrooms which are clearly signposted at the top of the main stairs. If the red light is on outside a bedroom, it is occupied".

"Right".

"It is easier to keep the other victims from getting startled too early on if you only do stuff to them in the bedrooms or the group room which is to the right of the stage. This ensures that none of the others can see what's going on until we are ready to finish them off. They are easy to lure up to the bedrooms because we have told them there are other activities in rooms upstairs which may require servicing from time to time. Is it all clear so far?"

Rod nodded, dumbfounded "Yep"

"The women in the plain red dresses know what we do here and are members of the club, though they do not take part in our major activities. They are minor shareholders of the company and offer sexual and other services to our major shareholders which you are on the path to becoming. You can trust these girls to help and advise you, or you can invite them upstairs or into the group room at any time if you want to fuck any of them. Feel free to have as many as three at one time if you want. They will perform lesbian shows for you if that's what turns you on. They can also arrange killings, torture sessions and rapes of the uniform girls if you ask them. They are adept at luring nervous girls upstairs for example. Don't worry about trusting them with your deepest darkest secrets as they have proved totally open-minded and trustworthy members of the organisation". Rod's mouth was open and he was looking rather gob smacked at the information he was receiving. Mike grinned at Rod before continuing.

"The red dresses will help organise your activities and watch if you want, but the red and gold girls, like Sherren for example are all major shareholders; they have all performed killings themselves and are on an equal footing with the men here. The only reason Sherren is serving drinks is because she is my colleague and like me is working tonight as part of the meet and greet function. We have to get all the women to wear colour coded outfits so our men can avoid murdering their fellow members. The red and golds are not staff, they are members with the same status as yourself, so please do not expect them to act like servants. Talk to them and learn from them about the organisation. They may well be taking girls upstairs or into the group room to perform activities on them just as you might. Some of our male members like to take part in activities with the red and golds because they love to see women abusing other women. If you can find a gold to act out with you, I know you'll enjoy it but don't mistreat them or you could get into the bad books of a very dangerous person"

Rod looked a bit wary and Mike patted him on the back. "Don't look so worried Son, most of them are very friendly. In fact you will find all of our members and staff to be highly approachable and helpful so just mingle, drink and have the time of your life. If you need any advice, I will be around all night. Just ask. Rod smiled weakly.

Mike gestured to a tall brunette wearing a red dress. As she walked over Rod studied her slim form and full bosom. Her legs were tanned and shapely and her shoes strappy and high. Her facial features were stunning. Rod had never even spoken to a woman as good-looking as this and felt a little intimidated.

As she approached she smiled at Mike and then at Rod. Her expression was very relaxed and friendly.

"Rod, this is Laura; Laura, Rod" She offered her hand to Rod who took it and gently shook. Her skin was soft. "Rod is a new member and a shareholder, I'd like you to look after him tonight please" Laura smiled again.

"Rod, I'd be glad to help you in any way you desire" she flashed her dark sexy eyes as she spoke. Rod's knees wobbled.

"Thanks" he mumbled. Mike walked off into the crowd. Laura stood close to Rod and laughed gently.

"I know its all a bit overwhelming at first. You should have seen me at my first party, I was a total wreck. Let me get you a drink. Is Champagne alright?".

"That'll be just great" replied Rod. He studied her figure as she walked away from him and disappeared into the crowd. The place was fairly full now but not packed. There was plenty of room to move around. As Rod surveyed the guests he was somewhat surprised to see that everyone seemed totally sane. The room was not full of weird psycho's who couldn't string two words together and killed as a twisted form of communication. The men and women all seemed decidedly normal, maybe even a bit more normal than average. The atmosphere was that of a carefree well-to-do party, a jolly gathering of successful and rich professionals. The women were all beautiful, glamorous and intelligent. It was like he had come home. Laura re-appeared carrying two glasses of Champagne and handed one to Rod with a smile.

"There you go Rod, get that down you and you'll feel more chilled." He took the glass and a big swig. The coldness and fizz of the liquid cooled his throat and livened his spirit. He grinned.

"So what happens now?" he asked. Laura took hold of his hand.

"Come with me, I'll show you around the place". Rod followed her to the back of the room where she indicated a set of double doors. "This is the group room. It's a bit early so I don't expect much is happening in here yet but you never know".

They went through the doors into a large room which was mostly covered in polythene, but in a classy way. The floor and walls had a layer of clear plastic sheeting professionally applied, not in the way of builders keeping sawdust off the floor but as a subtle protective layer over the expensive wallpaper and carpets.

There were a couple of tables in the corner, one of which had drinks on it, the other held a selection of knives, saws, swords and assorted instruments. There were other objects in a rack behind the table. The furniture was limited to a couple of sofas which were arranged to face into the room. "The sofas are for watching the action at close quarters. There is a much more comfortable viewing lounge through there" Laura pointed to another door at the far side of the room. There was a big mirror covering most of the wall. "The mirror is two-way, you can see into the room from there. Also be aware that everything which happens in this room, in the whole house in fact, is recorded. But don't worry, if you do anything interesting it will go on the website and you'll get a nice fat payment and royalties if members pay to download it" She smiled like a schoolgirl explaining all the best places to have a sneaky fag without the teachers finding out.

"I'm all for fat payments" Rod's eyes glinted with excitement as he thought of how much money he could make. The main doors to the room opened and a short man with blonde hair and round glasses entered with a woman. The woman was a little taller than him and had auburn hair and an attractive face. She wore a black and white uniform. Rod couldn't help but let out a little gasp as he realised what was occurring. Laura squeezed his hand and dragged him to the sofa.

"This looks like fun" she giggled. Her expression was one of rising desire and glee. Rod felt a tingle of excitement at her attitude.

The man walked with the woman into the centre of the room. By her expression it was clear that she did not know what lay in store at first, though she became a little alarmed when she saw the table full of knives and swords. "What's going on? What is this room?" she enquired nervously. The man replied by punching her hard in the stomach causing her to bend forward. He pushed her to the ground and kneeling on the floor, began to push up her skirt to reveal her shapely stockinged legs. The woman screamed as she realised that she was about to be raped. She spotted Laura and Rod sitting on the sofa watching and appealed to them. "Please help".

"O.k., we'll help" replied Laura, giving Rod a cheeky wink.

The man was rubbing the victim between her legs and she was squirming in an attempt to get away. Laura approached and smiled at the man.

"Need some help Bob?" she asked, grabbing hold of one of the woman's legs and forcing it down onto the carpet. "Come on Rod, get hold of her other leg would you, so Bob can rape her".

At this the woman freaked completely. She thought they were her saviours but they were joining in with the rapist. One of them was a woman too, smiling with joy at her panic. What the fuck sort of place was this? Before she could think about what, if anything, she could do to escape, Laura smacked her hard in the face.

"Shut it you stupid bitch, you're giving me a fucking headache". The woman went quiet, more from shock than pain. Her thoughts were full of confusion. All she knew was that she was about to be raped, maybe murdered if she wasn't careful. These were obviously people without mercy.

Rod moved forward and held the woman's other leg wide. Bob nodded politely and began to rub the woman's thighs greedily, pulling at her flimsy knickers and feeling her pussy.

Laura used her free hand to start undoing the zip which ran down the full length of the uniform the woman wore. Once it was unzipped, Laura pulled the bra up and away from the woman's breasts, which were full and firm. Her stomach was also hard and smooth. "Nice bod Darlin" said Laura, rubbing her hand over the woman's boobs and belly. "You picked a nice one tonight Bobby".

"Thanks" grunted Bob as he moved his head forward and began licking and sucking on the woman's tits. He had his trousers undone and slipped them down, revealing his hard cock. The victim braced herself for his entry into her, resigned to her fate at this stage and only hoping to survive the evening.

Laura gripped hard on one of the breasts and was obviously feeling very turned on by the whole thing.

"Get in there my son" she sighed. Her breathing was heavy with arousal and she was squeezing her own legs together with sexual pleasure. Rod found her reaction even more of a turn on than watching Bob's cock moving in and out of the woman's hole, though that was also getting him going. He gazed at Laura who smiled back at him with a look of such salaciousness that he knew it would not be long before he would be fucking her.

Bob was thrusting faster into the victim's body, gripping hard on her breasts as he rammed into her, until with a shudder he ejaculated inside her. He lay still for a while before slowly climbing to his feet. Laura produced a wad of tissues from somewhere and passed them to Bob who began to wipe the semen and blood from his penis.

"Thanks Laura"

"You're welcome Bob. That was a good one. Worked for me". She gave Rod a horny look. He grinned back, a little uncomfortable at her full-on approach. "I'll get Dennis to finish off here Bob, you go back to the party and enjoy yourself". Bob did up his trousers and walked back into the main party room, dropping the tissues into a bin on the way out.

Rod stood up as Laura got out her mobile phone and pressed a single number. Direct dial. "Dennis, can you come and finish off in the group room for Bob, I've got a bit of business to attend to myself". She listened for the reply.

"Thanks Den, you're a diamond".

Almost straight away a big, tough looking guy walked in and nodded a greeting to Laura and Bob. He looked at Rod in a friendly manner.

"Who's this Laura, a new boy?"

"This is Rod. It's his first time but I think he's having fun, eh Rod?" Rod smiled meekly at Dennis who grinned a big grin.

"If you've got Laura to contend with I'm sure you'll have a night to remember Rod" he laughed. Laura playfully punched him on the arm and he shoved her quite hard in fun. Laura moved next to Rod and took his hand, dragging him playfully towards the doors.

"Come on Rod, I've got something to show you upstairs". Rod smiled widely. Laura led him through the main room and out into the spacious hall. There was a wide staircase winding it's way up to the next floor. Rod looked at the large oil paintings which adorned the walls. They looked expensive. When they got to the top, Laura turned right and moved along a corridor. All the rooms had lights showing above the doors. One or two were red, most where green. She opened the door to room 7 and dragged Rod inside, locking the door behind them.

"Seven has always been my lucky number" quipped Rod.

"It certainly is tonight Rod" replied Laura, giving him a hot look. The room was spacious and comfortably appointed with a king sized wooden bed, a drinks cabinet, fridge and a big television screen hanging from a bracket. The walls were covered with mirrors. Protective polythene was applied to the carpet and any uncovered wall space. There was a wardrobe near the bed.

Laura opened it to reveal various outfits and a section containing various cutting instruments. "So what would you like me to wear, Rod? We've got all the classics, schoolgirl, nurse, policewoman, you name it". Rod thought about it.

"Have you got Birthday Suit? That'll do for me Laura".

She smiled. "That's my best outfit of all, good choice. Now do you want to watch some porn while we fuck?, we've got everything from gangbangs to double anal fisting. Whatever floats your boat".

"I reckon you'll be enough excitement for me without any additives" Rod moved towards her and took her in his arms, almost passionately. Laura responded by becoming passive and submissive. She could tell what a man wanted just by the way he behaved when they were alone together. Rod was a romantic who liked his women passive and willing. He wanted to do stuff *to* you rather than *with* you which was fine. She liked it any way it came, so long as it came.

Laura allowed Rod to lay her on the bed and lift her dress to reveal black hold-ups and lacy black panties. "Get stuck in Rod, do whatever you want to me, I'm a dirty girl and can take whatever you've got".

At this Rod felt lust explode throughout his body. He reached out and began feeling Laura's thighs, running his hands over the front of her panties and down the full length of her legs. Then he lifted her bottom from the bed in order to peel down her underwear and remove it from one leg, leaving her knickers around one ankle. He moved his head forward and opening her thighs wide put his lips against her vagina, gently inserting his tongue as deeply as it would go. He licked around her pussy and sucked her hole in order to get her musky taste in his throat. Laura moaned with pleasure as he began to flick his tongue across her clitoris, gently at first but increasing in speed and force as she got more excited and began squirming beneath him. It was not long before he had to grip her thighs with both arms and struggle to keep her on his mouth as she bucked and groaned.

"Oh yes, baby, yes, just like that" she whispered as he licked her harder and faster. "I'm coming, I'm coming, don't stop". Then she cried out from the orgasm that wracked her body. A mixture of pleasure and pain which brought a temporary unconsciousness as her whole body exploded in sexual bliss. Rod clamped his mouth over her cunt as she came, sucking up her hot juices as they flowed from her, swallowing them with a feasting hunger. After a few minutes they both flopped down on the bed, Rod's head resting on her pubic mound. As the orgasm wore off, Laura regained some control of her body and sat up.

"Where'd you learn to eat pussy like that? It was wonderful". Her eyes shone, blissed out but still lustful. Rod grinned smugly.

"I guess I'm just a natural".

"That makes two of us then" she replied, a naughty twinkle in her eye. Laura wriggled off the bed and moved into a position where she could undress Rod with well practised finesse. She gently positioned him so that he was laying on his back on the bed, his naked penis erect and ready for action.

Laura kneeled on the bed and took his shaft fully into her mouth, her tongue sliding up and down it as she began to gently suck on him. Rod groaned with pleasure as her hot soft mouth moved up and down his pole which was stiffer than he ever remembered it. She was a very good cock sucker and by the look on her face she fucking loved it too. What a woman.

Laura began to increase the speed of her movement and started to suck harder on his tool. He felt the sperm rise in his balls as he neared the ultimate moment. As his balls tightened, ready to explode, Rod gripped Laura by the back of the head and began to ram her mouth onto his prick harder and faster.

Laura allowed him to force himself deep into her. She loved to feel it almost gagging her as it banged against her tonsils.

Rod pushed himself into her mouth one last time and held her head still as his taut bollocks jerked and sent hot sperm into Laura's gullet, gushing into her cute pink mouth, his sack emptying as an acute feeling of ecstasy shook his whole being.

Laura let her throat relax; she felt the twitch of his cock as he came in her mouth. As the hot sperm made contact with her larynx, she swallowed hard, enjoying the sweet salty taste as squirt after squirt of hot fluid pumped between her lips, filling her mouth.

When he had finished ejaculating, Rod pulled his penis out and lay back on the bed, his eyes glazed over with sexual satisfaction. He watched Laura's face as she smiled down at him, then opened her mouth again to allow a trail of sperm to drip sexily from between her pretty pink lips and onto the bed. Rod pulled her to him and planted his mouth across hers, sucking some of the juice into his own mouth, tasting his own sperm as he swallowed it. Laura purred like a cat. "Ooh, that's dirty, very dirty. I love it".

As if in retaliation, Laura lifted herself up and reached down between her legs, inserted two fingers inside her pussy and brought her hand back up to her mouth. "I love the taste of my own cunt". She stuck her fingers into her mouth and sucked her juices in. Then she clamped her mouth over Rod's again and he tasted the cocktail of their sexual organs as he licked the inside of Laura's mouth, sucking on her tongue. When the taste began to thin, he lay back on the bed. Laura lay down beside him, her head on his chest, Rod's arm around her.

"That was great" he sighed.

"Truly" Laura whispered. They lay still for some time until Rod's penis began to twitch and harden once more. Laura felt it grow against her naked thigh.

"Oh yes please baby, put it inside me". Rod sprang to life and rolled on top of her, guiding his erection into the hot wet channel between her legs.

They fucked for a long time, rubbing against each other's bodies, thrusting deeply, gently. He knew that at this moment, if only for this moment, they were truly lovers.

After what seemed a timeless eternity of bliss, they felt their bodies click into a higher gear and began to push faster and harder until the pleasure rose to bursting point, the single being they had temporarily become melting into a long, slow-burning orgasm.

As she felt Rod's sperm fill her, Laura allowed her mind to be filled with an overwhelming feeling of love. Sexual fulfilment was truly the ultimate creator of love, that's why it was called making love. If it was done right it created an unbreakable bond between two people for a time. The better the sex, the more powerful the feeling of love and the longer it lasted. This time sex had been mind-blowingly good.

They wrapped themselves together and held each other tight, enjoying the feeling of connection and adoration which flowed between them like warm electricity. The bed was comfortable and they drifted in and out of a beautiful sleep for a while, maybe an hour. Gradually their normal senses reasserted control and they woke.

Laura kissed Rod lovingly on the mouth before climbing off the bed, pulling her knickers up and her dress down.

"Look lively boy, we've got a party to go to".

Jenny Yuce stood at the reception desk and tapped her foot. There was no-one around, no doubt because most of the staff had gone home already. Jenny had been waiting for someone to appear for over ten minutes.

She had arrived on time for her appointment with Ralph Higson but he hadn't turned up. That was a bad move on his part and put Jenny against him straight away. She hated being kept waiting, took it as a personal slight. It spoke volumes about Higson's lack of respect for the law. No doubt it was because she was a woman. If Jim Cutler had been here, Higson would have been punctual, no doubt with a cup of coffee in hand.

Jenny decided to go walkabout and cause a bit of trouble. That would ruffle the bastard's feathers. She moved across the reception area and pushed through a door marked 'Private. Staff Only Beyond This Point'. She found herself in a narrow passage with three doors leading into offices. There was nobody in any of the offices so she had a bit of a snoop. Just the usual company files and paraphernalia. She got to the end of the corridor and found herself facing double swing doors with a sign saying 'Factory'. There was a notice stating that only authorised personnel were allowed inside and on condition that they wore the correct boots and hard hat. Jenny pushed the doors open and walked in.

The factory space was not large by relative standards. It had a concrete floor and metal racking. There were big fibreglass mouldings in one corner and pallets of polythene pellets in sacks. A small fork-lift truck was parked in the far corner. The place smelt strongly of plastic. A sudden voice startled her a little.

"Can I help you?". Jenny turned to see a short stocky man who she estimated to be in his fifties. He had greying hair and a wrinkled face. He wore a blue overall.

"I had an appointment with Ralph Higson at Six. I got

fed up with waiting and thought I'd look for him".

"You just found him" said the guy holding out his hand. "Sorry. I didn't realise it was that time already. You must be Sergeant Yuce from Newbury C.I.D.?".

"That's me" replied Jenny tersely. "Is there somewhere we can go. I just need to talk to you about a couple of ex-employees of yours".

"Come through to the office" he motioned for her to go back the way she had come. They walked into the corridor and Higson opened the door to the first office on the left. He sat on a chair behind the desk. Jenny sat to the side of him. No way was she going to sit the other side of the desk and let the little twerp have the power seat.

"I understand you employed a woman named Gina Newman a while ago?".

"Yes, she worked part-time here as a cleaner".

"When did she work here?"

"She only stayed for a few weeks. Student type, didn't like having to get her hands dirty, so she legged it after she got her first month's wages".

"You do know she's dead?". Higson shrugged as if the information was of little interest.

"Yeah, I heard she got herself killed".

"What about Linda Sermon? Did you know her?" Higson raised his eyes to the ceiling. He was no doubt keen to get on with his important work of emptying bins.

"I know where you're going with this Sergeant but you're barking up the wrong tree. I heard she worked at our London office and also got herself murdered".

"And?" Jenny stared intently at Higson but he showed

265

no reaction at all.

"And?" he did an exaggerated Gallic shrug.

"And can you think of any reason why two members of your company would have been murdered by the same killer within weeks of each other?"

"The same killer? That's unlikely surely?"

"We know it was the same killer because of certain unusual features related to the murders".

"I never even met Linda. She never came here and I never went there".

"How well did you know Gina Newman?".

"Like I said she worked here for a month and then pushed off. We get a lot of that with young girls these days. They come, they go. I don't know them intimately, I just tell them what things to clean".

"Who would have known both girls, within the company?"

"Search me, I'm only the man in charge of cleaning this dump. You'd be better off talking to the boss".

"I did. He told me to speak to you". Jenny was sure she saw a smirk forming at the corners of Higson's mouth.

"Something funny about two of your colleagues being murdered Mr Higson?" her tone was stern. Higson's face became hostile.

"Not at all funny. Now if you've got no more pointless questions, Sergeant I've got work to do".

"Don't worry Mr Higson, I've finished with you. For now. Though I have a feeling we might be meeting again soon".

"I'll really look forward to that. Now if you'll excuse me,

I've got toilets to clean".

Jenny walked out into the reception area and through the glass door which led to the car park. She got in her car and sat fuming for a few minutes before firing up the engine and driving back to the station. What a sarcastic bastard Higson was. She'd bloody well do a full police check on him when she got back to her desk.

Mick Randall picked up the phone and dialled Karen's number for the third time that day. Where was the silly cow? If she didn't answer this time he was going round to her house to kick the fucking door in. He wasn't concerned, just annoyed. Karen had always been so reliable apart from the odd day's illness. But she hadn't even had the decency to phone in this time.

"Hello" croaked a voice.

"Karen, is that you?"

"Just about. That Mick?"

"Yeah its Mick. You sound like shit Karen."

"You want to see me, I look worse".

"What's the matter? I saw a strange note on your door when I came there yesterday".

"Just my attempt at humour Mick. I've caught something and its fucking bad".

"Not sexually related is it Karen?". If only the smartass knew how close he was to the truth.

"Not unless the flu is caused by masturbation. If that was the case you and the whole of Newbury fucking nick would have it. Now if there are no more questions officer, I'd like to get back to my deathbed".

"Sure thing Karen, please ignore my attempts at humour. I'll call you in a couple of days".

"Ok. Thanks for calling Mick. Take care, it's a dangerous world out there". she spoke in a mock American cop accent.

"See you Karen. Oh Karen, just one more thing" Columbo impersonation 3 out of 10.

"What?"

"Do you really masturbate?"

"Wouldn't you like to know you pervert. Now fuck off and do some police work and stop harassing innocent members of the public".

"No such thing". Mick hung up. His phone rang straight away, making him jump. He snatched up the receiver and barked into it.

"Yes?"

"Alex. I've brought in Yvonne Snelling, aka The Cat Woman. She found Rachael Heaver's body"

"I know who she is Alex, what about it?"

"She didn't want to talk so I gave her a ride in my police car. She's in cell twelve thinking about her attitude".

"And that's what you called to tell me is it Alex?".

"Just setting the scene you miserable bastard. Missing your au pair are you?"

"No, just busy solving multiple murders. Sorry if I sound a bit grumpy but I've lost Karen for a few days with flu and I've not had any good news for weeks".

"Well maybe today will be your day Mick. As I was saying Yvonne Snelling is saying nothing. Which is a bit of a change because when she first spoke to us, when the body was found, we couldn't shut the bitch up. Kept saying she wanted to be on 'Crimewatch' and shit. Now her lips are sealed tighter than a clam with arthritis and I'm wondering why that is".

"And you think something has happened to cause this change in attitude? You reckon the killer has had a word with her, threatened to put all her moggies in the blender ?"

"Something like that. Maybe they've paid her to keep schtum. I noticed she has a big new telly and her cats look like they've all been to the hairdressers recently. Last time I went there the place stunk of cat piss and fish heads. Now its all fumigated out and ponced up".

"Bit thin isn't it?"

"Might be thin Mick but it's better than nothing. Just call it a hunch". Alex laughed to himself.

"I don't believe you just said that. That's got to be a tenner in the clichéd cop tin at least"

"Maybe but my point still stands".

"I'm glad to hear it"

"Fnaar Fnaar".

"Alright Alex, let's assume she's been got at one way or another. What reason would the killer have for doing it? We've already questioned her fully. It's all been in the papers. If the Killer is Anton Russell he wouldn't need to do it because he's already been acquitted of the murder. So...."

"So, it might mean it wasn't Anton Russell and the real killer is getting nervous now that Russell is no longer in the frame. He's scared we might start digging a bit deeper".

"Which would mean the real killer thinks Yvonne knows more than she's already told us, right?"

"You catch on quick Mick".

"I am good aren't I?" Mick joked.

"But not as good as me. You see, if the killer thinks the Cat Woman knows more, then he must have a reason for thinking it. Such as the fact that he bloody well *knows* she knows more".

"Say that in English Alex if you would?"

"He knows she can lead us to him so he's putting the frighteners on her not to tell us. Which means that its very likely that she *does* know something which could help us. Which means that *we* can put the frighteners on her to tell *us*. Which means we can find out what she knows. Which means we can get at least a good lead to the real killer, maybe even a description or name".

"Its possible Alex, but why doesn't he just finish her off and get rid of the witness once and for all?"

"Maybe he thinks we're watching her place, or he hasn't had the opportunity, or he doesn't want to give us even more clues by committing another murder, or maybe she's his mum. I don't fucking know, but it's a potential clue is all I'm saying".

"You'd better follow it up then Alex. Let me know when you've got her to spill the beans. Oh, and well done Alex, you may be onto something here".

"You never know Mick, you never know. Talk t'ya later bozo". The phone went dead.

This was getting scary. They were obviously very dangerous and ruthless people judging from the website. As Jason Black surfed the site and found literally hundreds of video clips of real murders and rapes appearing on his screen, he felt sick to the guts. He must pass this on to the police.

Never mind the story glory on this one, it was well out of his league. If he got mixed up with this lot he'd end up deader than a dead thing.

There was also the thought that any delay in notifying the authorities would lead to more killings. He didn't want to be responsible for that. From what he had seen there were new murders being put onto the site every day. He had to pass this information on to the authorities. He had to. But what if he did? What would be the consequences of that?

Firstly he'd have to tell them where he got the web address from and that would put John Deller and his family at risk. Worse than that it would put his name in the frame for a starring role in next week's movie clips.

There was a special section on the website for revenge killings. This was one of very few sections in which murders of men took place. It was mostly sexually motivated deaths, rapes and mutilations of women, often young attractive women which filled the web pages he had seen. It was like the most extreme porn site ever. There was even a section for women to plan their own rape or murder if they were desperate enough to get famous. It was the cult of celebrity gone mad. Jason had watched a couple of these 'Death Star' murders to see if they were really willing victims or just drugged or confused women who had no real awareness of what was going on, like in some nasty porn sites where the girls are obviously drugged out of their heads and not enjoying the action very much.

To his horror he saw the brutal murders of attractive girls who knew exactly what they were doing. Their faces showed the gormless desperation to be 'known' by the public that Jason had grown used to seeing on hundreds of bimbos in reality TV shows over the years. He could not begin to understand the mental processes of women at the best of times but to let some madman cut your tits off just to have your name go onto a list with other dead bodies was just about the

271

sickest thing he could imagine anyone doing. Apart from filming the victims' deaths and selling the clips on a website of course.

The films were ranked by popularity in a section called 'Top of the Chops'. Number One this week was a pretty blonde with huge plastic tits being gang banged by four men before being doused in petrol and burned to a crisp. The clip, entitled 'Firing the Secretary' had been at the top of the chart for two weeks but was under pressure from a new entry at number Two called 'Sonya with Seven Slits'. It contained footage of a very sexy brunette using a knife on herself to create gaping wounds on her belly, thighs, arms and chest. Once the cuts had been made, another girl appeared on the screen, naked except for a black choker and high spiky stilettos. The second girl took the knife and began slicing the wounds even deeper, opening up the bleeding body in seven places before pushing her hands into the holes and pulling out internal organs which she began to stuff between the legs of the now screaming brunette. Once she had stuffed a considerable amount of the offal into the dying girl's vagina, she began to do the same to herself, masturbating with what looked to Jason like some sort of intestine before pulling the heart out through a gaping slit in the chest and ramming it between her open thighs, forcing it up her own cunt. Her face was on fire with demonic glee as she brought herself to the moment of vile orgasm. The screen went black momentarily before a short roll of credits began to appear on the screen. Jason noticed that the name of the girl who had just been killed - the supposed 'star' was Jenny Yates. Her name was up first in big letters which flashed on the screen in the form of ornate multicoloured fonts for a few seconds before disappearing to be replaced by the name of the second girl who had had fun with the gore. This girl's name was given as Laura Crowley. A tag line running underneath her name described her as 'Lethal Laura – Mistress of Mayhem'. She was obviously a bit of a favourite with the site's members because there was a link to all her other live events. Jason got the impression that girls were queuing up to be polished off by her. She had her own fan club and everything.

There were also a small number of men who had signed up for her fatal treatment but Jason found it impossible to watch beyond the point where she got out an electric saw and moved it towards a guy's erect penis. A strange kind of fame.

Jason surfed away from the website and sat with his head in his hands. A cold sweat covered his face. His heart was beating hard. A sense of evil crept up his neck and swamped his brain. It was too much for his mind to cope with. Beyond sick. For once in his life he was unsure what to do. Usually he just did the first thing that came into his head and damn the consequences. He could usually wriggle his way out of sticky situations like a snake shedding a skin. Now he was faced with a situation of a different calibre. The stakes were much higher than the disapproval of someone he had messed about. It would take a lot more than a bit of slick bullshit and a winning smile to extract himself from the web of organised murder he had discovered here.

Jane Race would be keen for him to go undercover and join the organisation. She would do anything for a chance to keep her name at the top of the success list. What's more she probably found the idea of people being murdered and mutilated for sexual gratification perfectly acceptable. Jason had never seen anything approaching a moral value emanating from Jane. She was a robot designed for two purposes only – getting fucked and getting power. She was good at both. Jason had never met anyone quite like her. She had no limits. Even his beloved Serena, dirty bitch that she was had some standards and taboos, though for the moment he couldn't think what they were. So, Jane would want him to call the number he had found in 'Razzler' and meet up with a gang of murderers in order to get the story.

But what about Serena? She would want him to come

273

home safely with the correct quantity of arms and legs. She had already made a fuss when he had been on undercover jobs before, telling him to watch out because there were some very bad people out there. As if he didn't already know that. He had won awards for his undercover reports. It was the one thing he was really good at. He had begun to make a name for himself. If he could pull this one off he'd be set up for life. But was he willing to risk his life for the acclaim? He didn't know.

Then there were the victims to consider. Not those who had already been chopped up but the ones who might not die if he went straight to the police. He could be the cause of innocent people dying if he went off playing private eye rather than letting the police sort it out. Maybe. Then again the police were a bunch of fuckwads who would startle the horses without actually catching them. The organisation would go deep underground and more people would be killed. All the leads would disappear if a bunch of heavy booted plod started stamping on toes before they had enough evidence to convict the ringleaders. Maybe. It was a tough call. The toughest.

Jason glanced down at the advertisement in the copy of 'Razzler' he had just bought. It was in amongst all the other cheesy offers for phone sex and cheap dildos. All it said was 'If you like it a bit harder. If you want to get extreme. If you want to take it to the limit call us and see things that will blow your mind. We have no limits'. A freephone number appeared below the photo of a sexy blonde with a knife in her hand. Blood dripped from the knife. It was kinky alright but no more kinky that some of the other adverts on a page full of kinkiness for sale.

Suddenly Jason knew what he had to do. Go down the pub and clear his head. A couple of pints would help him think straighter.

Rod and Laura went back down stairs and walked

straight into a scene from Hell. During the time they had been away the party had got into full swing. Laura smiled knowingly at the look of shock which passed over Rod's features when he saw a girl nailed to the wall being mutilated by two men and a woman in a red and gold dress. The victim had already had both of her breasts sliced off as her three attackers competed to see who could perform the most vicious act upon her. As they walked by, Rod noticed that the woman in red and gold was Sherren, the dark haired beauty who had been serving drinks when he first arrived. Now she was transformed into a knife-wielding maniac, her facial features twisted with evil delight as she forced the blade into the half-dead victim's throat and pulled down hard tearing open the body to let the innards fall out.

"Come into the group room Rod". Laura tugged at his sleeve and he allowed himself to be guided past scenes of carnage being acted out on the small stage. It was some sort of multiple rape scene but it was hard to distinguish how many bodies were involved or who was doing what to whom. The audience was rapt. Perhaps a hundred people stood gaping intently at the arcane misuse taking place upon the stage. Rod followed Laura into the room at the back where he had earlier helped a short man called Bob rape a woman. Now the space was filled with activity and the air with screams.

"There's Simon. Come on Rod, I know he wants to meet you". They made their way through the gore until they were standing behind a tall blond man. He was completely naked and in the process of fucking a long-haired beauty up the arse as if his life depended on it. Not surprisingly the girl was screaming. Rather more surprisingly was the fact that she was screaming with perverted pleasure as he forced his long thin cock into her back passage as roughly as he could. Although her outfit, which lay open and pushed half way up her back was white, Rod noticed that there were little green epaulettes on the shoulders. Laura spotted his confusion.

"This girl is a different sort of victim. A willing one. See the green bits on the uniform? They signify that she came here wanting to be abused sexually but not killed. She's likely to be a new girl at her first party who's trying out the depravities before buying shares and maybe becoming a red or even a red and gold if she has the guts to kill". Rod nodded.

"Oh, I see".

"But she's not a true victim, only very kinky. The real sickos are the ones with the purple tags on their uniforms. They are here by choice too but they don't just want to be fucked by strangers, they want to be slaughtered. They're murder groupies". Rod raised his eyebrows. "We're getting more and more coming along. Women who think its really cool to be chopped up live on the internet or on video phones all around the world. They get famous for five minutes, some of them go down in history. If you search the website you can find a role of honour for the most famous victims. Would you like to meet one?" Rod shrugged.

"Yeah, I guess so". He replied.

"Let's just have a word with Simon when he's finished with this little floozie and we'll find you a happy victim. Oh, and just so you know, you get paid at least double for the willing ones because of the weirdness of it all. You make a packet on royalties for them too. Very popular". Rod's eyes gleamed at the thought of the money. That was the best bit of all. Getting paid.

It was crazy but it was true. He felt much better when he thought of the money. It made him feel horny. They watched as Simon continued to ravage the girl's arsehole, groping her hard little tits as he pushed into her again and again. The girl's face showed a mix of pain and pleasure as he began to jerk and twitch, his cock shooting the hot white into her rectum. She let out a high pitched scream which was part orgasm and part overacting. As Simon pulled his dripping cock out of her, the girl

276

turned and smiled at Rod and Laura. Rod looked blank but Laura smiled back.

"Nice work Nikki" said Laura "That was really dirty". Nikki winked at Laura and moved around until she was facing Simon. His slimy cock was inches from her face. She leaned forward and began to suck the mix of red and white from his shaft, swallowing it down with exaggerated slut-like posturing.

Laura knelt down beside Nikki and began to lick her lips, sliding her tongue into the other girl's mouth, tasting her. Rod could tell that Laura was getting hot again. He watched as she began to fondle Nikki's tits, pulling on the nipples and sliding three fingers into her dripping cunt. Simon reached out to grip an object which lay on the floor nearby. It was a huge rubber vibrator. He turned it on and passed it to Laura who slipped her juicy fingers from Nikki's pussy and replaced them with the monstrous instrument, pushing it in as far as she could get it. Nikki moaned with pleasure as it went in. "There you go Nikki" said Laura standing up and sucking Nikki's cum from her fingers. "Finish yourself off with this". Nikki was too busy fucking herself senseless to reply.

"She's going to be an asset to this company, that's for sure" Simon spoke in a steady voice. He began to put his clothes back on. They had been neatly arranged on a chair at the side. Laura made a cum face, her mouth open and quivering with mock orgasm.

"She's a fucking natural Simon, where did you find her".

"She's my sister". he replied. Laura looked shocked. A very rare occurrence.

"You're kidding!" she exclaimed, wide eyed.

"Yeah, I'm kidding, she's someone from Dean's club, keen to get her face known and willing to do just about anything for a bit of dirty fun". Laura hit Simon gently on the arm, laughing.

"You sick fucker. You had me going there for a minute. If she wants to get her face known she's going the right way about it. Mind you it's her juicy little arsehole that Simon's going to remember, eh Rod?" Rod just grinned. This was all a bit extreme, completely beyond anything he had ever experienced before. Still, there was always the money to think of. Simon held out a hand which Rod took.

"Nice to meet you Rod. I saw your first event on the website and think you'll fit in nicely. Have you had a good time so far?"

"They always have a nice time when I'm looking after them Simon, you should know that by now" interrupted Laura. Simon shrugged.

"Too true". He looked at Rod. Hows about we get you a drink and a chance to earn yourself a lot of money Rod?". Simon looked at Laura who waved him away.

"You boys go and enjoy yourselves. I'm going to have a bit of fun with Nikki. I'll join you later". Laura was as good as her word. She dived straight on top of the delighted Nikki, whose hands were already tearing at Laura's dress in an attempt to unleash her firm breasts.

"Follow me Rod, I'll get you a drink". Rod followed Simon past a man who was busy slashing a woman across the face with a Stanley knife, her skin peeling in ribbons, blood streaming from empty eye sockets. They moved around a group of men and women who were holding a funnel between the legs of a young woman with red hair. As they neared, Rod smelt petrol. The funnel was taken out and a short blonde in a red and gold dress threw a match between the open thighs. The group moved back quickly as the petrol caught, flames appearing from inside their screaming victim's hole, her pubic hair a mass of fire.

Simon stopped to watch the woman burn from the inside out, her screams rising to a peak of agony before the fire began to blaze its way out through her cooked body, releasing an acrid smoke into the room alongside the scent of cooked meat. As soon as the girl was dead and the flames began to reach out around her corpse, two bouncers in smart suits rushed over and used CO_2 fire extinguishers to put out the fire. Simon began to walk again. Rod followed. He needed a drink.

When they reached the bar Simon gestured towards the bottles on display. "What's your poison Rod? Champagne? Or would you prefer some nose candy? We've got the best coke you can get if you're into it". Rod shook his head.

"I'll have a Scotch if there is any". His voice wavered a little as he spoke. Simon laughed, reaching for a bottle of Islay malt.

"We've got everything here Rod. Anything your little heart desires". He smiled and passed the glass to Rod who took a long hard swig. The bitter burn of the whisky brought his mind into sharper focus.

"That's better, I needed that".

"You go for it Rod, it's a bit of an eye opener here isn't it?"

"That's one way of putting it". Simon grinned and passed the bottle to Rod.

"Here take this, it'll make you feel a lot better." Rod took the bottle and refilled his glass. He looked across to the stage and saw that it was now occupied by a man using a hacksaw to cut a woman in half, longways, starting between her legs and sawing all the way up to her skull until the whole body fell in two. The effort he put into it was huge and he sat on the floor exhausted. There was a round of applause from the audience and the man stood up to take a bow, his clothing covered in the woman's blood. Rod recognised him. It was one

279

of the men from his induction meeting, the one who looked like a Nazi and had threatened to kill every member of Rod's family if he shot his mouth off and caused any trouble. Rod shivered involuntarily.

Simon spotted Rod's discomfort and made a face. "That's Martin, he's not a man to get on the wrong side of I can tell you. A real nasty piece of work". Rod raised his eyebrows.

"Do you know him well?".

"Not very. I've spoken to him at a few parties and meetings but to be honest he doesn't really fit in. He's not popular but he does his job well. I guess you would need someone that scary to keep tongues from wagging. Put it this way we don't get much trouble from police informers or the press since he taught some people a couple of hard lessons about loyalty a few months back. The things he did to those families makes my stomach turn and I'm a sick bastard. My advice is not to do anything which will get him to notice you".

"Don't worry, I won't". Simon nodded towards the doorway which led to the hall and the stairs.

"Let's go up and find your little treat Rod". The two men moved through the lobby and up the stairs. They passed groups and couples who seemed to be engaged in every possible sexual perversion, some fucking up against walls, others draped on the stairs. When they got to the top Simon turned left along the corridor. Rod saw that the lights above the bedroom doors were now mostly red, showing that the rooms were occupied. Every red light represented a murder or rape. What the hell did they do with all the bodies?

Simon opened a door on the left, about half way down the corridor. It was the only one still available. Inside the décor was the same as the room he had been in with Laura less than an hour before. A tall girl with mousey hair tied in a pony tail stood beside the bed. She had a shapely figure which filled out her white uniform well. She had purple epaulettes on her shoulders.

"Let me introduce you to your victim" said Simon. "This is Sarah. Sarah, this is Rod, your murderer". The girl looked a little scared and a little drunk but smiled and held out her hand for Rod to take. Her skin was soft and warm. A tingle of affection ran through Rod as he touched her.

"Nice to meet you Rod" said Sarah in a little girly voice. Rod just smiled, feeling quite uncomfortable. This was going to be a lot harder than killing Sandra had been. She had made him angry with her feeble minded terror and hope. Sarah showed no desire to avoid the path she had chosen, she was submissive and resigned to death. Rod took a big swig on his whisky bottle.

"I'll leave you two lovebirds to it then" Simon waved happily and left the room, grinning widely.

Rod sat on the bed, took another drink from the bottle and offered the whisky to the girl who stood beside him. She took it and drank deeply. "I don't really need this you know Rod, I'm all coked up with lovely snow. Makes me love everyone and everything". She laughed to herself and put her hand gently on his. "Are you ready then love, its just I've been waiting for quite a long time and I'm getting a bit sleepy. Do you want me to take my clothes off?". She began to unbutton her uniform.

Rod watched as she revealed a pair of large breasts straining to escape from the lacy pink bra, a shapely waist and long smooth legs. Sarah then took off her bra, letting her full boobs hang free. She slowly rolled down her lacy panties to reveal her pubic mound which matched her hair. When she had slipped her knickers off she stood with her legs slightly apart, her pussy inches from Rod's mouth. "Do you want to lick me out?" she asked innocently. Rod stood up.

"You do know why you're here, do you Sarah?" he

asked.

"Yes I do Rod, do you?" her voice held an edge of aggression now. "Just so we can get on with this event I'll explain it for you. I'm here because I want you to rape, abuse, torture and murder me in no particular order. I imagine you're here because you want to do those things. That's what I was led to believe anyway". She looked annoyed.

He was spoiling her big moment. Didn't he know that this was all being filmed and would be on the internet before morning? He was going to ruin her chances of getting onto the roll of honour if he didn't buck his ideas up.

Rod felt a blush of embarrassment creep over him. He was making himself look weak and stupid. Even the fucking victim thought he was a loser. He took one last swig before putting the bottle on a table and turning to face the naked Sarah.

"As long as you're sure sweetie" he said sarcastically "You'd better brace yourself 'cos this is gonna hurt". Sarah's face lit up with pleasure and excitement.

"Oh goodie" she giggled, then squealed as Rod's hand made contact with her cheek. The slap brought tears to her eyes, which showed arousal rather than fear. Rod moved forward, grabbed her by the shoulders and threw her backwards onto the bed. He gripped her thighs and pushed them wide apart, burying his tongue deep inside Sarah's wet pussy. Sarah moaned with delicious pleasure as his tongue explored and stimulated her juicy hollow. Rod felt his cock go hard and stood up to take off his clothes. While he was doing so, Sarah sat up to watch him undress. Rod punched her hard in the face. Sarah screamed, her head rocking back from the force of his fist.

"I never told you to sit up, did I bitch". All softness was gone from his voice. As he undressed he looked at Sarah's face. Now that real pain had been inflicted upon her she was having a bit more difficulty convincing herself that this was her moment of glory. It was just beginning to dawn on her that it was more likely to be her moment of gory. Death didn't bother her. Life had given her nothing. It was just that she was thinking it might hurt a lot more than she thought it would, even with the cocaine in her bloodstream.

As soon as Rod was naked he climbed on top of his victim and inserted his erect penis into her moist cavity. He began to slide in and out of her spread legs. As they both became more sexually aroused, Sarah's face brightened. It was feeling real good now. There was nothing she liked more than a good hard fucking. That punch was being replayed in her mind as a real turn on now that the interface between pleasure and pain was being blurred by the sexual excitement. The mind could not hold two opposing experiences simultaneously. As long as she was being fucked, all pain was going to feel like a mind-blowing orgasm. She hoped Rod was a horny bastard.

Rod was enjoying himself. There was nothing he liked more than giving a woman a good hard fucking. His earlier lack of confidence was forgotten now that he was sexually aroused. As long as he stayed turned on he would be able to finish the job. He could enjoy killing this horny slut because it was just the extreme end of lovemaking. Many women liked it rough. Sarah was someone who liked it very very rough.

He had once read how some philosopher or psychologist had described the moment of orgasm as a 'little death'. It was a moment of oblivion from which the mind returned slowly. As the mind re-focussed on ordinary reality it was always a disappointment. The world felt dark, cold and lonely, just like a bad come down from speed or some other drug. It was similar to those stories you hear from people who had supposedly died on the operating table and been dragged from their heavenly bliss back to a world they found unpleasant and frightening. Sarah was obviously looking to prolong her orgasm eternally. She wanted to permanently escape the pain of living but didn't have the guts to do it herself. She was using him to commit her suicide for her, hoping for the ultimate orgasm that would last forever.

Rod moved up so that his face was level with Sarah's. He put his mouth over hers and they began to eat each other's faces. Rod loved a passionate snog with a hot woman. Sarah was obviously on the same wavelength. Her tongue moved inside his mouth, exploring him, tasting him, allowing her mind to imagine that he was her lover, taking her to heaven on the end of his cock. Rod felt the semen inside his balls begin to stir.

He slowed down the fucking, letting his fluid recede from the stem, then moved forward, his cock slipping completely out of her vagina as he did so. Sarah moaned with disapproval at this so Rod slapped her hard across the face causing her to lay back on the bed. The slap felt horny because she was feeling very hot indeed, on the verge of coming in fact. She let the pain transform into sexual arousal and lay back, waiting for Rod to get back inside her.

Rod reached forward into the wardrobe and felt around for an implement. He gripped a random handle and pulled the weapon out. It was a dagger with an ornate design on the side. Sarah saw the knife and felt her heart flutter. It was a thrill of pleasure. There was no fear, just delight at the thought of the long blade slicing deep into her body, sending her to a blissful forever. She felt Rod push his cock back inside her and to move in and out. It felt wonderful. As the pumping gathered pace once again, Sarah felt a hard orgasm begin to build deep inside. She could feel Rod's pole twitch as he got close to ejaculating. Her orgasm began to explode. Sarah let out a soul-deep scream of ecstasy.

Rod began to groan with the pleasure of his impending moment. His balls were tight and began to jerk as what felt like gallons of sperm squirted into Sarah's bursting cavity. As he came, he used all the strength he could muster to bring the knife down between her breasts, pushing the sharp blade through her ribcage into her pulsating heart.

Sarah felt the knife go in a split second before her orgasm blasted her into oblivion. The intense burning pain was transformed into sexual energy, her bliss levels going into hyperspace as her heart exploded along with her mind.

Rod felt his whole body jerk with pleasure as the knife went in at the exact moment he came. As he simultaneously shot his cum between her thighs and forced the knife into her flesh, Rod's mind took him to a place of such intensity that he lost consciousness for a short period. He was rising up into a white light, his body eternally linked to Sarah's. Then he began to regain some awareness and found himself back in the bedroom, his semi-soft dick still inside the bleeding body of the woman he had just murdered.

The computer whirred as it processed the data. Jenny Yuce tapped her finger on the desk impatiently. Information began to appear on the screen. The report revealed that Ralph Higson had form. He had spent eight years in Reading prison for the manslaughter of a woman he had been living with at the time. Her naked body had been discovered on some waste ground with it's head bashed in. Higson had been suspected from the word go due to his reputation for drunken violence towards women.

It hadn't taken the police long to gather enough evidence to convict him of murder; but somehow the jury had been unable to return that verdict. In court Higson had some Harley Street doctor state that he could not have known what he was doing at the time due to a combination of alcoholism and depression leading to a period of diminished responsibility.

Jenny fumed. Just bloody typical. The police catch the guy quickly and provide the evidence to send him down for life and some fucking paid expert scares the lily-livered jury with a few big words and the cunt gets off with a poxy eight years of which he serves just over four after convincing a bunch of liberal do-gooders that he's a reformed and repentant character. Never mind Higson suffering from diminished responsibility it was diminished justice that this country was suffering from. They should string the bastards up and get rid of them once and for all. Why waste tax payer's money feeding scum like Higson. Well, the smirking smart-mouthed cunt had met his match this time. Cross Jenny Yuce and you live to regret it.

Somewhere else a computer whirred as it carried out a Tracert routine. A Mac address was found. A cutting edge spyware programme was sent to the Mac address. The program included a keylogger which went to work and quickly began to upload data.

After a couple of pints and a bit of reflection Jason made his decision. He smiled at the luscious Terri as he crossed the floor on his way outside. She winked and licked her lips suggestively as he passed. One day soon he was going to have to teach that little fox a lesson she would never forget. Jason walked through the door of the pub. Three killers were waiting outside.

Jane Race picked up the phone.

"We've got your boy Jason".

"Who the fuck's this and what do you want?".

"I'm the person who's got Jason Black locked up in a

dungeon. What I want is your flaky ass outside the Rosey in twenty minutes or he's dead". Click.

"Oh Shit".

"Mick, I've got something on Ralph Higson". Jenny walked into the inspector's office holding a sheet of paper. Mick looked up from his computer.

"What ya got Jen?"

"Higson served a term in jail for the killing of his then partner. He got off with a manslaughter conviction but the jury were wrong. I've looked through the evidence which was gathered at the time and he should have gone down for murder". Mick looked a bit confused.

"Sorry Jen, but who is this Higson again?"

"He's the guy in charge of cleaning at a company where Gina Newman worked. I went to see him and he was so full of shit, I thought I'd do a little search into his background and bingo, one rap sheet for manslaughter". Mick sat up straight and reached out his hand.

"Give" Jenny passed the paper to Mick who spent a bit of time studying it. "Looks like you've got us our first decent lead Jenny. Well done".

"Do you think we've got enough to bring him in for a chat?"

"I reckon we've got plenty. He's killed a woman before and works at the same company as one of our murder victims. Go get him Jenny". Jenny's face lit up with a big smile.

"Yes!" she punched the air. "Got you you bastard. You mess with Jenny Yuce, you pay big time".

Mick laughed. "Oh, and take that useless fucker Jim

with you, he could do with the exercise".

"He's not Yuceless when he's with me Mick". Jenny was looking smug now. Mick had heard her favourite pun a hundred times and grimaced.

"Just fuck off and get on with it Sergeant". They smiled at each other as Jenny turned and walked out of the office.

Karen stretched and carefully climbed out of bed. Her pain was still bad but the painkillers had finally started doing their job. She could at least get about a bit now, though it still hurt like hell to sit down. It had been four days since she had last spoken to Mick Randall. At this rate she would need another week off work and that would cause a bit of interest at the station. Better to knock the rumours on the head before they started. She needed a good story fast.

Yvonne Snelling, aka The Cat Woman lived in a flat on the 3rd floor of a block of council flats on the Turnpike estate. It was a run down area of Newbury which had a bad reputation. Unless you liked drug dealers, violent criminals and psychos, it was best to keep clear of the place.

Alex Hinton and his D.C. had woken her nice and early. She had not been pleased to see him or Malky and had pretty much clammed up from the start. Now, after six hours in one of Newbury Police station's best hotel rooms, Alex hoped she would feel like talking. He waited while the uniformed constable jangled his keys and unlocked the door.

Yvonne was sitting quietly on a thin plastic mattress which covered the wooden bench attached to the wall at the back of the cell. The cell was clean, otherwise empty, and stunk of sweat, no doubt Yvonne's contribution to the ambience. Alex walked in and motioned for the old woman to follow him.

"Right, Yvonne let's have a chat, shall we?"

The woman looked worried and frowned as she followed Alex out into the cell block corridor and through a set of heavy locked doors into the interrogation room. It was sparsely furnished, containing a simple table, two chairs each side and a large tape recording machine on the table which Alex went over to, pressing a button on the side. The tape started to whirr, recording the conversation in the room.

"I need to feed my cats" Yvonne's voice was frail and breathy, her posture poor. She shuffled when she walked.

"Take a seat Yvonne". Alex used his stern interrogation voice. Any sympathy he felt for the woman was put aside now. Yvonne sat down. A tall man, in his twenties, with a friendly face walked into the room and sat in one of the chairs opposite her. Alex sat next to the man. Both men stared at the woman for a few moments, like they could see right through her, see all her secrets and fears.

"I need to feed my cats" Yvonne repeated.

"For the tape, I am Detective Sergeant Alex Hinton. Also present is my colleague Detective Constable Malcolm Jordan and Yvonne Snelling, who has declined our offer to get her a duty solicitor"

"Coppers in disguise" mumbled Yvonne. "I need to feed my cats".

"As soon as you've helped us with our enquiries Yvonne, you can be out of here and see to your cats". Alex spoke softly but with no sign of friendliness. If anything he seemed more menacing when he spoke like this. Yvonne shook her head.

"I already went through everything last year. I told you all I know then. I've got nothin' else to say".

"That's a shame, I was hoping to use your cell for a nasty drunk we've got coming in soon. She doesn't like to share but I'm sure you will learn to love each other after a few hours". It was a complete bluff. Alex was pretty sure she would see through it but it added a bit of pressure, set the tone and created an uncomfortable sense of the future for Yvonne if she stayed at the station much longer. Her best bet would be to spill and get back home as soon as.

"Look, I know how you coppers work, you know. What's he the nice one then?" she pointed at Malky who sat smiling, mostly to himself. Alex Ignored her comment.

"All I'm trying to get you to understand is that we are in the middle of an investigation into a brutal murder. You were a major witness at the trial of Anton Russell, so we need to go over a few of the details, just in case we missed something".

"A lot of good that did before, the bloke got off with it". Malky fought to hold back a grin. The flea ridden old hag had a point.

"Listen love, I need to know who's been threatening you and your cats. We know you've been frightened off by someone." Alex went for the oldest one in the book. Pretend you know what's happening and if you say it with enough conviction they believe you and come clean. Some coppers used the maxim 'conviction leads to conviction' as a way of convincing themselves of the merits of this age old ploy. It was layer upon layer of bluff but it was amazing how often it worked.

"I've nothing to say to you".

"We know you're scared but we can't help you, or your cats if you clam up and say nothing. In fact that course of action will mean we have to waste our time and yours by keeping you in here even longer. If you tell us what's been going on we can protect you".

"So you reckon, do you?". The woman sagged in her chair, a sign that she was coming round to the idea of getting whatever was worrying her off her chest. Alex remained silent. Now was the most crucial moment of the whole process. Whoever spoke next would be the loser in this battle of wills. This was a technique used by sales people and coppers alike. It was very productive at pivotal moments of a negotiation or an interrogation. Alex prayed to a God he didn't believe in that Malky wouldn't open his gob and spoil the whole thing by asking an inane question about the weather or some such nonsense in a misguided effort to play the soft cop and start to build a rapport with the woman. The heavy laden seconds inched forward. The atmosphere grew tense and uncomfortable. Malky shifted on his chair. Alex flinched.

"Look, if I say anything, you've got to stop them hurting my cats". Alex let out an audible sigh. Thank fuck. Now was the time to change approach and coax the information out of Yvonne carefully. Time for Malky to use his boyish charm. Alex nudged Malky gently. Pick up the hint, you lemon. Malky looked at Alex who widened his eyes at him.

"You don't want your cats to starve so let's sort this out as quick as we can. Would you like a cuppa and a couple of chocolate digestives? My colleague will go and get us some, won't you Sarge?". Alex gave Malky an 'I'll get you for this you little twit' look.

"Sure, what would you like, tea or coffee?"

"Tea". grumbled the old woman. "And make it strong, not like the usual gnat's piss you get in here. And give me three sugars".

"And I'll have a coffee Sarge, two sugars and a couple of chocolate Hob Nobs on the side". Malky's face spread into a wide grin as his superior went to get the order. He would have to pay for his little bit of fun later but it was worth it to see Hinton's face. It was a picture. Malky turned to face Yvonne

Snelling.

"You'd better not drop me in it with 'em, they said they'd kill my little ones and I believe 'em. After all if they killed that girl, they won't care about animals will they?".

"Who won't?"

"Three men came round to my place a couple of days after the case finished and that Anton Russell was let go. They told me to shut my mouth and I'd be alright. Otherwise they'd kill all my cats".

"Why would they threaten you Yvonne. What would be the point?"

"I guess they're mixed up in the murder in some way"

"Yes, but in what way, Yvonne?"

"I don't know. I told you all I knew before didn't I?"

"Did you Yvonne?"

"Well yeah....everything that happened on the day when I found the body of that poor Heaver girl. I used to see her walking in the park some days. Seemed a good girl she did. I mean, what's wrong with people?"

"What didn't you tell us at the time Yvonne?"

"I told you everything I knew about finding the girl and seeing that nasty man walking away from the girl. Or it looked like he was walking away from the girl".

"Yes, love you've told us all this. What else didn't you tell us?".

"Well I never thought it would be important. Not until the men came to my place. Then I thought that maybe it *was* important because why would they threaten my if it wasn't important eh?".

"Go on love". The door opened and in walked Alex Hinton with a tray. Malky grimaced. What a fucking moment to interrupt. And they had made him a Sergeant.

"Tea, three sugars wasn't it Yvonne?" Alex spoke in a slightly sarcastic tone. "And coffee with two lumps for you Detective Constable. I couldn't get the Hob Nobs so I brought you some Rich Tea fingers. I hope that's all right". Malky hated Rich Tea, they always fell into his cup when he dunked them.

"Thanks Boss. I really appreciate the thought. Yvonne was just about to tell me some really important new information when you came in". Stick that up your sarcky arse.

"Oh, yes, Yvonne" Alex said in the most coaxing voice he could muster at short notice "And what was that?". Time to play the 'silent game' again. Yvonne looked a bit annoyed at the intrusion, though she appreciated the tea. Not too bad considering a copper made it. She took a bite of one of three chocolate digestives Alex had put beside her on a saucer. Make the fuckers sweat for a bit. She knew their games. A long silence was broken only by Yvonne's contented nibbling and slurping. Alex and Malky began to glance at each other nervously but neither of them said anything. Finally Yvonne spoke again. A self-satisfied smile on her face which both men noticed. Outwitted by an old cat woman who stunk of urine. If this ever got out, their suffering would go down in piss take history.

"Right then, I guess I'd better put you boys out of your misery".

"In your own time, we can take all day if you want". A slight threat entered Alex's voice. Malky smoothed things over.

"Yvonne's been very helpful Sir, she's just having a bit of a breather. It takes it out of you, being stuck in those cells you know". Back of the net. Hinton would go spare after this bit of humiliation but fuck him, he nearly blew it with his

293

impatience.

"Ok young man, I'll tell you everything else but do you mind shutting up for a minute and letting me get a word in?". Alex grinned widely. Take that you cocky little bastard.

"Sorry Yvonne, please continue". Malky said quietly. Bollocks.

"As I was saying, I told you everything about what happened before. I saw Russell walking away from the dead girl's body in the park. You arrested him, took him to court and he got off with it".

"Thanks for reminding us" quipped Alex. Malky shot him a look.

"So what happened since which may have caused those men to come around making threats?".

"I think they think I know something else. I don't really know what they think I know but I know they think I know it". Was she taking the piss now?

"Can you be more precise?"

"Well the only thing I can think of is that Anton Russell was involved with them in some way. Maybe they think I saw them with him or something". Alex was losing patience with the old bag now. Get to the fucking point.

"Listen Yvonne, we can piss about all day or you can just tell us and get home to your cats" Alex couldn't hold it in. The old bag was overplaying her part now and needed bringing back down to earth.

"Alright. Look I may have seen one of them talking to Anton Russell near the body. He walked down the path towards the tennis courts and there was another man standing just near the pavilion. I never took much notice at the time but he may have been waiting for Russell. They may have been talking".

"Is that it?" asked Alex.

"Well I guess its enough for them to come round to my flat and start making nasty threats".

"I guess so, Yvonne, thank you. Now what did these men look like. Can you describe the one you saw talking to Anton Russell first?". Yvonne stared into space, attempting to recall the scene.

"He was a fat man. Short, a bit of a slime ball, hair all greasy. I didn't like the look of him".

"Was this man one of the ones who came round to your place?"

"Yes, he was the one doing most of the talking, the other's were just muscle. I guess he needed a bit of back up in case I turned nasty" Yvonne quipped wryly. Alex smiled indulgently.

"Would you recognise any of the men if you saw them again?"

"The fat one I would. There was also a quiet man with ginger hair who didn't seem all that happy to be there, just stood at the back watching really. I'd remember him for sure because he reminded me of one of my neighbours".

"Who's your neighbour?" Malky jumped into the conversation. Yvonne was not impressed with his question.

"It's not my neighbour sonny, I would have known if it was him wouldn't I? I said he looked a bit like my neighbour. Same sort of general colouring and appearance". She looked at Alex. "Where'd'ya get him from, The Pound Shop?". Alex couldn't help but laugh out loud at that one. It was priceless. Malky forced a smile he didn't feel.

"If I let you look at some photos would you be able to pick out any of these men?" Alex kept his tone professional even though he still felt like laughing.

"If it means I get out of here and can feed my poor cats, I'll do it. Preferably before my next birthday" Yvonne was enjoying herself now, giving these wet coppers a good battering. Serves them right for being such a pair of smart arses in the first place.

"I'll get the books" Malky took his chance and bolted out of the room.

Rod logged into his PayPal account. He smiled and punched the air with glee when he checked his balance. It said £23,900. He quickly withdrew the money into his personal bank account. Time to start spending.

Jane raced to the rendezvous point and waited. She had arrived early and stood tapping her foot impatiently. Her heart was beating fast even though she had not had any speed yet. Her hands fiddled with buttons on her leather coat. Five minutes to go before....

A black car pulled up onto the kerb. A dark skinned man with several days stubble leaned out of the passenger window. His attitude was pure street punk. Jane did not think he was the brains of the operation.

"Get in bitch" he said in a cartoon gangsta voice. Jane flipped him the finger.

"Miss bitch to you asshole". There was no way she was going to let a hired thug like this intimidate her. She felt fairly safe for the moment, guessing that the real brains would be waiting wherever it was she was being taken. They would probably get into trouble if they hurt her without the permission of the big cheese. Jane opened the rear door of the vehicle and climbed in. The driver smiled sheepishly. He was younger and blinged up big time.

"Please ignore my associate, he's not used to civilised company". Jane did up her seat belt.

"Who said I was civilised, shit for brains". The driver smiled widely but said nothing. He put the car in gear and moved off into the London traffic.

Jason stared into the darkness, letting his eyes adjust to the gloom. He was in a small stone-walled room. There was no furniture. Maybe it was some sort of cell, like a dungeon in an old castle in a movie. He had definitely walked down a lot of stairs to get here but had not been able to see due to the blindfold that had been wrapped around his eyes. Before that all he remembered was a long drive in the back of a windowless van. His best guess was that he was still in London because he heard traffic noise as he was being moved from the van to the building. Apart from that he had no idea where he was, why he had been brought here or who had abducted him.

The only reason he could come up with was that somehow the people John Deller had been mixed up with had found out about him. Maybe Deller had bottled it and decided to tell his colleagues that a reporter had been snooping in his office in order to get himself off the hook. None of that mattered now. The who and the why could wait.

Jason squinted into the blackness and found he could make out a door. A big locked door. He walked over to it and rattled the handle, but it was useless. He'd expected no less but you had to try even the most obvious things in these kind of situations. At least that's what they always did in the movies and Jason had no experience of such situations in real life from which to draw. He sat on the dusty concrete floor and glanced through the murk to see if there were any other escape options open to him. There weren't.

"It's Me"

"That you Karen?". Mick asked. His voice conveyed a mixture of anger and relief which would have gone unnoticed had she not spent the last few years working closely with the old sod.

"Of course its me, who the hell do you think it is you old stoat. I thought I'd better call in before you put out an a.p.b. on me".

"You've been watching the wrong movies love, more likely to send you your P45. Where the fuck have you been Karen?". Now that he knew she was all right he was narked.

"I've had the worst fucking case of P.M.T. in the history of womens' problems. You wouldn't believe it if I told you". Karen felt pretty sure that a man like Mick would feel uncomfortable if she mentioned menstruation. Men just hated the subject, which made it a good excuse for covering up all kinds of mischief.

"Never mind that, you could at least have phoned in couldn't you?"

"I guess I could have Mick but I really didn't want to do anything other than dose myself up with painkillers and sleep as much of it off as possible". It looked like it was going to work.

"Any idea when you are going to be back in here and ready to help the team solve crimes? You may not be aware but we found two more bodies last night. It's not been released to the press yet but both of them were gruesome and local. A woman named Briony Wellson was battered and stabbed to death on some waste ground at the back of Randsomes Building Supplies near the railway track and a blonde girl of about eighteen was found strangled to death in Victoria Park".

"Fucking Hell. What the frig's going on lately?"

"I wish I knew Karen but it goes without saying that we need all the help we can get just now".

"I'm sorry I didn't call in Guv but I'm really not in any shape to come back yet. I spoke to my doctor earlier and she said I should definitely take the whole week off. Sorry, I know it's really inconvenient Mick".

"As long as you know it then I guess we'll just have to struggle on without you. Still as long as you've not run off to Corfu with a Greek waiter or got yourself run over trying to cross the road in a drunken stupor, I suppose we'll just have to look forward to you making a very swift recovery".

"I'll get back in as soon as I can walk, lie down or sit without agonising pain then shall I?" Karen's voice hardly showed her relief at having got away with her excuse for being off work. Only someone who had worked with her for years would have noticed it.

"Make sure you do".

Karen replaced the receiver and sighed. Well at least that's done now. Should give her time to heal enough to crawl back to work in a few days without the constant worry of someone from the nick popping round to see if she was dead or not. She would have to endure a few saucy comments and sly remarks when she returned but that was nothing compared to the thought of the truth coming out. Karen shuffled back to the bedroom and climbed back into her big cosy bed. She closed her eyes and began to drift off into a painless sleep. Moments later she was brought back to a startling reality by a loud banging on her front door.

Karen slowly got out of bed and looked out of her bedroom window through a gap in the curtains. It was Dean from the club. What the fuck did he want?

It took her a while to get downstairs but she eventually made it. Dean smiled as she opened the door.

"Surprise surprise. I didn't wake you did I?" he asked, noticing her dressing gown.

"As a matter of fact you did Dean but I'll let you off this once".

Dean followed Karen into the sitting room, taking a seat in a high backed armchair situated near the door. Karen sat on the sofa and fixed him with a quizzical stare.

"So what brings you all the way out here to the wilds of Newbury then Dean? It must be something important". Dean smiled his best boyish smile.

"I was just passing...."

"And I was just designing a new military aircraft for the Russian Airforce". Karen rolled her eyes and glared. Dean became a little more serious, though his smile didn't disappear altogether. It was his premier weapon of choice. He had plenty of others if needed.

"Can't kid a kidder eh, Karen? Ok I'll come clean. I wanted to ask you if you'd heard any more about the murder that happened in my club. I had whisper from a guy I know that it was your pal that was up snooping the other night".

"So I believe. To be honest Dean I've hardly been in any state to speak to him about it yet. Still, knowing Mick Randall he's probably just sniffing around on some hunch".

"Do coppers still have hunches these days? I thought it was all psychological profiling and computer tracking?"

"Mick isn't like other coppers. He's old school with the emphasis on the old". Dean nodded and laughed.

"So what was he doing out of his jurisdiction. He must think he's onto something or he wouldn't have driven all that way late at night when he should have been wrapped up in a shawl in front of the television with a mug of hot chocolate".

"I'll have a dig when I get back to work Dean. Until then I can't really help. Are you worried about something that I should know about?"

"No, honestly Karen, it's nothing, I just thought I'd look you up as I really am in the area on business" Dean stood up. Karen struggled to her feet, wincing in pain as she did so.

"That bloody Horse has really done me in this time Dean". Dean winced in sympathy and then laughed.

"If you will hang out with those sorts of people I guess that's the kind of pain you should get used to. I wouldn't fancy it myself but plenty do. Enough to keep me in flash motors anyway". Dean leaned forward and kissed Karen on the cheek. "Take care, I'll see you when you're better. Soon I hope".

"I might come up for a drink and the cabaret but I don't think I'll be visiting the back room any more". Dean nodded, giving her a knowing wink.

"You'll be back Karen, you wait and see. You just can't get enough".

"Yeah, right"

Jenny and Jim drove to Powerbox Auditorium Ltd and parked in the staff car park. It being past 7pm the place looked deserted apart from two cars near the entrance. The officers smiled to each other as they walked over to the main doors of the building. There was nothing quite like the buzz you got when you were on your way to arrest a piece of scum like Higson; it made the job bearable and was only surpassed by the feeling of a job well done when the criminal finally got locked away for a long time.

The reception area was empty as it had been before when Jenny had been there. This time she had no qualms about going into the restricted area and pushed the door open forcefully. As they walked along the corridor flanked each side with offices, the detectives checked each room but there was no sign of Higson, or anyone else. They reached the end of the corridor and opened the door which led into the factory area. At first sight it looked just as it had on Jenny's recent visit but she noticed that a large crate had been placed at the far end with a tarpaulin over it. They looked around.

"Is that him Jen?" Jim was pointing to a man who was moving swiftly towards the far exit.

"That's him alright. It looks as if he doesn't want to talk to me again."

"Must be something you said last time". Jenny raised her eyebrows before calling out to Higson.

"Mr Higson, I'd like a word with you please". Higson bolted out through a steel shutter which led into the car park at the rear. The officers jogged across the factory and ducked down under the lowering shutter. Higson was opening the door of a blue Nissan Micra.

"Mr Higson, stop. Police!". Higson started the engine and reversed the car in a tight arc before slamming it into first and wheel-spinning forward towards the car park exit. As the car came towards them, Jim and Jenny moved out to block as much of the forecourt as possible, waving their arms. The car began to slow a little, then accelerated directly at them. Jenny caught a glimpse of Higson's fearful but determined face as he drove the car forward. Both officers jumped aside when it became clear he was not going to stop.

"Quick go get the car Jen, I'll phone the nick and get some back up" shouted Jim.

"To kill is the most fundamental, the most natural thing in the world. It is the basic motivation which burns within the males of every species on earth, man's reason for living. The ultimate victory against all aggressors. And believe me all males are aggressors. Those who seem peaceful simply do not have the strength to dominate and so take a meeker role, perhaps eventually convincing themselves that they are of a different breed and do not have the urge to kill all other males so they can have all the females and mate with them, seeding limitless offspring and thereby slowly becoming God, the founder and Father of all mankind." Martin spoke with grim tones as he stared semi-vacantly into the near distance, a thin smile spreading over his taut face.

Jason watched silently as a girl was brought into the room, dragged by two men in blue mechanic's overalls. The girl, a standard blonde bimbo, struggled uselessly and half-heartedly to no avail. She was made to stand directly in front of Jason.

"This girl has been drugged in order to keep her from struggling too much when you rape her, Jason"

Jason raised his eyebrows in astonishment. "You what pal?"

"Jason, I know that if I tell you that you can do anything you like to this girl, without her consent, and that I can guarantee you will never be found out or punished for it, you will at first feel shocked and horrified. Years of conditioning will forbid you to even consider the fact in terms of a genuine opportunity to experience total power over another human being and to assert your manhood in a way that is totally fulfilling and energising. However, if I leave you alone with her for a long time, keeping her sedated and pliable for you, it will only be a matter of time before you convince yourself that it wouldn't hurt to just cop a feel of her tits, or kiss her pink

303

mouth. Eventually you'll do it and enjoy it more than you have ever enjoyed anything before in your life. You will begin to feel powerful and superhuman, like your destiny is being fulfilled at last; and you will go a bit further with her, maybe cop a feel of her pussy, sliding a finger or two into her, knowing she cannot stop you, that you are her master. Once you've gone this far its only a matter of time before you are inside her, brutalising and beating her as your orgasm builds, all your false morals swept aside by a dose of super-reality which transforms you into the hunter you were born to be and have always been. Then we can talk again as men". With a gesture of his arm, something akin to a military salute, Martin and his two acolytes left the room, locking it behind them.

Jason stared incredulously at the place where Martin had been standing, glad that they had at last turned on the lights so he could see where he was.....

A Man Becomes Part of a Novel, Discovers an Inter-Dimensional Über-Criminal and Gets a Big Surprise

......"Wakey Wakey Grant, we've got work to do". I had fallen asleep on the comfy chaise. I slowly came to and saw the mind-blowingly gorgeous Orba standing beside me.

"Uh?" was all I could manage. Orba laughed; a warm sea of love washed over me.

"Don't just lay there drooling Grant. We've got a mission to complete". I sat bolt upright.

"You mean I'm in the team?"

"Yep. But first I've got to go through the file with you to explain exactly what it is we'll be getting into and which character you'll be playing". I laughed now; a boyish grin spreading over my face. I was fairly certain I knew which character I was to play, his personality being so similar to mine.

"I bet it's Jason, isn't it". Orba beamed a saucy grin back at me, making my legs go weak at the knees.

"Not that you're naturally anything like the irresponsible womanising user though, eh Grant?" I almost blushed.

So off we go into a realm that I think is sort of the time and place I was happily, then insanely, living in not so long ago (not that ideas such as 'not so long ago' mean anything to me now that I know the score).

It's the Orba and Grant show now, apart from the fact that the aforementioned honey is not playing any of the characters as such; no she's got a much more specialised role in all of the horror we are about to plunge into in order that we might save a little segment of spacetime from the disfiguring clutches of a reality-manipulating supercriminal who uses the pseudonym 'The Mesmeriser'.

The plan is that I'm to temporarily kindof sortof take over the person called Jason Black who I read about in a sorta kinda novel given to me by the most beautiful goddess I've ever seen, while residing in a higher realm I went to after a long period of madness and philosophical questing which came to a head when I took hallucinogenic drugs in order to somehow get one over on my erstwhile life partner and lover with whom I had become increasingly competitive careerwise in the arena of cutting edge art and film. (It sure don't sound too likely when I say it like that).

Orba is in for a rough ride in more ways than one; she's got the unenviable task of taking the roles of what are to become my many victims; whom I am called upon to abuse and kill in an effort to convince the bad gang of murderers that I am the new gore-king on the block in order that I might get to meet the puppetmaster who is none other than the fucking Mesmeriser (who I first met in my lunatic period of transmogrification from nearly normal artist and bon viveur to interdimensional law agent along with several other aspects of myself I had played insanity games with during my most florid times in the asylum).

We've all got to take a bit of moral, psychological and physical punishment if this convoluted and terribly dangerous Scenario is going to play out like the clever good guys on cloud nine want it to. Mind you I'm not sure I'd want to be a murder victim for any cause; so obviously it proves just how far above me Orba is in the scheme of things; I guess the rapes will be fairly simple; maybe even pleasurable for her as it's just going to be a case of me fucking her quite brutally from time to time: and based on what I've learned recently about the higher souls' attitude to sex, that should be a walk in the park for her and a dream come true for me. It's the beating, mutilating and murdering bit that I'm going to have trouble with. Because we are going to be in a real life Scenario rather than a reality menu game, the pain I inflict upon Orba is going to be real. I'm sure she knows what she's doing; probably done similar stuff on previous missions, but I'm hoping I can throw myself into the role enough to convince those I need to convince that I'm an extraordinarily vicious and evil son of a bitch.

A little flick of a very clever switch and I'm standing looking into the eyes of the drugged girl in the stone dungeon room. She's as described in the file I read back at what I shall henceforth refer to as HQ 'a standard blonde bimbo'. Quite pretty though. I make Jason move toward the girl who is laying on the stone floor and say "Oh what the hell, if you can't beat 'em, join 'em" in a loud voice, hoping that the hidden microphones all pick up my change of heart; my moment of transformation; my switching of sides from 'good guy' to 'bad guy'.

I see my intended victim cringe at my words; Orba is obviously not too impressed with my overblown theatrics; she must think I'm a right numpty with my phantasmagorically instant and complete change of personality; I really should have played it more subtle; if the Mesmeriser is watching me I've probably tipped the fucker off that higher powers are on his case: not a very believable crisis of conscience, slowly overcome by the promise of vast opportunities to satisfy the lust and rage I normally hide even to myself blahdy blah. If it's only nasty humans watching I may get away with it: I doubt that the M. has disclosed his secret identity to many, if any, of his henchmen. Whatever. I've cast my dice now, better just play them and hope for the best. So now I have to rape and murder my totally awe-inspiring, love transforming boss in order to convince the guys upstairs that I'm bad enough to be one of them.

I flop down onto the floor next to the girl and lean close to her.

"What's your name then Honey?" The girl grins a drugged grin but doesn't speak. I roll nearer and rest my hand on her bare thigh, enjoying the feel of the smooth flesh. The girl just lays there. I run my hand a bit higher and lift the skirt of her dress up so I can get to her panties; nice lacy pink ones with a purple polkadot trim. I place my hand on her knickers, massaging her mound with my fingers, then I slip my hand down the front, getting a feel of her pubic hair which is quite wiry for a blonde. It is only when I slip a finger between the lips of her vagina that the girl reacts; snapping out of the semi coma like she's been stung by a wasp, and sitting up. She grabs my hand and pushes it away.

"What the fuck are you doing you freak. Get away from me" she screams at the top of her voice. I pull a 'hurt' face.

"Aw, don't be like that". I pull her down onto her back and make a grab for her pussy. "I'm just tryin' to be friendly". She struggles feebly and attempts to slap my face. I grab her hand and push it away, following up with a hard slap to her pretty face. She shrieks in pain (Orba shrieks in pain) and tries to get up. I grab her leg and pull her onto the floor again.

"If you don't settle down I'm going to have to really hurt you, understand bitch?" She stops making so much noise while she considers my proposal, then she moves away a bit and sits looking at me with a sleepy frightened look on her face, like she's trying to figure out her best option: fight; or acquiesce to being raped but not get beaten too; maybe save her life. She decides to fight me (obvious really when you think about what's really going on; it has to be brutal to be convincing).

So battle commences and I lay into her pretty face with my fists, knocking her to the floor. She lays there in a sort of curled up position and I stick my boot into her body and face. I connect particularly well with her chin once and think I hear a bone crack. I also kick her hard between the legs (right in the cunt) when she tries to squirm away from me. Soon she has been subdued enough for me to continue with a leisurely rape.

First I have a feel of her thighs, before tearing open the front of the dress and lifting up her bra so I can have a good hard suck on her breasts; my hands kneading the soft flesh before moving lower and inside her pink panties once again, fingers sliding (unopposed this time) between her soft lips into her hot (and surprisingly, wet) hole (Orba you dirty bitch). Thus encouraged I quickly unbuckle Jason's belt and get his well proportioned dick out. Within seconds I have it inserted into the girl's slit and am pumping in and out of her with genuine pleasure and abandon. (A couple of times I swear I feel her pussy clamp onto me, offering me support in my difficult task and, I hope, signifying genuine pleasure from Orba).

After a few minutes of screwing her cunt I flip the bitch over and ram it up her shitter; I rape her tight arse hard, enjoying the way my cock goes a bit red as blood begins to lubricate her sphincter. I could see the blonde's face, contorted in pain as she was buggered with ferocity.

I feel myself getting close to the point of ejaculation and grip onto her long blonde locks, pulling her head back viciously as I push into her torn anus. Her distress increases in line with my fuck speed. As I shoot hot burning fluid up her shit hole, I grasp her around the throat from behind and pull her head right back, clutching her under the chin and trying to crack her neck. I squeeze her throat as hard as I can as I cum; slowly relaxing and letting her head drop forward. She lays still as I press against her back, my penis still inserted in her rectum, until I have fully completed my orgasm. Then I roll her onto her back and grope her breasts before shaking a few drops of semen and blood over her face. She just lay there whimpering.

I had a sudden dreadful thought that I had actually brutalised an innocent girl. I was relieved to see a secret twinkle in her eye and knew that Orba had been coping beautifully; a look of lust flicked across her face for an instant before contorting into utter distress. I knew what I had to do next; it was time to kill. For a few seconds I faltered, feeling a wash of dread at the thought of ending the life of another person. Then I thought about all I had been taught by Martu and tried to steel my flashing nerves. In the end my victim whispered in my ear as I leaned forward over her sagging body; she said 'Do it Grant': only Orba would know my 'true identity' (if there really was such a thing, which I was very doubtful of given my recent multi-dimensional experiences).

Reassured that I was not going to become a murderer, I got a real good hold on the blonde head and with all my strength I smashed her face into the stone floor; there was a nasty cracking noise and an horrendous scream of pain; I lifted up the head and saw that the nose was squashed almost flat; blood poured from the nasal orifices; I cracked my victim's face several more times onto the flagstones until the skull cracked open and the screaming (Orba's screaming) finally stopped: brains spilled out over the ground and mingled with the blood and other liquids which were splashed all over the place. I stood up, a genuine look of alarm on my features.

"Hey there Jason, you Tiger!" the female voice spoke with a sexy French accent. I turned around and saw to my utter amazement that Serena, my girlfriend, was standing there with Martin; both grinning. I did a double take.

"What the fux going on Serena, what are you doing here?" She laughed her dirtiest laugh (the cheap slut one) and moved forward to take my bloody hand.

"Don't be cross Jason, but I'm running an international murder business which is responsible for the rape, murder, mutilation and torture of thousands of women worldwide. Let me show you my Empire of Gore and Lust. Jason, it's a really beautiful thing". I stood there looking stunned (I was also totally unsure as to how to proceed in this game without my leader

Orba, who I had unfortunately just raped, buggered and murdered, oops!).

"Er.."

"Don't worry about it for now Jason, come and get cleaned up; there's plenty of time to get your head around it later" she purred. I let myself be led away from the scene of carnage and up several flights of stone steps. We went through a metal door into a plush, carpetted corridor. A short ride in a gold plated lift, brought us out into the vast penthouse which, I soon discovered was where Serena went when she wasn't keeping up the charade of living in a flat with me. All those sales trips had been fiction.

"Relax Jason" purred Serena "Give yourself time to get your head clear. Maybe we could take a shower together?"

"I might just have one on my own Serena, calm myself down a bit". She shrugged.

"I must say, I'm quite surprised that you went all the way with that girl Jason. I thought you would be squeamish. I guess we've both managed to shock each other today, eh?"

"That's an understatement". Jason moved across to the en-suite bathroom, slipped out of his blood-soaked clothes and into the shower. The water felt good against his skin, helping him shake off the surreal feelings that engulfed him. He had to work out what to do next in this crazy Scenario. He had to avoid being put into a position where he would be expected to kill anyone else. Unless somehow that person was able to look at him with the eyes of Orba, to reassure him that things were under control at a higher level of reality. It was all very strange and fatiguing. He needed sleep.

After a while everything began fast-forwarding. I could see the police grabbing Higson after a bit more zany chasing, ending up in a sliding crunch just by St. John's roundabout. Jenny Yuce kneed the cunt in the face as she wrestled him to the ground. When they got him back to the station Jenny and Carver gave him a bit of interrogation soup and made him cry like a little lost boy, so out of his depth now that the Scenario had changed from 'cool big-time murder gang employee' to 'frightened little coward locked up in a small cell with scary police officers'. Anyway the little fucker ratted on his chums, giving a major breakthrough to the rozzers. In the end even they managed not to fuck it up and got video evidence on eighty murderers and rapists. Some of the organisers turned out to be government ministers, press barons, police officers and leading clergy. No surprises then. Jane Race was found giving a blow job to one of the cheeky drivers in the back of a limo; she made a packet on the story of how she and her colleague Jason Black had been working undercover, at great risk to themselves, in an attempt to make the public safe from these deadly killers.

Art Fux – End Game

I wake up and I'm in a hotel room in London with a needle in my arm. Standing beside me is a tall, dark-haired woman with a smirk on her face. "Hello Fuck Head, how's it goin?" I freak out a bit and shake my mind to set it back on it's foundations. The bitch is looking good, dressed in leather jeans and spiky boots. I groan and hold out my hand for her to take which she does. She tenderly sarcastically helps me to the lift, tells the hotel manager to fuck off and gets me into her limo. Soon I am sleeping like a baby on the M4 motorway, heading back to Marlborough.

"I've been freaking my tits off about you, you complete dickhead. Four fucking days and not so much as a text. Then we find your useless Greg spy and we kinda make him tell us what you were up to and all the drug crap you'd been spouting. You never could handle the shit, not like me eh, fancy taking ten year old acid for fuck's sake you prat".

"Nearly forty fuckin' year old acid if you don't mind bitch" I managed to sort of gabble. I felt it was important to let her know just what sort of a hero she was dealing with.

"What a total wank-arsed cunt of a twat fuck you really are". I could tell I had really impressed her. I reckon I've won the cool drug battle. It wasn't easy but it just had to be done. I must be a total legend by now, or soon will be once word of my daring adventure leaks out. That should blow Derren LeVine and those poncy film bandits totally out of the water. Not only have I managed to go completely insane and take a lethal drug cocktail but I have survived to tell the tale. I felt really pleased with myself for some time; maybe a week or two, then the mind freaks started coming back and I had to spend a lot of time in a warm room with nice spongey wallpaper. But to give her her due, the slut had kept on poking her head around the padded cell door from time to time and collected me once they said I was no longer a danger to myself or others.

She let me just slob around for a month or so which is when I decided to fuck the lot of them over and piss off to somewhere totally quiet and drug free. I told her I needed to go die somewhere less crowded. She just shrugged and told me I'd soon be back once I realised how needy I was.

"Fuck off Shithead. See you later". That's her way of saying she loves me and desperately awaits the day I have sorted my vapourised head out and realised I want to live in semi-domestic pseudo-bliss with her in our big house, with our big arty careers. Like bollocks I do, I'm out of here permo.

"Whatever" I say nonchalantly.

She drops me at the airport but doesn't wait with me. I get semi-trolleyed in the airport bar and then climb into my first-class seat and sleep most of the way to my destination.

Epilogue: Ice Smoker

Finally I am here alone; the plane has gone, after several hours re-fuelling, checking, testing, repairing. Now it's just me, ice, cigarettes. A small building, temporarily erected twenty years ago, attempts to protect it's single occupant from the worst ravages of the climate.

I laugh and light a cigarette; a Marlboro red, always destined to be my significator, my flag of freedom. I suck in it's sensual bite, feeling the ice fire in my lungs. A combination of intense burning smoke and frozen ice air, blazes in my lungs. The hit is intense, significant, euphoric. I flick ash onto the floor and laugh; it always gives me such a sense of freedom not to be constrained by the limiting confines of an ash tray: the symbol of repression of spirit, masquerading as a civilised value.

I have always felt a subtle insistent irritation towards anything which represents an unspoken 'moral standard' to which we are all supposed to subscribe and aspire; any behaviour which falls even marginally below, or indeed above such 'standards' and 'values' is hated and assassinated. Make a note of this: it could be important when you next go to Magdalen College to study some sort of obscure subject related to arcane mathematics, historical occultism and special business opportunities. Ha ha ha.

Why anyone in their right mind would want to end up smoking themselves into the grave in the middle of the Arctic, beats me to death. And how unlikely that a grave could be dug in the solid white shelf of land on which I perch like a splayed crab.

It's obvious that I'm running away from something in my past; after all isn't that the underlying motif of every novel? If only it were that exciting. Most of the time I'm out of my skull, trying to run away from some unspoken dark secret which pursues me to the far corners of the earth. I welcome such horrors as these. They are indicators of something alive; something other than tortured clutching inner mind fingers cob-webbing over my eyes, taking the lifeblood from my once-fat and juicy soul. I creep slower and lower, my belly dragging the ground both physically and emotionally; and metaphorically and fucking euphemistically. Ha ha ha.

I light up another smoke and puff away merrily for a couple of minutes as I gaze, bemused and slightly horrified at my present geographical location. It's just ice; mostly white ice, but some cool blue ice which sort of makes me laugh for some reason. Lots of unfunny stuff is starting to make me laugh: it must be the clean cold air of the arctic circle that is causing it.

I love to feel the bite of the ice in my lungs, mixing with the smoke burn as I suck in a massive chest-full, body-full of ice blue Marlboro red. It is a heavy cocktail that sends my psyche spiralling into space, French kissing stars, riding on the galactic swirl; some sort of unification with all things: or some other bollox. Never mind all that now. Don't let even this be just about the Mind. I came this far; I refuse to be taken back so soon, so easily.

So you think you know my secret; you think I came here to escape my mind? But what can you possibly know of it? Don't even kid yourself. If I took you on a journey through the screeching microcosm of my thoughts, you'd be a gibbering wreck in five minutes flat, no matter how many cigarettes you smoked.

It's nowhere near as simple as you think it is. Even the convolutions have plot twists; mostly very unwieldy ones. Still, that's enough for now. It's getting cold, I'm going to heat up

316

some water and make myself a cup of coffee. Oh, when I glibly say 'it's getting cold' what I really mean is that I am beginning to feel the cold; it's cold here all the time, which was the whole point of my coming here in the first place; a cool temperature leads to a cool mind. My personal yoga is to freeze the soul.

I shuffle over to the stove and open the little door which covers the controls. As far as I know, they have set it up for me to use. I click the dial and press the ignition button twice. Nothing lights up. I peer more closely at the controls and see a little tap thing, so I wiggle it and it turns clockwise, half a turn. I hear a rushing noise and press the ignition button again; this time the gas head bursts into flame with a startling pop. The flame is nearly a foot high and burns the sleeve of my padded jacket. I quickly fiddle with the dial and get it turned down to a couple of inches. So it's gas then. I had expected an oil burner for some reason. Perhaps the stove is plugged straight in to a Russian gas main or something. They didn't tell me much and I didn't ask. Not the sort of detail I want to get involved in any more. Just chillin'.

I fish about in my holdall and find some coffee and a small bag of sugar. There is no milk so I'll have to drink it black. That's a change; that's a tiny part of my new life revealed to me. So the new me drinks black coffee. Interesting. I guess I'll be drinking it with no sugar too very soon. Then I'll be drinking hot water once the coffee runs out in about a fortnight. Fascinating really; though not as fascinating as when my food runs out in two months time. That'll be a corker. I reckon I can handle it though, as long as my vast supply of cigarettes lasts. I think I've got enough to really go for it smoke-wise for a good six months. After that I'm really up shit creek. What will I do then? Die perhaps. That was always part of the deal. The likelihood of my demise.

Then again I'm just as likely to make a million bucks selling ice to the Inuit or whatever they're called. Not that I've seen any of them around here; just a couple of American pilots and a Polish fur trapper looking for ice weasels.

I move across the room at a lumbering pace and lean over as I rummage in my rucksack. I pull out a carton of Gitanes Blond and tear a pack of twenty from the cellophane wrap. I walk outside, flick my Zippo, the one with a stag on it. I begin to walk into the far distance as I suck in the arcane subtleties of the French cigarette; the javelin prick of hot toxins at the back of my throat makes me grin like a jacked up smack head. I experience the sexy explosion of über-sophistication which is contained within all exotic smokes, especially French ones. It is like pulling a real hot bit of French totty out of my pocket and gorging myself on her yielding, grateful flesh; smoking is the poor man's equivalent to the feeling of power which comes from having a massive amount of money. Never mind 'Think and Grow Rich', I prefer to Smoke and Feel Rich. It works every time. When I smoke I am a world leader of wealth, power and attractiveness.

I look around and not surprisingly see only ice in every direction. I have a little death wish and want to see what the outcome will be if I walk and walk until something happens. It's a variation on the theme which is the underlying basis of my entire reason for being here. What happens to a person, namely me in this case, if they, or in this case I, do nothing; if I let fate, pure unalloyed and unlimited, make my choices for me. Until this moment I have made decisions which have had consequences, my life has been under my own control. But it became too boring to walk from A to B. It held too little significance; an arbitrary whim on my part; you have to do something with your time don't you?

So the world is made busy with people doing stuff and getting results, but so fucking what? Everyone gets a result every time and the only thing it really proves is that they never take time out to think about whether or not all this 'doing' is actually achieving anything of 'true' value or is it all just a case of filling time until we drop dead and finally find an answer of some sort about what the fucking hell is really going on here after all. I'm sure I have not got a damn clue and never had if I'm honest, whatever that means.

So I have decided to let fate take charge from now on. I sold up (lies!) and moved out here to the middle of a white cold nowhere to take what comes. And yet is this anything more than another decision made by me which will have consequences, just like everything else I have ever done? Have I just set myself up to die in days, if not hours, in a frozen wasteland? Probably.

It's an urge I have had all my life, a desire to have no control over my life; a sense of freedom from my own blundering, or the desire to feel that some higher power is guiding my life. Some spiritual yearning which I never understood.

I strain the last of the poison lust from the butt and flick it away, watching it burn into the ice. Tee Hee.

Appendices

Appendix 1:

The Institute of Infinity Sciences

Over time, as the Institute and University become more established within society, we will increase the areas of research undertaken by our students, academics and fellows. Currently we are, through the work of Professor G. De'Ath, conducting major research into Reality Engineering, through the basic Holographic Model.

In practice we are developing the theories of Bohm & Pribram, with a core aim of expanding and applying those theories in order to better serve humanity. Our underlying drive is always to improve the lot of living beings and to expand human knowledge and freedom.

How we Engineer Reality

The theory underlying our engineering work states that there are an unlimited number of Simultaneous Realities (usually called Parallel Universes). The realities make every possibilty and every combination of possibilities a potential experience. There is a reality where everything is exactly the same as the one you are now experiencing apart from the fact that your eyes are a different colour. In another simultaneous reality, your hair is shorter, or longer, or you have no hair. There are also realities where very little is the same, or nothing whatever is the same. Every possible experience (we call them Perceptions) and combination of experiences (we call them Scenarios) exists at some location within the entirety of the manifested universe.

Traditionally there is an idea, generally accepted, that reality changes continually. One day it rains, the next is sunny. We in the Faculty of Reality Engineering, you may be surprised to hear, do not ascribe to the notion of change. We subscribe instead to the concept of MOVEMENT. This is the basis of many of our reality engineering hypotheses. We do not change reality when we cut our hair, we MOVE BETWEEN REALITIES, we travel through uncountable simultaneous realities every minute of every day and don't even realise it!!

Far from being strange inaccessible mysteries, parallel universes (simultaneous realities) are an everyday mundane occurance. Each discrete reality that we pass through (each frequency) is unchanging, static. It is our flowing movement between these static realities which cause us to feel that things are constantly changing.

By discovering and utilising various mechanisms by which we can control the speed and direction of movement from one reality to another, we can engineer reality by deliberately moving to Scenarios we have chosen or designed through the tool of our imagination. If you can imagine it you can experience it. If you can dream it, you can go there.

The research we are undertaking in the Reality Engineering Department of the University is centred around developing ever more accurate and powerful 'Steering Mechanisms' by which we might move to a place more in line with our needs and desires.

Our initial research, with regard to development of the Steering Mechanism concerns the creation of audio programmes - targeted building blocks of thought, which grow into networks

324

over time and develop into powerfully focussed convictions and desires. It is high focus, conviction and desire which are the basis of the steering mechanism.

Time is Distance

The concept of time has long intrigued and baffled scientists. Fairly recently they came up with the idea of time being linked to space - they called it SPACETIME. Reality engineers describe Time as DISTANCE.

There are an infinite number of simultaneous realities. Every day we move through many thousands of Scenarios without noticing. People often travel more or less randomly from one place to another with little idea of where they are heading or where they want to be. We often just drift through Spacetime, covering the distance between point A and point B in a winding or meandering course. There are infinite routes, or paths between points of the manifestation. The shortest path between any two points is zero distance (instantaneous travel).

The work of reality engineers is to devise, develop and discover ways of making our journey from any two points as short as we can. We do this mainly through the use of technological, psychological and philosophical methods and systems based around our ability to control the Steering Mechanisms of Desire, Commitment and Focus.

If our options are infinite, then how do we choose where in all the manifest worlds we should be heading on our journey? Its an easy question to answer - and in line with much current 'spiritual' and 'New Age' thinking - you go where your heart, your, joy, your bliss, leads you. It is only by following your deepest desires that you can enjoy your journey. To put it bluntly - if you are not doing what you want to do - life sucks!!

Our paths should lead to joyful places which hold the very essence of who we are. The stronger our desire to be within a given Scenario (to perceive certain manifest circumstances), the more our determination to reach it, and the more we focus on it - the quicker we get there.

To give an everyday example - You want a new car (your heart desires to perceive a Scenario in which you own a new car) - you want it (desire) so much that every day you imagine (focus) how joyful it would be to drive it - this leads to a strengthening of your determination (committment) to have it. So you start working extra hours and saving like crazy until you get the car.

The actions you take are the indicators you need to tell you where you are heading in life - they are fed by the steering mechanism - it is only when you begin to manifest actions that are in line with your desires that you begin to move swiftly toward them. So action is the proof that you are getting nearer your desired Scenario. If there is little or no action then one or more elements of the steering mechanism need strengthening or re-tuning - this is what our audio programmes do.

Appendix 2:

European Jesus Lecture

The Mesmeriser laughed as I closed the book and thought that I was after all his plaything. I wondered if it was true that he had total control of my brain and mind like he had been telling me he had. Now that he had come out from behind the shadows, I knew who was pulling my strings when I got confused about my identity, and why I often worried that I was mad and just deluding myself about my desire to serve God and raise this planet up to its place in Heaven sitting on the right hand of my Glorious Lord. There was obviously a battle going on for my soul; they were using all kinds of technologies, psychologies and media to do it and I was the pawn in the game. But something told me I was also the prize. It seemed both absurd and banal that somehow my own personal mind was linked to the ultimate destiny of the planet earth and maybe the entire galaxy and the whole of creation. Dare I even hope that this was all just a dream; That when I cleared the debris and mist from my mind's eye, I would at last remember that I was in fact the Creator. Why does the Mesmeriser laugh when I tell myself this? Is he scared? Or is he laughing at the fact that he has fooled me into being ungodly in my thoughts, after all my efforts to dedicate my life to the Father?" I decided to give him a lecture of my own. So I transferred us into a big cathedral in Cologne and let him have both barrels: He fucked off into the ether after only a few minutes. He just couldn't take it. I really kicked some rant arse with my powerful diatribe of intergalactic transformation.

European Lecture: 'Let This Be A Lesson To You'

"I will now attempt to help anyone who is deeply entrenched in a religious or philosophical ideology; which sees free thought or independent action as a sin; or which has the effect of causing feelings of guilt as a result of acting in ways which support the self". The congregation sit silently; their faces show expressions of sacred awe, brought about by the holy presence of the European Jesus.

The great man continues; his voice warm and reassuring but with an underlying note of absolute power and control.

"There are many belief systems around today which only serve to make shadows and robots of people. I know that people deserve a better life and to feel happy and positive about themselves, about others, and about the wonderful world in which they live".

"Not everyone believes in God: That is their choice as a free being. A belief or disbelief in God makes no difference to whether or not God exists. My aim in talking to you today is not to prove the existence of God, but to improve the quality of life of those people here today who believe in the existence of a punishing despotic God; those of you who are not at ease with your own beliefs concerning God's nature: those who have been taught to fear God's wrath, should they dare to breathe without permission or have a free thought".

European Jesus looked around the audience at the upturned faces. His big heart went out to them, poor creatures. He took a drink of water before continuing.

"I will attempt to comfort those who suffer through their personal religious beliefs, and who fear that there is no escape from damnation. I sincerely hope that one day you shall be freed from such crippling ideological slavery; for you are the slaves of the modern world; caught up in chains of twisted dogma. I will simply say this: however you came to be made, or to exist upon this planet, it cannot be disputed that you *are* here and that you are made in a certain way".

"If you believe God made you and that God is infallible; then it cannot be doubted that He made you that way deliberately. He did not leave out any necessary components or aspects of you; neither did He include any unnecessary parts of you. It is also reasonable to assume that He intended you to live in line with how you were made; he did not make you tall in order for you to walk around making yourself short. He did not give you two legs so you could hop around on one".

"Given this proposition; if you have a certain feeling, then that feeling is meant to be there. However: the judgment of what the feeling may mean, represent or indicate, is open to interpretation, given that you have free will. The facts which exist are created by God; the interpretation of things is given to us, his creations. In the same way; the power to take action is given by God, but the choice of how we use that power is given to us. We can either interpret things in harmony with our natural perspective - which God designed us to have - or we can interpret things in a way that goes against the viewpoint He gave us". Sounds of amazed approval from the crowd.

European Jesus smiles a beautiful smile of beatitude. "Alternatively, given our free will, we can choose to accept someone else's view of the world. By deciding that our own viewpoint is incorrect we are saying that God is wrong and that Man is correct over Him. Now we have to choose which man to believe and take our viewpoint from. There always have been people who are willing to tell you what viewpoint or opinion to take. Often these people are religious leaders, philosophers, media harpies, self proclaimed 'experts' or politicians. There are thousands of different religions, sects, cults, political parties, pressure groups, charities, pop stars, social commentators, journalists, critics, family, friends, neighbors, colleagues; and so on ad infinitum; who think it is their business to tell you what to think. All of them state, or imply, that the last thing you must do is to rely upon your own viewpoint, or give any credence to your own perceptions or opinion – the very viewpoint that God has given you. Each of these groups or individuals is convinced they speak the truth and that all the others are wrong. What sort of God would put you in the situation where you have only a few years to live, but during that time you have to choose from among a million conflicting viewpoints and select a single truth?".

A murmur of joy rippled through the audience. Jesus smiled meekly but powerfully at the flock who stood in awe of his majesty.

"If that were true it would mean that your lives were nothing more than a big puzzle; set for you like rats in a maze; you would have no greater value to God than an experimental animal to it's abuser. In such a Scenario he is simply playing with us. Not what a loving God would do is it?" A few mumbled "no's" from the front row, made Jesus laugh to himself; but he went on like the true professional he is.

"After all, would you, as a fallible and supposedly sinful human being, do that to your own children or loved ones: would you use them as amusements in a pointless experiment?" A few groans of assent and a ripple of applause. It was clear that the majority of the crowd were completely transfixed, if not transfigured, by this lecture, such was the powerful enlightenment of his inspired words.

He took another sip of holy water and looked around the rows of seated pilgrims who filled the ornate cathedral of Cöln. They were a sorry looking lot, but that was not their fault; they were suffering from spiritual malnutrition, and he was here to see that the hungry got a good healthy meal for once in their dismal lives. He took a Yogic breath and continued masterfully.

"So, if God does not expect you to spend your lives

searching for the one truth among many; is it not reasonable to conclude that He gave you a personal viewpoint with the intention that you would make use of that viewpoint? If mankind is given free will; to interpret facts and experiences as each sees fit, then is it not likely that different people; given that God gave them different ways of seeing the world, will interpret the facts they encounter in different ways to each other? Given that their interpretations differ, is it not likely their actions will also differ? Therefore, my followers: what is right for one person may not be right for everyone. In fact it is unlikely that what is right for any one person will be exactly right for anyone else; unless that person is an exact clone of course. I don't see any clones here today, do you?"

"No" the audience responded in unison.

"You are all made differently; so it is right that you should all see things differently and act differently from one another. Mass religions, beliefs, philosophies and ideologies represent nothing more than large groups of people who have traded their own God-given viewpoint – the very free will that He gave you – for a pile of man-made dogma which fits the true nature or viewpoint of no-one".

"They do this for various reasons: all show a lack of faith in a loving God. One reason is the illogical conviction that the more people who profess to believe the same thing, the more likely it is that they are correct. Therefore the bigger a religion can get, the more weight it carries. Another reason why so many people subscribe to mass thought forms is that these belief systems have been very cleverly designed to make it difficult for people to feel confident enough to break away from them. They get their victims while they are young; by commanding that the adults 'do their duty', and take their kids to church, political rallies, and so on. By the time the child becomes an adult they are so full of fear and guilt and so repressed that they dare not even think a free thought. After all, they have been told that such thoughts are put there by Satan in an attempt to lead them astray; and will result in them going to Hell and burning in fire forever!"

At this point Jesus looks around and sees frightened faces at the mention of the Underworld. He laughs and waves his hands wide. "Fear not my little ones, for I have literally been to Hell and back to bring you the light. And let me tell you there is nothing in Hell but a railway station and a post office. Honest." A loud laugh erupts and some cheers and clapping.

"Ok, Ok, restrain yourselves my little iniquities, I have more to tell you; to set you free". (Have another drink of water, just to give them time to settle and control their heaving sides. It's going well and they are lapping it up. Twas ever so, old friend, twas ever so. Begin again in earnest.)

"It is not surprising then, that many unlucky people succumb to such powerful brainwashing. Most religions work actively towards the undermining of the individual; stating that it is sinful and wicked to believe in your own view of the world – the one God gave you. This has nothing to do with God's will and everything to do with control. What sort of God is going to create a being and then eternally torture it for doing what He designed it to do? An Insane one. Do you want to follow an insane God? There are plenty to choose from. Take your pick. If, on the other hand, you find it makes more sense that God is not insane (how can an infallible being be insane?), then it must follow that Mankind is more likely to make errors of judgment and misinterpret facts, than God is. It is not only more logical, but also more faithful to God, to live as He designed you.

To do this, you have to interpret His world in the way that He designed you to interpret it: have faith in your own viewpoint – in yourself – and you are showing faith in God. What d'ya think of that for a mind-blowing statement my little munchkins?"

Jesus stood upright and glanced once more at his

feeble underlings. What a bunch of Muppets. Still, best not rub their noses in it too much, hey; after all I am the King of Kings and the Glorious Future of Mankind. I'd better give them some more of my Golden Prose of Empowerment so I can get out of this toilet and back to more luxurious revelations amidst the enigmatic giants of Heaven. What a blast it is being so Great. I'm brilliant.

"Pin back your ears, worms, 'cos I'm gonna lay it on ya some more!". Drink of water for effect. Look at 'em, just standing there, dumbfounded like a bunch of ninnys. I'm really messin' with their heads today. Ha Ha. Well here goes perfection on a stick.

"To believe what others tell you above what God has told you, shows no faith in Him and puts man above Him. Religious dogma is a substitute for faith. To be yourself, and to think for yourself, is to have faith in, and love for, God. You are then in a position to receive His love for you".

"You may have difficulty in believing that God can have such a joyful life planned for you. I know I find it pretty incredible that he even bothers with you at all if I'm honest; but that goes to show just how fucking amazing a guy he is, doesn't it?" A couple of disgruntled jeers are heard in the auditorium; which Jesus hears as a type of adorational murmur. "But hey, is it really that surprising that God wants the very best for you; after all, isn't that what you want for your own imperfect children? Don't believe the bullshit that others speak, oh lost and lonely cretins, for I am here to bring you the Good News. Listen not to those who would have you take note of their warped and inane preachings. Beware those who speak as if God has given them the right to undermine you and fill you full of fear and guilt in the name of their twisted religions of the Ego".

"I do not think a loving parent would take too kindly to someone who chose to thwart His very plans for you. God

333

would be rather cross with anyone who preached lies in His name. To truly follow God you must follow your hearts: for He lives in them".

"God has been on the receiving end of much bad press for far too long. It's about time you mere humans started to understand that God is bigger and more far-reaching than you are capable of conceiving. The ways that God can be visualized or experienced are infinite. Move on from your outdated idea of an old man with a beard who lives in the sky and whose greatest delight is to punish sinners and to wreak vengeance and eternal damnation at the drop of a hat, so to speak, if you dare to breathe without His written permission. Through your unique perspective... Oi you in the front row, bloody wake up you lardy-arsed twonk! Can't you hear the Son of God Almighty himself; addressing you with benevolent majesty? That's better pal, now don't do it again, now where was I? You've made me lose my place now, ow! And just as I was building to a mighty magnificent crescendo an' all, Ok now just pin your flaps back and catch a load of this wazz, once I've had a drink of water". Has a drink of water. Sees two people talking to each other near the back but chooses not to draw attention to their lack of civilised standards.

"Through your unique perspective you have been given a gift of immense wealth and beauty. You have been given the opportunity to see God in a way that nobody else ever will; to experience an exclusive relationship with the very love-filled core of the Universe. Do not let this gift be stolen from you by people who are so lacking in faith that they spend their sad lives attempting to undermine you and your faith in a God of goodness, beauty and kindness; to replace your lovely God with their third-rate God of fear and brutality".

"However you experience God; be aware of one thing and know that it is true: God is love incarnate, and wants nothing but your highest good. God wants more for you than you are even capable of conceiving. God is your greatest wish fulfilled. God is your every fear gone forever. God is so good and kind and full of love for you that you would explode with happiness if you even got a glimpse of one-thousandth of it. God is total Heavenly bliss. All your hopes and needs and desires fulfilled completely and forever".

"God has not got a big list of rules: God does not watch your every move and thought, in the hope of catching you actually enjoying yourself so that he can punish you. That is what religious people do. God is not a religious fanatic; he is not religious at all. If you think up the nicest, kindest God you can possibly imagine, you will not come even close to how nice God actually is or how much He wants you to have all your dreams come true, and to have the best life you can possibly have, forever".

"So the next time some religious fool, puffed up with pomposity, attempts to lay a guilt trip on you; or tries to keep you down, by spouting threats of eternal damnation at you, in God's name of course: then just cling tight to your own God's hand and know that their nasty little God is simply a reflection of their own lack of faith. By their Gods shall ye know them!"

European Jesus steps back from the lectern and stands with his arms spread wide, as the audience erupts in a swathe of sacred merriment: their souls lightened by the immense and radiating presence of the Son of God, and his sacred and joy provoking words of healing light. He is truly the hero of these people, and they love him with all their hearts; for he has saved them and released them into joy everlasting.

Amen.

Made in United States
Troutdale, OR
10/25/2024

24126621R00189